Solving problems is her job…even when it may cost her life.

When Councilor Allerton sends Stanzie to investigate a territory dispute between tiny pack Stony Fell and the British branch of much larger Mac Tire, it seems routine until someone sets a bear trap. A young Stony Fell man pays with the loss of his leg and now it's up to Stanzie and Murphy to figure out who set the trap--and why--before more members of the packs are maimed.

Add a pair of star-crossed lovers, one love triangle, a grief-stricken bond mate with jealousy issues, and bad blood all around and the resultant twisted hell brew reveals the darker side of inter-pack politics that could prove too difficult--and dangerous--for even Stanzie to untangle.

Books by Amy Lee Burgess

The Wiolf Within Series
Beneath the Skin, Book One
Scratch the Surface, Book Two
Hidden In Plain Sight, Book Three
Inside Out, Book Four
About Face, Book Five
Across the Line, Book Six

Published by Kensington Publishing Corporation

Across the Line

The Wolf Within Series

AUTHOR

LYRICAL PRESS
Kensington Publishing Corp.
www.kensingtonbooks.com

Lyrical Press books are published by
Kensington Publishing Corp. 119 West 40th Street New York, NY 10018

All Kensington titles, imprints, and distributed lines are available at special
quantity discounts for bulk purchases for sales promotion, premiums, fund-
raising, and educational or institutional use.

Special book excerpts or customized printings can also be created to fit
specific needs. For details, write or phone the office of the Kensington
Special Sales Manager:
Kensington Publishing Corp.
119 West 40th Street
New York, NY 10018
Attn. Special Sales Department. Phone: 1-800-221-2647.

First Electronic Edition: September 2013
eISBN-13: 978-1-61650-484-7
eISBN-10: 1-61650-484-6

First Print Edition: September 2013
ISBN-13: 978-1-61650-857-9
ISBN-10: 1-61650-857-4

Printed in the United States of America

This one is for Kristen Malone. We met in New Orleans and had so many magical times there. Now we're both living in Houston and the good times roll on!

Acknowledgements

I never know until my beta readers tell me whether the next Stanzie novel is going to fly or if I have to go back and start again. Kim Murphy, Portia Scott Palko, Chris Wilbanks and Nerine Dorman–you all keep Stanzie's adventures on track. Thank you, Antonia Tiranth, for your editing expertise and to all my Lyrical Press family for their continued support. You all are awesome!

Chapter 1

The red dress on the back of the bathroom door called to me. Short, but not indecent, filmy but not see-through. Sexy but not trashy. I stared at it from my vantage point in the tub and couldn't help but smile.

I loved to wallow in my favorite mint-scented bathwater until my fingers and toes pruned, but I couldn't ignore the siren song of that dress.

Tonight marked an entire year since Liam Murphy and I had exchanged vows at the Great Gathering bonding ceremony.

Once on the bath mat, I toweled off, never taking my gaze from the new dress. The peridot and pearl bond pendant Murphy gave me that night shifted around my throat as I drew the towel across my arms.

Murphy didn't know it, but I'd made reservations at an expensive French restaurant in the heart of Dublin. If we didn't hurry, we'd be late.

A pang went through me as I briskly rubbed the towel through my wet hair. All day I'd waited for him to remember the date, but so far he hadn't said a word. Thankfully, it wasn't one of his bad days—when he brooded about Paddy and his father, but it wasn't a great day either.

He'd spent most of it behind his laptop connected to the stock market. He made money for our pack, Mac Tire, that way. For us, as well.

For all I knew, he might have been using his work as a shield against grief—it wouldn't be the first time, but I preferred it to the days when he sat on the sofa with a cold cup of coffee and stared into space. Those were the days I hated.

I'd managed to smuggle the red dress into the bathroom so he wouldn't see it until I had it on. The cherry red stilettos I planned to wear with it were from Paris. I'd worn them the night we'd met.

I smiled, remembering that moment. Polite, yet reserved when we'd been introduced by Councilor Jason Allerton, Murphy had obviously resented my presence at the table. He'd barely glanced in my direction until one of the other people there asked me if I was the Constance Newcastle who'd killed my bond mates in a stupid, careless car accident. Then Murphy looked at me and his polite facade crumbled, replaced by disgust. He'd left the table and stranded me in a sea of British pack members who, after they'd had their fun making me squirm, cold-shouldered me out of subsequent conversation.

To hear Murphy tell the tale, he'd been smitten the moment Jason Allerton led me to the table. One of the stories he told people about us featured my red dress and how he'd known from the moment he saw me in it, we were destined to bond.

I didn't all the way believe him, but maybe the truth was somewhere in between. All I knew was that he'd protected me at the Great Gathering and saved my ass by bonding with me.

Now a year later, we both had admitted our love for each other, but instead of wine and roses, we had grief and an invisible wall.

We talked—about inconsequential things. *What should we have for dinner? How about this movie tonight? Jesus, the weather's awful, isn't it?* But if I brought up Paddy, Murphy would shut down as if he were one of those animatronic robots at Disneyworld and it was closing time at the park.

Fee couldn't make him talk about Paddy either, but he listened to her talk about him. Listened and held her when she sobbed against his chest while I dealt with Fee's new baby, Will.

Four nights out of seven Fee and Will slept at our apartment—Will in his portable crib, Fee, Murphy and I tangled together on the bed.

What must it be like to have a twin? Murphy was endlessly patient with his sister and she relied on him with a faith that must weigh so heavily, but he never said a word of reproach.

This morning, after Fee packed up Will's crib and his diaper bag and left to go home, I'd held my breath waiting for her to return. Usually when she left, she stayed gone for at least twenty-four hours, but with Fee it was hard to predict. All I knew was she'd be back, I just didn't know precisely when.

So when I heard her voice in the living room, just as I reached for the sexy bra that went with the dress, my heart sank. Should I get dressed? Could I? How could I walk out there and remind her I had something to celebrate and she didn't?

Paddy had been dead for three months. Fee was swamped with pain and guilt she hadn't known he was in trouble, that he hadn't shared his fears with her. I kept waiting for her to turn on Murphy in anger because he'd known everything, but so far she hadn't. Murphy and I knew the stages of grief from bitter experience. We'd both lost our first bond mates to the conspiracy.

The bitter conflict between the Guardians, who wanted our world to remain as it was and Pack First, who wanted the Pack to reveal itself to Others killed them as it killed Paddy. Fee, Murphy and I were members of an exclusive, horrible club. Devastated survivors because our bond mates paid the ultimate price. I was determined the ranks of this club would not swell with more reluctant members.

That was why I was Jason Allerton's Advisor and worked to reveal members of the Guardians, who took matters in their own hands and murdered Pack First members or sympathizers.

In the living room, Fee's voice rose to a shrill pitch. I winced. Murphy's murmured response was meant to soothe her, but she overrode him and now I discerned the thread of anger. She was bitching about her bond mates, Colm and Deirdre, especially him and since that was nothing new and I'd heard it all *ad nauseum*, I didn't pay much attention to actual words. I was too busy mourning the fact my night out with Murphy had been torpedoed. So much for my red dress and fancy dinner reservations. Most likely it had been a bad idea anyway.

In the bedroom, I hastily hung the dress at the back of my side of the deep double closet. As always when I saw my shoe collection piled in a sorry-ass heap beneath my dresses and skirts, I heaved a sigh and mourned the loss of my walk-in closet in Boston. Dublin had taken a lot of getting used to and sometimes the lack of a walk-in closet seemed the deepest cut.

I threw on a pair of jeans and the red hand-knitted sweater Paddy's mother, Maureen, made me. She ran a small mail-order clothing line. Sweaters, vests, jackets, baby clothes—all knitted by hand. Some of the other members of the pack contributed their talents and recently one built her a website. The website made me nervous. Too high tech for some of the Guardians. I hoped we'd rooted the bad ones out with the deaths of Grandfather Mick, Declan Byrne and Glenn Murphy, but didn't know for sure. So I kept an eye on Maureen and the girl who'd designed the website, just in case.

When I walked into the main room of the apartment, Fee still stood in the doorway, her face flushed red with fury. Will dangled in his car seat from one of her clenched fists and made fussy noises indicative of hunger.

Did we have any breast milk in the refrigerator? With Fee so caught up in her anger, the last thing she probably wanted to do was take a time out to nurse.

I didn't bother to say hello. She'd left not even seven hours earlier. Instead, I tacked right, into the galley kitchen.

Score. Three bottles of breast milk and all of them within the expiration date. I popped the oldest into a cup of hot water to warm and walked over to where Fee stood yelling at Murphy.

She'd crossed the line from shrill to shout in the space of time it had taken me to get the bottle. Murphy listened to her patiently. He had one hand on her shoulder. Touch was important to Pack. Did he derive as much comfort from the touch as she did? Did she even know his hand was there?

Perversely, I was glad to see her mad. For the first time in ages she was angry. A good sign she was beginning to move on in her grief. But I predicted it was going to be loud around our place for a few weeks.

Will's little rosebud mouth puckered into a bow as he let out a protesting wail when I lifted him from the warmth of his blanketed car seat. Fee had bundled him up in one of Maureen's knitted jackets and a blue cap with an adorable white yarn puff on top.

"You greedy, hungry baby, you just wait a few more minutes," I told him as I struggled to hold his small arm still so I could take off the jacket. The heat was too high in the apartment again but Fee was always cold so we kept it up. Neither of us had remembered to turn it down. Murphy had been wrapped up in the stock market and I'd cleaned. Guests with babies left an awful lot of disarray in their wake. I suspected Will had more blankets, binkies and clothes here than he did at the house Fee shared with Colm and Deirdre.

I found one of his cloth rattles—the one in the shape of a lamb—and shook it in his face to distract him from the fact he was hungry and there was no food. He was having none of it. His face scrunched up into a miniature red-cheeked version of Fee's and he let out another indignant blat.

Born three weeks after Paddy's death, he was just over two months old. He mostly slept and ate, but when I spoke to him, he swiveled his head in my direction, and I swore, listened to me. Did he recognize my voice? He'd spent much of his young life cradled in my arms as Fee wept in Murphy's.

His eyes had settled into their permanent color. Left eye blue, right eye brown. Just like his father. His hair was growing in black and curly, also like his dad's. Otherwise, he was a carbon copy of his mother. He would have her quicksilver good looks. She and Murphy closely resembled each other, so maybe when Will grew up he'd look like his uncle Liam. That thought made me smile, and I pressed a kiss to his wrinkled little old man forehead, which made him squirm. He cooed, his earlier temper tantrum forgotten. If only adults' bad moods could be as swift and mercurial as babies'.

Occupied as I was with Will, I'd tuned out most of Fee's impassioned diatribe, but once he was settled in the crook of my arm, greedily sucking on his bottle, I spared some of my attention for her.

"He's just doing it to be difficult, because he knows damn well I don't want to fuck him. I don't want to fuck anyone at this point, Liam."

"I think he's doing it for the pack's sake, Fee," Murphy told her. "Think about this for a minute. None of us seem to be getting over the shock and pain very well. This could help us."

"I don't want to get over the grief. Do you hear me, Liam Murphy?" The tendons in Fiona's neck stuck out from the force of her shout. Will gave a convulsive jerk in my arms and the nipple slipped from his mouth. He added his scared wails to her angry shout and I hastily plugged the nipple back in and hoped the poor thing wouldn't choke.

Jesus, could she not take three minutes to calm down and let her poor son drink his milk?

"Getting over the grief doesn't mean forgetting him, Fiona," I said.

Both Fee and Murphy turned in my direction as if surprised to find me there. That was nothing new. Half the time I thought I must invisible to them. Just a ghost who took care of the baby. A housekeeping ghost who put food on the table they rarely bothered to eat then cleaned it all up again.

I told myself to be nice because I knew what it was like to lose loved ones.

"I won't be forced into this. You know that sonofabitch has called the hunt for tomorrow morning? Without my consent, he's called the hunt and all the pack has known about it for days now. He finally bothered to inform me an hour ago. Bastard."

"I didn't know about it," Murphy said. He took a deep breath.

"It was posted on the pub wall, and he's been making phone calls. But he didn't call you, Liam, because the gobshite knew I was here with you."

"Why did he leave us out? Why is calling a hunt so awful, Fee?" I was confused. A hunt sounded like fun to me. Since Paddy's funeral, Murphy spent most of his time with Fee and on the computer. Also, many, many members of Mac Tire managed to drop by to see him or ask him to go somewhere so they could talk.

Everyone knew Murphy and Paddy had been best friends. Mac Tire was reeling from the blow of losing their Alpha male and also their Regional Councilor, Glenn Murphy. It was a one, two punch nobody seemed able to deal with.

Murphy knew how to listen. He knew how to say what was needed. He guided, advised and sometimes just lent a shoulder to weep on. I'd watched him do it a dozen times and more these past three months.

Consequently, we didn't have much time together. We'd made love exactly twice since Paddy's funeral and neither time shifted because Fee showed up before we could get to the forest.

I'd hoped tonight after a leisurely dinner, I might seduce him and we would shift. That wouldn't happen now because it would take hours to calm Fee down. But a hunt tomorrow could make up for losing out on the dinner seduction scenario tonight.

I wanted to let my wolf free. She was gloriously normal now and last time she'd run with the pack, it had been at Paddy's funeral and it had been a sad, solemn, gut-wrenching hunt. I wanted something upbeat and blood-stirring. I missed Paddy like hell, but we had to go on. Things like hunts would be small steps in the right direction.

"Because the high-handed bastard intends to administer the pack bond before we do, that's why, Stanzie. And he needs my blood for it. Are you that stupid, I have to explain it to you?" Fee's voice dripped sarcasm, and I gulped.

Pack bond. A terrible chill swept through my body. My fingers slackened enough around Will's bottle that it slipped out of his mouth again. He wailed as the bottle slid with a wet thump to the hardwood floor at my feet.

"Now you've done it." Fee swept across the room to snatch her son out of my limp arms. She rocked him and crooned something in Irish as she fumbled with one hand to unbutton her jacket and blouse. "And how old is that fucking milk you've been poisoning him with?" She gave the bottle a contemptuous kick with her boot so it skittered across the floor somewhere beneath the dining table.

"I...it's not old. I checked the date first." My lips were numb. Was I going to pass out? Everything seemed so oddly bright and yet frighteningly dim.

"It's all right, Stanzie," said Murphy. He sounded so kind. So understanding. Could he possibly understand the tumult of emotions gripping me right now?

My wolf was normal. Free of the yoke of the unactivated pack bond my father forced upon me when I was a baby. I'd shifted three times since it had been lifted. Once when my wolf was out of control because it was the first time she'd ever been free of the pack bond. That had been a giddy, scary, roller coaster of an experience. Once after Paddy's murder when she and I had been wracked with grief and then again at his funeral. She'd never run free and unfettered just for the hell of it. I'd waited and waited, patient because if anyone understood the grief of losing a loved one, it was me.

But now a new pack bond would be thrust upon us, While intellectually I understood it wouldn't hurt her, cold terror settled in my heart.

"A pack bond right now would be the best thing for Mac Tire." Murphy stepped around Will's car seat so he could sit beside me on the sofa.

"You don't understand a feckin' thing," shouted Fiona and Will, who had been calming down, gave another frightened wail. Fee shushed him by sitting in an arm chair and giving him her breast.

Paralyzed, I couldn't turn my head to look at Murphy. I wanted to see his face, but couldn't move.

"Stanzie, if you can't stop stinking up this room with your fear, can you please go somewhere else?" Fee glared at me. I couldn't see her face, but the burning wrath of her gaze was hot on my cheek. "What the hell are you scared for anyway?"

"The pack bond, Fee," Murphy reminded her. He stressed her name as if to jog her memory. Maybe it was a reproach too because she sucked in her breath as if struck.

"For fuck's sake," she snarled. "We don't have time for your petty little fears right now. Get over it. A pack bond won't hurt your precious wolf and you know it. Why can't you sympathize with me and what I've got to go through instead of wallowing in your own self-pity?"

"I've been wallowing in yours for three months. Do you suppose I could have two minutes for myself?" The words rushed from my mouth before I could take them back.

Again I told myself she was grieving. She'd lost Paddy. Sick to my stomach, I remembered what it was like to lose Grey and Elena.

Shocked silence for a beat, then Fee burst into ugly tears. Will howled and Murphy cursed beneath his breath.

Tears pricked my eyes. Poor Murphy. I'd made his night even harder because now it would take much longer to talk Fee around. I was such an idiot. Fee was right. I had no time for self-pity or fear. I needed to suck it up and deal. The pack bond would supposedly help everyone. I had no idea how because I thought they were devices from hell, but I was a member of Mac Tire and if they took a pack bond, so would I.

My lips trembled and I leaped to my feet, brushing away the hand Murphy stretched out to me. He didn't have time to deal with me too. He needed to concentrate on Fee.

"I'm sorry, Fee." My voice was choked. "I'm sorry."

She refused to look at me and buried her face in Will's sweet-smelling hair. I retreated to the bedroom and curled up on the bed.

* * * *

"Want to talk about it?"

I jerked in the bed and rolled over to see Murphy assembling Will's portable crib. He'd switched on the desk lamp and the yellow light spilled across his tired face as he worked.

I must have dozed. A glance at the clock on the nightstand revealed it was the middle of the night. Nearly one o'clock.

"Fee?" I whispered.

"Sleeping in the chair finally," he answered. "I'll carry her in after I settle the baby."

"I'll get him." I slid to the edge of the bed and rubbed my sleep-encrusted eyes.

"Will you be all right? Colm's determined to do this thing tomorrow. I called him and couldn't get a word in edgewise. Five minutes of impassioned screaming. In stereo. One ear was him, the other Fee."

"I must have slept through it." I yawned guiltily.

He cast me an amused look, but he looked so damn worn out. "Good for you."

He finished setting up the crib and turned toward me. "Will's in his car seat and they can both sleep where they are for now if you want to talk."

"What about?" I tried to find a brave smile, but was fresh out of such luxuries.

Murphy scrubbed along the edge of his jaw. His fingers rasped against his beard stubble. When was the last time the poor man shaved? He'd verged past sexy stubble two days ago and was now closing in on unattractively prickly.

"Really, it's the best thing for the pack," he said. "All this fucking grief, we're mired in it. We're not moving forward. A pack bond will help." His tone was wistful, as if he only half believed in his own bullshit.

I swallowed hard and slid off the bed. I wanted to talk to him in the worst way, but it wasn't fair. It was one o'clock in the morning and he was flat-out exhausted.

"I believe you," I said, and his smile turned affectionate. He took a step toward me, as if he meant to hug me, but Will chose that moment to cry out. The poor thing disliked his car seat intensely.

"I'll get him." I darted out the door and across the living room floor to rescue him before he roused Fiona.

She was sprawled in the arm chair, still with her jacket on, blouse buttoned wrong. Tears had left shiny streaks across her cheeks and her sandy blond hair was lifeless and bedraggled around her shoulders. She looked so pathetically alone, tears rose in my eyes.

What the hell, Paddy? Why did he fucking have to die? Irrational anger bloomed within me. *He* was supposed to have given me the pack bond. I trusted him. I loved him. I didn't know Colm O'Reilly and the thought of drinking his herb-infused blood sickened me. Terrified me.

I scooped Will from the car seat and bounced him against my shoulder, cradling his little head in my hand.

As soon as his face pressed against my skin, he quieted. Pack children needed touch. Hell, so did Pack adults.

Murphy lifted Fee's limp body and moved ahead of me into the bedroom. He set her down gently on the bed while I placed an already sleeping Will in his crib. As I looked at him, he gave a hitching, little sigh that tore at my heartstrings. This little boy would never know his father. He'd hear stories and see pictures, but he'd never, ever know his father's touch.

Anger bloomed inside me again and I beat it down. Pointless. Useless. What was done was done and now it was time to pick up the pieces and move on.

By the time I turned away from Will and the crib, Murphy was stretched across the bed next to Fee, sound asleep. He hadn't even undressed or crawled beneath the covers.

I shook out a blanket and drew it over him. When I smoothed the back of my hand across his stubbly cheek, he murmured something in his sleep. My name. This time when tears choked me, I let them fall because no one else could see them but me.

Chapter 2

Fee's hip bones protruded alarmingly above the waistband of her blue-and-white striped bikini panties. She wore a short blue robe, untied, over them. How had she gotten so thin?

Any weight she'd gained from her pregnancy had melted away and then some. She was so scrawny I probably could have pushed her over with one finger.

I rocked in the chair by the window. Murphy brought the rocker home one afternoon shortly after Will's birth so Fee would have a place to nurse him in the middle of the night.

Will was in my arms, fussy and hungry, but freshly washed and changed. I'd bathed him while Fee showered. Halfway through Will's bath in the kitchen sink, Murphy had returned from the store with a bag of groceries. He'd looked marginally less exhausted, and he'd shaved, but all the sleep in the world couldn't erase the weight of the sorrow he carried.

"I'll take him," said Fee as she padded across the hardwood floor and tossed her damp towel across the unmade bed. Her sandy blond hair was wet against the side of her thin cheek, and she pushed it away impatiently.

"You can finish dressing," I told her. Will was a barrier between me and the morning. As long as I could hold him, I didn't have to get dressed and take the pack bond.

I'd woken with a sour, churning stomach and a dry mouth I'd tried to fix with chamomile tea, to no avail. Holding the baby helped. Small and frail, he was someone I could protect and keep safe. He'd need a sitter while Fee and the rest of the adult pack attended the hunt. Why couldn't the sitter be me?

"Nah. I'd just have to take half it off again to feed him, wouldn't I?" She gave me a lopsided smile which didn't reach her greeny-gold eyes. I smiled back at her to show there were no hard feelings from the night before, though I was pretty sure she didn't even remember how bitchy she'd been to me.

With reluctance, I shifted Will in my arms so I could pass him to her. She surprised me when she reached out a hand to touch my face.

"I love you like a sister. You know that, don'tcha?"

"Of course," I answered. "Right back at you, Alpha."

I listened to her croon an Irish song to her son as Will nursed while I threw on jeans and a turtleneck sweater. It didn't matter what the hell I wore to the hunt—I'd only have to take it off to shift. But maybe there was a ceremony or something for the pack bond part.

In the kitchen, Murphy was stirring a pan of scrambled eggs. His attire was no help—jeans and a sweater.

Ah, fuck it. I'd change if he and Fee dressed up, but I could eat breakfast in jeans. If I could eat. My stomach gave another ominous churn. I found my mug of tea on the table and took a hasty sip. Cold. Barf.

"You're my rock, you know that?" Murphy kept his attention focused on the eggs, so he missed my shocked stare. "I'll take you to that French restaurant soon, I swear, Stanzie."

"How did you know?" I hadn't told him in case things hadn't worked out. Good call on my part because they hadn't.

"Restaurant called to confirm the reservations last night," he said. I winced. Damn. Why hadn't I taken my cell phone into the bedroom?

"There will be other times." I headed for the electric kettle to boil more water. Cold chamomile tea was disgusting.

"But we'll have to wait a whole year for it to be our anniversary again," he said, and a flood of warmth rushed through me. He remembered. I hadn't been sure he would. It was not as if our bonding had been all hearts and flowers romantic. He'd done it to save my ass from Councilor Celine Ducharme. We hadn't even slept in the same bed the first night. He'd been fleeing the ghost of Sorcha, and I'd ended up drunk and sad on a bottle of champagne. Fun times. But still, he remembered.

"Pack don't celebrate anniversaries like Others do. It's not a big deal, Murphy."

He took the kettle out of my hands and set it down on the dark granite counter so he could hug me. In the cocoon of his arms, I felt safe. Loved. How long had it been since we'd hugged each other? I couldn't even remember.

I buried my face in his neck and inhaled his unique, beloved scent. Autumn wind and leather. God, I loved this man.

"You've been so damn patient, Stanzie. I keep waiting for you to get angry, but you never do." His mouth was so close to my ear, the warmth of his breath sent shivers down my spine.

"Angry about what?" I was honestly confused.

"You see? That's why you're my rock. Everyone in this damned pack is falling to pieces expecting me to pick them up and put them back together but you don't. You suffer just as much, more even, and you don't come crying to me to be fixed."

I swallowed past an obstruction in my throat. So many times I'd wanted to cry in his arms, and let him cry in mine, but Fee or their mother, Siobhan, or any number of Mac Tire pack members had always gotten there first.

"I know you don't want to take the pack bond, but I can't wait. They'll turn to Colm after that. Colm and Deirdre because they know Fee's too close to the grief. I'm walking such a fine line, honey. I try to send them to Colm, but they won't go."

I hadn't thought of the pack bond from that perspective. Nor had I considered Murphy might be uneasily aware he was close to usurping Colm's position as Alpha. In times of crises and grief, a pack member's natural inclination was to turn to his Alpha, but they'd been turning to Murphy. But the realization they hadn't also turned to Colm and Deirdre was new to me.

That had to be a dilemma for Murphy. Another one. More than ever, I was glad I hadn't added my neediness to his already heavy load.

"I guess they remember what a wonderful Alpha you were." I brushed my fingers along the side of his face and his lashes swept his cheeks.

"You'll be fine today, Stanzie," he told me when he opened his dark eyes. "You and your wolf."

For a shiny moment I even believed him. No wonder the whole damn pack turned to him.

* * * *

The moment the three of us alighted from Murphy's black BMW, a crowd of jostling pack members surrounded us. Intent on getting to Fee, Murphy or both, I soon found myself on the outside of the cluster.

I took Will in his car seat out of the BMW and shouldered his diaper bag. The kids of the pack, including the more responsible teens who would not be shifting, were inside the castle and would watch over the baby during the hunt.

I shuddered when I looked at the cold gray stones of Mac Tire's castle. Technically, it belonged to the Ireland and UK Mac Tire packs, who contributed to its upkeep. Also a safe house, both the Regional and Great Councils paid into the funds used for taxes, grounds keeping, and general repairs.

But the Dublin pack truly owned it. We shifted here on the private land that abutted the Donadea Forest Park.

I hadn't been here since Paddy's funeral. I'd come here after his murder, broken and grieving, to attend the tribunal of the man who helped kill him. Murphy and Fee's father, Glenn, tried to strangle me on the main staircase and if not for Ryan Kelly knocking him down the steps where Glenn broke his neck, I would be dead too.

I wasn't a huge fan of the damn castle.

Gwenith McCarthy, one of the pack's young teens, rushed down the gravel walkway, her face aglow. She adored babies and I let her take Will and his diaper bag so she could coo over him as she walked back to the castle.

The day was cold and dismal and I thought about lecturing Gwenith over her lack of a jacket, but couldn't find the heart. She loved babies so much. I didn't want to burst her happy bubble. Christ knew, I wished I had one.

The pack gathered in the front courtyard. No one but the kids went inside the castle.

Every step I took seemed to take more and more effort. On the castle steps, Colm's bright red hair shone even in the muted November daylight and he had one large, muscled arm around frail Deirdre Collins's shoulders. She was nearly six months pregnant and the round bump of her belly swelled beneath her tight blue winter coat. Paddy's death at least ensured Deirdre's baby would live because Fee bonded with her and Colm after the funeral.

Only Alphas could have children. Deirdre discovered she was pregnant a few days before Paddy's murder. She'd been scheduled to have an abortion until Grandfather Mick's knife ended Paddy's life and reign as Alpha.

Sour bile rose in my throat. Had they made the pack bond elixir yet? Didn't they need Fee's blood too? Maybe Colm took her blood yesterday. Shouldn't it be fresh? What would it taste like? Hopefully not as vile as my father's blood mixed with herbs had tasted when I drank it to break his pack bond.

What would the new bond feel like inside me? Would it chain my wolf the way my father's shackled her?

Panic, white-hot and nauseating, gathered into a fist in the pit of my stomach. Oh God, I couldn't do this. I couldn't willingly swallow any Alpha's blood and chain my wolf to his and the others in the pack. No.

I darted into the bushes beside the gravel path and puked. My legs went out from beneath me and I crouched on the gravel so it dug into my kneecaps. The brittle sticks of a winter-sleeping bush scraped at my cheek. I spewed again, half-digested chunks of eggs and toast, and the smell made me gag.

"Mother of God, tell me you haven't gone and gotten yourself pregnant," scolded someone I knew well. And dreaded. Siobhan Carmichael—Murphy and Fee's mother. She hated me. Hated me for bonding with her son. Hated me more for causing her bond mate Glenn's death. She thought he'd had a heart attack under the strain of the tribunal which I'd called against Declan Byrne. She had no clue he'd been knee deep in the violent faction within the Guardians and contributed not only to Paddy's death, but to his son's bond mate's years earlier. If she had, she'd probably hate me even more. She was like that. Irrational and mean as dirt.

"I'm not pregnant, Siobhan." I wiped my mouth with the back of my hand and wished I had a breath mint. A cough drop. Some damn thing to rinse the taste of puke from my mouth.

"Are you sick? You pick a hell of a time to come down with a virus. Have you passed it along to my grandson? He's too little to be sick, you selfish twat."

"I'm not sick.," I spat into the bushes. "Do you happen to have a breath mint or some gum?"

She rummaged in her purse and came up with a stick of what smelled like spearmint chewing gum.

Grateful for the opportunity to clear the vile taste from my mouth, I hastily unwrapped the stick and shoved it in my mouth.

Siobhan wrinkled her delicate nose as surprise dawned in her eyes. Her expression turned suspicious.

"You're not sick. You're scared spitless. Of what?"

I chewed the gum and swallowed until the taste of bile was gone.

"Taking the pack bond." I braced myself. Her hazel eyes narrowed. Here it came.

"It's nothing to be scared of, you silly bitch. Didn't Liam and Fee explain this to you?"

"I know all about pack bonds." My chin jutted. God, this woman was infuriating. I tried so hard to like her because she was Murphy's mother, but just couldn't do it.

"Then you know they're nothing to shiver and shake about. Nothing to puke about either," she said, her tone derisive.

"Look, I have my reasons. Thanks for the gum." I tried to walk past her, but she grabbed my elbow and spun me around to face her. She and I were nearly the same height, but she was strong and scrappy. Every goddamn member of Mac Tire was a fighter. Except for me. I hadn't grown up brawling for fun. The Irish baffled me at the best of times. Just my luck, I'd fallen head over heels for an Irish bond mate.

"What are your reasons?" Her gaze was flat and unconvinced, as if I was full of shit and she just couldn't wait to call me on it.

I spat out the gum and wished I had the guts to punch her.

"When I was a year and a half old, the red virus swept through my birth pack," I said and she was thrown for a moment. She hadn't expected to hear something like that. I half anticipated her to argue or ask me what the hell the red virus had to do with pack bonds. Only everything.

"Half my pack died and in desperation, my father, the Alpha, forged a pack bond with the ones left because he'd heard the pack bond promoted healing."

Understanding flickered in the hazel depths of her eyes. Siobhan Carmichael was in her fifties, but thanks to Pack genetics could pass easily for early thirties. She was damn good looking. Like Murphy in female form. Her face always threw me. She looked so much like Murphy, I expected her to *be* like Murphy. Only she wasn't.

"He gave it to the children too because some of us had the virus. I was sick and I was the fifteenth generation in the pack. I know that means shit to packs like Mac Tire who go back a thousand years, but it was pretty damn significant to us. Mayflower is the third oldest pack in America. I'm not such a provincial little nothing like you think, Siobhan. I have a pedigree, maybe not as much of one as you, but I've got one."

"I haven't got a pedigree. I come from a tiny pack in Northern Ireland that isn't even in existence anymore. It only lasted three generations. Mine was the last and when I left to bond with Glenn, I pretty much sounded the death knell for the damn pack. When I bonded with him, my entire pack joined with Mac Tire. So you've got me beat, if you think how many generations you can count from the founding members of a pack mean anything. Go on with your story, damn you. Your idiot father gave children the pack bond. That's not right. It wouldn't make a damn bit of difference to children because the pack bond doesn't activate until you shift after you take it." Siobhan's laugh was harsh and yet, was there a touch of sympathy in there somewhere?

I tried not to show her I was surprised at her confession. I'd figured her for the bluest of blue bloods. "They were desperate. But it does make a difference when the children grow up and shift for the first time with someone in the pack."

"How the hell could that be?" She frowned. "By the time you grew up enough to shift, your father would have long since ceased being Alpha. Small packs keep the Alpha status longer, don't they? But twenty years? Wasn't there an entire generation between that lost an opportunity to have children?"

"He wasn't Alpha by the time I shifted the first time. He just never dissolved the pack bond even when he stepped down," I said.

Siobhan whispered in horror, "But that's evil, Stanzie. Against Pack law."

I nodded. Tell me about it. "Anyway, I never shifted with anyone from my pack. It's a long story. I ran away with someone from a different pack and we joined Riverglow and my pack bond was never activated."

"I don't understand." Of course she didn't. What my father had done was monstrous and unheard of. He'd not only not dissolved the pack bond, he'd given it to children.

"You know my wolf wasn't normal," I said and her breath hissed between her teeth as she sucked in a mouthful of air.

She'd been so angry at me because I'd kept Murphy from returning to Mac Tire after we'd bonded. We'd worked on my wolf together. He'd been afraid to bring me and my wolf to his pack for fear of what my wolf might do in a big pack. Rules existed that she didn't know and wouldn't have followed or understood even if she had. Siobhan had been less than tolerant about the whole thing.

"The pack bond?" Siobhan guessed. "It interfered somehow with your wolf?"

"Yes," I said. "It's broken now and my father was exiled. So much for my pedigree. I come from a fucked-up pack and my family is the most fucked-up branch of it. The only time my wolf's ever been normal was Paddy's funeral. I haven't shifted since and I'm afraid, that if I take another pack bond, she'll be like she was. I know it's irrational and I know I'm being ridiculous, but I can't help how I feel." Tears choked me and I bit my lip, miserably aware I was on the edge. "Now tell me how stupid I am. Go on, you know you want to."

Siobhan stared at me for a long moment. "Fee knows the whole story, doesn't she? Liam as well?"

I nodded. What the hell was she waiting for? I'd bared my throat and she had me down. All she had to do now was rip me to pieces. I'd given myself to her on a freaking platter.

Angry blotches appeared on Siobhan's cheeks. "The idiots. What the fuck were they thinking? They weren't, that's the truth of it. Colm and Deirdre have no clue, do they?"

Was she angry at her children? Not me? What alternate universe had we been sucked into? "I don't think so," I managed to choke out. Goddamn tears. I always cried at the most inopportune moments.

"You wait here. Don't you move and don't you puke again, you poor thing." Siobhan whirled and stormed down the gravel path toward the courtyard.

Poor thing? Huh?

Alarmed, I tried to call her back, but she ignored me. Over the past few months, she'd gotten very good at ignoring me. Unless she specifically wanted to skewer me with unkind words, she pretended I didn't exist. Was she actually going to go rip Murphy and Fee new assholes? On my behalf? And I was stuck out in the cold and supposed to wait? The woman was diabolical even when she apparently wanted to help.

"Shit," I muttered and kicked some loose gravel. I wrapped my arms around myself. Right on cue, a gust of cold autumn wind attacked. My hair blew into wild witch snarls as dead leaves rattled down the path around my boots.

A cold stone bench tucked into a hedge more brown than green provided scant protection, but I retreated to it anyway. The chill from the stone penetrated through my jeans and I shivered. Shifting was going to be a bitch those few moments when we were naked and in this form. The temperature wouldn't matter a damn once we'd achieved wolf form, but I didn't relish freezing my ass off in the interim. I didn't want to take the pack bond either. I didn't want to make love in a group. Murphy and I hadn't had sex in over a month. I wanted to be alone with him, not surrounded by other people. Was he going to be mad at me because his mother yelled at him in front of the whole pack and embarrassed the shit out of him? Was she going to shame him that way or had she just marooned me here so I wouldn't ruin the whole fucking hunt?

I tucked my chin beneath my turtleneck sweater in a vain attempt at warmth.

The top of the hedge blocked my view so I couldn't see what was happening in the courtyard or if everyone had gone into the castle to escape the bitter cold. I didn't hear shouting. Just the goddamn wind and the relentless cold splash of water into the fountain. If only I could go into the castle. Fires would be burning in the massive fireplaces and there would be food and hot coffee.

Murphy told me there was a huge room full of mattresses and blankets where the pack orgy took place when it was too cold or rainy to have sex outside in the meadow by the lake. Even though I wanted to be alone with him, I still wished I could be in that room right now. Or I had a hat. Why hadn't I worn my knit hat to keep my ears from freezing? Or my gloves? Or another shirt under my turtleneck?

Was Siobhan telling the entire pack about my father's pack bond? At the top of her lungs so nobody was left out of hearing range, not even the kids?

My father's face mocked me from my mind's eye. Cold and superior. Handsome. Reddish blond hair, disdainful smile. From the time I'd hit puberty, I'd never been good enough. Nothing I'd done had been right. He'd waited and schemed for the day I'd fall underneath his pack bond. The day he could make me do whatever he wanted.

Just like Colm, Deirdre and Fee would be able to do in a few hours. No, it wouldn't be like that. Mac Tire was over a hundred members strong and the pack bond would not be potent enough for the Alphas to have absolute control the way my father had over the twenty poor members of Mayflower. Everyone told me that. Only, what if it wasn't true?

What if my wolf wasn't the same? What if she felt the yoke of another hated bond and refused to come out ever again? Maybe I would lose her forever because I was fucking stupid enough to willingly take another pack bond. I wasn't just chaining myself, but enslaving her as well.

Paddy's funeral had been brutally sad, but my wolf had been perfect. She'd known me and I'd known her. We'd been fused in a way we'd never been before. She completed me in a way I'd never known was possible. I'd wanted so much to be with her again, but Murphy was busy and grief-stricken and nobody would let him alone, so, of course, he hadn't had time for me or my wolf. I'd been content to wait. Stupid me, I'd forgotten about the damn pack bond. Now it was here and I'd only been with my wolf three times. It wasn't enough.

* * * *

I was crying when two people sat beside me on the cold bench. I smelled them before I saw them. Colm and Deirdre. Two out of three of my Alphas. Great.

Deirdre wrapped her arms around me and that made me cry even harder. Colm took one of my hands between both of his and squeezed. We sat together until I could stop the waterworks. They were so patient, my heart hurt. Why were they being so good to me? I was a pain in the ass. They didn't have time for my stupid bullshit. They ought to be mad at me, but instead were comforting and kind.

Gravel crunched beneath someone's booted feet. I looked up and saw Fee, her face contorted with shame and sorrow. She lowered herself to her knees before me and buried her face in my lap. Her shoulders shook with sobs and I combed my fingers through her wind-snarled hair.

"Don't cry, Fee." I'd made my Alpha cry.

"You're all the time helping me and letting me take over your life and your home. You're more of a mother to Will than I am. And this is the thanks you get. When you need me, I'm not there, am I?" Fee lifted her tear-stained face to mine and wrapped her fingers around my wrists. "I knew what you went through with that evil bastard father of yours and even last night when you were scared, I told you to suck it up and get over it instead of letting you talk about it like you wanted."

"I don't like to talk about it," I told her. "I haven't talked about what happened with anybody. Not even Liam, so don't blame yourself, Fee, please."

"When she drank the elixir that released her from the pack bond, it hit her hard." Fee looked at Colm and Deirdre, her eyes wide with shame. "I think because it had never activated in her. She shifted totally on this plane. All the pain intensified. It was horrific, Paddy told me." She swiped at her eyes with the back of her hand.

"Paddy wasn't there," I reminded her. "Nobody from Mac Tire was there."

"Of course they weren't, you poor thing, because we've been piss-poor pack mates to you. It's a wonder you still want to belong to us. If Colm and Deirdre had known about this like they should have because I ought to have told them, this hunt wouldn't be happening like this. They've been waiting and waiting for me to be ready to do it and I kept putting them off. This is my fault."

"I'm sorry, Stanzie." Colm's voice was soft and gentle. Totally at odds with his massively muscled body and harsh features. "We'd put this off entirely, but Deirdre needs it and she won't be able to shift soon. One of the main reasons we want it done is for the babies. They need the help."

"Is something the matter?" My fears were forgotten and I turned to Deirdre in shock. She was so tiny and Colm was nearly seven feet tall. "You're having twins?"

"Triplets," she said and a mix of anxiety and joy crossed her face. "Andrew says I'm going to end up spending at least the last two months on bed rest. This will be the last time I shift."

"And the pack isn't recovering from the blow of losing Paddy," said Colm.

"Because of me. Because I'm not," Fee whispered. Colm reached out a hand to touch her hair. His expression was affectionate and for a moment he looked like Paddy except with straight, red hair. They were half-brothers, but I'd never seen the resemblance until just now.

"I'm sorry I'm so impatient, Fiona."

Fee's mouth twisted. "I'm sorry I'm so awful. I've been so mean to you, Colm O'Reilly. And to you too, Deirdre. To everyone." Tears slid down her cheeks, and Colm got up so he could pull her into his arms. Deirdre stood too and the swell of her pregnant belly made her arms and legs look stick-like. Triplets. Jesus.

She wrapped her arms around Fee from the back and the three Alphas held each other. Which was how it should have been from the start, only Fee hadn't let them get close.

A measure of scared relief flooded me. I still was afraid of the pack bond, but knew my wolf would want to protect her Alpha and the babies. Even if it meant she wouldn't be free anymore. Babies were treasures. Every pack member believed that.

This pack bond was not forever. Not thirty years like Paul's. This triad's time as Alphas would be up in two years and a new Alpha duo or triad would step up. It might even be me and Murphy. It probably would be unless I completely blew everything and turned the pack against me. Which I just might, if I didn't stop being a baby about the pack bond.

What would it be like to give the pack bond instead of receive it? I knew I would never, ever abuse it. I looked at Fee, Colm and Deirdre and realized they wouldn't either.

No, the opportunity for control and domination was slight, but the chance for promoting good will and healing was great. The pack would stop looking to Murphy and start looking to Colm and everyone would move on from the grief.

We wouldn't be losing Paddy. He was already lost to us. We'd lose the mindless, soul-sucking grief. Maybe even be able to remember him with laughter instead of tears.

Just a few feet away, he'd spilled his life's blood on the gravel, victim of a stabbing. I'd knelt in his blood so I could smooth the curly hair from his pale, clammy forehead and hold his hand as he'd lain dying.

The pack ring was cold on my finger. I twisted it, trying to find comfort. He'd presented it to me at my tribunal, He told me I was family and I belonged to him. I gave myself to him that day. A part of me would always be his.

Would a part of me also be Colm's? Deirdre's? Fee already had me. We were best friends. She was my Alpha, no question.

Deirdre sat beside me and put her arm around my shoulders. Colm continued to rock Fee as she sobbed against his muscled chest.

Colm had been the first member of Mac Tire I'd met in person when I'd come to Dublin. Standing guard outside the pack's pub, An Puca, he'd seemed all brawn and very little brain. He'd challenged me and denied me admittance to the pub, but I'd stood up to him at first before I retreated miserably. After that, he'd become my protector, but I'd been so wrapped up in Paddy and Murphy and their drama, I'd barely given Colm a second thought.

Over the past three months in Ireland, I'd begun to know Deirdre. I spent a fair amount of time playing the harp at An Puca on nights Fee or Murphy wanted to get out of the stifling apartment. Between songs and on breaks, Deirdre always supplied me with cold cider or Guinness. Alannah Doyle, the bartender, wouldn't spit in glasses she poured for Deirdre, but she had the one time I'd been rash enough to approach the bar on my own.

Alannah Doyle had been bonded to Declan Byrne—traitor to the pack. He'd given Grandfather Mick the knife he'd used to gut Paddy. On directions from Glenn Murphy.

Alannah occupied a unique and uncomfortable position in Mac Tire. On one hand, she was the ex-bond mate of the notorious and despised Declan Byrne. On the other, she was the half-sister of the beloved, dead Paddy O'Reilly. So people both reviled and revered her.

She'd bonded with another duo who were said to be poised to be named contenders for the next Alpha election. The duo was obviously banking on Alannah's status as half-sister to Paddy and full sister to the current Alpha male, Colm.

An icy shiver slid down my spine. If Alannah became an Alpha female, I'd have to take a pack bond from her. She hated me. Blamed me for exposing Declan. She couldn't hate him. He was dead. So she transferred all her malice to me, his accuser.

I'd had such rosy thoughts of belonging to a pack again. But Mac Tire was full of rage, grief and churning confusion.

The pack bond would help.

"You can take the pack bond later, Stanzie." Deirdre pressed her forehead to my cheek. Her skin was cold.

"You ought to be inside. It's freezing," I said.

"It would have to be after the babies are born." Deirdre took a deep breath. The thought of giving birth obviously frightened her. No wonder. Triplets. Colm-sized triplets. "I can't shift after today. Andrew's not even happy about today."

Andrew Brody was the pack's doctor. He was also bonded to Paddy's mother, Maureen O'Shea, and now, Siobhan Carmichael as well.

"When he was Alpha, his first bond mate almost died in childbirth. The babies did die." Deirdre shivered, not from the cold. I took her hand in both of mine and squeezed. "I think he's a little overprotective. I feel fine, Stanzie. Tired, of course, but fine."

"I think you ought to listen to him. And I don't want to wait until after the babies are born. I want to be part of this today. I'm scared, but I don't want to put it off. It'll just hang over me if I do."

"The sword of Damocles," she said with an understanding laugh. "And, listen, if you need someone to talk to, I'm always here."

My throat constricted. *Did* I want someone to talk to? I never really talked about my fears or the things that had happened to me. I just wanted to put them all behind me where they couldn't poison me anymore.

Besides, Colm and Deirdre knew nothing of the conspiracy. At least not yet. I sure as hell didn't want to be the one who told them.

The rotten branch of the corrupt movement within the Guardians had been pruned away from Mac Tire. Now all that remained was the positive force of Councilor Etain Feehery. Not part of the underground movement, she'd been the one who decreed Colm and Deirdre should be kept in the dark, at least until Deirdre gave birth.

Everything was so tangled I couldn't even talk about it without tripping if I tried.

That was Murphy's problem too. He couldn't talk to his Alphas about the loss of his father or best friend without going into the conspiracy angle. Fee was too close to it and she relied on him. Murphy constantly listened to her and took care of her and soothed her. He couldn't then turn around and confide in her—she didn't have the strength for it yet.

And he wouldn't talk to me. At first Glenn's and Paddy's deaths had brought us together. We'd clung to each other until Fee and the others descended upon our apartment and infiltrated nearly every moment we had.

"This will be a good thing, Stanzie. You'll see," promised Deirdre. "We'd best go inside. Everyone's waiting." She dug a tissue from her pocket and held it out to Fee, who took it gratefully.

"I've been such a bitch," Fee said after she'd blown her nose.

"You've had your reasons." Deirdre extended her hand for help off the bench. Colm stepped forward, but Fee moved faster. Once Deirdre was standing, Fee wrapped her arm around her bond mate's waist and they walked down the gravel path toward the castle.

Colm held out his gargantuan hand to me. Mine was dwarfed within it when his fingers closed. He drew me to my feet and kept hold of my hand, his fingers laced with mine.

"I always wanted to be Alpha," he confided as we walked. "But I sure as shit never wanted to be Alpha in a situation like this. I miss Paddy, Stanzie. He was my little brother and I wish it could've been me instead of him to die bleeding on the ground the way he did."

A groan of grief escaped me. I didn't want to talk about Paddy. Especially when we were at the spot where he'd fallen. A glance down confirmed there was no blood—the gravel had been washed clean. But I still knew.

"Right here," I said. Colm made me think of it, so now I'd share the wealth. I tugged him to a stop and he followed my gaze. "He fell right here." The splash of water from the fountain beside us was gratingly loud. Stinging cold droplets sprayed over us, but we didn't move.

"They say you stayed with him. Here, and in the ambulance. You even tried to go into surgery with him but they wouldn't let you." Colm's voice was hushed, and I squeezed my eyes shut against the memory.

"He asked me to stay with him. I promised him I would. I broke the promise, Colm. They wouldn't let me stay with him." My voice wobbled and the next thing I knew, I was in Colm's arms. He was so warm, I burrowed into him for comfort.

"No, you didn't. Allerton told me Paddy was out of it by then. He never knew you weren't there. But you were there when it counted."

"Why me? It should have been Fee or you or somebody he loved." Guilt choked me until I couldn't breathe. Poor Paddy had been dying and all he'd had with him was me and Jason Allerton. Virtual strangers. A cold tear slid down my cheek.

"He loved you, woman," Colm said harshly. "Didn't he always brag about you when he'd had a few shots of whiskey?"

"Bragged? About what?"

"How brave you were at that tribunal. How clever you were to outfox that bastard Alpha. You saved that girl."

"She died," I said. "I didn't save her, didn't save him and I wasn't clever, Colm. I was desperate and scared. He was the one who got me through that damn tribunal. He did." Sobs overcame me again. Why did it still hurt so much? When would it stop? Why did I have to lose everyone who meant anything to me?

Colm rocked me, his face buried in my snarled hair.

"Will the pack bond make this better?" I asked. When I tilted my neck back so I could look up at his face, I discovered he was crying too. I brushed his tears away with my fingers. Alphas shouldn't cry. I shouldn't make them cry.

"I hope so," he said forlornly. "Right now I feel like the shittiest Alpha that ever was, you know that?"

"You aren't," I said. "Don't say that, Colm."

A small smile tugged the corner of his mouth. "Worst one in the whole history of Mac Tire."

"Bullshit," I argued.

"Most people think of your Liam as their Alpha more than me. I'm a fucking afterthought to most of them."

I shook my head.

"He was a fine Alpha in his time and he'll be a better one with you by his side, but it's my turn now. I think the pack bond will help me prove myself. I let Fee get away with putting it off and I shouldn't have. Etain argued with me about it. Deirdre didn't argue, but she was upset with me. All my people counseled against putting it off, but I have a soft spot for that woman. She was my brother's bond mate."

"She's your bond mate," I reminded him, and he snorted.

"I can barely handle Deirdre. Fee's a fucking whirlwind, Stanzie. Always has been. Dancing around—Paddy's the only one who could keep up with her. Well, Paddy and her brother. I'm putting a lot of hope into this damn pack bond, you know that? Because it's a symbol. A starting point. We bonded at Paddy's funeral, for Christ's sake. Nobody sees me. I'm just filling in for him. But that's not who I want to be. You understand?" He gave me a shake and I grabbed his elbows to steady myself.

"You and Liam could support us. You could try to do that."

"We do," I objected.

"You don't," he said. "You harbor Fee and her baby. You let the other members of this pack turn to you and don't bring them to me and Deirdre. You and Liam walk into An Puca and everyone flocks around like you were rock stars. Deirdre and I could stand on the bar and shout for three hours before someone bothered to notice us and then it would only be to yell at us to shut the fuck up. You want to be the next Alphas, fine. Go for it. But, damn it, you give me and Deirdre our shot." He shook me again, his brown eyes full of frustration.

"I'm so angry, Stanzie Newcastle. At you. At your feckin' bond mate. At this situation. Something's got to give."

I bit my lip. A pack bond formed with an angry Alpha. An Alpha who was furious with me.

"You're the lynch pin, don'tcha see? Liam listens to you. Fee does. And you sit there and play your fucking harp and don't say a fucking word. Why?" Colm shook me again.

Far ahead of us, Fee and Deirdre were nearly to the top of the staircase to the massive castle doors. The courtyard was deserted. Just me and angry Colm.

The wind whipped my hair around my face, but I couldn't brush it away because Colm held my arms. His fingers bit into my flesh even through the padding of my sweater and jacket.

"Let go of me." I tried to jerk out of his grasp, but his fingers were like iron. "You have no fucking clue what I do or don't do. You want the respect of your goddamn pack, do something besides cater to Fee. Take control, you pussy-whipped bastard."

I waited for him to hit me, but instead, he threw back his head and shouted with laughter.

The sound was incongruous in this cold, bleak setting. Paddy had been mortally wounded on this very spot and now Colm was laughing. The funny thing was, Paddy would've been laughing too. Maybe he was. Fee had seen his spirit lingering in this world and I'd asked him to go away, but what if he hadn't? He could be here right this second. I swore I could almost smell his cologne.

"You're right," Colm said as he wrapped a beefy arm around my shoulders and all but dragged me down the gravel path. "So this is what I'm doing. Forging the pack bond like I ought to have three months ago. You with me?"

"All the way," I vowed and he laughed again. I sneaked a look at his face in profile. His red hair stood up like a rooster's comb. A tingling shivered down my spine. My Alpha. He was my Alpha. For the first time, I felt it more than I understood it.

* * * *

The fireplaces at either end of the massive room roared. Choked with logs, they gave off stultifying heat when close to the flames. The middle of the room was chilly. The pack members nearest the blaze had shed their jackets and some even their sweaters. Those in the center huddled together for warmth, jackets on. Most of them had bottles of water. The mattresses on the floor were piled with brightly colored sheets and pillows. Three or four couples had already claimed theirs, but no one was making love yet, although I did see several couples kissing.

Colm left me near the fireplace on the north wall and I held my frozen fingers out to the flickering flames. God, the warmth felt good. When my fingers thawed, I removed my pack ring, bond pendant and earrings and put them in my purse for safe keeping until after I'd shifted back. Purses were piled in a heap in a corner of the room, and I threw mine on top of the stack. I searched for Murphy and spied him near the French doors that opened onto the garden overlooking the lake. A woman with bright red corkscrew curls halfway down her back had her arms wound around his neck while she stood on tiptoe whispering something into his ear.

He had a half-hearted smile, one hand on her shoulder as he listened to whatever proposal she made, but when he saw me, gently set her aside. The redhead turned around with a pout and I wasn't surprised at all to see it was Alannah Doyle, the conniving witch. A big, evil smirk lit her pretty face. Any hopes I'd harbored that Siobhan had kept the story of my father's pack bond between herself and the Alphas crumbled into ash like the logs in the fire. Shit.

Conversation ceased as the people around me stared.

"God, your mother has a big mouth," I said when Murphy got close enough so I didn't have to shout. Although I should have.

A pained smile twisted Murphy's lips. "She was really pissed. She actually boxed my ears."

A horrified laugh burst from my mouth, and I covered it with my hand.

"She hasn't boxed my ears since I was sixteen and caught me making out behind the bushes with Caitlin Bell. We're cousins, you know. And to this day, Caitlin won't even give me a hug if my mother's anywhere near. And she's always near." Murphy shook his head.

I stared at him, struck speechless as he'd no doubt intended. I'd met Caitlin at the pub and she was pretty enough to turn any boy's head, even her cousin's.

"How old was she?" I couldn't help but ask.

"Fourteen or thereabouts," he said with a wince. "I know I took shocking advantage, but it was all her idea, although she'll deny it. She's a liar, Stanzie. 'Wonder what it feels like to kiss somebody on the lips,' she said. 'Do you think it would be gross, Liam? Maybe it would be nice. Want to try it maybe?' What was I supposed to do with her puckered up and adorable and me frigging sixteen and never been kissed?"

"Stop." I gave his shoulder a gentle shove and the people closest to us burst into laughter. The tips of Murphy's ears were red, but he'd embarrassed himself on purpose to divert attention from my humiliation. One more reason to love him.

Murphy grinned and I rolled my eyes.

"Colm and Deirdre talk to you? Everything okay?" he asked.

"I told Colm he was pussy-whipped." I'd get Murphy back for the Caitlin Bell story if it killed me.

He choked on strangled laughter. "Did he cry?"

I dissolved into laughter. Jerk.

"I would have cried," he added and I smacked his shoulder again.

"You wouldn't have and neither did he. He laughed at me."

"I'll bet he did." Murphy looked proud of me. He lifted my chin with gentle fingers so he could look me in the eye. "You are all right, aren't you? You going to go through with this today? Did Colm give you a choice?"

"Deirdre did, but I chose to do it today," I said.

The skin around Murphy's eyes crinkled when he smiled. "That's my brave girl."

I wrapped my fingers around his wrist so he couldn't move away and his smile faltered.

"You'll stay with my wolf, won't you?" I asked. I didn't know what she'd do when she felt the pack bond. Everyone's wolves would want to run with Murphy's, and she'd get crowded out. The way I did in human form whenever more than three people were in the room with him.

Even now, several people were making steady progress in his direction. Those around us hung on our every word, no doubt waiting for their chance to swoop into our conversation and take it over.

"Every minute," he promised. He gave my chin a squeeze and kissed my forehead. His expression was stricken and sad.

* * * *

When my father released Mayflower from the pack bond, he'd mixed his blood with herbs and the vile concoction had been served up in glass test tubes.

Today, we were lined up and given bottles of obviously doctored water, judging by the bits of leaves and petals suspended in the liquid. The water was cloudy, but not with blood. Where was the blood? My gorge rose at the thought of drinking the contents of the bottle, but everyone around me chugged theirs as if it tasted great.

Murphy and I were in middle of the line. I hadn't wanted to go first, but I also hadn't wanted to be at the very end. The suspense would've killed me. I figured with just as many people in back of me as in front, I wouldn't have time to chicken out, but wouldn't panic because I didn't know what the hell to expect.

Murphy kept one arm around me as we shuffled along. I craned my neck to see what the hell the Alphas were doing with those at the front, but it was just my luck to be in back of three tall, broad shouldered Irish men with their equally tall bond mates. I could have stepped out of the line to see, but sure as hell didn't want everyone gawking at me more than they already were.

My friend Ryan Kelly was behind Murphy. He reached out to touch my shoulder and I nearly dropped my damn bottle of suspended crap. Herbs. Elixir. Whatever.

"You gonna drink that or beat me with it?" Ryan took a wary step back and I realized I was brandishing the bottle at him.

"What does it taste like?" My question came out more of a petulant whine than an inquiry, and I grimaced.

"Dunno. Kinda minty," said Ryan. His bottle was empty. "You really need to have it drunk by the time you get up to the Alphas, Stanz."

"Thank you for that newsflash, Ryan." I rolled my eyes. Next to Murphy, I thought Ryan Kelly was the most attractive man in Mac Tire. Young, though. Not even twenty-four. No bond mate, but I was sure he made hearts swoon at Regionals. We'd gotten close during Declan Byrne's tribunal. He saved my life when Glenn Murphy tried to strangle me. His memory was still fuzzy, thanks to the vicious knock on the head he'd taken tumbling down the stairs. He was lucky that's all that happened to him. Glenn Murphy fell too, and he'd broken his neck.

Ryan, Murphy, Fee and Etain Feehery were the only members of Mac Tire who knew that. Everyone else believed the heart attack story, although sometimes I caught Siobhan staring at me suspiciously. I shuddered to think what she'd do if she knew the truth. Finish what her bond mate had started probably.

Murphy's arm tightened around my shoulders. I was being mean to Ryan, but honestly, I knew I had to drink the damn water. I had time, though—we weren't near the front yet.

"You nervous?" Ryan asked. "I was scared shitless the first time I took the pack bond from Paddy and Fee."

"Really?" I tried to relax my death clutch on the bottle. "I don't remember taking it with Paul."

"That was fucked up, Stanzie," said Ryan. Now that I'd brought it up, he was free to as well. "Mac Tire's not like that. Give us a chance, you'll see."

"I'm standing here, aren't I?" My smile felt weak and fake.

"Yeah. And not drinking the elixir," Ryan pointed out.

"Shut up," Murphy told him in a low voice full of friendly exasperation. "Don't push her, Ryan."

Ryan gave Murphy a look of pure frustration. "No worries, Liam. Maybe you've been too busy looking after everybody and their brother in this pack, but while you've been everyone's handy shoulder to cry on, Stanzie and I have become good friends. I know when to speak and when to shut the fuck up around her."

I winced at Ryan's bluntness.

"Yeah?" Murphy's jaw swelled. "It's too goddamn bad you don't have that same level of intimacy with me, isn't it?"

Ryan's eyes widened and he took a step backward. "Don't start something up. I'm not saying we've been screwing behind your back."

"What the hell are you saying then?" Murphy demanded.

"Please don't do this," I whispered. "I'm nervous enough as it is without you two going territorial."

"This little shit better shut his mouth. That's all I'm saying." Murphy snarled and Ryan paled.

"You know damn well you're the only man she looks at in this pack. All right? Cards on the table? Peace." Ryan spread his hands in smoothing motion as if he could erase everything we'd said.

"Liam, this is a hunt," said one of the brawny men ahead of me in line. I thought his name might be Ronan. It was hard to keep everyone straight. Mac Tire was so big. He and everyone else in the general vicinity had been listening intently. "The gobshite's smelling everyone's lust and it's gone to his frigging head. Give him a break. Everyone knows you don't do threesomes. Jesus, Ryan, get some sense into your feckin' skull before I break it open for you."

"Sorry." Ryan's face flamed with humiliation.

Murphy clenched his jaw so tightly my own ached in sympathy. I wrapped my arm around his waist and leaned my head on his shoulder. Did he really think I would have slept with Ryan behind his back? Just because he didn't sleep with me himself?

"We're all friends here," said Ronan. "Right? Liam?"

Murphy gave a jerk of his head that looked like it hurt. Ryan nodded nervously. I wanted to tell him it was all right but was afraid if I spoke to him, Murphy would rip his frigging head off. Irish tempers were nothing to poke at unless, of course, a person enjoyed stirring up a hornets' nest of fury.

A brawl before a hunt was something this pack enjoyed, but we were also taking the pack bond so we had to be on our best behavior. At least I think that's what Ronan was trying to telegraph to me with his eyebrows. I sure as hell didn't want to be the one to light the match to Murphy's powder keg of a temper. Fuck that.

"Ryan, come up here, love, with us." The blond woman who was bonded with the man in front of Ronan gestured for Ryan to move up in line. "Have you got a partner yet for the hunt?"

"No, Cass." Ryan looked torn between acute mortification and hopeful lust. Cass O'Connor was very pretty.

"Well, now you do." She grinned as she held out her hand.

With a mumbled apology, Ryan slid past me and Murphy so he could stand between Cass and her bond mate, Sean. He gave Ryan a welcoming clap on the back. Obviously he had no issues with threesomes.

Murphy's muscles were hard as rocks beneath his skin. I wished he would relax. He was making me more nervous. I twisted the cap off my bottle of doctored water so I could take a swig. Bits of sweet mint plus other herbs danced on my tongue. Was that marjoram? Lavender? Something similar? I forced myself to swallow and tried not to gag. This elixir tasted completely different from the one I'd drunk to break my father's pack bond. No blood, also the herbs were sweet not sour.

Cautiously, I took another sip, aware Murphy watched me. So was everyone else around. A bug on a pin, that's what I felt like in this pack. Thanks to Siobhan Carmichael.

"Not that bad, is it, Stanzie?" Ronan winked at me before he finished his own bottle. One of the grandmothers passed by with a bag and he tossed the bottle into it. Murphy discarded his as well. I'd have to wait for the next time around. Maybe by the time she'd worked her way back up from the end of the line. I'd have the bottle emptied.

Another minty swig. I wished the bits had been chopped finer, but maybe they needed to be this size. The recipes were very exact for a reason.

"Why does the pack bond work?" I asked Murphy. "Is it metaphysics? Magic? What?"

He shrugged. "I don't know, honey. It just works. Like shifting."

"Others don't have bullshit things like pack bonds," I muttered beneath my breath, but he heard me and gave me a hug.

"The Native Americans had some interesting rituals," he told me. "Vision quests and all that. The Egyptians too. Modern man has lost a lot of his connection to the earth and the otherworld."

"The pack bond belongs to the otherworld?" This was a concept I hadn't considered before.

"I don't know," he said again. Did he know *anything*? How could people blindly take something like a pack bond and not know its origins?

I took another swallow. Either the bits weren't as big as I'd thought or I was getting used to them. The taste was growing on me too. Something tugged inside me, like a fish nibbling at a baited hook. Was it my wolf? Did she like the taste too?

I bit my lip and gulped more. Definite warmth was spreading throughout my body. Did everyone feel it?

I touched my fingers to Murphy's cheek. His skin was hot, but he was not particularly flushed. Couldn't be the heat of the fireplaces, we were nowhere near either of them.

Those who had been in the front of the line were now spreading out. The mattresses by the fireplaces were being chosen first.

I watched Andrew strip off his sweater. Siobhan and Maureen were sprawled across a mattress. Siobhan had let her blond hair down from its customary twist and Maureen was running her fingers through it, her eyes half lidded. Andrew sank to his knees before his bond mates and they moved into his arms together.

Siobhan bit one of his earlobes playfully while Maureen kissed his throat.

I turned to face forward again. My jeans chafed the inside of my thighs, which had suddenly gone tender.

Ryan and Cass were making out and when the line moved up and they didn't, Ronan gave Ryan a good-natured shove.

"Drink it all, dearie." The grandmother's voice was kindly, but she still scared me. Where'd she come from? I jerked in shock and nearly dropped the bottle. Two or three mouthfuls were left and since the grandmother didn't appear inclined to move without my empty bottle in her bag, I hastily swallowed the rest of the elixir in one gulp.

Fire lit in my stomach and branched out in glowing tendrils throughout my body.

"It is magic, isn't it?" I whispered to her when I tucked my bottle into the bag. She gave me a mysterious grin.

"The magic part is you," she told me before she moved on.

* * * *

We didn't *drink* the blood. We mixed ours with the Alphas'. Three chairs had been placed on a small riser so the Alpha triad could sit while the pack advanced by them. Colm was first. He had a small silver knife and used the sharp point of it to prick the meat of his thumb until blood ran. Then he handed the knife to the person in front of him, who also pricked their thumb. Skin to skin, thumb to thumb, the blood mingled. Contact might last fifteen seconds or forty-five. It seemed to depend on the relationship between the Alpha and the pack member.

Murphy went ahead of me. He and Colm exchanged a long, silent look before Colm nicked his already bleeding thumb with the knife before passing it, handle side out, to Murphy.

A flash of silver, and Murphy's thumb bled. He and Colm pressed their thumbs together. One heartbeat, two. I held my breath and let it out with a whoosh when Murphy moved to stand before Deirdre.

My turn. I squared my shoulders. Part of me wanted to run away. But the heat inside me was a fire that needed more. Almost against my will, I dragged myself in front of Colm.

He was solemn, no smile for me. Paddy would've smiled, I just knew it.

Colm handed me the knife. When had Murphy given it back? The blade was hot to the touch, warmed by the blood and body heat of countless others.

The metallic tang of blood coated my sinuses. The crackling flames in the fireplace nearly deafened me. So did Colm's steady heartbeat. Mine was as fast as a humming bird's gossamer wings. Hot. So damn hot.

Right hand? Left hand? Fuck, I'd known only a moment before. Left. It was the left.

The sting of the blade made me gasp, and I bit my lip. Blood welled on the sides of the slice and ran down to my knuckle.

Colm took the knife back and held up his bleeding left thumb. The slightest twitch of his mouth. Was that a smile?

I pressed my thumb to his as the world stopped spinning. My vision blurred as if someone had thrown a silver veil over my head. I couldn't breathe. I was drowning in invisible water. My lungs burned then, shock, the world spun on its axis again. A rush of cold air smacked me in the face as I sucked in a deep breath. The veil lifted.

What the fuck? Colm did smile then and I stumbled as I moved over three steps to Deirdre.

I didn't need her silver knife., My thumb still bled. Her smile lit her pretty face, but she was exhausted. When we pressed our thumbs together, I sent her some of my strength. A small push of energy from me to her. Electric tingling as she absorbed what I sent. Her eyes widened gratefully. Then the world stopped again and everything went silver for several heartbeats.

Fee's eyes were still red-rimmed from crying and, when I pressed my bleeding thumb to hers, she gave me her grief. I don't think she meant to, but maybe she couldn't help it. She missed Paddy so much. For a dizzying second, my perspective shifted and I was the one sitting on the riser, Paddy beside me. I smelled his cologne and his blood. We were thinking about Murphy, who'd just lost his bond mate and wouldn't take the pack bond, wouldn't stay in Dublin with us. All this happened four years ago, not tonight, but it made perfect sense to me in the moment. Time was fluid and it skipped like a stone across the flat surface of a dusky lake.

The world ground to a halt as everything turned silver. I was myself again. Fee and I stared at each other. Had she been me? Had she experienced my sense of terror at the prospect of tying myself to her and the rest of the pack? Maybe seen with my eyes as I'd drunk the unbinding elixir in Scott and Faith's basement? She'd seen something, of that I was sure.

Murphy waited for me a few steps away, near the wall. His dark eyes gleamed amber. His wolf was awake inside him somehow. The pack bond woke him, just as sex did?

All around us, bodies writhed on mattresses. I stepped over a pair of red shoes and a crumpled sweater, arms inside out. I hissed aloud when Murphy closed his fingers around my wrist. He was burning up.

He slammed me against the stone wall and moved so every inch of him pressed against me. His cock was hard as a stone in his jeans and he groaned when I slid my hands down to cup his ass. He kiss burned my mouth. Our teeth clicked together as we dueled for dominance with our tongues. He fisted my hair with both hands and pulled possessively. The heady scent of his blood tangled in my hair. I left bloody thumbprints on the back pockets of his jeans. One of us growled. I think it was me.

"I want to be inside you." Murphy lifted me up and I hooked my legs around his waist. His cock pressed tauntingly against my pussy, but there was too much fabric between us still.

I undid his belt buckle—why the hell did he wear a belt and button-fly jeans, the teasing bastard? He let go of my hair with one hand so he could unzip my jeans.

With his help, I wiggled them down over my hips to my knees, while his jeans dropped to his ankles. Wonderful, beautiful man, he was going commando. Wished I'd thought of that.

My panties ripped beneath the assault of his determined fingers. He slid the probing tip of his wet cock between my legs. I shifted my ass as I used the stone wall for support so I could move up and—yes. Murphy's cock rammed home. We both cried out.

"Harder," I urged as he pumped into me. The stone wall scraped my skin, but I didn't care. I locked my ankles and dug my heels into his ass.

"You're perfect," he told me as he devoured me with brutal, drugging kisses. "I love you, Stanzie. I love you so fucking much."

My wolf leaped beneath my skin, stretching over my soul like cold purple fire. She danced through my veins and scratched down my spine.

When the orgasm hit me so hard I saw shooting stars, I let out a throaty scream as I ripped to glorious pieces. An invisible wire snapped tight inside me, pulling every muscle I had into screaming pleasure pain. The wire stretched from me into Murphy and from him into the couple four feet away then from them to a triad and out farther and farther until the entire pack was enmeshed in a hazy net of pure energy.

"Fee?" I thought dreamily and came again, so explosively I screamed and banged my head against the stone wall.

"*I'm here, Stanzie.*" It was not Fee in my head but Deirdre, and I could taste Colm in the back of my throat. His sweat as it dripped from his face into my mouth as he thrust into me. I felt them all then. The whole pack become as one together in a litany of names, faces, skin, scent, taste, texture. Surreal and terrifying, spinning out of control until everything was a silver blur and I couldn't think, couldn't breathe, couldn't see or hear.

I opened my eyes only to see Murphy's face, contorted with lust as his climax pulled his muscles tight before going slack.

He sagged against me, warm and sweaty. I unhooked my ankles to let my legs slide away from his waist. Rubbery and weak, if not for the wall, I would have fallen.

"The fuck was that?" My voice was rusty croak. My throat burned.

"Pack bond," Murphy answered, his voice as hoarse as mine. He buried his face in my sticky neck and shuddered. I ran my hands along his back. He still had on his sweater, so I helped him take it off.

Mine was gone. I didn't remember taking it off, but there it was on the floor by our feet. We both still had on our boots. My bra chafed. Murphy undid the front clasp as I slid the straps down.

We kicked off our jeans, boots and socks then staggered, hand in hand, for an empty mattress. I would have fallen if he hadn't held me up. He was none too steady on his feet either.

I sprawled face first on the soft blue sheets and Murphy fell beside me. He draped one arm and a leg over me protectively.

The couple on the mattress six feet away from our heads was still going strong. When I smelled them, their sweat sparked something inside me.

Murphy as well. He moved so he was on top. I raised up on my knees so he could take me from behind. When he slid inside me, he felt so good I wanted to scream, but if I did, I'd come and I wanted to prolong the pleasure.

I'd missed this so much. Him inside me, us together. My wolf awake and itching to take over my skin.

He nipped my shoulder, his teeth so sharp against my skin I gasped. I wanted to bite him too. When he touched my cheek, I turned my head so I could sink my teeth into one of his fingers. He laughed, and a sensual shiver slipped down my spine. I arched my back and he moved faster. Perspiration dripped down my face onto the sheets. Murphy's sweat was slick against my shoulders and ass.

He whispered something in Irish which sent me tumbling over the edge into what seemed like an endless orgasm that turned me inside out.

Cold wind blew across us from the open French doors. People were leaving in twos and threes, headed for the meadow above the lake.

I wanted to go too. The wind was a siren song in my blood, singing not only to me, but my wolf as well.

Murphy pulled me to my feet and we dodged around writhing couples, discarded clothing and rumpled mattresses.

Gray clouds full of rain hung in dark spirals across the sky. Light mist drifted across my sweaty face as I moved away from the stone castle and off the paved terrace to the wet grass.

Murphy's eyes glowed feral amber as we paused for a long kiss, our bodies slick and hot against each other.

Ryan rushed past us and dropped to all fours in the green grass. His body contorted and shuddered as the shift swept over him.

Murphy kissed the side of my mouth and stepped away. Never taking his gaze from me, he went to his knees then pitched forward, breaking his fall with his palms. His back arched, but he didn't bow his head, even as the shift boiled over him.

He was smiling when he blinked out of existence. When he flashed back, he was fully wolf, but I still swore he was smiling.

My wolf howled to be free. Cold purple fire flamed beneath my skin as she stretched her claws and ripped at me. I dropped to my knees then let my hands take the rest of my weight. Pain plucked at me, but it was fleeting.

Everything turned silver and then…

* * * *

Rain, wet on my fur. Feels good. Friend looks at me. I love Friend. I lick him behind the ear and he nuzzles my throat. He tastes good. Ryan Wolf wants to run. I chase him, steer him back to the pack. Our Alphas lead the hunt. We follow. Friend runs so close our fur brushes, but our legs do not tangle. Ryan Wolf runs beside me. He sniffs me. Friend tackles him. They roll together, teeth snapping, but do not bite. They play, but Ryan Wolf rolls to Friend. Good.

The pack is far ahead. We must run fast to catch up. My paws slip in the wet grass. I smell the lake and the rain and Friend's wet fur. I sneeze, but I still run.

Siobhan Wolf breaks from the pack. She comes to us, lips wrinkled back in disgust. Why are we so far behind?

Play with us, Siobhan Wolf? She snaps at me, growls, but does not bite. She herds me ahead. We must catch up. Friend nips at Ryan Wolf's flank. He dodges away and zips first one way then the other. I want to play that game!

Alpha Colm howls. No time for play. Siobhan Wolf snarls at me, glares with golden eyes. Yes, I know. Catch up.

My pack sits in a ring around the Alphas. Alpha Fee is beautiful, but so sad. I want her to be happy again. She misses her mate. I miss him too. One blue eye, one brown. He is gone forever. He runs with Him and Her and the Thems from my old pack. Big Them and Little Them. In the otherworld now. Running there instead of here.

Alpha Deirdre is heavy with young. This is good. Cubs are good for my pack! She is tired and cannot run and play. I sit with her. Leave her alone. She must rest.

Mother and father of Alpha Deirdre are pleased with me. I guard my Alpha. You can run and play, your Alpha cub is safe with me.

Friend stays too. He wants to play, but we must protect our Alpha.

I roll to her. She nuzzles my throat but does not bite. Nudges me up. Up. Friend rolls too. Up, Friend. Stand up now.

We sit together while our pack hunts. The rain is wet against our fur. The grass is soft and smells of good things. I would like to drink from the lake, but I must stay here with Alpha Deirdre.

Alpha Fee does not want to play, but Alpha Colm is patient. He sneaks up behind her. Pounce! They roll. I feel them inside me. All my pack. My brothers and sisters. We are together.

Alpha Fee howls. I howl back. Friend howls too. We are safe together.

Chapter 3

Shepherd's pie had never tasted as good as the three heaping plates of it I shoveled into my mouth after the hunt. Spicy meat, flavorful potatoes, crisp kernels of corn. The combination was pure magic.

The minute I cleaned my plate, Murphy refilled it. He managed to devour four platefuls himself and, between us, we drank at least a gallon of fresh, cold water.

We sat shoulder to shoulder in the massive chamber where we'd made the pack bond. While we hunted, the older teens cleared away the sheets and mattresses. With the help of the grandmothers and grandfathers who had chosen not to shift, they'd set up trestle tables full of food and water. There were a few tables and chairs, but not enough for all one hundred fifty plus of us.

Murphy and I cheerfully sat on the floor, backs braced against the wall near the northern fireplace and its crackling heat, which was comforting as hell. My hair was plastered to my skull and I was chilled to the bone, but it was good. I felt alive and my head clearer than it had been in months.

Murphy had a slab of homemade crusty bread on his plate only half-eaten. When he turned his head toward the sound of someone laughing, I snatched it and stuffed it into my mouth as far it would go. The piece was bigger than my mouth, but I chewed as fast as I could.

He laughed when he saw me and sheepishly, I tore a chunk away with my teeth and gave him what was left.

"I'm starving," I apologized.

"Save room," he advised. "There's apple amber for dessert."

I moaned in anticipation. Apple amber was like apple pie with meringue, and I fucking loved it.

After Murphy wolfed down the chunk of bread, he carried our plates to one of the bins by the door. He went to the dessert table where he took his sweet time selecting the proper pieces.

While I salivated in anticipation, Colm sauntered over and slid down the wall into a graceful squat beside me. His red hair was muted with rainwater. Blood stained the left cuff of his sweater. He looked tired but happy.

"You okay?" He tipped a bottle of water to his mouth so he could suck down a huge swallow.

"It was the weirdest thing. I swore at one point I was with you, not Murphy," I said. Someone had lit the candle sconces on the wall so the flames cast dancing shadows on the stone walls. The room smelled of sweat, wet hair, shepherd's pie and sex. Not a bad combination at all.

Colm smiled but didn't say anything.

"I don't feel it now, though. The pack bond." I searched inside myself for proof of it, but felt nothing.

"It's there. When you need it, you'll draw on it. You might be doing it now, for all you or I would know."

"Tell me to do something." The soft paws of panic unsheathed claws inside me and scraped along my nerve endings. "Order me to do something."

"You'll do it because I'm your Alpha, not because of the pack bond."

"Make it something you wouldn't ask me to do as Alpha," I urged. "Please, Colm, I need this."

"I think you're panicking a wee bit myself." He sighed. "Fine then. Go spit in Liam's face. Go on."

I gaped at him. "Why can't you be serious?"

"Spit in his face. And then make out with Ryan right in front of him."

Colm obviously heard about the altercation. Pack grapevines were insidious. It hadn't even been three hours and the Alphas knew. Christ.

"Who told you what happened? You couldn't have heard it."

"You're sitting on your ass and I told you to do something," Colm reminded me. He nudged me in the side with his beefy elbow.

I burst out laughing.

"Nothing, huh?" Colm ruffled my wet hair and grinned at me. "You got yourself all panicky about nothing."

"Spit in Liam's face. Make out with Ryan. Jesus," I said between giggles.

"You're the one giving me the orders and I'm the one following them. God, maybe the pack bond got frigged up somehow and you're the one pulling the strings!" Colm gave a very realistic girly shriek. People all around us swiveled their heads.

"Move along. These are not the droids you're looking for." Colm waved their attention away and snickers filled the air.

Murphy returned with two huge pieces of apple amber and Alannah Doyle literally clinging to his elbow. All moist and doe-eyed too.

"Liam promised to share his dessert with me," she announced. Her eyes were green as grass, the color of jealousy. The greenest eyes that ever were, as Paddy once referred to them. Well, he would wax poetic about her. She was his half-sister.

"How nice of him," I said. "You seem to have forgotten a third fork." Murphy had only two in his hand. I took one and the biggest piece of apple amber.

"We don't need one. We can share." Alannah giggled and I gritted my teeth.

Murphy had the smile of a man with his balls in a vise. He tried to give her the fork and the whole piece of apple amber, but she waved both away and continued to cling to his elbow.

"It's going to be hard for him to eat with you hanging onto him like a redheaded barnacle," I observed and Colm shifted uneasily beside me.

"I'm not the clingy scared rabbit in this scenario," said Alannah with a toss of her springy curls. "Have you finished whimpering yet? Have the flashbacks to your father stopped?"

My cheeks burned.

"I really would shut the fuck up if I were you," I advised. I shoved the goddamn apple amber into Colm's surprised hands. I couldn't swallow now, I was so pissed.

Alannah's lips peeled back from her teeth in a malicious smile." The scared rabbit is going to roar like a lion now? A little late to act like you actually have a spine, isn't it?"

"I may be a rabbit, but at least I'm not an ostrich with my head fucking buried in the sand while my bond mate helps murder my brother," I declared.

A wild little scream burst from Alannah's throat and she kicked me in the face. Or she tried to, but I dodged to the right. When I toppled into him, Colm fell over, apple amber going everywhere.

"Fuck," said Murphy.

I bounced to my feet and ducked Alannah's fist just before she would have buried it in my right eye. Little bitch was fast.

"Come on, you feckin' cunt. Fight me," Alannah screamed. Every person in the room came to attention and a surge of bodies pressed together as they struggled for ringside positions to watch.

From the corner of my eye I watched Ryan hold up a twenty beneath Sean's nose. Sean fished out his money, and the bet was on.

"You'd best be betting on me, Ryan Kelly, or I'll kick your ass too," Alannah shouted. Her eyes had a crazy glow and, for a short person she seemed very big.

"If Stanzie loses, I'll *let* you kick my ass, how's that?" Ryan retorted. Laughter filled the room.

"Better get ready to bend over." Alannah's grin was ferocious.

"I'll bend over for you, sweetheart," someone said from the back of the room.

"I'd rather bend her over," called someone else to more laughter.

"I'd rather bend the two of them over at the same time," another witty bastard shouted. He meant me and Alannah. Next thing I knew someone would toss us into a kiddy pool of mud or Jell-o.

"Eat shit," I snarled. Colm snorted with laughter.

"God, you're classy. A fucking classy coward. Just what Mac Tire doesn't need," drawled Alannah as she slowly circled me. I moved with her, wishing like hell I was somewhere else. Why did I have to have such a big mouth?

"Yeah, like we need a stupid, clueless bitch like you," I muttered. Alannah hawked up a wad of spit and aimed it for my face.

I dodged out of the way, grimacing with disgust.

"You can't fight for shit. Too scared," jeered Alannah.

Murphy looked like he wanted to reach out and yank her out of the room by her hair, but he couldn't do that. Nobody fought anybody else's battles in this pack. Except for me the night I leaped on Declan Byrne's back when he'd fought dirty with a piece of glass against Paddy.

Murphy faded back to give us room, his expression apologetic when he met my gaze.

"I'll be twice the Alpha you'd ever make." Alannah lifted her bond pendant so we could all see the small Celtic knot next to the triad pendant on the chain. I had a knot pendant just like it on my chain. So did Murphy. Fee had given them to us when she backed us as her choice for the next Alpha duo.

Colm winced. "I wish she'd let me announce that myself," he muttered.

So, it was official. Alannah, Petra and Dane were up for Alpha against me and Murphy. Great. So this fight would have double the meaning. If she wiped the floor with my face, I could pretty much kiss Alpha goodbye. No baby for Murphy and I knew how much he wanted one. Hell, I did too. Now that my wolf was normal.

"You're such an asshole." Would she really throw away her shot on one stupid fight? She had just as much to lose as I did. More, because some people in the pack had not forgiven her for being bonded to Declan.

Her new bond mates looked less than thrilled. They were in the front of the crowd. Petra's face was thunderous with rage and betrayal. Dane glared at me.

"Well, fight her, for Christ's sweet sake," he shouted at me.

I calculated the odds. If Alannah won, was it really over? We still had nearly two years to election. A lot of things could shift in two years, including opinions. Especially opinions.

On the other hand, if I lost, Alannah would never let anybody forget it. I was pretty much screwed. So was Murphy, which was worse.

If Alannah were elected Alpha, she would never, ever agree to let me and Murphy run for the next Alpha pair so I'd have to wait ten years for another chance. I'd be forty-three by then, and I might still be fertile, but it was pushing it.

Alannah was already nearly forty and if she didn't make Alpha at the next election, she'd never have a baby. Babies. Why must so much hinge on them? Why could only the Alphas have them? It wasn't fair.

At that heretical thought, I froze. Alannah took advantage of my lapse of attention to dart in and land the first punch. A sucker punch right to my jaw.

I saw stars and tasted blood. I'd bitten my tongue. Damn, that hurt. The pain snapped me back in focus. I ducked her next blow aimed at my nose.

"Ah, my God, you don't know how to fight, do you? You never fought in your frigging American pack, did you?" Alannah's face crinkled in disgust.

"Stupid us, we preferred to discuss our differences instead of beating each other like fucking barbarians." I licked my lip. Was it bleeding too? Damn it.

Alannah rolled her eyes. "I won't hit you again, you poor thing. Just tell me I'll make a better Alpha than you and we'll shake hands and act all civilized as shit, how's that?"

"There's only one problem with that," I told her.

"Oh, yeah? And what would that be?"

"You'd make a terrible Alpha," I said.

"At least I don't hide behind my wolf and let her fight my battles. What's the matter, Stanzie? Scared? Why don'tcha let your wolf out to rip my throat open? That's the only way you know how to fight, isn't it? Not so fucking civilized when you're furry, are you?" Alannah smirked.

"I'm so sick of people talking about my wolf." The red veil of rage descended until everything was tinged bloody.

Front foot forward, I spun toward her and brought my other leg around in a perfect roundhouse kick. My self-defense teacher would've burst into excited cheers. I hadn't spent *all* my damn time decorating after Murphy left me in Boston.

I took Alannah out, my left foot planted smack into her stomach and she flew backward a gratifying five feet before she smashed, breathless to the floor.

"You bitch," she said when she got her breath back.

Dead silence around the room for three beats as everyone waited for her to get up.

I gestured for her to hurry up and come get me then as I swallowed a mouthful of blood. Tongue blood was sweet, but damn my jaw hurt.

She lumbered to her feet, her gaze murderous. The room erupted in cheers and screams.

Colm's grin was incredulous and Murphy looked deliriously proud. Fee jumped around pumping her fist in the air like she was Rocky after the big fight. I would punch her next, I decided.

"Lucky shot," sneered Alannah and I rolled my eyes. My self-defense instructor would beg to differ. That move had taken me three weeks to even approximate.

"Wanna try again and prove it?" I asked. The crowd went wild. Alannah scowled at them, her expression sour as curdled milk. Could I help it if they were on my side?

"So what does it feel like to kill someone?" Alannah asked. "What did it feel like when you saw their dead bodies after the car crash and knew you'd been the one to smash them into bloody pieces?"

At first I'd thought she was talking about Nate, but when she said 'car crash' the red veil of rage strangled me again. In my head, Elena's scream cut off with the snap of her neck. Grey's eyes went wide with shocked agony as he was sucked out the open door and flung into space, his spine crushed.

"What does it feel like to fuck a murderer?" I wondered. Alannah's face went black with absolute rage.

She rushed me with a wild, banshee scream and I let her come close enough so I could grab her arm and flip her over my shoulder. It *was* all leverage. My damn instructor had been right.

She hit the stone floor hard and for a moment didn't move or make a sound.

Fuck. I'd killed her. She'd cracked her skull open on the goddamn stone. No. Screw this. She could be Alpha. No problem. I didn't want to kill anyone else. How did it feel to kill someone? Cold, dark. Like the end of the world was a bullet and I was the one who pulled the trigger.

"You fucking bitch. You broke my back," Alannah screamed into the dead silence. Her eyes were full of shock and malice. "I'm paralyzed and it's all your fault."

"You're not fucking paralyzed," I yelled at her. I could see her arms and feet moving. "You wouldn't be able to yell so damn loud if you were paralyzed. Get up, you baby. Unless you're done? Are you done? Am I the next Alpha?"

"The fucking pack votes, you don't get to say who's next," she whined.

"Fine. Then tell me I won the fight and get the fuck up. Or do you need help?" I extended my hand and she spat at it. She had to move her neck to do it. Paralyzed, my ass.

"Fifteen second rule, Alannah. You lose even if you don't say uncle," Ryan said from the sidelines. He snatched the twenty from Sean's fingers triumphantly.

"Bugger off, Kelly." Alannah rolled into a slumped sitting position and gingerly touched the back of her head. "I'm bleeding," she announced and held up her red-smeared fingers.

"What the hell do you want? A choir to sing you sleep with lullabies?" I grabbed her hand and hauled her to her feet. She tried to kick me in the shin, the bitch, so I socked her in the jaw.

She flung herself at me and Colm waded in to grab her around the waist. He was laughing. Murphy pressed against my back, one hand on my shoulder, but didn't hold me back, just let me know he was there. He was laughing too.

"Where the hell did you learn those moves? They were frigging awesome." His mouth was so close to my ear, I shivered.

"After Nate Carver, I swore I'd never be defenseless in this form ever again," I answered and his laughter stopped. "I took a self-defense course at the YMCA in Boston."

I turned around so I could look at him and the guilt on his face made me wince.

"Came in handy, didn't it?" I tried to make him smile, but he was having none of it.

* * * *

We left shortly after. People spilled out of the castle and down the steps to follow us to the car, most of them reaching out to touch me and tell me how bad ass I was. I wished they'd all drop dead.

"Are you mad?" I asked after fifteen straight minutes of silence as we headed back to Dublin. The rain beat down in a steady rhythm—ticking against the roof and windshield until I wanted to scream. Late afternoon traffic clogged the road. I didn't think I'd ever get used to driving on the wrong side.

Murphy gave me a glance, as if inviting me to clarify.

"That I took a self-defense class?" I said. "You haven't said one word since I told you I did."

Murphy's mouth thinned. "I'm angry you felt you had to. Angry I wasn't there to beat the shit out of Nate Carver myself. Angry I didn't listen when you insisted Bethany hadn't hitched to an abortion clinic. I'm angry about a lot of things, Stanzie."

I scrunched down in the seat and tried to make myself as small as possible.

"Did you really think for one minute I'd let your wolf face the pack alone today?" He flung me a look of betrayal. His fingers were so tight around the steering wheel they were bleached bone white.

"No. Your wolf's always been there for mine," I whispered.

"My wolf," he ground out. "But not me. Not in this form. I'm never there for you when you need me, am I?"

I swallowed and tasted blood. My jaw ached like a bitch.

"Answer me," he said with a snarl.

"What am I supposed to say? You did what you thought was best. Your intentions are always—"

"Don't give me any crap about my intentions. You think I'm not there for you. You think I won't be when you need me." He slammed his palm into the steering wheel and I winced. I was petrified we'd crash.

"Tell me what you think, Stanzie!" Murphy struck the wheel again.

"I think you'd better calm down before you wreck us." I dug my fingers into the upholstery of the seat.

"Don't be so fucking paranoid," he suggested, but didn't yell or slam the wheel again.

"Look, all I did was take one class. One six-week class so if I ever got cornered again by someone bigger than me, I wouldn't need my wolf to get me out of there." A sob hitched in my chest. "Is that so bad?"

"I never should have left you alone that day. You could've made those calls from the car with me. I'm so, so sorry, Stanzie." He took a deep breath, fighting for control.

"It's not your fault," I said. "I'm the one who ran off without a cell phone, without telling Jossie where I was going. And, anyway, it's over. The bad guy's dead. Didn't you hear Alannah? My wolf ripped his throat out."

Murphy winced. "You handled yourself well today."

"Bullshit. I let her goad me into a fight."

"And she respects you a hell of lot more now than she ever did. You won't hear her mouth flapping anymore."

"Oh joy." I stared out at the wet Irish countryside. It was an alien landscape far from home.

"We brawl in this pack," Murphy told me. "I thought you knew that."

"I may be a member, but I don't like settling disagreements with my fists. And I don't like it when other people do it, either."

"There hasn't been a good fight in this pack in months." Murphy gave a small laugh. "You were in the last one too, as I recall."

"You weren't there." I could have slapped myself. His smile dried up and his mouth got small and tense.

"That's becoming a running theme with me, isn't it?" he asked.

"I only meant you didn't see it. I wasn't *in* the fight, I just brought an end to it. Paddy and Declan were the ones fighting."

I remembered the rage that had ripped through me when I'd seen Paddy's throat dripping blood from the piece of glass Declan Byrne clutched in his cheating hands. If there was one thing I hated worse than a fist fight, it was a fight where one person fought dirty and used a weapon when the other person had nothing.

"He would have had a scar on his face after that fight," I whispered. If he'd lived.

"I really don't want to talk about him, Stanzie." Murphy looked ready to bail out of the speeding car.

I knuckled a tear from the corner of my eye. Of course not. I wasn't Fee or anyone else in the goddamn pack. He was probably sick of talking about Paddy. But who did I have to talk about him with? Why did I always have to keep my grief to myself? I guessed I should be used to it. I'd done it when Grey and Elena died, so why should Paddy be any different?

"I thought the pack bond was supposed to make things better," I said bitterly.

"It's not a fucking cure, Stanzie." Exasperated, Murphy drove a hand through his hair.

Something inside me snapped. "Maybe if somebody would bother to tell me what the fuck it *is* instead of what it *isn't*, I wouldn't make stupid assumptions like that, would I? It won't control you, Stanzie. It won't fuck you up. It won't hurt your wolf. It won't make you feel better about the mess of your life and it won't cure a damn thing. What the fuck good is it then?" I drove my fist into the side window and welcomed the wallop of pain.

"I'm sorry your life is such a mess. That's what you get for coming here. I tried to keep you out of it, but no, you had to come chasing after me," Murphy snarled.

"Yeah, just another example of how you protect me by abandoning me like garbage. I love how you get to decide how my life is going to go. Because yours is so fucking great, everyone wants to be you, don't they?" I snorted.

"You want to be abandoned? You want to be left on the side of the road like garbage?" Murphy twisted the wheel and the car slid across two lanes to the shoulder while cars already in those lanes blared their horns.

I wrapped my arms around my head and stopped breathing—waiting for the accident. I'd go out the same way Grey and Elena had. And this crash would be my fault too.

I didn't want to live if Murphy didn't. Fate could not be so cruel as to kill Murphy and leave me alive. Not again.

Murphy's harsh breathing and the relentless pound of the rain gradually alerted me to the fact we weren't moving and we hadn't crashed. Not even close.

Billy Idol's *White Wedding* played in my head. Elena's scream choked off. The wet snap of her neck. Grey reaching out to me as he was sucked out the yawning door. The Mustang flipping over the guard rail, sheering off the top of the small tree. *Crash*, the shriek of tortured metal, the deafening silence when it was over.

When I could look at him, Murphy was slumped over the wheel, forehead braced against it, fingers white knuckled around the steering column. His heart was as loud as his breathing.

I found the door handle and yanked on it. The damn door wouldn't open at first, until I remembered it was locked. The roar of the rain seemed to rouse Murphy. He reached for me as I slid onto the pavement. I would never, ever let him drive me anywhere again. I was through with cars. Fuck them.

The rain drenched me to the skin ten steps away from the shelter of the BMW. My jaw ached and I winced when I touched it. Bruised probably. I didn't belong in this pack. I wasn't Mac Tire material. I wanted to go home in the worst way. Somewhere I fit in.

"Please get in the car." Murphy guided the BMW next to me and kept pace with my stride. I ignored him. After I blinked rain out of my eyes, I shielded them with my hand so I could look down the road for a street sign. Anything that would tell me how far away I was from Dublin. I cursed. I had no money. No purse. Where was I supposed to go? I was damned if I'd go to the apartment. Maybe I could call Fee. She might lend me some money for a hotel. Only she'd want to know what was wrong between me and Murphy and screw that.

"Stanzie." Murphy tried again, but I didn't look at him. He'd pulled across two lanes of oncoming traffic so he could throw me out of the car. Just because he hadn't actually gone through the throwing me out part didn't excuse any of it. The only person in the world I'd felt safe driving with, and now I couldn't trust him anymore.

Did that sign say ten miles or kilometers? Jesus, everyone in the pack talked miles but the street signs were in kilometers and I couldn't figure distances out. Why couldn't anything ever be easy? What was the difference between ten miles and ten kilometers? Whatever it was, it was too goddamn far to walk. At least to Dublin. In the rain. Maybe there was some fucking little town or something. Anything.

"Please," Murphy begged.

"Aren't you going to yell at me? Scream at me to get into the car?" I glared at him. That was next. If kindness didn't work, yelling might.

"No," he answered. "I know I scared you."

"You're damn right, you did. You didn't just scare me. You scared the shit out of me. You pulled across two. Fucking. Lanes. There were cars coming. It's raining and you know I'm scared of driving, especially on the wrong side of the road. Do you have any fucking idea how pissed off I am?" I kicked one of his BMW's damn tires. I hoped I left a mark. I kicked the side panel too. If I didn't make a dent, I'd at least smear mud on his precious paint job.

"We need to talk," he said.

"Not in the fucking car, we don't. I think we've pretty effectively proved we suck at talking in the car."

"Okay. We won't talk until we get home. I swear. You get in and I will drive silently and carefully. Please?"

"You're an asshole, Liam Murphy," I told him.

"I know. A very huge asshole. I know," he agreed.

"Don't think I'll forgive you just because you know you fucked up." I wrenched open the damn door and flung myself into the passenger seat. "And don't think I'm going to buckle my seatbelt. I'm fucking done doing things your way. I'm going do things my way for a change. No more seatbelts. No more waiting for you to finally remember I'm there. No more you telling me when I get to talk about Paddy and when I don't and I'm not cleaning up after Fee or the baby. I'm not waiting to go out to eat until you want to. I'm not putting my life on hold so you can make everyone in the whole damn world feel better while I sit there alone. I don't want to be your rock. You hear me, Liam Murphy? I don't want to be your fucking rock!"

"I bet you'd like to hit me with a really big one right about now though," he said and it was either explode or laugh.

I laughed.

* * * *

We didn't get three feet through the apartment door before he had me on the floor, tearing at my clothes. I ripped at his too. He kicked the door shut with his foot while simultaneously slamming his cock deep inside me.

I sank my teeth into his shoulder and he yanked my hair hard.

"Are we playing rough?" he asked me.

For an answer, I head butted him. "That's for being a giant asshole."

When he gave one of my nipples a twist, I hissed in painful pleasure. We rolled over and over, smashed into the coffee table and knocked the lamp in the corner over. The crash of the bulb shattering was loud as hell.

"We're not rolling around in glass." Murphy managed to lift me up while he was still buried inside me. I locked my legs around his waist and he staggered us over to one of the sofas. We crashed down and the springs gave a protesting wail.

I scratched his back with my nails and he bit my lip until we both tasted my blood. It smeared across our faces as we kissed and he shifted so I straddled him on my knees as he sat upright.

"I love you," he said as he tongued one of my nipples. He sucked on it, sending a shooting burst of pleasure traced a line from my breast, down my stomach to my pussy.

"I love you," I told him. When he lifted his head, his eyes gleamed with tears he blinked away.

"Say it again," he begged. "Tell me again."

"I love you." I cupped his face with my hands. Beneath my fingers, his cheeks were smooth and warm. When his wolf colored his eyes amber, my wolf reached for his through me. He pulled me down so he could kiss me and our lovemaking turned slow and gentle. His touch was reverent and lingering, his kisses a drug that pulled me into him, so my heart beat in time with his.

He brushed his lips, feather light, across my bruised jaw and bleeding lip, whispered to me in Irish as we moved together in a slowly building rhythm until he drew his breath in with a hiss and said, "I'm gonna come, Stanzie. Come with me. Please, honey, now. Now."

A rush of energy, my soul to his, and I buried my face in his sticky warm throat as the orgasm rocked through me. God, I loved this infuriating man.

Chapter 4

Murphy's smiling face was the first thing I saw when I opened my eyes the next morning. At some point we'd made it to the bed, but my recollection of how and when was hazy. The muscles in my thighs and stomach were exquisitely sore and I was starving.

The tip of his nose was approximately two inches away and he scooted across the sheets so he could bump it against mine.

"I've got an idea." He sat up in bed, covers pooling around his bare waist.

"Me too." I traced the narrow line of hair from just above his belly button down his flat stomach.

He grinned. "I suppose my idea can wait half an hour."

"An hour," I decided, and he grinned again.

* * * *

"So what's this idea?" I asked as I poured a thick stream of ketchup onto my scrambled eggs. After stirring them with my fork, I scooped a pile into my mouth. Sheer bliss.

Murphy buttered a piece of rye toast and set it on the edge of my plate. That made four slices. If he had his way, I'd eat the entire loaf and he'd butter it piece by piece for me.

"Road trip." He winked at me. "Just you and me. Pack a suitcase with a change or two of clothes, and in your case, seventeen pairs of shoes, and go wherever we fancy."

"In the car?" I crunched into a piece of the toast. Damn, it was good.

"How else would you suggest we took a road trip? Pack mule?" he deadpanned.

I swatted at him with my free hand and shoved more toast into my face.

"What part of I'm never driving with you again didn't you understand?"

"The part where you got in the car yesterday afternoon and I drove you here."

I threw the crust at him before I attacked my eggs again.

"For how long would we go?" I sucked down half a glass of orange juice, took a breath, then drank the other half. Murphy pushed his glass toward me and I drank that too. Eggs and toast made me thirsty.

"That's the beauty of it. It doesn't matter. However long we want. All you've seen of Ireland is Dublin. There's a whole lot of countryside out there and the coast and I know it's frigging November and cold as midnight in a graveyard, but we can bring coats. You can wear your boots with the fur on the inside."

"Faux fur, thank you very much. I don't wear real fur. Well, except when I'm shifted." I giggled and he rolled his eyes. "What about your job?"

"What job? The stock market?" he scoffed. "So I'll bring my laptop. We'll try to find accommodations with WiFi and if we can't, oh, Jesus, it'll be a tragedy, won't it?"

"What about my job?" I debated licking the butter off my fingers but pictured my mother's shocked expression and opted for a napkin instead. Damn manners. Always got in the way.

"Allerton's done without you for three months, what's another few days?" For the first time, wariness and frustration crept into Murphy's tone.

"You ever think about working for him again?" I selected a blueberry from my bowl of mixed fruit and popped it into my mouth.

"Are we really going to get into this now?" Murphy's frown was about to become an outright scowl. He was adorable.

"No." I forked up more eggs. "But you are going to be his Advisor again someday, Murphy. I've made up my mind."

"Well, let's all bow down in submission," he said, but at least he was smiling again.

I smiled too. My mind was made up. He would take his Advisor's job back again someday. Jason and I agreed on it the day of Paddy's funeral even if Murphy hadn't been there to accept.

* * * *

My phone chirped forty-five seconds after Murphy left the apartment to buy supplies for our road trip. He had a picnic lunch in mind even though it was freezing out, but I was game if he would be there with me.

I'd barely dragged my suitcase from beneath the bed when the damn phone went off.

I scooped it off the desk and paused to glance at the screen before I answered.

"We were just talking about you," I said. My stomach sank a little and my spine stiffened as I waited for the words that would ruin our road trip.

"I'm flattered," said Jason Allerton. "At least I think I am. Should I be?"

"We were just planning a road trip and Murphy said you could wait a few more days to put me to work since you've ignored me for three months anyway."

"I see." I really doubted he did.

"If you give me just a little bit more time, I'll talk him around into being an Advisor again," I promised somewhat rashly. Damn it, it wasn't right that Murphy quit because he thought he wasn't good enough to be an Advisor after stabbing Grandfather Mick in the heart. That bastard killed Paddy, if Murphy hadn't killed him, I would have. Or Jason would have. We'd all been there.

"I don't think that will be necessary anymore," Jason said, and my heart sank in unison with my stomach.

"Why not?" I didn't really want to know, but had to ask.

"Because I've already replaced him," Jason told me and if he'd been standing in front of me I would've thrown the phone at his face.

* * * *

Murphy found me slumped on the sofa, pillow stuffed to my chest. While he'd been gone I alternated between punching the pillow and hugging it. When I punched it, I pictured Allerton's face. When I hugged it, I saw Murphy. I knew I was irrational, but Jason Allerton was the most annoying man on the face of the earth.

"What's the matter?" Murphy let the plastic bags of food slip gently to the floor before he came to sit beside me. His face was grave as if he braced for bad news. The urge to punch the shit out of the pillow again was overwhelming.

"Our road trip is fucked for a while." I gave the pillow a vicious uppercut. In my mind, Allerton reeled backward, blood spurting from his shattered nose.

"What the hell now?" Murphy gently pried the pillow from my grasp and set it aside. He took my hands and gave them a squeeze.

"That bastard. He promised me we'd get you to come back and now he goes and does this? I can't trust him. I just can't. Maybe I should quit too. That's it. I'll quit."

"Are we talking about Allerton? What the hell's he done now?" Murphy gave my hands another squeeze.

"Sent me on a job right when you and I were going on a road trip, for one thing," I snapped.

"And for another?" I could tell by his expression he suspected. Only he didn't know the half of it.

"He's replaced you," I said and because I didn't have the damn pillow anymore, I kicked the leg of the sofa with my heel. I forgot I wasn't wearing shoes and bit back an agonized curse.

"Careful." Murphy took a breath. "I suppose that was always the risk, wasn't it? So he's replaced me. So what? I didn't want the job anyway. Go on the investigation, honey. The road trip will wait." He squeezed my hands again.

"It's not just that he's replaced you. It's who he's replaced you with." I pulled my hands from his and bounced indignantly.

Murphy's face became a blank mask. "Who?" But he knew. I could tell he knew.

"Colin Hunter, who else?"

* * * *

The night Murphy's first bond mate, Sorcha, fell down a dark flight of stairs and hemorrhaged to death, she'd been nearly four months pregnant. Murphy was pretty sure the baby had been his, but there'd been a chance it might have been Colin Hunter's. The three of them were in negotiations to form a triad. This was tricky, because Murphy and Sorcha were the Alphas at the time. Through them and their newly formed triad, Colin would have become Alpha too. Colin was an outsider to Mac Tire, so the situation had to be handled delicately. Nobody in Mac Tire had much liked Sorcha, but they adored Murphy. I suspected they would have done anything for him if he'd asked.

Although Murphy loved Sorcha with everything he was, she hadn't loved him back. She'd been in love with Colin. Murphy suspected Colin mainly saw Sorcha as his ticket to being Alpha of Mac Tire, the largest, continuous pack in Europe, but because she'd wanted Colin, Murphy had been willing to form a triad.

Before they could, Sorcha died, and Colin accused Murphy of murdering her so he wouldn't have to share Alpha male status. The pack and the Councils had done everything but laugh it off and Murphy hadn't even been brought before a tribunal. An investigation had been convened only because it was Pack law.

After it was over, Colin slunk back to the Mac Tire branch of England from which he'd come and Murphy retreated in grief-stricken pain to Belfast. He'd bought a cottage where he'd grown vegetables in the back garden for two years until Paddy and Fee convinced him to attend the Great Gathering in Paris.

Where he'd met me.

Colin Hunter eventually bonded with a woman named Devon Talbot from a small pack in England and, when the Mac Tire branch forced them out, Jason Allerton stepped in and arranged for them to join my old pack, Riverglow, in Connecticut.

He'd done this by dangling the possibility of Colin becoming one of his Advisors. That would have been a coup for ambitious Colin. Jason wanted someone in Riverglow to monitor them. He'd suspected all along that Grandfather Tobias had not acted alone when he'd tampered with the brakes of my Mustang in the name of the conspiracy.

He'd been right, of course, and Colin tried to play a role when Murphy and I had gone to Riverglow after Grandfather Tobias's tribunal, but I was the one who smoked out Callie's involvement. Colin hadn't done a damn thing except give Murphy and me a ride to a coffee house to meet Jason after we'd been shot at in the woods after shifting together. And for a while, we'd thought *Colin* had been the one who'd shot at us.

Now he was Jason's Advisor, just like I was.

Murphy hated him and I didn't blame him. Hunter had apologized for what he'd done after Sorcha's death. He even admitted he'd been after Alpha status the whole time. He'd tried to ingratiate himself with Murphy, but only because Murphy was an Advisor and in a position to help him out.

I didn't trust him because Murphy didn't. I sure as hell didn't want to work with him and I resented the untenable position in which Jason Allerton had placed me.

When I uttered Colin Hunter's name, a burst of dark fury turned Murphy's brown eyes almost black. I knew he must have felt betrayed and sold out. I would have.

Murphy had watched his best friend and Alpha get knifed to death. A person didn't recover from something like that overnight. Jason Allerton had the patience and cunning of a stalking lion. He didn't have to replace Murphy this quickly.

All the time he'd been pulling our strings and Murphy had been suspicious but played along. I'd been the one to swallow everything Jason said without any doubt. Consistently, Jason manipulated me and kept crucial information from me. He'd even bonded with my mother. One moment I thought he was the most inspiring leader I'd ever encountered, the next he was a diabolical player in a game where I didn't know the rules and didn't want to.

"I'm quitting as his Advisor. Screw this." I bounced to my feet so I could go find my phone.

"You're not quitting." Murphy's jaw was so tight I had no idea how he managed to get the words past his lips.

I stopped my headlong rush for the bedroom where I'd left my phone and whirled. "Stop telling me what to do." Hadn't he listened to a word I'd said yesterday? "I'm not telling you what to do, I'm just telling you you're not quitting," he said. Incredibly, he kept a straight face the entire time.

"How is telling me I can't quit not telling me what to do?" I scowled. "You're telling me what to do and I'm not going to listen to you. We're going on that road trip and that's it, Murphy. Screw Jason Allerton."

"I'm not going on a fucking road trip." Murphy's tone was cold and decided. I hated when he closed himself off like this. Now he'd sit and brood on the sofa for the rest of the day and I'd have to tip toe around him like a mouse. Fuck that.

"Yes, you are." I swooped upon the two plastic carrier bags of food for our picnic and slammed them down on the dining table. Something cracked ominously. "Come help me make sandwiches. Or go pack. We're leaving in an hour."

"I'm not going anywhere."

"Fine. I'll go by myself," I threatened. He didn't even look at me, just fished the car keys from his pocket and set them down on the coffee table. Hard.

If only I had the guts to drive on the wrong side of the road. The very sight of the keys sent a worm of fear slithering down my spine. "Murphy, I don't want to work with him."

"Why?" he spat. Now he looked at me and his eyes blazed ferociously. I took an involuntary step backward. "What did that bastard ever do to you?"

"He hurt you." I bit my lip to keep it from trembling.

"What he did to me doesn't concern you."

"How can you say that? I'm your bond mate. Everything that happens to you concerns me." My stomach clenched. I hated it when he shut me out like this.

"This doesn't."

"Why? Because it's Sorcha?" I rushed into speech before I could muzzle myself. It was sick to be so jealous of a dead woman, but I was.

Murphy loved me, but he'd never love me the way he'd loved her and that stung. "Because I'm not her and you don't need my support for anything that has to do with her precious, precious memory?"

"Don't you ever compare yourself to her. Do you hear me?" Murphy didn't shout, but his furious tone froze me in place. "Do you hear me?" He took a menacing step in my direction and my paralysis unthawed enough to allow me scoot backward.

"I hear you," I whispered because if I didn't say something, he'd keep coming at me.

"Now finish packing. You're going on that investigation." He glared at me.

Every bit of intimacy we'd built up and shared from yesterday disintegrated into cold ash. Why couldn't I be half as much to him as that bitch? She'd never loved him. She'd screwed around on him behind his back and made a mockery of being Alpha, of his Alpha status too.

Maybe that's why he didn't want my support in anything. He'd trusted her and now he couldn't trust anyone. Not even me.

Blood pounded in my ears, deafening me to everything else. I retreated to the bedroom and carefully closed the door so I didn't have to see him while I packed.

My suitcase was still on the unmade bed. The room stank of spent passion and sweat. My J'adore perfume. His cologne. I scrubbed my face with my fingers and stood by the bed for a moment before I began packing.

Who did Murphy talk to about the things that hurt him? Had it been Paddy? His vegetable garden? Sometimes I found him behind his laptop typing, not manipulating stocks in an online trade. Letters of inquiry to investment houses? Maybe he kept a journal.

I never touched his laptop. He left it on the desk most of the time, sometimes even propped open and on, but I'd never once looked at the screen.

Maybe he wrote love letters to Sorcha. He surely never wrote any to me.

"Balls," I muttered as I zipped my suitcase closed. I spared one last look at my side of the closet. I'd packed six pairs of shoes, but my heart hadn't been in it. Maybe they'd go with the outfits I'd chosen, maybe they wouldn't. Who gave a shit?

Courage. I needed a healthy dose of it if I was going to apologize. How Murphy felt about Sorcha and Colin Hunter was none of my business.

Just like what he typed on his laptop when he wasn't trading. I didn't get to decide the level of intimacy he felt comfortable offering me. He did.

I'd been starved for his attention and when I'd gotten some, become greedy. I ought to be ashamed of myself. I *was* ashamed of myself.

"Murphy?" I opened the bedroom door, but the living room was empty. So were the kitchen and bathroom. No one stood on the cold, wet balcony. Murphy's keys were gone and so was he.

* * * *

My phone rang from the depths of my purse. I sat on an uncomfortable chair at what would be my departing gate for London once the four earlier flights went through. My departure was scheduled for six PM. It was barely noon.

I set aside the book I'd been pretending to read. The words kept blurring and made absolutely no sense even when they were in sharp focus. I'd been on page fifty-nine for nearly an hour.

A fat businessman sat squashed next to me on my left, a harried mother of a toddler and an infant on my right. In order to dig out my phone, I had to elbow the businessman in the side. He shot me an indignant look and rattled his paper. Next to me the mother said in tones of hopeless exhaustion, "Robbie, don't touch trash on the floor. You know better. Don't put that in your mouth. Give it to me."

She held out a weary hand and the toddler screamed "No" and popped whatever it was into his mouth.

The mother lunged for him, nearly dropping the infant in his car seat in the process. I grabbed for the handle of the carrier and my purse flew off my lap. Everything in it scattered onto the filthy green carpet.

"Shit," I said. The mother wrenched the baby carrier out of my grasp and glared at me.

"What the hell do you think you're doing?" she yelled at me.

"Saving your baby," I snapped. She flushed with either wrath or humiliation, but before she could say anything, the toddler started screaming.

The fat businessman harrumphed, lumbered to his feet and stalked off, crushing my favorite tube of lipstick on his way.

I stooped to gather up what things of mine I could find. Stuff that had rolled between other passengers' feet presented a dilemma. Most of them kindly helped me out, but a few were oblivious and when I reached around their feet, gave me death looks.

Goddamn Others. I was surrounded by them. Drowning in a sea of them. My phone had, of course, stopped ringing by this point. I didn't even know where it was, but pinpointed its location when it began to peal again. Bell tone. Murphy's ring.

The phone was underneath the row of seats opposite mine. I snatched it before a curious teenager with blinding red hair could grab it.

I retreated at a fast walk to the most secluded corner of the gate I could find. Just as I pressed Talk, the gate attendant behind the counter opened the intercom and blared out the beginning of the boarding call for flight whateverthefuck that wasn't mine. My ears nearly bled from the volume.

"I'd ask you where you were, but it's pretty apparent," Murphy said when I could hear myself think again. Tears burned my eyes and I knuckled them away angrily. "What time's your flight leave?"

"Six." The clock on the wall read twelve fourteen.

"I would have driven you, honey."

"You weren't there." My voice was flat, but I'm sure he took it as yet another accusation. I braced myself for his anger.

"I needed to take a drive. Clear my head," he said, and he didn't sound mad, but I couldn't see his expression so I didn't know for sure. "How about if I come down there? You could meet me at one of the restaurants outside security."

"Why?"

"Because I want to see you. I don't want to let you go, angry at me."

"I'm not angry," I denied.

"Sure you are."

"Now in addition to telling me what to do, you're telling me what to feel? Nice," I snapped.

"See. Angry."

"Why don't you let me be angry? I don't want to meet you at a damn restaurant full of eavesdropping Others so you can make yourself feel better while I have to sit there in silence because I can't talk about anything that matters."

Rows twelve through twenty were invited to board and I gritted my teeth until there was relative silence again. The screaming toddler was corralled and dragged onto the plane. The fat businessman was no doubt buried behind his paper in a first class seat, fortifying himself with a pre-flight beverage of his choice.

"I always listen to what you have to say." Murphy's tone was reproachful. Hurt.

"Unless it's about Sorcha," I said. Fuck him. He couldn't tell me who I could or could not talk about. "Or Paddy."

Amy Lee Burgess

He sighed. "When you get home, we'll go on that road trip, honey, and we'll talk about everything. I promise."

"No, I'll talk about everything and you'll listen. And you'll shut me out of what you're feeling like you always do. Go write in your goddamn journal or whatever the hell it is you do on your laptop when you're not trading. Spill it out there. Why should you talk to me? I'm only your bond mate."

"Anything I have on my laptop, you can read if you want," he said. Was that a small chink in his armor? If he couldn't talk about it, he'd let me read about it? Or was it simply because he didn't have anything relevant on the damn thing anyway so he didn't give a shit? "My password is Stanzie7. Okay?"

My name. His password was my name? My heart hurt. My whole soul ached.

"I've never looked at your laptop," I told him.

"I know. But you can. No secrets, Stanzie. I know how you hate them."

"Liam?"

"What, honey?"

I gripped the phone so tightly my fingers ached. "If I wanted to come home, could I?"

"Of course. You can come right now if you like. I'll pick you up."

A rush of relief left me weak. I leaned against the wall for support and held my breath for a moment.

Rows twenty and above were cleared to board. I found a seat at the extreme edge of the gate, as far away from passengers and the agent's counter as I could get.

"I didn't want to come between you and your job as an Advisor," Murphy said when there was relative silence again. "You do good things as an Advisor. For the Pack and for yourself. It gives you a sense of purpose."

"You give me a sense of purpose," I told him.

He laughed a little. "I hope being with me is more of a pleasure and less of a job than being an Advisor. Maybe I'm fooling myself. I know I'm not easy to live with."

"Neither am I, with all my fears and fuck-ups," I said.

"Stanzie, please don't let me wreck your work as an Advisor."

"I am so angry at Jason," I whispered. "I talked to him just last week and he asked me if you'd agreed to act as his Advisor yet. And then he pulls this shit. I don't understand. Murphy, he's always doing things like this to me. I just get back on my feet and he pulls the rug out from under me again. I don't want to work with Colin Hunter. I want to work with you."

"That's not going to happen," said Murphy. "So the question becomes what you want to do now. I know I hate the bastard, but Hunter's never done anything to you. You could forge a decent working relationship with him. I know you. You can do anything once you set your mind to it."

"He's a self-serving ambitious prick," I said. "You and I became Advisors to help people. To make sure they didn't lose the ones they loved the way we had. All he wants is power and glory. Jason has to see that. I don't understand why he'd even want Colin on his team."

"Allerton's very good at sensing a person's potential, regardless of what crap he has armored himself with on the surface."

"Are you saying deep down, Colin Hunter is a decent person?" I was skeptical.

"No, I'm saying he's got to be one of the pieces on Allerton's chessboard. I'm hoping a pawn, personally, that he'll trade away or sacrifice on purpose, but I'm a bit biased." Murphy laughed again, bitterness mixed with exasperation.

"You can stop with the chess analogy right here because I don't know how to play. And if I'm one of his pieces, that's a stupid idea on his part because I don't play strategy games."

"Honey, with that man plotting your moves, you don't need to know how to play."

"That just makes me a manipulated fool. I don't want to be that. I'm coming home, screw this," I decided.

"Stanzie, you've known this about Allerton from day one. I've told you and you've seen it for yourself. Why now are you going to act all furious and betrayed?"

"I've acted furious and betrayed with him plenty of times," I said. "Every single time he sends me on an investigation there's one point where I blow up at him and tell him I'm tired of him pulling my strings. It's just at the beginning this time, not the end. So maybe I'm making progress finally."

Murphy snorted laughter. "What's this investigation about? Tell me. If you can."

"Some territory dispute between Mac Tire and a tiny pack in the Lake District in England."

Murphy was silent for a moment. "That tiny pack must have balls to go up against Mac Tire and try to take some of their territory. The English branch is the largest next to us in Dublin."

I shifted the phone to my other ear. "Other way around. The little pack says Mac Tire's muscling in on their territory."

"In the Lake District?" I imagine Murphy's frown. "Mac Tire's had territory there for years."

"So does this little pack apparently. The land abuts. They need the Councils to decide who gets what. I don't even know why it can't be the Regional. Territory disputes are usually handled by Regional Councils."

"Not when it's Mac Tire. Regional Councils in the UK are made up of nearly all Mac Tire members. It wouldn't be fair."

"See, you know more about this stuff than I do. And what does Colin know?"

"A lot probably. He used to belong to the English branch of Mac Tire," said Murphy. Something suspiciously like glee entered his tone and I remembered Hunter had been all but thrown out of his pack for daring to call a tribunal against Murphy.

So Colin was going to help investigate a territory dispute against his ex-pack? The ones who had treated him like shit? Did this mean Allerton was on the small pack's side? Councilors were supposed to be impartial until their Advisors presented them with their findings. Advisors were supposed to be impartial too. Would Hunter be capable of playing fair? That guy?

"What is Allerton thinking?" I pushed an annoying strand of hair behind one ear and groaned.

"Why don't you find out?" Murphy suggested.

"But our road trip."

"We can take it next week as easily as this."

"Will you be all right? Alone?" I asked. Now that the pack bond had been taken, Fee would stay with Colm and Deirdre. I suspected her overnight stays at our apartment were over. The thought of Murphy sitting alone in the apartment with just his laptop for company was not a good one.

"I'll be fine. You'll call me from time to time, won't you?"

"Every day. Probably a hundred times," I said and he laughed. "Murphy, I don't like this. I don't like the idea of working with Colin Hunter or leaving you alone."

"Give Hunter a shot. Just one so you know if you decide to stop being Allerton's Advisor, you'll have made an informed decision. Okay?"

"Okay," I agreed, but reluctantly. "You still want to meet me for lunch outside security?"

"On my way," he said, and it was true. The purr of the BMW's engine rumbled in the background and I wondered if he'd been on the road the entire time we'd talked.

I smiled.

Chapter 5

The enticing scent of bacon roused me from a deep but uneasy sleep. I shifted on the mattress and reached for Murphy, but encountered only empty space.

That's right. I wasn't in Dublin. I was in Windermere, in the Lake District. England. The safe house owned by the British branch of Mac Tire. I opened my eyes and blinked at the emerald green walls. The paint jobs in the guest rooms were on the darkly vibrant side. My bed was full sized with a brass headboard and footboard. The comforter was wildly geometric. Black-and-white ovals within ovals, larger on the outside, growing steadily smaller. I stared at the pattern, lost in it for a moment, until the lure of bacon broke the spell. The safe house was staffed by a triad—two grandmothers and a grandfather, who also used the house as their permanent residence.

One of them definitely knew how to make bacon.

The wooden floor was cold beneath my feet as I padded to the bathroom. My cosmetics were spilled haphazardly across the cream tiled counter. I'd gotten in late last night and had been tired as hell. My damn toothbrush had been at the bottom of the zippered cosmetic bag and in a weary frenzy I'd thrown the contents of the bag around until I found what I wanted.

I peered at my watch. I hadn't bothered to take it off, although I had managed to shuck my jeans and sweater. No wonder I was cold. I wore just a pair of panties and a bra.

The radiator in the corner of the room clanked, but it was too little too late. I turned the taps to the shower and waited an impossibly long time for hot water. Damn it. Would there be any bacon left by the time this frigging shower decided to let me have some warm water?

I brushed my teeth while I waited and peeked through the slats of the blinds. My room overlooked a sunken garden with a rock staircase that led to a terraced garden below. I could see the gleam of a lake over the trees and buildings across the street.

The trees still wore some of their autumn foliage, but most of the leaves were scattered on the ground in brown and red drifts.

I'd never been to England before. Would I like it? More importantly, would they have ketchup for my eggs?

* * * *

The first person I saw after I descended the stairs into the communal dining room was Colin Hunter. He sat at a small gate-legged table beneath a window overlooking the street, sipping coffee. Impeccably attired in crisp jeans that looked ironed and a green crew neck sweater beneath a tailored tweed jacket with actual elbow patches, he looked contemplative. A calculated pose. He knew damn well how attractive he was, with his angelic blond curls and electric blue eyes. He looked like a prince from a fairy tale. I did like his boots—brown suede chukka boots, perfect for walking in the woods. Were they waterproof though? I'd find out if I accidentally shoved him in the lake, I supposed.

Cheered by the thought, I was grinning as I approached his table and he turned on all the charm of his hundred-watt smile and rose to his feet. He touched my elbow and guided me to the empty chair across from his. Did I look like I needed help to sit down?

I opened my mouth to snarl at him, but one of the grandmothers arrived with two plates of fried eggs and bacon. Bacon.

"I took the liberty of asking Grandmother Nan to make your breakfast along with mine. I hope you don't mind. We said we'd meet at nine thirty." Colin reseated himself and gave me another million dollar smile.

Allerton had set up the meeting time. I looked at my watch. Damn. Nine thirty on the nose. I'd totally forgotten what time we were supposed to meet for breakfast. If I'd remembered, I would have made sure to have been late.

"I guess you were early," I said. Duh. Where the hell was the coffee? Ah, there was a pot in the center of the table. I poured some into my cup and frowned. Okay, not dark enough for coffee. Tea. Crap.

"I haven't gotten into the American habit of coffee with breakfast, I'm afraid." Colin's apology was more of a dig, perhaps because of his snide smile. Maybe I was reading the sarcasm into his expression. I reminded myself that Colin Hunter was Jason's new Advisor. I had to work with this man and, if we got off on the wrong foot, my job might become hell. But the thought of Murphy facing a possible tribunal after Sorcha's death because of Colin Hunter enraged me. Murphy had needed his pack and their support and instead he'd had to answer a lot of intrusive and painful questions from the Councils.

Colin had been helpful the last time I'd seen him, although even then he'd been angling for an Advisor's position.

"Congratulations," I said. "You're an Advisor to one of the highest ranking men on the Great Council."

"I'm well aware I wouldn't be if your bond mate hadn't stepped down," he answered. Was that another subtle dig or was he struggling to be polite?

I reached for the milk for my tea and he frowned. What had I done wrong now?

"What happened here? You're bruised." He touched his fingers to my jaw.

With heroic effort I resisted the urge to bat his hand away and instead leaned back in my chair so I was out of reach. After breakfast I needed to rush up to my room and do a better job with my concealer. I did not want the Alphas of the two disputing packs to ask me any awkward questions.

"Souvenir of a little altercation with a pissed-off pack mate," I said and the asshole actually grinned.

"Welcome to the Irish branch of Mac Tire. Where fists and fur fly first, rational conversation comes a distant second. Did you win, I hope?"

"None of your business," I said and the friendly edge to his grin faded. He picked up his fork and began to eat.

"He didn't hit you because you had to work with me, did he?" Colin kept his gaze on his plate.

"Who? Liam?" My cheeks burned. "I said a pissed-off pack mate, not bond mate. Do you have a hearing problem or are you trying to be deliberately offensive?"

"Sorry." His tone was clipped and he kept his head down.

"Are you really?" What could I throw at him? The toast rack? The jelly? My hot tea?

"I am sorry. That was offensive. Liam Murphy doesn't hit women. He never laid a hand on Sorcha and if anyone in Mac Tire ever gave him ample provocation, it would have been her. Flaunting her affairs. She treated him like shit and all he ever gave her in return was a smile and an understanding shoulder to cry on when things didn't go her way. He was a saint actually. Of course he hasn't changed since she died. Why would he?"

I tried to picture Murphy smiling when proof of Sorcha's disrespect had been flung into his face. Or offering her comfort when her flings went south. He hadn't fought with her the way he did with me? Not that I had flings, but we did argue.

One more painful reminder I wasn't as good as her.

My jaw tightened. "You must be really nervous to face the pack that threw you out on your ass. That must be why you're talking about my personal life. We need to get some ground rules set here. Liam Murphy is out of bounds. We don't discuss him or your history with him or my pack or your pack or anything that doesn't directly pertain to why we're here and what we're doing. We have to work together, so we obviously need some boundaries or I'm going to walk around in a high state of piss off for the next few days and I don't want to do that."

His face flushed at the words *threw you out on your ass* and by the time I'd finished my rant, his anger was evident.

He lifted his gaze to mine, eyes gleaming. "Why do you get to set the rules? Pulling rank on me? Do you have any? I wasn't told that I was your subordinate. Should we drag Allerton into this little discussion?" He smacked his cell phone down on the table by his plate. "I've got him on speed dial."

Did he think I wouldn't call his bluff? He obviously didn't know shit about me.

"Stop making snide cracks about Murphy," I said.

"I called him a saint." The word seemed to taste bitter by the grimace he made.

"I know sarcasm when I hear it."

Colin took a deep breath. "Eat your breakfast. It's getting cold."

"There's no ketchup," I complained, but picked up a piece of bacon and sank my teeth into its crispy goodness.

We ate in silence for a few moments until Colin said, "I am nervous to face my damned ex-pack, honestly."

"I'll bet you are." I unbent enough to give him a sympathetic look. I pushed some damp hair behind my ear and made a mental note to pull it back into a pony tail when I fixed my concealer. "Jason has this habit of thrusting his Advisors into really uncomfortable situations. You should probably get used to it."

Colin flashed me a grin that lit his attractive face. Murphy was cuter, but I could see how this man might have intrigued Sorcha. "This can't be easy for you either, can it?"

I shook my head, not bothering to falsely reassure him. This was hell.

"So how are we going to play this? Are you going to ignore the fact you used to belong to Mac Tire or use it?" I asked.

Amy Lee Burgess

Colin's blue eyes twinkled. "Hadn't decided really. I suppose it would depend on how offensive the Alphas are about it. I'm pretty certain they're going to be. At least she will be." His smile died somewhere in the middle of the last sentence to be replaced by a grim frown.

"Have you got history?" I guessed.

He snorted. "You could say that. I was once bonded to Mary Lancaster." I choked on a sip of the strong tea and grabbed for my napkin.

"Shut the fuck up? And Jason sent you here anyway?" An exasperated half growl, half groan escaped me. "That man is unbelievable."

"He's our employer," Colin reminded me and I grimaced. "Is it true he's bonded with your mother? His bond mate came with him when he met with me in Connecticut. She looks a hell of a lot like you and her last name is Newcastle, so I wondered."

I didn't answer because at that moment my emotions were not strictly under control and I tended to say unadvisable things when they weren't.

"Sorry," Colin apologized with a sheepish grin. "That's your personal life. I forgot."

"It's going to make things really difficult if we have to step around each other's sensitive feelings every second. We need to present a united front or the Alphas will tear us apart."

He laughed a little. "Agreed. They will. Without compunction. At least the Alpha female of Mac Tire at any rate. She'll be looking for a weak spot, knowing her. But you've set these ground rules and I'll tell you this much. I'm not very good with rules. As you can probably tell by the fact I'm now in the smallest pack in New England and barely clawing out an existence. These clothes I'm wearing? Don't let them fool you. They're from my former life. These days I can't even afford Wal-Mart."

"Your salary as an Advisor will fix that." I tried not to feel so bad for him. He deserved his fate after what he'd done to Murphy. But I thought of Devon, his bond mate, and her jolly smile. And of Nora. Even Jonathan, that stupid little dickhead. Was Riverglow really in such dire straits?

"I won't pretend it's not a godsend." He picked up his tea cup and focused on it. "Things got very bad after Callie and Peter's funerals. They'd racked up several thousand dollars' worth of bills. Fertility drugs mainly."

"Fertility drugs? But she was Pack," I protested.

He shrugged. "I managed to pay everything off, but it wiped Riverglow, and me personally, out financially. Now the pack can't afford the luxury of a baby, so Devon's threatening to leave me again. That woman. I deserve everything I've gotten, don't I?"

I flushed as if he'd read my mind. Damn.

"Wouldn't Vaughn help you?" I asked.

Colin gave a bark of derisive laughter. "Vaughn pretends we don't exist. Anyway, I don't imagine he's got much extra cash. Maplefair never has, have they? Besides, you can't blame the bastard. Why on earth would he help us? He's put us behind him. Well, Riverglow at any rate. He barely knew me or Devon. I can't possibly take it personally."

But he had. He'd asked Vaughn for help and had been rebuffed.

Jesus, Vaughn. Just like him to walk away and not help clean up a mess he'd helped to make. My irritation must have shown because Colin quirked his lips into a wry smile.

"It is imperative I do a decent job with this, Stanzie. More than decent. Stellar. I intend to shine and I'd really appreciate your help. If you can't do that, at least don't sabotage me. Please?"

I pointed to the bruise on my jaw. "Alannah Doyle. Remember her?"

"Declan Byrne's bond mate," Colin said at once. "Paddy's half-sister."

I must have grimaced at Paddy's name because Colin's expression became sympathetic.

"I heard about what happened." He lowered his voice although no one was in the room but us. "The real story, I mean."

The Pack believed Paddy died trying to avert the assassination of Jason Allerton. Mick Shaunessy had been Allerton's first bond mate's grandfather and supposedly had never forgiven him for taking her away from Mac Tire and keeping her away from her family after she'd gone insane when her baby had been stillborn.

No one in Mac Tire much liked Jason Allerton, but he'd attempted to fix that by taking on me and Murphy as his Advisors. I suspected only Murphy could have gotten away with something like becoming Jason Allerton's Advisor. I didn't count. I was too new and by the time I'd joined Mac Tire, was already working for Jason.

After Paddy's death, an upswing of feeling against Allerton surged, but the swift resolution of rounding up the conspirators and their subsequent deaths appeased Mac Tire's thirst for revenge. Jason had wisely attended Paddy's funeral but departed shortly after before good will could evaporate.

I looked at Colin Hunter and a thought struck me. Maybe Jason hadn't had much choice in appointing Colin his Advisor. Colin knew about the conspiracy—how much I wasn't quite sure—but enough so he wouldn't have bought the assassination attempt. With Mick Shaunessy involved, he would have known it was conspiracy related. Maybe Jason was consolidating his position by awarding Colin a coveted Advisor role. He'd keep quiet about his suspicions then.

Politics made my head hurt.

"I'm deeply sorry about your loss, Stanzie. Paddy O'Reilly was a brave man and from all accounts, a good Alpha." Colin reached impulsively across the table to lay a hand on my arm. My head swam with visions of Paddy, bloody and weak, clutching at my hand, afraid to die, but knowing death was stalking him. Ten more seconds and I'd be bawling like child. I bit my lip and turned my head so I could look out the window.

Outside, rich autumn sunshine poured over the street in a golden glow. The souvenir shop across from the safe house boasted an impressive display of mugs, t-shirts and calendars emblazoned with gorgeous views of the Lake District. I made a mental note to buy Murphy one of the mugs.

I missed him. He ought to be the one sitting across from me as we plotted strategy, not this stranger with an angel's face and a demon's character.

"I'll be back down in a bit. I've got to fix my hair." I shoved back my chair and escaped.

* * * *

Colin wasn't at our table when I returned after applying more concealer to my jaw and tying back my hair. Five people stood on the porch. I spied Colin's curls glowing in the sunlight and zipped my windbreaker. Beneath it I had on a hoodie and that, combined with a thin pullover, I hoped would be good enough against the autumn temperatures.

Our destination was the disputed territory in the forest. The Alphas wanted us to walk it with them as we discussed their grievances.

I stuffed my wallet, keys and cell phone into my pockets and braced myself before I twisted the knob on the front door.

Everyone turned when they heard the jangling bells above the door. Colin's expression was neutral, but I thought I detected temper dancing in his eyes. Two women and two men, the Alphas of the disputing packs, stood with him.

The taller man had mahogany hair and a supercilious smile. The shorter was well-muscled, with a reddish beard and close-set, dark eyes. The taller was arrogantly handsome, the shorter possessed a rough, masculine appeal, like a Highland warrior. On the whole, I thought I'd prefer the shorter man. He, at least, didn't radiate superiority.

The women were as different as could be. The short, plain one with red hair and freckles stood by the bearded man. She had a nervous smile, and a hand tucked into the crook of his elbow.

The taller woman had sleek black hair pulled into a long French braid with the end tucked up. The style emphasized her high cheekbones and almond-shaped dark eyes. I knew her face at once and by her self-important smile, she recognized me as well.

The witch at Murphy's table at the Great Gathering in Paris.

"Hello, Mary." I gave her a confident smile and her dark eyes turned calculating. Now I recognized the mahogany-haired man as well. He'd sat next to her that night. Likely the entire table had been made up of members of the British branch of Mac Tire. Except for Murphy and me. We'd been loners back then. Pack with no pack. Why the hell had Murphy been at a table with British Mac Tire and not the Irish branch? Paddy, at least, had been in attendance. I'd met him later during the Gathering. Presumably, other members of Mac Tire from Dublin had been there.

I'd never thought to ask Murphy that question until now. One thing was sure—I couldn't waste time thinking about the past.

"I don't believe we were formally introduced, were we?" The mahogany-haired man moved forward to shake my hand. "Richard Croft. I see you remember Mary."

"Very well," I said and Colin's eyes narrowed speculatively.

"You're looking lovely today, Constance." Mary eyed my windbreaker. Her smile was smug. Attired in designer jeans, a black cashmere turtleneck and a black-and-white houndstooth tailored jacket, she could have hobnobbed with the Queen at a country estate. Her riding boots gleamed expensively. All she needed was a riding crop and a black stallion. God, what a bitch.

"Love your boots," I said. I did, actually. Mine were brown Timberlands. Perfect for hiking wooded trails. I sneaked a glance at the other Alphas' footwear. Richard Croft had on riding boots that matched his bond mate's. Tweedledum and Tweedledee. Murphy and I would never wear the same style shoes at the same time. Jesus. Barf.

The bearded man had on a pair of well-worn brown hiking boots. The redhead wore black lace-up Oxfords with a textured sole good for walking. Certainly not shabby, but definitely not the same league as the Alphas of Mac Tire.

"Angus Finch, Alpha of Stony Fell." The bearded man stepped close to me to offer his calloused hand. Here was a man who performed manual labor. Construction, I guessed. Many Pack worked in construction. He had a definite Scottish burr.

The redheaded, freckled woman moved up when he nudged her. She gave me a shy smile and introduced herself as Evelyn Crowley. "Evie for short," she added. Her accent was English. The dusting of freckles across her cheeks and the bridge of her nose disappeared when her skin flushed. A timid Alpha? One not used to socializing with people outside her pack?

She seemed anxious, but then I would be too if I were Alpha of a small pack being harried by a larger one.

"We'll take my Land Rover," said Richard, and he walked for the stairs. A pretty flagstone path edged with autumn flowers led to a small gravel car park. An obviously new white Land Rover held pride of place in a front parking spot, while beside it crouched a blue Ford Focus station wagon. Or estate car as they called them in the UK, I'd learned. The Ford was elderly, but meticulously maintained.

Angus stomped behind me down the steps, breathing hard. He couldn't afford a Land Rover, but had nothing to be ashamed of. Most Pack couldn't afford vehicles like that. Sometimes Mac Tire and their privileged superiority grated on my nerves. The British branch was more insufferable about their wealth. The Irish branch didn't flaunt it, but they were mostly oblivious to how many other packs existed.

Not everyone in Mac Tire was wealthy. Status, job skills and family determined the standard of living for each individual, but in a pack everyone shared, so if one family couldn't afford something, another would generously provide. Basically, the pack was as rich as its most wealthy members—usually the Alphas, since they had access to the shared pack funds as well as whatever they earned on their own.

Stony Fell was not rich, obviously.

Colin and I took the seats in back while Angus and Evie sat together in the middle.

"Something wrong?" Colin leaned close to whisper in my ear so the others wouldn't hear as we all adjusted our seatbelts. I probably looked pale. Sick even. My heart squeezed itself into a tight, painful ball.

Driving. Bad enough I'd had to take a cab from the train station to the safe house, now I would have to be driven by the Alpha male of Mac Tire. I didn't know him or trust him. I wished Colin had a car. He'd driven me once and hadn't crashed us. I didn't really trust him either, but he was better than Richard Croft who, for all I knew, drove like a frigging maniac.

The smell of my fear was pungent and Mary Lancaster twisted around in her luxuriously padded leather seat to give me a fake look of concern.

"Constance, is there something the matter?"

"I'm fine." My nails bit into the flesh of my palms and sweat trickled down my back. Damn windbreaker. I fumbled with the zipper, hands shaking, miserably aware of everyone's scrutiny.

"Are you having a panic attack?" Evelyn Crowley asked, her face pinched with sympathy. "I get them sometimes in enclosed spaces." She pressed a button and fresh, lake air blew into the car. I took a deep, grateful breath.

"Perhaps you ought to sit in the front," suggested Angus, much to Mary's evident dismay. I wasn't sure if she was more horrified at the thought of sitting beside her ex-bond mate or being relegated to the back of the vehicle.

"No." My voice was shrill. The passenger seat was a death trap. Just ask Grey. "I'm fine. Can we please go?" One more reason why Murphy should be here with me. He'd have figured out a way to drive me himself. Maybe rented a car of our own. Something.

Damn Jason Allerton.

Colin, his expression guarded, sat very still beside me as if he wasn't sure what I might do.

"Oh, I remember," said Mary as Richard switched on the ignition and a fresh burst of panic thrilled through me. "You were in an awful car crash, weren't you, Constance?" Derision dripped from her tone. A flush of anger ripped through me, chasing most of the fear away. For someone who wanted a decision made in her favor, she was treating the person who might be the key to her victory rather poorly. Was she that sure Mac Tire was in the right, she could afford to alienate the Great Council?

"Poor thing." Evelyn reached out a hand impulsively to touch my knee. Maybe she wasn't shy, just not used to being formal.

Colin's eyes widened as he obviously put two and two together. He looked a little disgusted with himself as if he thought he ought to have figured things out.

"I'm quite a conservative driver," said Richard as he carefully backed the Land Rover into the center of the car park so he could shift to first gear and pull forward. "Mary often chaffs me that I drive like a grandfather."

"You do, darling," Mary said with an indulgent laugh and ran her talon-like fingernails through his dark brown hair. The gesture looked calculated, as if she played a part on stage.

Beside me, Colin rolled his eyes. He wasn't taken in either. What was the story of his break-up with Mary? Had she left him for Richard? Had he left her?

Had Murphy known he'd sat at a table with Colin Hunter's ex-bond mate? He'd seemed to know Mary fairly well. He'd told her to shut up when she'd wondered aloud why Jason had seated me with the group since none of them were murderers.

Ah. The pieces clicked together. For the first time I understood. Murphy hadn't left the table that night at the Great Gathering because he'd been appalled I'd driven my car over an embankment and my bond mates had been killed, but because of what Mary had insinuated.

"We're not murderers here. Are we, Liam?" she'd said. A dig at him for facing an investigation after Sorcha died because Colin accused him of her murder.

Bitch. Rage churned in my gut. As an Advisor, I was honor bound to remain impartial, but hoped Stony Fell had a good case. I'd love to crush Mary Lancaster beneath my booted heel. Slowly.

* * * *

The territory in dispute was a small stretch of private land that abutted the Lake District National Forest. One of the problems lay in the fact the land was surrounded on the three other sides by Mac Tire's.

"My great-gran deeded the land to me," said Evie as we walked together through the crisp autumn woods. We had to cross through Mac Tire's territory to get to the area of dispute. Each time Stony Fell members wanted to shift, they did too. Another point of contention.

"She did, yes," Mary said with a stinging smile. "When you were a member of Mac Tire yourself. That land was never meant to go out of Mac Tire."

"All you have to do is come back to Mac Tire. All of your pack." Richard paused so he could snatch up a fallen tree branch in the path and toss it away with a crash into the underbrush.

Angus bristled visibly. "I'll not give up Alpha status."

"We've promised you both will be one of the two duos in contention to be the next Alphas."

"You know damned well we don't have a prayer of being elected. Even if we did, the election's five years from now," spat Angus. "When Evie will be forty-two. Maybe she'll conceive, maybe she won't. But you know she has a better chance before forty. Why should we trade precious years of Evie's fertility so you can claim twenty more acres of land?"

"Because it's the right thing to do. We're making a huge concession, offering you a chance at the next Alpha slot. In Mac Tire, remember. Not some—tiny pack." Mary obviously bit off something more derogatory, but it was an effort. Of course, her smug smile said it all. She put about as much stock in Angus and Evie being elected the next Alphas of Mac Tire as Angus himself did. None at all.

Angus shook his shaggy red head and continued to forge ahead of us on the path. Smoldering anger emanated from three of the four Alphas. Evie kept her head down, chin tucked, gaze on the ground. She wasn't angry—she was anxious. I wasn't feeling all that cheerful myself.

"Land titles pass from generation to generation, but I thought it was understood that the individual doesn't own the land, the pack does," I said.

"And that pack is Stony Fell," said Angus. "Evie's got a title to the land. Pack law says the individual holds the land in trust for the pack. Her pack is Stony Fell. It's a clear-cut case that shouldn't need arbitration." He cast a sly look over his shoulder. "We might consider rejoining Mac Tire if we were named Alphas now, not in five years."

"You insufferable bastard." Mary clenched her fists. "If you think for one second you're going to knock Richard and me out as Alphas, you're dangerously delusional."

Angus merely smiled before he turned back to face forward.

Colin surged ahead to walk beside him and they conferred in low voices while the Mac Tire Alphas stalked behind them, shoulders stiff with furious tension.

Evie kept her gaze fixed on the brown carpet of fallen leaves beneath our feet, her face flushed.

"I hate all this drama," she confided.

"Why did you leave Mac Tire?" I asked. The day was glorious. Birds flashed between colorful branches while patches of dark blue sky dotted with fat white clouds floated above us. The forest smelled rich and brown. My wolf stirred within me as if she could sniff the air as well.

Evie shot me an anguished look. Her freckles stood out in sharp relief against her cheeks.

"I never stood a chance at Alpha in Mac Tire. I've never been popular. I was bonded before to someone in Mac Tire and when it didn't work out, Grandmother Beverly gave me the land. She knew somehow she was dying, poor thing. I've known Angus for years and he and a few others from the Mac Tire branch in Scotland wanted to leave and form their own pack. My land was a godsend."

"So how long have you been bonded?" I asked.

She flushed again and this time I saw adoration in her eyes. "Just six months."

"Why is this coming to the fore now?"

Evie grimaced. "Our youngest pack member has been sniffing around a popular girl in Mac Tire. They want to bond and since she's Mary's cousin, there's been an awful uproar about it.

"We can't seem to come to a satisfactory agreement, and so now you're here. Colin as well. And that's not really fair since Colin was once Mac Tire himself. How can he be impartial?"

Did she not know they threw him out?

"And you're Mac Tire too. Angus says we're doomed." Evie bit her lip and turned her face so I wouldn't see the wet gleam of tears blurring her eyes. "Everyone's Mac Tire in the UK and Ireland, that's the bloody problem." She wiped her eyes with the back of her hand and sighed.

She was right. A few small packs were scattered here and there in the UK and Ireland, but mostly it was straight Mac Tire. Small packs must have it hard, trying to coexist with the giant entity of Mac Tire.

The hike provided us with quite a workout and even though the day was cool, after an hour of steady walking, sweat trickled down my back. We'd parked as close as we could in one of the National Forest's lots, but it didn't seem as if we'd ever reach Stony Fell's land.

Just after we'd forded a small brook by skipping nimbly across the broad, flat backs of three slippery rocks, we came to a small clearing. Evidence that it was used for shifting orgies was apparent by the flattened grass, odd bits of discarded clothing, bottle caps and empty water bottles. To me, more care could have been taken to keep it less cluttered. Mac Tire never left their meadow in anything but pristine condition and in Riverglow, we'd been scrupulous about packing out what we packed in.

Richard must have seen my expression because his mouth tightened. "Mary, we need to get some of the teens here to clear away this mess."

Mary's eyes were narrowed as she gazed past the clearing into a wide stand of aspens. She shaded away the slanting sun with her hand. "Richard," she said. "Listen."

I heard it then too. Crashing in the underbrush, panicked breathing, and a low, steady whining. A dog perhaps, but more likely a wolf.

Ten seconds later a small red wolf plunged out of the darkness of the forest into the streaming sunlight of the clearing. Running flat out, ears pressed to her skull, the young female zipped past Angus and Colin and made straight for Mary and Richard.

Eyes huge with terror, she rolled before them and presented her throat and belly. The high pitched whining never stopped.

"What the hell?" muttered Richard. He knelt by the young wolf. "Tracy?" His voice was soft.

"Tell her to shift back." Mary's tone was sharp.

"The poor thing's terrified," said Evie, her face full of compassion and worry.

"You keep out of this," snapped Mary, and Evie flushed. Angus glowered and stalked back to his bond mate.

Colin gazed into the woods then turned back to look at the young wolf speculatively.

"Tracy," said Richard as the wolf continued to whine and pant. She rolled to her feet and dashed back to the trees, but pulled up short just before darting between them. As she turned back to gaze at us pleadingly, she uttered a series of high-pitched yips.

Sympathetic fear began to claw down my spine. What the hell had frightened her?

"Get back here and shift, damn you," Mary all but shouted and Richard cast her an impatient look before he held out his hand.

"Tracy, come back here, love. We can't understand you in that form. You must shift and tell us what's wrong, darling. It's all right. You're safe here with us."

The young wolf uttered more frantic yips and danced in a frustrated circle, tail tucked between her hind legs. She switched her gaze from the forest back to us and whined low in her throat.

"Where's her partner?" Colin asked at the same time I said, "She wants us to follow her."

Colin and I exchanged a lightning fast glance of understanding. Her partner was in trouble.

"Shift back and tell us what's happened, you bloody little twit," Mary demanded and shook off Richard's hand when he touched her arm.

"Snarling at her isn't helping, darling." His tone was sharp with irritation, but he spoke barely above a whisper. She cast him a spiteful look and opened her mouth to argue with him, the bitch.

"Come on," I said to Evie and Angus. Colin was already in motion and when the young wolf saw we meant to follow her, she streaked off into the woods.

"How the hell are we supposed to keep up with a wolf?" Mary complained from behind us. "This is why I asked her to shift back. We'll never keep up."

We didn't, but when we fell too far behind, the red wolf waited, trembling violently, for us catch up.

The scent of pine needles, decomposing leaves and fresh air was poisoned by the stench of the wolf's abject terror. As we rounded a corner, leaves crunching beneath our booted feet, the sour reek of fresh blood invaded our nostrils.

Evie gasped and put one hand to her throat where the pulse fluttered rapidly. Angus's brow lowered and Colin, ahead of us by quite a few paces, jerked to an abrupt halt, body tense with shock.

"Good Lord," he said. I pulled more speed from somewhere and ran to his side.

I flailed to a stop when I saw the carnage. Clumps of leaves had been flung around the pathway exposing raw, bloodstained dirt. Off in a small gap in the trees, lay another wolf—this one black. His fur was dotted with blood, his lower left leg mangled in the jaws of a pitiless steel trap. Exposed bone gleamed in the weak autumn sunshine and I swallowed back a surge of bile.

The red wolf cried out and nuzzled the black one behind his ear. When he moaned, it was one of the eeriest sounds I'd ever heard. Soaked with pain, terror, and complete exhaustion.

Mary pulled up short, a hand over her mouth before lurching to the other side of the pathway to puke. Evie hid her face in Angus's shoulder. He held her, but never took his gaze away from the stricken wolf.

"What is this? A trap? On our territory?" Richard's body vibrated with fury. "Is this your way of fighting back, Angus?"

"You bloody bastard." Angus didn't raise his voice, but a chill went down my spine at his tone. "Funny how you think I've set a trap when it's one of my pack mates trapped in it, isn't it?"

"We don't have fucking time to debate which one, if any, of you set this thing." I shoved past them and dropped to my knees beside the black wolf. The red female cried in my ear and I put an arm around her. She pressed against me, trembling.

Colin knelt by the trap, his face taut with pity and rage.

"Can you spring it?" I asked him as I smoothed back the fur on the black wolf's neck. He snarled at me, his amber eyes glazed with pain and shock and snapped his teeth around my wrist. I held still even when I felt his teeth break the skin. A bracelet of pain tightened around my wrist. "Easy, sweetheart," I murmured and he released me.

"We need him to shift back," said Richard. "We can't bring him to the hospital in wolf form."

"Let's just get him out of the fucking trap first, shall we?" Colin explored the edges of the trap with gentle, swift fingers but the young black wolf growled. I was well within biting range and hoped he didn't go for my throat. The red wolf whined anxiously and pressed her nose to his and he relaxed a fraction.

"Keep him calm, that's right," I told her.

"Tracy, shift back," ordered Richard.

"Let her alone." I kept my gaze south of the black wolf's eyes so he wouldn't take my stare as a challenge, but I could keep him in sight. I pitched my voice very soft and slow so I wouldn't startle him. "She's keeping him calm and I need her to do that. She can shift later. Colin, can you get that thing off him?"

"I need to find the bloody release. Ah, here you are, you bitch."

The black wolf thrashed in agony.

"Hold him down, Stanzie," Colin snapped at me and I used my body to pin the wolf to the forest floor. He snarled, ropy saliva dripping from his mouth, but couldn't twist around to sink his teeth since I was careful to keep out his reach. My wrist was bleeding, not hard, but it hurt. My own damn fault.

"This is going to be bad," warned Colin and he pulled apart the jaws of the wicked steel trap. The black wolf struggled beneath me, shrieking with agony and the little red wolf cried out too in sympathy.

Something crashed in the underbrush. The trap after Colin had flung it away furiously.

"We'll need that as evidence," I told him.

"I know, but I need the bloody thing out of my way. Stanzie, what do I do? I've never seen so much damn blood. I don't know what to do." Colin's voice was remarkably calm for someone who was panicking. I knew he was. I could smell him.

"A tourniquet?" I suggested. I had no clue either. If only Allerton, the doctor, were here.

I heard Colin unbuckle his belt. I couldn't see because I was facing the other way. The black wolf struggled and moaned beneath me and I murmured to him that everything would be all right. I was glad I couldn't see his leg. Warm blood soaked through the back of my windbreaker.

"We need him to shift back," said Richard. His tone was not as calm as Colin's. "We can't bring a wolf into a hospital and I'm damned if I'll bring someone Pack to a vet."

"We'll damn well do whatever it takes," said Colin.

"Who the fuck do you think you are?" Mary's voice was shrill, and if I hadn't been holding down the poor black wolf, I would have backhanded her. "You slimy little weasel. You may have wormed your way into a

Councilor's good graces, but that doesn't give you the right to speak to the Alpha of Mac Tire that way."

"Shut up, Mary," said Colin. I don't believe he even bothered to look at her.

"If you get my phone out of my pocket, Jason's on speed dial. He'll know what to do," I said. "I'm afraid to let go. He's so scared and in so much pain. He has to lie still, I know that much."

"I've fastened the tourniquet and the bleeding's slowed way down," Colin told me as he fished in my jacket pocket. "Sorry, if I'm getting too familiar."

"Not a problem."

"Tracy, shift your bloody ass back right now." Mary stalked through the crackling autumn leaves and the red wolf cowered against me.

"Will you keep your bond mate away from here and muzzle her while you're at it?" Colin snapped at Richard.

"You bastard." Mary hissed.

"Mary." Richard's tone brooked no opposition. "Come over here. Get the bloody hell out of the way."

"Richard, we need her to shift back. If she does, maybe the black wolf, whoever the hell he is, will too."

"Don't make him shift when he's like this. You don't know what it might do to his leg. Will you please keep out of this?" I tried not to yell so I wouldn't agitate the wolves, but, damn, it was hard. Where the hell were Angus and Evie? They were this poor wolf's Alphas.

I looked around as best I could while Colin moved down the path trying to find a signal for the damn cell phone. I wished him luck.

Evie and Angus were just standing there on the path. She had her face buried against his shoulder and his eyes were blank with shock. Great.

"What's his name? Angus?"

He jerked when he heard me say his name and gulped. "Ben," he answered after a moment. "Ben Hastings."

"Ben." I turned to the black wolf, who had stopped thrashing. His breath was shallow and the thready beat of his pulse weak. He was going into shock. "Ben, sweetie, you just hang on and we'll get you some help. Okay?" I sat up, ready to pin him down again, but he didn't move. The glaze over his eyes frightened me. What if he died? I couldn't let that happen. I looked at the red wolf. She leaned into me, head down.

"Honey, I need you to shift back so he can hear your voice. Can you do that?" I smoothed her ears back to her skull and pressed my forehead to hers. The musky scent of wolf was drenched with the acrid stench of fear.

The wolf moved away a few feet and whimpered as the shift boiled over her furry body and left her nude and human a few seconds later.

The woman who replaced the wolf had long red hair and when she rolled over, I saw she was very young. Twenty, tops. Ben probably was the same age. This must be the young Romeo and Juliet couple Evie referred to earlier.

The horror of the situation pressed down on me so hard, I had to squeeze my eyes shut to keep from sobbing.

Ben's wolf's leg was a mangled mess of shredded bone and tendon. I didn't see how it could be repaired. An hour ago he'd been dashing through the autumn woods without a care in the world, and now this.

Rage shuddered down my spine.

"Someone give her a jacket." I didn't recognize my voice, coated as it was with wrath. The leaves crackled and the redhead reached out to take Richard's hacking jacket. It swamped her, the cuffs coming down nearly to her fingertips.

She knelt beside me and put out a shaking hand to touch Ben's wolf.

"Will he be okay?" Her voice was soaked in anguish. "We didn't know there was a trap."

"How could you?" I put an arm around her and she huddled against me gratefully. "Talk to him, sweetie. So he knows you're there."

Tracy smoothed back the fur at his nape and in a breathless, tear-filled voice, began to talk about how much fun they'd had together last night, did he remember? Did he know she loved him, because she did. Even though they came from feuding packs, they'd never let that come between them, would they?

* * * *

"No fucking reception." Colin's frustration was evident in his expression and the way he looked like he was going to take my cell phone and throw it against the nearest tree.

I snatched it away before he could and said, "I'm going to shift and run until I get to the parking lot. There's bound to be reception there. Can you put the phone in my jacket pocket and tie my jacket loosely around my neck so my wolf can get it off, but it won't fall off as she runs?"

Colin sighed. "Yeah. Meanwhile I'll try to get these useless fuckers to help me rig a travois. Worthless Alphas. One's puking, one's hysterical, the other two are fighting over vets versus doctors. Such bullshit, Stanzie."

"We'll get Ben through this," I said and a tense smile lit up his face.

"Hurry up. Shift."

I began to strip off my clothes and Colin picked up my jacket so he could put the cell phone in the pocket and knot the sleeves together before hanging it around my wolf's neck.

Richard obviously saw what we were doing and hurried over to me. He kept clear of Ben and Tracy and I cursed him in my head. As Alpha, he ought to be with his pack member. Mary had taken one horrified look at Ben's ripped-to-shreds leg and puked in the bushes again. Now she sat with her back against a tree trunk, face averted. Perspiration stood out on her pale face and she looked ready to upchuck at the slightest provocation.

Evie was sobbing against Angus's chest and he soothed her, but he radiated fury and suspicion.

"I'm going with you," Richard announced and bent to pull off his expensive riding boots. "I can call the pack doctor and have him here in less than an hour."

"Henry is at the clinic which is two hours from here." Colin snarled. "We can't wait that long for help to arrive. Are you frigging serious, Richard? Does this poor bastard look like he can wait over two hours to you?"

Richard glared at him threateningly and Colin stared back without fear.

"It'll take us an hour or more just to get him back to the parking lot. By the time we got him there, Henry would only be another hour out. What else do you suggest we do?"

"Call nine nine nine," Colin said.

"For a wolf?" Richard's voice had risen incredulously.

"Just shut up and shift if you're coming. We'll work out the details when we get there. Jason will know what to do, he always does." I said.

Richard peeled off his sweater and threw it on the ground. Beneath, he wore a t-shirt, which he shucked off. He put his phone in one of the sweater sleeves and tied a knot at the end to keep it from falling out. Then he fashioned it into a small noose.

"Put this around my neck. Advisor." He sneered the last word as he cast the sweater at Colin, who snatched it out of the air with a mocking smile.

I kicked my panties away and dropped to all fours. My wolf was so close to the surface of my skin that the shift was almost instantaneous.

* * * *

Colin puts the clothing thing around my neck. I need to run fast. Smell of blood chokes me. Ben Wolf is hurt. I want to lick his wounds, but I cannot stay here. I run. Fast. Leaves crunch beneath my paws and I run fast as I can. My leg hurts. It bleeds, but I run on it anyway. Pain is not bad. Alpha Richard is behind me, but he cannot catch me. My leg slows me down, but he still cannot run as fast as me. Thing around my neck bothers me. Want to shake it off. No. Need that. Need that later. Run. Run fast.

* * * *

"Stanzie." Jason's voice was crisp and clear, and I sagged with relief when I heard him. I had two bars of reception on my phone and hadn't been sure the call would go through. I was sick to my stomach from running. Clammy with sweat, hot, yet chilled to the bone.

A cold autumn wind cut through the windbreaker, which covered my nakedness but left my legs and feet exposed. I hid behind the Land Rover as two male hikers lingered by their car, sharing a thermos of what smelled like hot tea.

Richard's wolf hadn't caught up yet. Perhaps he was lurking in the woods waiting for the hikers to leave. Maybe he was having a heart attack from running so fast for so long.

"Jason, we have a situation," I said and, when I caught my breath, explained the problem.

"I'll have people there in forty-five minutes. It's not optimal, I know, but let's hope Colin's managed to get Ben at least halfway back to the parking lot. You stay there so you can guide them in if need be." He disconnected without waiting for my acknowledgment. Every second counted.

The male hikers climbed into their Volvo and the driver backed carefully from the parking space.

A flash of pale gray between the trees. Richard's wolf. I blinked and he disappeared. A moment later Richard, in just his sweater and a pair of blue boxer briefs, hurried to my side. He clutched his cell phone and the keys to the Land Rover. His sweater sleeves had come in handy for storage. Good thinking.

He got behind the wheel to make his call and I got in too so I'd be out of the cold wind. My legs were red and goose pimpled.

I rubbed them with my hands and said, "Jason's taken care of everything. You can call your people, but his will be here first and will have everything we need."

He shot me a look. His hair was plastered to his head with sweat. "Forgive me if I indulge myself and still make my call."

I shrugged. "Up to you."

He stared at the phone for a moment then swore beneath his breath. "How the hell did a trap get there?"

"Someone set it," I said and he cursed again.

"You think someone from my pack did that? It was our territory."

"So you're saying someone from Stony Fell did it? How far were we from the border to their land?" I asked.

He flushed. "It's not their land, and I don't know precisely. I'd say within a few yards."

"The border then. Anyone who wants to shift there has to cross Mac Tire land. Can't they get in through the National Forest?"

"Yes," he said tersely. "But it would be a hike of at least four hours. The way through our land is the shortest."

"Bear traps like that have been outdated for decades. And are there bears here in the first place?" I asked.

"Not for centuries," he said as if I ought to know. "Wolves either." That I did know. "So if we're seen in this damned car park with an injured wolf, how the hell are we going to explain it, Advisor? Does your Councilor have a fix for that too?"

"Ben's wolf is black. He could pass for a big dog," I said and Richard bristled. One of the worst insults a person could make was to compare our wolves to dogs. Stupid, really, because dogs were wonderful creatures. If our apartment in Dublin weren't so small, I'd adopt one in a heartbeat. I'd always wanted a dog, but when I was little my father wouldn't consider it. Later, when I was bonded and belonged to Riverglow, Elena had loved cats so much but they wouldn't tolerate her. I'd hardly thought it fair to introduce a dog into our household and somehow I'd never had the heart to adopt one when I was alone in Boston. Stupid of me because a dog might have made things more bearable, but then I'd wanted to suffer, hadn't I?

"I'll pretend I didn't hear that," he said and looked down at his cell phone so he could make his calls.

A gust of wind kicked up and rocked the Land Rover. God, I would have killed for a cup of coffee.

My cell phone chirped.

"Everything's been arranged," Jason said when I answered. "I want your opinion. Do you think someone from Mac Tire or Stony Fell set that trap?"

I gazed out the windshield at a stand of aspens. Nearly bare branches trembled in the restless wind, and the few remaining leaves fluttered. As I watched, one or two spiraled down to join the others on the mossy ground.

"I don't know what to think. But it's incredibly hard to believe that some random Other managed to set a bear trap on the border of the disputed territories."

"My thoughts exactly," he said. "I'll arrive early tomorrow morning. I'm on a flight that leaves in an hour and a half. The Regional Councilor will arrive late tonight. I'll need you and Colin to work closely with us on this. We can't let this go unsolved too long. Stanzie, it is imperative to find the guilty party as quickly and quietly as possible. I want both sets of Alphas to move to the safe house immediately, where they'll stay until further notice. They are not to tell anyone in their packs about what's happened."

"What about Tracy? The boy's girlfriend?" I asked.

"She can remain at the clinic with him if you think she'll stay, otherwise she needs to come to the safe house as well. No access to phones and get her cell phone if she has one. I'll have one of the nurses at the clinic look out for her if she goes there or one of the grandmothers at the safe house if she doesn't. Try to keep this under wraps as best you can. I'll be there soon." He disconnected before I could ask to speak with my mother, but I had no idea if she was with him anyway.

"Well, the Great and Regional Councils are now officially involved," I told Richard, who had finished his calls. "Aside from the doctor, who else have you told about this?"

"No one. I didn't actually speak to Henry. He's already on his way. I spoke to one of the nurses at the clinic. Victoria. She already knew as well. You and your Councilor work fast, Advisor." Richard pulled at the collar of his sweater as if it choked him. Maybe he wanted to choke me. He wouldn't be the first one.

"Councilor Allerton has asked that you and the other Alphas move to the safe house until further notice. Also, he would like you not to share the news of what's happened with the rest of your packs." I hoped I sounded diplomatic but by Richard's scowl, suspected I fell short.

"Why am I not allowed to tell my pack? They have to stay out of the forest, and how will I stop them if I don't tell them why?"

"You're the Alpha, you figure it out," I suggested. I twisted in my seat to look around for food or beverages. "Is there anything to eat or drink?"

"Mary keeps candy in the glove box." He reached over to pop it open. Licorice All Sorts. Hmm. No chocolate. Damn.

I opened the box and tried a bright pink piece with a white middle. Not bad. Richard fished in the box and popped a handful into his mouth. The pungent scent of licorice filled the car.

"I'm not Alpha three months, and this bloody fiasco has to happen." Richard closed his eyes for a moment and, when he opened them, they were hot with rage. "This is so typical of my luck. My brother, Rob, coasts along for five years without a murmur of complaint, has twins, and retires covered with laurels. I, on the other hand, am confronted with a damned territory dispute gone lethal before I can even catch my breath. My twin has always had the luck. The good luck that is. I've gotten all the rotten luck."

"Welcome to the club," I said before I popped a black-and-white candy into my mouth and let it dissolve deliciously on my tongue.

Chapter 6

True to his word, Jason had people on the scene in forty-five minutes. Forty-three, by the dashboard clock. The rest of the day passed in a blood-soaked blur as Ben was rushed away, still in wolf form, Tracy by his side.

Colin and I didn't get back to the safe house until nearly eight that night. I went straight up to my room for a hot shower and half an hour later discovered him in a small lounge at the back of the ground floor.

An amber glass of brandy clutched between his hands, he sat with his head down on a plump red-cushioned sofa beneath a large print of an English fox hunt. Brown-and-white brindled hounds chased ahead of several handsome horses with braided tails and manes. Men in bright red hacking jackets paired with cream breeches, shiny black boots and riding helmets were perched on small English hunt saddles with the stirrups drawn tight. One horse seemed to fly over a green hedge while another stretched, neck out, tail streaming as it raced after the hounds.

Colin hadn't bothered to shower. He'd gone straight for the alcohol. His tweed jacket was smeared with blood, as were his jeans and boots. His blond curls were wind-whipped out of shape and he didn't look up when I entered the room.

"You okay?" I asked and, after a moment, he lifted his head. A crimson streak of Ben's blood disfigured one cheek. His fingernails were crusted with more blood and dirt.

"No." He took a gulp of brandy.

I sat beside him and put my arms around him. He put his glass down so he could clutch at me as if he were drowning. He buried his face in my neck, shuddering. The first sob was silent, but the one after was not.

"It's okay," I said as I rocked him. I wanted to cry too, but held back my tears as best I could so he wouldn't feel he needed to comfort me. He'd taken the brunt of it today, the poor bastard. He'd had to carry Ben's wolf out.

Ben's condition was not good.

"They had to amputate his leg," Colin choked out against my throat. "Stanzie, they cut off that poor boy's leg and he's barely twenty years old. For what? What for? Why is land so fucking important that a twenty-year-old boy has to lose his leg in the fight for it?"

I tried to smooth out his tangled curls and he clung to me like a child.

"Stanzie?" The voice was familiar, but how could he be here?

"Murphy?" I looked in disbelief toward the doorway, where Murphy stood. He looked shocked—his face very pale and his eyes haunted.

"Sorry to interrupt," he said stiffly. "They told me you were in here."

"What are you doing here?" I was off the sofa like a shot so I could fling myself into his arms. He held me, but let go so quickly it was like being hugged by a gust of weak wind.

"Surprise," he said with a smile that didn't reach his eyes. "You're looking at the UK Regional Council's newest Councilor."

"Councilor?" At first I couldn't concentrate on what he'd said because of that smile, but the idea slowly took hold. "Murphy, this is great news. Of course! Now I see why Jason replaced you."

"Yeah, everybody's replacing me it seems," he said and his smile died. Hurt glimmered in his eyes and he stared at me as if I'd betrayed him. What had I done?

"Liam, I know what you're thinking and you're wrong," said Colin from the sofa. His voice was rough with tears.

"Am I?" Murphy looked at Colin and his voice trembled when he talked. "I walk in here and you're in each others' arms. What am I supposed to think?"

"Not that." Colin pressed the palms of his hands to his bloodshot eyes. "I've just had one of most foul days of my entire life. Believe me, a seduction scene is the last thing on my mind right now."

Murphy stared at him and seemed to see the bloodstains saturating Colin's clothing for the first time. Still, hurt lingered in his expression.

At first I didn't understand then it hit me. Murphy thought Colin and I were screwing behind his back. No, worse. Falling in love.

I couldn't speak or breathe for a moment, the betrayal was so immense. Horrible pity also clawed at me. How could he believe I'd do that to him? Were the foundations of our love so shaky? I guess they were on his side, but then I'd always known that, hadn't I?

The stupid thing was that Sorcha, the one he'd adored and loved so damn much he had only so much left to give me, *had* betrayed him with Colin. I never would. Ever.

Blind with tears, I shoved past Murphy and out into the hall. I raced to my room on the third floor and locked the door.

I flung myself across the geometric comforter on the bed and gave vent to my frustration and hurt. Was I crying for Ben? Because of Murphy? For every shitty thing that had happened lately?

"Stanzie, please let me in." Five minutes later, Murphy knocked softly on the door. He'd tracked me by my scent, I was sure. "Please, honey."

After a moment, I slid off the bed and unlocked the door. I retreated to the bed and sat—head down, but couldn't resist peeking at him through my lowered lashes.

Murphy locked the door behind him and appeared so tired and remorseful my heart hurt. Colin and I had looked incriminating together, I suppose. Especially to Murphy when he'd had to go through what he had with Sorcha and Colin in the past. How could I blame him for jumping to conclusions? Emotion often raced ahead of intellect. He knew he could trust me. Didn't he? Maybe he was afraid of himself.

"You'll make a wonderful Councilor," I told him and his eyes widened with shock. I guess he'd expected me to yell at him. "You always know what to do, what to say to people."

"Except you." He sat beside me and when I moved closer so our bodies touched, put his arm around my shoulders.

"Even me." I let my head fall to his shoulder and inhaled his scent. Autumn wind and leather soothed my soul somehow. Most of the dreadful tension that had me twisted into knots relented. "I know how it looked, but I was just trying to comfort him. Colin went through a lot today, Murphy."

"Yeah, and so did you. He spent the past five minutes making sure I fully understood what you'd done. Hunter said without you, that boy would have died."

"No," I said. "Colin's the one who got his leg out of that trap."

"Yeah, but you took charge. That's what he said. He said he did what you told him to and he was damned grateful for the direction. Allerton said the same thing. How proud he was of you."

I shook my head. "I just did what needed to be done."

"That's right," he agreed and kissed my forehead. "You always do that. It's like a thing with you."

I burrowed closer. Outside the safe house, autumn rain beat upon the roof and the night closed in until there was just darkness and us within it.

Chapter 7

The rain tapped like inquisitive fingers against the windows as we gathered after a hurried breakfast. All four Alphas were not well pleased about being confined to the safe house, especially Angus. His glowering countenance cast a pall across the room as he sat on the sofa beneath the hunting print with Evelyn.

Her eyes were red rimmed with crying and the tip of her snub nose was red. She clutched a tissue in one hand and a mug of tea in the other.

The Mac Tire Alphas sat beneath the rain-streaked window. Mary's hair was down today, the front drawn back with a silver barrette. Richard looked arrogantly elegant in obviously expensive clothes.

The Stony Fell Alphas' clothes, while dressy, were obviously of less quality material and cut, and made them look shabby in comparison.

No one had given me a dress code, so I was in comfortable jeans and one of Maureen's hand-knitted sweaters. My high-heeled black ankle boots were the most expensive thing I wore. Mary Lancaster eyed me askance when I entered the room with a mug of coffee, and I flashed a grin that made her grit her teeth.

Suiting his new role as Regional Councilor, Murphy was dressed up. He looked sexy enough to attack and I wished we had the time even though we'd made love before we'd gotten up for breakfast. On fire for him, I made sure to sit on my own on one of the stools in front of the old-fashioned bar, so I wouldn't drape myself all over him.

He winked at me as he took one of the arm chairs by the fireplace. A crackling fire lent warmth to the room and, if not for the serious reason we were all gathered, the room could have been a cheerful place to spend a rainy Sunday.

Colin sat on another bar stool, but kept one empty between us, while he nursed a cup of what smelled very much like Irish coffee. Jason Allerton made a late, no doubt strategic, appearance and shut the door. Jason barely had the chance to take the second arm chair by the fire before Angus Finch said, his Scottish accent thick with indignation, "I protest, Councilor Allerton. A Regional Councilor from Mac Tire is hardly going to be unbiased. This is why we requested the Great Council handle this situation in the first place. If we must have the Regional Council involved, isn't there any one else but Councilor Murphy to represent them?"

Jason looked thoughtful as he settled into the chair. Murphy's expression was neutral as he gazed across the room at the Stony Fell Alphas.

Jason said, "Councilor Murphy has just been appointed and as the newest Regional Councilor, he has never worked on a case in this region before. You could hardly ask for anyone less biased."

"He's Mac Tire," spat Angus.

"So is ninety-five percent of the UK Regional Council, I'm afraid. And the one Councilor who is not is at the bedside of her daughter who is having a baby and, therefore, is not available. I'm afraid you'll have to bear with us, Mr. Finch. Can you do that?"

"Have I got a choice?" Bitterness twisted Angus's rough features.

"It does seem a trifle incestuous," said Richard, although he was smiling a little. "Councilor Murphy and Advisor Newcastle are bonded."

Murphy's eyes darkened and I expected Jason to speak first to keep Murphy from exploding, but he kept his peace.

"Advisor Newcastle is Councilor Allerton's Advisor, not mine," Murphy said. "She'll report to him."

"Yeah, and pillow talk to you," sneered Angus.

Jason said, "That is extremely insulting and you will offer Advisor Newcastle an apology. These proceedings will not advance until you do."

"It's a valid concern," I said before Angus could say anything, and Jason steepled his fingers before his mouth—a posture I'd learned hid anything from anger to amusement. I think in this case he was smiling. "But since I'm only interested in finding out the truth, Angus, you shouldn't worry unless you've got something to hide."

Murphy didn't bother to hide his grin.

"Well said." Colin lifted his mug to me before he took a sip. He rolled his eyes when he noticed Angus's scowl and added, "You can hardly accuse me of being biased in Mac Tire's favor. Although I was once a member, I was not an influential one, nor did anyone weep at my departure. I certainly hold very few fond memories of my time spent with them. Something I have in common with your bond mate, I imagine. If anybody ought to be crying foul, it's them." He glanced at the Mac Tire Alphas.

Evie flushed and blurted, "I may not have been popular, but I don't hold any grudges, Advisor. Please don't insinuate I do."

"Never meant to, I'm sure," Colin said, but his expression was on the sarcastic side.

Jason looked pointedly at Angus, who took a deep breath. I wasn't sure if he was about to erupt with rage or give in and apologize.

"I beg your pardon, Advisor Newcastle," he said. As apologies went, I'd had better, but at least he'd made one.

"Now I'm going to offer both packs one opportunity to confess to setting that trap. If you admit it now, the only penalty will be the revocation of your Alpha status. I'll ask you step aside voluntarily without Council censure. However, if you decline, and we find out you did it, the penalty is removal as Alpha and exile from the Pack." Jason's tone was matter of fact, but a chill slipped down my spine.

"You really think an Alpha did it?" Angus's face was as red as his hair. "That's bloody cheek, Councilor."

Jason's jaw tightened. "The offer was made to the entire pack, not just the Alphas. If you know who it was, give him or her up, and you'll keep your Alpha status. Shield them and you'll lose it."

"Why would I or anyone from Stony Fell set a bloody trap? The land's ours by rights. We would not jeopardize our position with such stupidity," said Angus.

"The land is not yours by right." Mary's tone was venomous. "You know damned well it belongs to Mac Tire and has for over a century."

"Here's the deed right here, madam." Angus reached into the pocket of his jacket and withdrew a piece of paper which he waved contemptuously in her direction. She stiffened with rage.

Richard's eyes began to dance with anger as well. "Must you be so offensively disrespectful? Act like an Alpha. If you know how."

"Should I model myself on you maybe?" Angus gave a derisive snort. "Let Evie call the shots and tell me what to do, the way you let that black-haired witch tell you?"

Richard whitened. "You will take that back and apologize or we'll have to step outside to settle this."

"I've already apologized one time too many to suit me. I'll be glad to step outside. Let's go." Angus rose to his feet and so did Richard.

"Gentleman, take your seats." Jason didn't raise his voice, but the authority in his tone was undeniable. "This proceeding will not devolve into a brawl or neither one of you will continue your involvement in it. If you'd rather fight than cooperate, that's fine. But there will be repercussions."

"He insulted my bond mate." Richard could barely get the words past his clenched teeth.

"He insulted me," said Angus.

"Do you suppose we could put aside egos for the sake of what happened to Ben?" I asked. "That's the important thing isn't it?"

"There's also the little trifling matter of who gets the land," said Angus. "I know you're hell-bent on righting the wrong done to Ben, but it never would have happened if Mac Tire hadn't started this whole bloody thing."

"Won't solving who set the trap also decide the matter of who gets the land?" I wondered.

"Maybe," Angus conceded. "But if the only basis we're going on is who set the trap, that's not looking at the bigger picture. If this ever happens again to two other packs, what's decided here could avert another damned investigation."

"Very true," said Jason. "But my Advisor is right. I'm more interested in getting to the bottom of who set that trap at the moment. After that's settled, then we can look into the territory dispute."

"What if we never find out?" Angus scowled.

"We will," Jason vowed. "I'll see to that personally."

"As will I." Murphy's expression was dark and determined. "Ben Hastings has been permanently disabled and not only will we find out who was responsible, there will be restitution made."

"How? By giving him one of our legs?" Angus scoffed.

"Mr. Finch, you are out of order and have been from the first words out of your mouth this morning. I'm a tolerant man, but my patience has been exhausted. If you cannot contribute to this discussion in a respectful, calm and orderly manner, you may leave. The door is not locked." Jason's dark brows made an angry slash above his eyes. I nearly strangled on the scent of his powerful rage when I tried to take a deep breath.

"I'm trying to be respectful. I don't understand how we can make it right with the lad. He's missing a leg and he always will be." Angus took care to speak calmly.

"He'll be given a prosthetic leg and will be compensated monetarily as well."

"Stony Fell hasn't the money for something like that," Angus admitted.

"Let's hope someone from Stony Fell isn't responsible, shall we?" Jason steepled his fingers in front of his mouth again. This time, I suspected he strove to hide his impatience and anger.

"It wasn't Mac Tire," said Richard.

"You're certain of that?" Jason elevated his eyebrows.

"I know I didn't do it," Richard said, sounding exasperated. "You won't let me tell my pack what happened, so how I'm supposed to know it wasn't any of them, I'm not clear."

"Exactly my point. You can't be sure it wasn't Mac Tire, can you?" Jason asked.

Richard flushed. "We're not barbarians, Councilor."

"Oh? And people in Stony Fell are?" Angus was quick to anger again, but a look from Jason quelled his agitation and he fell silent.

"I'm putting my original offers on the table again," said Jason. "Confess now, whether it was you or a pack member, or this is going to get ugly, I promise you that."

Thundering silence. Tension so thick my stomach ached gripped the room. Jason looked at each Alpha in turn. Angus met his gaze belligerently. Richard's expression was cold and determined. Mary tilted her head with an arrogance that made me want to slap her. Evie's eyes filled with tears, but were they inspired by guilt or fear? Jason was formidable. I was never so glad not to be in the hot seat as that moment.

"I need a cigarette," said Mary.

"Five minutes." Jason looked at his elegant wrist watch and Mary all but bolted for the door.

Evie escaped too, tissue pressed to her nose and with a muttered oath, Angus followed. He probably didn't want her left alone in case she said or did something unadvisable. Fear made people stupid.

Colin refilled his mug with coffee from a silver urn on the bar and went behind it for the whiskey bottle. I shoved my mug in his direction and he obligingly poured me a shot of Jameson's.

"What if it was Stony Fell? And they can't afford to help Ben?" I looked at Jason, who sat still as a stalking predator. Murphy was gazing at the leaping flames, but at my words, had turned.

Richard was peering out at the relentless rain, but now he faced forward too. I suppose I ought to have kept my mouth shut since he was in the room, but I wanted to know.

"The Councils will not let him suffer, Stanzie," Jason told me.

"He'll never be an Alpha," Richard said from the window seat. "Can you make that up to him, Councilor?"

"Why can't he be an Alpha?" I was outraged.

Richard grimaced. "Maybe he might in a small pack like Stony Fell, but I doubt it sincerely. And never in a pack like Mac Tire. Alphas cannot be disabled. How can you not know that?"

I thought about my wolf and how she hadn't been normal because of the pack bond. How even small Riverglow had conspired behind my back to keep me from being Alpha. Of course I knew it, but that didn't make it fair and I didn't have to like it.

"If he can't be Alpha, who would bond with him?" I asked.

Richard shook his head pityingly. "That's what Councilor Allerton means. He'll never bond. Maybe when his female peers in the pack are past child bearing age or perhaps as spare to a pair. After they've been Alpha, of course. He'll need to be taken care of."

"Unless he bonds, he can't be a true member of any pack." My voice shook. "He'll be a loner."

"No, he'll be taken care of," Richard said. "Loners don't have pack support. Ben always will. If Stony Fell can't do it, Councilor Allerton, Mac Tire will take him. We're not guilty, but we'll take him into our pack if he'll come to us."

"That's a generous offer, Richard." Jason gave him a weary smile. "That would be the best thing, in my opinion."

"No, it wouldn't," I argued. "Because he'll never be an Alpha in Mac Tire. He might in Stony Fell. Tracy will bond with him. She loves him."

"Tracy is Mac Tire," Richard said. "Her whole life and her family are here. She'll be Alpha someday, but not if she bonds with him."

"Then she can leave and go to Stony Fell."

"If the Councils decide in Mac Tire's favor over the land, there will be no Stony Fell. With no land, they aren't big enough to petition for another territory. Mac Tire will take them over. It's our land, Stanzie." Richard stared at me and, true Alpha, wouldn't look away. "I know you like to champion the underdog, but there are advantages to belonging to Mac Tire a small pack just can't offer. Surely, you see that?"

"How do you know anything about me?" I glared at him. "Twenty acres. A small piece of land and you're too greedy to give it up."

"It's not the land so much as the principle. Small packs don't work. Not enough income, not enough gene pool, not enough of anything. Even in America most packs number at least twenty, don't they?" Richard refused to rise to the bait and become angry.

"My birth pack was decimated by the red virus when I was a year old. My pack was never larger than sixteen my entire childhood. Then I joined

Riverglow and we never got bigger than nine. So perhaps I can see the other side of this equation a little better than you obviously can," I said.

"I see." Richard probably didn't. "Your opinion may be valid, but it doesn't count for much in this proceeding, does it? You're an Advisor. Your role is to listen and report, not cast a vote."

"Lovely of you to explain her role, Richard," Colin said, the barest hint of ire in his tone. "But maybe you ought to concentrate on your own."

"You don't get a vote either," Richard said with a shrug. "I don't even know why either of you are here, frankly. Shouldn't you be off gathering evidence in the field? Or fetching coffee for the rest of us?"

"Ah, he's angry," said Colin with a smile. "Stanzie, you must have gotten under his skin with the logic of some of your observations. Good for you. If you want coffee, Richard, the urn is full. Help yourself."

Colin slid off the bar stool and walked out the door.

"I'd be happy to go out into the field." I climbed down from the bar stool and gulped the last of my Irish coffee. "Sitting around arguing has never been my strong suit anyway."

"We're not arguing, we're debating," Richard said with a smile. "Please don't let me give you the impression I'm arguing with you. I value your insights and appreciate your candor, Advisor."

I had to bite down on the impulse to tell him to stuff it up his ass, but my face probably gave me away because he laughed.

I headed out the door, intent on going outside for some fresh air. The porch would shelter me from the worst of the rain, and if I didn't get out of there, I would do or say something even more regrettable than I already had.

Evie and Angus sat at one of the tables in the dining room. She was crying again and he was whispering something to her I couldn't make out. Damned Scottish accents.

Chilly, damp wind whipped my hair back the second I opened the front door. Mary Lancaster huddled in a protected corner beneath an eave, smoking.

"Beastly weather." She cast the rain a baleful look. She held out her pack of Players. I shook my head. "Thanks, but no. I just need some fresh air."

"There's an abundance of that, I'll grant you." She took a drag from her cigarette and held the smoke for a long moment before exhaling. How anyone Pack could smoke, I couldn't understand. Wolves needed full lung capacity so they could run. Didn't she appreciate that?

She studied me with her imperious, dark eyes. "We're going out for dinner this evening. At a rather upscale restaurant. I do hope you packed a decent dress."

"No. I was in a rush to get here. I guess I'll wear what I've got on," I said. Bitch.

"You're not serious?" Her black brows elevated.

"I am." I had a nice dress. Two of them, in fact, but I was damned I'd wear either to appease this arrogant witch.

"Well, you and Evelyn will make a dowdy pair then, won't you? It's easy to see where your sympathies lie."

"She's wearing a lovely dress today," I said.

"Bargain bin. Maybe she even made it herself. It's entirely the wrong style to suit her. It makes her look the most atrocious frump. Though with that carroty hair and those freckles, I suppose anything she put on would look awful. And she would attempt to wear yellow. Redheads should never wear yellow."

"And affluent Alphas should never look down on their less wealthy counterparts," I said. "At least in my opinion."

"Well, that's just what it is, isn't it? Your opinion," she snapped. "God, you're as provincial as she is. How on earth did you get to be Jason Allerton's Advisor? I pegged you for a small town, tiny pack nobody the second I saw you in France. You might have been wearing a decent dress and fashionable shoes, but you know the saying. You can't make a silk purse out of a sow's ear, can you?"

"If anyone's walking proof of that, you are," I said with a smile. I hadn't been on the receiving end of Siobhan Carmichael's best shots for nothing. Mary was amateur hour compared to that woman. It was almost too easy to return her clumsy serves.

Mary shuddered with rage and flung her cigarette into the rain before glaring at me and storming back inside. I couldn't follow until I stopped laughing.

* * * *

The rest of the afternoon passed miserably slowly. Trapped in the lounge with the rain hammering down and tempers kept barely in check, I thought I would go crazy. My sole contribution to the proceedings was to take down a list of names from the Alphas of people from both packs who might possibly have set the trap.

Just the idea of pointing fingers pissed the Alphas off and I wasn't thrilled with the process either. How did they come up with names for something awful like this? It seemed a terrible sort of fishing expedition to me, but as an Advisor, I wasn't asked for my opinion, only my administrative skills.

Colin kept his mug full of coffee and whiskey and, at some point after lunch, switched to straight whiskey. I kept watch on him, but he didn't appear to show any drunken effects. I suspected he wanted something to occupy his hands, maybe to keep from beating the Alphas senseless.

Dinner reservations were set for seven. At five, Jason called a halt to the proceedings and when I came back to the lounge after a much-needed bathroom break, several bottles of wine had been opened to breathe on the bar.

"Red or white?" Colin, perched on his bar stool, gestured at the bottles.

"Red," I decided, and he poured me a generous glass of pinot noir.

During the break he'd donned a fawn colored blazer and combed his hair.

Defiantly, I'd remained in my jeans and sweater.

He eyed me up and down as he handed me the wine glass. "You're a bit under dressed."

"Long story," I said and at that precise moment, Mary Lancaster made her appearance into the room. As with most things, it was staged for maximum effect.

She'd changed into a dramatic black velvet sheath dress, black tights, gorgeous silver-trimmed ankle boots with stiletto heels and a ruby-sequined bolero jacket. Her bond pendant—a gleaming emerald and diamond duo—dangled from a thick, twisted platinum choker. Diamond earrings winked from her earlobes and she wore an exquisite emerald cocktail ring. Her distinctive silver bracelet I guessed was the Mac Tire pack jewelry, as Richard sported a more masculine version on his right wrist.

Mary had let her witch black hair down in a shimmering mass to just above her waist. While not what I'd consider beautiful, since her personality poisoned her looks and made her hard, she was certainly striking.

Beside her, Richard was sophisticated and sharp in a black dinner suit. His tie was ruby tinted, no doubt to play up Mary's bolero jacket.

"You really aren't going to wear jeans, are you?" Her tone was incredulous, but a smug smile played across her scarlet lips. Plainly, she believed she outshone me and the thought pleased her.

"I really am." I lifted my glass, aware of Colin snickering beside me. "Cheers." I debated whether I ought to be truly gauche and swig half the glass in one swallow. It might be fun to watch her have a stroke, but it was a shame to waste good wine that way and I'd already made my point by not changing.

"I shall speak with Councilor Allerton about this." Mary flounced to the sofa and draped herself across it.

Richard approached the bar.

"Why must women play such petty games?" he asked Colin as he poured white wine into two glasses.

The impulse to dash the contents of my glass in his arrogant face was almost too strong for me to resist. Colin angled his body between us as if he sensed my dilemma.

Petty? I'd show him petty. And damn Jason Allerton, if he thought he could get me to wear a dress to this frigging dinner.

The Stony Fell Alphas walked in and Angus zeroed in on the wine. He wore a kelly green dinner jacket that had seen better days and a plaid kilt, socks with garters and black brogues.

I'd never seen any man wear a kilt before, outside of a Renaissance festival I'd attended once with Grey and Elena in upstate New York. No man in Mac Tire wore one, that I'd ever seen.

Richard moved aside so Angus could reach the bottle of red and his expression hadn't altered. I supposed this must be normal after all. I'd learned something new every day since moving to Dublin.

Angus had rather nice legs. I couldn't help glancing at them when he stood next to me at the bar.

"I didn't know there was a Finch clan in Scotland," I said, no doubt revealing my horrible ignorance. Richard's lips quirked and he quickly strode away with his wine. Colin cleared his throat in a not very convincing attempt to cover his laughter.

"This is clan MacKenzie," Angus explained. "My da's British. My mother's a MacKenzie."

"Oh," I said. That didn't make a lot of sense to me since Pack sons took their fathers' names and daughters their mothers', but this was the United Kingdom and the rules seemed different here.

Angus gave me a cheerful grin. "Okay, you got me. I like kilts. I saw you peeking at my legs. Nice, aren't they? They're my best feature. Can I help it if I take every opportunity to show them off?"

Colin did laugh then.

"Cheers, mate," he said and touched his glass to Angus's.

Evie smiled tentatively, as if she were unsure of the joke. Her evening dress was on the elderly side. My Grandmother Carolyn would have loved it. The hem hung an unfashionable inch below her knees and the long sleeves were loose and bunchy. The ruffles down the bodice were the most unfortunate effect. The color was wrong for her too. The weak green shade washed her already pale skin into an unhealthy pallor.

Her short, bright red hair had no volume and she hadn't bothered with makeup. Maybe she never wore it.

Black pumps with ugly square heels did nothing to improve the overall look.

From the corner of my eye I saw Mary glide over to greet her. Hell, she'd come over to gloat and most likely say something mean. I braced myself.

So did Evie, by the stiff set of her shoulders. Angus handed her a glass of wine and moved off with Colin for a discussion by the fireside. Rats deserting a sinking ship.

"What an interesting dress," Mary drawled. "If I ever have a daughter, I'll remember those ruffles, Evelyn."

Evie swallowed hard and mustered a forlorn smile. "I rather like ruffles."

"You would." Mary reached out for one of the baked cheese sticks on the bar. Evelyn, unfortunately, stretched her hand toward the bowl at the same moment and Mary jogged her elbow.

Red wine splashed all over the ruffles of her dress.

With a curse, Mary leaped backward to avoid staining her dress.

Wine puddled on the wood floor at Evelyn's feet.

"Clumsy bitch," spat Mary. Had she bumped Evelyn deliberately? I wouldn't put it past her. One of those accidentally on purpose mishaps.

Tears rose in Evelyn's brown eyes as she surveyed the utter ruin of her dress. Red wine. Angus couldn't have poured her white.

"Evie, come on. I'll help you clean up." I slid off my bar stool and plucked the empty wine glass from her fingers so I could set it on the bar. Wrapping an arm around her shoulders, I steered her for the door.

Murphy and Jason stepped aside to let us out on their way in. Both looked sympathetically at the wine stain.

"A little accident," I said. "Can I have the room key, Murphy?"

He fished it out of his jacket pocket and handed it to me.

Evelyn allowed me to herd her up the narrow, carpeted stairs to the third floor and my room without protest.

Once inside, she stood by the door in a dejected slump.

"Take off that dress." I moved to the armoire in the corner, where I'd hung the two dresses I'd brought with me. "What size shoes do you wear?"

"Six." Her expression was bewildered.

"Ha. I knew it." I fished out a pair of silver pumps with rhinestone encrusted accents from the shoe rack in the bottom of the armoire.

Beneath her dress, Evie had on a white slip with more damn ruffles.

"That too. Off," I said, and she bit her lip.

Evie and I were the same basic shape. She was less well endowed than I and maybe an inch shorter, but I thought my dresses would fit her nevertheless.

I selected the sapphire pleated A-line dress and tossed it at her.

The other dress, the cherry red, one-shoulder draped evening dress, was the one I'd planned to wear to dinner with Murphy on the anniversary of our bonding. The rhinestone embellishment on the shoulder sparkled in the light when I took it off the hanger. Richard was right. It would be petty to wear jeans just to irritate Mary.

I was an Advisor, not a child.

Evie, still in her slip, stared at the red dress. "Sleeveless? It's cold outside." She looked at the rain-streaked dark window and shuddered.

"I have a heavy black velvet shawl. I'll be fine." I found my Paris stilettos and straightened.

"Come on, Evie, I never got to finish my wine and I'd like to before we leave for the restaurant." I cast her an impatient look as I unzipped my jeans and shimmied out of them.

"This is a lovely dress. I might spill on it. I spill a lot." Evie gave the dress in her hand a dubious look.

"Lose the slip and put on the dress," I said.

"I don't want to lose the slip. It hides panty lines," she argued.

"Fine. Keep it on, Grandmother," I said and she stared at me for a moment before two tears trickled down her cheeks. I stifled an impatient curse. "I'm joking with you. Please don't cry. Put on the dress and I'll do your hair and makeup. I have a couple shades of eye shadow I think will look equally good on a redhead as a blond."

"I don't wear makeup." She held up the sapphire dress and must have realized it had a zipper. She pulled down the tab and looked at it again. At this rate she'd be dressed by Tuesday.

I'd already donned my dress. I adjusted the draped shoulder in the armoire mirror. Would Murphy like this dress as much as he'd liked the one I'd worn in Paris? That had been ruined by red wine just as Evie's dress had been. Funny how things went in circles.

I twisted my hair into a French knot and, holding it in place with one hand, went into the bathroom in search of pins. Evie had better be in that dress by the time I came out or I was going to dress her myself.

After pinning my hair, I redid my makeup and put my bond pendant on the thick silver chain I wore at night.

Evie was in the dress, but needed help with the zipper. I came to her aid and had her sit on the bed while I did her makeup and hair.

With some foundation, eye shadow and mascara, she transformed from plain to gamine. I tousled her hair with gel and, with a tiny rhinestone barrette to hold her bangs to the side she really looked different.

She gasped when she saw herself in the bathroom mirror. "Is that me?" A smile pulled at her lips. I'd glossed them with a nude tint which made them shine.

I glanced at the clock on the nightstand and winced.

"We'd better go," I said as I snatched my black velvet fringed shawl and evening clutch.

The men came to attention when Evie and I made our entrance into the lounge. I stepped to the side so Evie could take center stage and smiled when Angus's eyes lit with appreciation.

I signaled to Murphy to go to her. He grinned and brought her a glass of wine. As he handed it to her, he leaned close to whisper something into her ear, making her giggle, and Mary's expression turned sour.

Richard had abandoned his bond mate the second Evie and I entered the room. Now he handed me a glass of wine.

"The wait was worth it," he told me. "A truce, Advisor? I know you think I'm an irritating bastard, but I can be very nice on occasion."

"Don't let me get in the way of your natural inclinations," I said, He laughed.

A short while later, we left the safe house and headed to the car park. Umbrellas were unfurled, jackets donned while Evie expressed doubt she could walk on the cobblestones in the pumps I'd lent her.

"You can hold onto me." Colin offered his arm gallantly and Mary sneered at them both as she brushed past them to get to the umbrella stand.

She paused by me as I wrapped my shawl around my head and shoulders. Murphy held the door for everyone.

"You may have moved up in the world, Advisor." The title was an insult. She pitched her voice low so presumably only I could hear her. "But inside you'll always be a small town, tiny pack nobody. I hope you know that."

"As long as I don't morph into a big city, large pack bitch like you, I'm cool with it," I remarked with a smile. I didn't bother to keep my voice low. Murphy turned his head away from the door to stare at me.

"Your bond mate is rude, Councilor." Mary flounced out the door, her dark eyes dancing with temper.

"And sexy as hell in that red dress," Murphy said as I passed him. I winked and he grinned.

I made sure I rode in Jason's car. He let Murphy drive, no doubt for me, and I climbed into the back seat of the rented white Vauxhall Ampera. Inside, the doors and seats were black with red accents. New car scent was strong. I wrinkled my nose.

Jason waved Colin toward the Mac Tire Alpha's Land Rover.

"Yeah, good call. He can be a buffer so they won't rip each other to shreds if they're left alone," I remarked as Jason slid into the passenger bucket. He shook out his black umbrella and quickly shut his door.

Murphy started the car and waited for me to buckle my seatbelt.

"Evelyn looks wonderful, Stanzie." Jason settled the umbrella at his feet and his gaze met mine in the rearview mirror. "I appreciate the gesture you made."

"You don't think it makes it look like I'm favoring Stony Fell?" I asked as the car bumped out of the parking lot and Murphy turned left onto the smoothly paved road.

"Are you?" Jason sounded genuinely interested.

"I don't know. As obnoxious as the Mac Tire Alphas can be, I can't imagine them setting that trap. It's equally hard for me to picture Angus and Evelyn doing it. Besides, one of their pack members was hurt."

"The trap was technically on Mac Tire's side of the disputed territory," Jason pointed out, but his tone was neutral.

"Anyone from Stony Fell who wanted to hunt on what they consider their land would have to pass that area. Tracy from Mac Tire could just as easily have stepped into that trap."

"They shifted on Mac Tire land and were on their way to Stony Fell's when Ben was caught," said Jason. "They were chasing each other. Perhaps if they'd been paying more attention to their surroundings they would have smelled it or seen it."

"Who on earth would ever expect a trap on Pack land?" I gave an indignant bounce on the seat.

"In Montana, we have to be very careful of traps and poachers who hate wolves." Jason stared out the windshield into the rainy autumn darkness.

A shiver of fear slid down my spine.

Amy Lee Burgess

"Lauren—" I began.

He turned his head to meet my gaze in the rearview mirror. "Is safe, Stanzie. We post sentries at all times at the access points and hunt at night. I'm just trying to say perhaps some of us have become a bit complacent and it might do to become more vigilant and aware of our surroundings."

"Wolves are extinct here. Nobody would hunt them down like they do in Montana and Wyoming. Are you trying to suggest an Other did this? Traps like the one Ben was caught in haven't been used in decades. They're illegal in the States."

"This is not the States." Jason frowned.

I shook my head ."It was a replica of an antique bear trap. There haven't been bears or wild wolves here in over a century. At least according to Richard and he would know better than me. There's nothing big to hunt here. Deer, rabbits, maybe foxes. But wolves? I don't think so. Not unless you think an Other hunter has seen Pack wolves. It's private land."

"Which abuts a national forest. I'm merely exploring all possibilities. You don't like to think it's any of the Alphas but you don't like the idea of it being Others, either. The truth is somewhere in there though, isn't it?"

I was silent.

"What's your impression of Colin?" Jason changed the subject and I darted a glance in Murphy's direction. Aside from tightening his fingers on the steering wheel, he remained relaxed, but I knew he was fiercely interested in my response.

"Devon's threatening to leave him because Riverglow can't afford to support a baby. Callie ran up thousands of dollars of debt on fertility drugs and he paid them off."

"I'm aware of that," Jason said.

Murphy's mouth twisted as if he tasted something bitter, but he didn't say anything.

"So he wants to do a good job, but yesterday kicked the crap out of him emotionally," I said. "He'll need a thicker skin if he wants to work for you. People die around you all the damn time, Jason."

"How are you handling that?"

I shook my head. "Just when I think my skin's developed the requisite thickness, something like this happens and breaks my heart into pieces. But I don't know what else to do except keep going so I can stop the people who hurt the ones around them. I don't know what Colin's motivation is, but if it's to earn money and prestige so Devon can have a baby, you're going to have one fucked up Advisor on your hands. Just my two cents, Jason."

"Noted," he said and faced forward again.

* * * *

Our table at the restaurant had a sweeping view of the lake. Or would have in the daylight. Tonight there was nothing much to see because the rain and heavy cloud cover shrouded everything.

Jason was a consummate host and never allowed conversation to lag, but even he could do nothing about the stilted nature of it. I mainly kept silent and listened because I was worn out from the emotional tension that had battered us all day.

Tonight no one seemed much inclined to talk about territory disputes, how to make Ben Hastings's life as endurable as possible, or who the hell might have set that damn trap and why. Instead, topics switched rapidly and were superficial and as upbeat as possible.

I sat between Colin and Angus and did my best to demolish the huge plate of roast beef and Yorkshire pudding I'd ordered.

Colin picked at his rack of lamb, but kept his wine glass topped up with expensive Cabernet.

"Colin." When he made to pour the rest of a bottle into his glass, I moved mine next to his. After an entire day of drinking, he was fraying at the edges, his eyes slightly glazed and when he did talk, chose his words carefully and spoke slowly as if to avoid slurring.

"Sorry, love." He gave me a wan smiled and aimed the flow of wine into my glass. His hand shook, but he managed not to spill.

Angus was involved in a spirited discussion about some damn sports team. Soccer, football, whatever the hell they called it, with Murphy and Mary. Surprisingly to me, Mary knew more about scores and player statistics than either of the men.

Evie, Jason and Richard were discussing the goddamn weather. Poor Jason. I'm sure he didn't give a rat's ass about how this rain would usher in winter sooner than need be and maybe even cause local flooding, but he contributed gamely to the conversation.

"Why don't you eat something?" I gestured at Colin's mostly full plate and he grimaced.

"I'm really not hungry, Stanzie."

"Have you talked with Devon lately?" I watched him shake the last drops of the bottle into his glass and gulp it down.

Another bottle of red was half-full at the end of the table, and I angled my body so maybe he wouldn't see it and ask Angus to pass it down.

"Devon doesn't want to hear about amputated legs and feuding Alphas." Colin drained his glass, looked around and snagged the bottle of white in front of Evie. Without bothering to switch glasses or even rinse the one he had with water, he filled it to the brim.

He sensed my disapproval and set the bottle down on his knife. It nearly went over, but he saved it at the last second.

Jason glanced up briefly from his riveting discussion about the last time the stream behind Richard's house flooded, and just as quickly looked away again.

"She told you that or you're trying to shield her?" I set my fork down. A screened porch ran the length of the restaurant on the lake side. Could I get Colin out into the bracing autumn air on the pretext I needed a break? Did he smoke? Could I use that to my advantage?

"Devon doesn't like to hear about the darker side of life." A muscle in Colin's jaw twitched. Frustration? Anger? Humiliation?

"You've got to have someone to talk to," I said.

A derisive smile twisted his mouth. "Like who? You? And have your bond mate come down on the both of us like a ton of bricks? A real understanding bloke, that's Liam Murphy. We ought to drink a toast to his appointment to the Regional Council. Yeah. Let me lead that one, what do you think?"

He pushed back his chair and I knew he meant to get to his feet to propose the toast. Disaster.

"Yes, I would like to go out for some fresh air." I raised my voice and scrambled out of my chair. "Let me get my shawl."

Conversation around the table stumbled to a halt as everyone looked at me.

"My head hurts a little. I'm going to out on the porch for a moment with Colin." A very thin excuse, but I hoped at least some of them would buy it.

Murphy's eyes narrowed as he gazed at Colin. Jason gave me an almost imperceptible nod. He hadn't missed a thing, I'd bet.

Colin was not so drunk that he'd plow on with his toast. He did snag his wine glass on the way to the French doors leading to the porch.

I'd vowed to myself he'd leave it, full, on one of the small tables out there.

"I've got some aspirin in my purse. You can have it when you get back," Evie called after us, her face creased with sympathy.

Our waitress cast us a surprised look, but held the door open for us to escape outside.

Colin stalked to the end of the porch and I hurried after him, scheming how to separate him from his wine.

"I've made some crap decisions in my arsed-up life, but becoming Jason Allerton's Advisor has to be among the very worst." Colin's voice was savage as he glared out at the cold lake.

Waves hissed to shore like discontented gossipers. The rain had let up, but the gutters still ran with overflow and the darkness smelled damp and sullen.

"Then why did you go after the position the way you did?" I leaned against the porch railing and pressed my face to the cold screen. Tree limbs rustled and moaned in the pitch blackness, and I drew my shawl tighter around my shoulders.

He shot me an incredulous look. "Have you not been listening to me? Hasn't Allerton told you how I was booted out of Mac Tire for having the temerity to accuse Dublin's precious Alpha of murdering his bond mate? So I had no pack and Devon was about to leave me, but Allerton swooped in like the bird of prey he is, and offered me Riverglow. For a price. Be a fucking spy for him.

"They were babes in the woods. They never suspected a thing. Well, perhaps that old man did, and I suppose Callie must have, but the rest of them? They actually welcomed me." A gasp of laughter escaped him. I bit my lip. "Now I'm their frigging Alpha and Jonathan and Nora just accept it when I tell them I can't give them their monthly stipend this month, but maybe next, and oh, do you mind getting a second job for a bit, mate? And contributing all of the income to the pack's fractured funds?

"And Devon, going spare because she can't have a baby and looking at me as if to say what a fucking failure I am. I had enough of that shit with Mary. Why do you suppose I broke it off with her? So she couldn't do it first, that's why. And now she tells everyone I dumped her and has turned all my former friends against me, when they have no idea how I felt when she begged me to get us nominated for Alpha. I couldn't even get us into the running. You should have seen her disappointed face the night the duos in contention were announced and we weren't one of them. Just the way she looked at me was enough to make me want to slit my wrists. So I broke it off with her. Gave her a chance to be with somebody who would get her to Alpha. And you see, Richard has. So I did the right thing.

"Do you think she loves Richard?" He bared his teeth at me in a feral smile. "I did all of it for her and to this day she still bad-mouths me. After I dissolved our bond, I couldn't stand to stick around and watch her throw herself at Richard, so I went to Dublin to lick my wounds in private and Sorcha pounced me the second night.

"For God's sake, Stanzie, I wasn't the one who started it with us. She did. I thought she wanted a fling and I was more than willing to oblige there. A bit of an ego boost, wasn't it? She's the one who dreamed up the idea of a triad. I never would have. I told you before, I didn't love her. I'm still in love with Mary. Always will be.

"But I had a shot at Alpha of the Irish branch of Mac Tire. The jackpot, don't you see? I could have shown Mary I wasn't useless and I could accomplish something prestigious and important.

"And then it got fucked up because of that goddamned conspiracy. Bloody Guardians and their bollocky ideas of keeping us in the background like the world's dirty little secret.

"And now here I am working for the leader of the bloody idiots. And I come here and Mary still thinks I'm a fuck-up, doesn't she?" He turned to glare at me as if I'd done something wrong, but I held my ground.

"I'll tell you something else." He shook his finger in my face. "She wasn't such a shrew when I was bonded with her. She's changed. Richard got her to Alpha, but he's twisted her into a bitch in the process."

Tears streaked down his face, and he leaned his forehead against a wooden post that separated one screen from the next.

I pried his fingers away from the wine glass and carried it to a table behind us. I thought about drinking it myself, but set it aside. Murphy stood in the shadows by the door but I didn't acknowledge him. Was he spying on me? Or trying to protect me? What had he thought of Colin's confession that it had been Sorcha who'd chased him? Murphy had been there, had no doubt seen it firsthand himself. Sorcha didn't seem like she'd been the type to hide her actions, even if they were hurtful.

"Everything I do, I do for Mary and she doesn't care, does she?" Colin's shoulders heaved.

I put my arm around his waist and leaned my head against his. "You don't have to be Alpha of Riverglow or Jason Allerton's Advisor. I think you ought to do what you want, Colin, not what you think other people might expect of you. Being an Advisor is a shit job and it will tear the heart out of you. Especially if you aren't doing it for yourself. To hell with Devon and Mary and Jason Allerton. Who cares what they want?"

"I'm not a fuck-up," he whispered. "I'm not."

"No. For what it's worth, you did a hell of a job yesterday. And you've done your best for Riverglow as Alpha. I'm not going to run Mary down, but I'm not impressed with her Alpha behavior. You've got twice as much grace under pressure."

"She's always hated the sight of blood," he said.

"I don't particularly like it either. I'm sure you don't." When he shuddered, I tightened my arm around his waist.

"You need a better partner than me," he said. "I should resign. Liam—"

"Leave me out of this, Colin." Murphy stepped out of the darkness. "I'm a Councilor now. I would like Stanzie to have a partner she could count on."

"That's why I need to quit." Colin shrugged out of my grasp and moved a few feet away. He didn't seem startled to see Murphy. Maybe he'd known he was there all along? "You couldn't even let her come out here alone with me because you don't trust me."

"I loved Sorcha." Murphy kept to the shadows so I couldn't see his face. "Being accused of murdering her devastated me. I was already reeling with grief and you made it a thousand times worse. Can you understand that? You allowed your pitifully bruised ego to influence you to do something truly evil. You knew how much I loved her. You knew I wasn't standing in the way. I argued for you, you bastard. To my pack, who didn't particularly care for the idea of some stranger, British Mac Tire or not, waltzing in as Alpha right off the frigging bat. Sorcha wasn't the most popular Alpha. Surely you figured that out. You're smart."

"You didn't do me any favors, you miserable prick. You did it all for Sorcha, not me."

"So that's how you sleep at night? Telling yourself I stood up for you because of Sorcha? I tried to be your friend, you asshole. Do you remember that part or have you convinced yourself it was an act performed for Sorcha's benefit too?" Murphy's tone was scorching hot with derision. "Who welcomed you that first night you arrived? When nobody knew what to think. Who bought you your first Guinness at An Puca and introduced you to everyone? Kept you at my side the whole night so everyone would know I accepted you?"

"You were just being a decent Alpha. It wasn't for me. It was the right thing to do and Liam Murphy always does the right thing, doesn't he?"

Murphy laughed darkly. "If you didn't feel so fucking sorry for yourself, maybe the people you surround yourself with would respect you more. It's just a thought. You make it easy to despise you. You make it simple to walk all over you. Believe it or not, I've held back."

"And now what? You want me to throw myself at your feet and grovel? Thank you for your patience and understanding? Sod you. You and your bond mate and Mac Tire and this whole fucking joke of a situation."

The screen door slammed behind Colin then he stumbled down the stairs in the dark and crashed into the woods.

"If we're lucky, that asshole will fall in the lake and drown." Murphy kicked something. The leg of a table maybe or one of the slatted deck chairs.

"You two are more alike than you know," I rushed out the screen door after Colin.

Murphy was two steps behind me on the stairs and at the bottom he moved to my side.

"If he does fall in the lake, you're the one who's jumping in after him. I just bought this dress." My cherry red stilettos were not made for rushing down muddy paths. When I stumbled over a rock, Murphy grabbed my arm to keep me upright.

"And it's a really nice dress. Shorter than the one you wore the night I met you, but it puts me in mind of it just the same. And you know what the dress did to me. That dress is why we're bonded today." Murphy let go of my arm so he could take my hand and we twined our fingers.

"Celine Ducharme is why we're bonded today," I said, and he laughed softly in the cold darkness. The rain had ceased, but the ground beneath our feet was soft and squishy. Damn Colin and his mad drunken dashes.

"I think this path leads to the car park not the lake," said Murphy and, sure enough, we rounded a corner and had to squint against the sudden blaze of lights in the lot. Colin sat on a parking curb in one of the empty spaces, face buried in his hands.

"What a fucking bastard," Murphy muttered with an exasperated sigh. "I suppose you want to go sit beside him and give him a hug, don't you?"

"Hell, no. That curb is filthy. Remember the dress, Murphy," I said. "I think you're the one who ought to go sit beside him."

"I am not hugging him." Murphy declared.

"Did I ask you to hug him? I just said go sit next to him and talk to him."

"About what?" Murphy lowered his voice to an incredulous whisper. "I have nothing to say to that feckin' idiot. Unless I can call him a feckin' idiot? I don't have to sit next to him to do that. I can say that from here."

"What an understanding and compassionate Councilor you'll make," I marveled.

"He's not before a tribunal," Murphy told me. "Are you going to start making sarcastic remarks about me being a Councilor every time I do something you don't think is nice, Stanzie? Because I'm not gonna be a very happy person if you do. Fair warning. I didn't really want to even be a Councilor but I thought it was a way to get here to be with you."

"Oh, that's a wonderful foundation for the work you'll do on the Council," I said, and he groaned.

"You're on the Regional Council and I work for Jason and the Great Council. The odds of us ever being on the same case together after this one aren't that great, Murphy. Did you think of that when you leaped to accept?"

"I just wanted to be there for you. I'm never there and I wanted to change that. So, no, to answer your question, I didn't really think things through before I accepted. But I'm thinking now. And you'll have to deal with the Regional Council on some of your investigations and I'll be there in that case. So if I can't be an Advisor with you, I can be a Councilor there a decent amount of the time. Unless Allerton starts sending you on cases outside the UK, which I don't put past him, but I'll deal with that when it happens.

"Right now we're together on this investigation and I, for one, am grateful for the opportunity. Judging by last night, I think you're a little bit pleased yourself."

"I can hear every word you two are saying." Colin's words were muffled by his hands. "I'm already not feeling very steady. You're going to drive me over the edge and I'm going to be sick all over the side of Richard's fancy-ass Land Rover. If you kiss her, Liam, I will puke on you. I swear I will. Bastard."

"Serves you right for eavesdropping," Murphy said.

"How is it eavesdropping when you stage your bloody lovers' quarrel ten inches away from me?"

Murphy pinched the skin between his eyes and struggled with his temper. "I think you'd better come back inside with us. The rain's let up, but not for long. Can't you smell it? It's going to piss down at any moment."

"Bugger off." Colin's tone was malevolent. "Do you think I give a shit about rain?"

"Since you're so damned big on making good impressions, you might give a thought to how you'll look, soaking wet and pathetic in front of your new boss."

"Sod him."

Murphy's laugh was more of a snarl. He looked at me. "Okay. I give up. What do you suggest we do with the bastard?"

"Stuff him in our car? You've got the keys, right?" I asked.

Murphy grinned and fished in his pocket.

* * * *

"You fucking cunts, I'll just get out again once you leave," Colin ranted at us as we dragged his ass to the Vauxhall.

"Not if I bash you unconscious." Murphy looked at me over Colin's wildly twisting head. Holding onto his arm was like taking hold of a bag of writhing snakes. I debated kicking the bastard in the shin, but if I broke it, we'd have to carry him and the Vauxhall was still halfway across the parking lot.

"Can I, Stanzie? Can I cold cock him? You have no idea how much I want to."

"Hit me and I'll kick your ass, Liam. You think you can take me? Me?" Colin roared and nearly ripped my arms out of their sockets as he struggled to be free.

"No one would blame me for hitting him, Stanzie. Look at him. He's drunk and disorderly. I'd be thanked for shutting him the hell up," Murphy told me.

"I'm thinking about it," I said.

He grinned. "I'm going to toss you the keys. Let go of him and I'll take it from there," he said and the jangling keys flashed silver bright under the lights.

I caught them neatly and Murphy had Colin's arms twisted behind his back in one impressive move.

"Smooth." I grinned. Colin kicked out at me as I opened the car door and Murphy dragged him backward.

"Why can't we fight, Stanzie? I really want to fight him. Sincerely."

"He's drunk off his ass. It's no fair fighting with a drunken idiot who doesn't know what he's doing."

"I do so know what I'm doing," Colin shouted. "I want to fight him, Stanzie!"

"You see? We both want this. You're the only thing standing in our way," Murphy said.

"You'll thank me in the morning. Can you imagine what Jason would say if he came out here with the four Alphas and found Colin in a bloody puddle on the ground and you standing over him with bruised fists and a maniacal grin?" I asked.

"Oi," yelled Colin indignantly.

"Shut up and get in the car." Murphy manhandled him into the backseat of the Vauxhall. "And stay there if you know what's bloody good for you."

Colin's obscenity-laced response was cut off by the slamming car door.

"Lock the damn thing," Murphy said, and I did.

"He'll have to climb into the front seat to get out. I child-locked the back doors," I told Murphy as we walked back to the restaurant.

Murphy gave a shout of laughter. "I love you."

"I know," I said. "But I'm pretty sure Colin's going to hate me after this."

"Good," said Murphy and I elbowed him in the ribs, but he only laughed more.

* * * *

"Murphy?" The rain drummed on the roof above us and I snuggled into the warmth of his body. He was pressed against my back, one arm thrown over my waist in our usual sleeping position.

"Mmm?" He was three quarters asleep and struggled to respond to me. Maybe I should just be quiet and let him fall all the way.

"Did you really take the Council position so you could be here with me?"

He pressed his lips to the bare skin above the neckline of my nightshirt.

"Yeah." His voice was thick with sleep. "I want to be there for you. I never want to let you down again the way I did. Not bringing you with me the day Nate put you down in that frigging root cellar from hell. The tribunal. Leaving you behind in Boston. It haunts me, Stanzie. Your face and the way you looked as I walked out that door. I don't ever want to see that expression again."

"You were trying to protect me," I reminded him, and he pulled me even closer as if he could somehow merge our bodies into one. "I understand that and I more or less understood it then too."

"You always understand me. It makes it worse when I disappoint you anyway."

"Be a good Councilor. Because the Great Pack needs you. Don't do this for me. Do it for us all. Do it for yourself."

"It'll always be mostly for you. Everything I do," he said and twined his fingers with mine. "Go to sleep, honey. It'll be another long day tomorrow. You need your rest."

Chapter 8

"Oh my God." Colin held his head gingerly between both hands and looked miserable.

I piled thick-cut marmalade on my toast and took a huge bite. Colin watched me chew with a sick fascination.

"If you eat something, you'll feel better." I pushed the toast rack in his direction. He gagged and squeezed his eyes shut in horror.

"You're looking bright-eyed and bushy tailed this morning," Murphy observed, pulling out the chair next to mine. "Want a wee shot of Jameson's in that coffee, Hunter?"

"I know you hate me, but you don't have to be vicious," Colin muttered.

"Oh, but I think I do." Murphy grabbed a slice of toast and slathered on marmalade. "You'd better drink your coffee and, if you're the least bit drunk still, you'll not be driving Stanzie anywhere today no matter what Allerton's orders are."

"I'm not drunk. I'm hung-over as hell, but I'm not drunk. Stanzie can drive, can't she?"

"On the wrong side of the road? You're crazy as well as hung-over," I said. "You better get it together. Jason's lending us his rental car to go interview people and if it doesn't come back in the same condition as it went out, I'm not the one who's going to catch hell for it."

"Americans," said Colin bitterly as if the word was a curse. He grabbed his mug of coffee and slurped. It seemed coffee was good for breakfast after a night of drinking. No tea in sight today.

He set the mug down and took a deep breath. "So? You and me, Liam? We might as well get that fight over with before you eat too damn much and can't get out of your own way. It'll clear the air between us, don't you think?"

"A fucking hurricane gale force wind couldn't clear the air between us, you devious prick," said Murphy cheerfully between bites of toast and scrambled eggs. "But I'll fight you regardless."

Colin bared his teeth in what might have been a smile, but looked more like a snarl.

Murphy spread more marmalade on another piece of toast and I snatched a link of sausage from his plate. He pretended not to see me.

"I'll tell you what you can do for me." Murphy waved his toast in Colin's direction and Colin gritted his teeth.

"Oh, what?" he asked.

"Be Stanzie's friend. A real one, not a back-stabbing fuck like you were to me. While it won't clear the air, it might make me think you've got a least a hope of being a decent sort of person."

Colin looked at me, then Murphy, then back to me.

"Seriously? You want me to be Stanzie's friend. Your *bond mate's* friend?" Colin seemed to forget his hangover in the face of the utter madness Murphy proposed.

"You're not my first choice for a friend for her. Or my second. Or my five hundred and twelfth, but, damn it, you're Jason Allerton's Advisor and so is she. I won't always be able to be there on every investigation with her. You'll be there more often than me, I suspect. So I would like to think she's got a partner she can count on. I know this is a difficult concept for you to contemplate, let alone aspire to, but give it a shot, will you?"

"Will you lay off the sarcasm for once?" Colin demanded. "Jesus Christ, I've only apologized a hundred times for what I did to you. It was a shitty thing, I know, but I've paid for it. Yeah, you were humiliated and pissed off, but I lost everything. Do you think I like being Alpha of Riverglow? A frigging four-member pack? We're the joke of New England, did you know that? Even Maplefair, who had a fucking lunatic serial killer for an Alpha, gets more respect than we do. I'm this bloody close to losing my second bond mate and if she walks, I won't even have the joke pack anymore. Maybe you'd like to see that happen? I bet you would, wouldn't you?" Colin's eyes were storm dark.

Murphy tossed down his piece of toast. "The hell I would. Knowing Jason Allerton, if that happened, you'd end up back in my pack. That I'm even contemplating asking you to be Stanzie's friend makes me a bigger fucking joke than you are." He shoved his chair away from the table and stalked out of the dining room.

Appetite gone, I dropped what was left of the sausage on my plate and pushed back my chair.

"Oh, for fuck's sake, you're not leaving too." Colin smacked the table with his palm. The Stony Fell Alphas jerked in their seats two tables away and stared. Colin glared at them until they looked away.

"That joke of a pack was all I had at one point, you know," I said and stalked out onto the porch. Fuck him. Fuck everybody.

More rain threatened, judging by the ominously dark clouds and the heavy scent of water that nearly drowned out the other outdoor smells of earth, gasoline, old wood and dying flowers.

Light wooden chairs lined the porch, and I chose one with a golden cushion that didn't seem quite as soggy as some of the others. The damp air sank into my bones, and I shivered. Maureen's sweaters were warm, but I thought longingly of the jacket I'd left over the back of my chair.

The bells above the front door jangled, and Colin stepped out on the porch. His expression was hangdog, and he had my jacket over one arm.

"I said way too much last night. Now you think I'm some kind of an asshole." He handed me the jacket and took the chair beside me. The red cushion must have been wet, judging by the grimace he made.

"Hey, I thought you were an asshole way before last night." I shrugged on the jacket and zipped it against the autumn chill. "If anything, last night explained a few things."

He cradled the mug of coffee he'd brought with him and stared into the inky depths as if he could divine some hidden secret if he looked hard enough.

"Look, Vaughn may not have the money or inclination to help you, but I do. Will you let me?" I shoved my hands into my pockets and stared across the street at the lake. The buildings opposite the safe house blocked a direct view, but tantalizing glimpses between them made me want to go explore the windy shore.

My wolf stirred restlessly inside me. My blood heated. Instead of interviewing members of Stony Fell and Mac Tire the Alphas reluctantly indicated *might* be sufficiently pissed about the territory dispute to plant a trap, she wanted to run on the cold sand and between the dark trees.

Murphy and I would have to stop having so much sex, I decided. My wolf was distracting me. Yeah, we could start that whole no sex thing tomorrow. Or maybe the next day, but we'd have to stop soon. Or shift. My wolf perked up inside me again as if she understood the thought. Maybe she did.

"Are you laughing at me?" Colin's bitter voice brought me back to reality with a snap.

"No, I'm thinking about my wolf," I blurted then he smiled, but reluctantly, as if he didn't really want to.

"I'll take all the help I can get. I'm not too proud to reject an offer that could help us." He studied his coffee, his shoulders stiff.

"Then that's settled. I'll send you five hundred a month until you don't need it anymore. And maybe five thousand up front?"

"I'll pay you back," he vowed.

"No, you won't. Riverglow was my home for ten years. Grey left his money to the pack, but Elena gave hers to me. If she hadn't, you'd be fine today."

"We can leave our money any way we like," he said. "It was a damn good thing for you she did leave you hers, wasn't it?"

"I might have rejoined the Great Pack sooner if she hadn't. Her money gave me the opportunity to exile myself for two years."

"You and Liam are a lot alike, aren't you?" Colin set his mug aside and gazed toward the lake shore. "There's no way I could ever be a loner. It's my biggest fear."

Funny how some people tumbled toward their fears, kicking and screaming the whole way, but somehow never thinking to just step aside.

The door bells jangled and Mary Lancaster stepped out onto the porch, cigarette between her lips, one hand cupped to protect the flame from her pale blue lighter.

When she saw us, her dark eyes narrowed. She blew a cloud of gray blue smoke in our direction and said, "Am I interrupting something?" Her tone was snide and full of innuendo, as if she'd blundered across a lovers' tryst. I thought of the scene with Murphy when he'd first arrived, and grimaced

"I'll get the car keys from Jason," I rose to my feet. Colin's expression froze into blankness. As I moved for the door, Mary sauntered past me, intent on claiming my vacated seat. Colin sat there like a sacrificial lamb to the slaughter and I ducked inside before I had to watch the axe fall.

The warmth from the crackling fire in the grate of the corner fireplace in the dining room was a welcome change from the sodden cold. Jason sat at the table beside the fireplace with the remains of a country breakfast on the table in front of him. He had half a cup of black coffee in his hand as he stared at the flames. His cell phone, car keys and an iPad rested beside his plate.

"High tech." I slid into the chair opposite him, unzipped my jacket and pointed at the iPad. A smile quirked the corners of his mouth.

Jason Allerton was a handsome man with straight dark hair, a square jaw and deep blue eyes that missed nothing. He had a politician's good looks. Nothing bad boy about him. Yet in the year I'd been associated with him, he'd brought me more trouble than anyone in my whole life except my father.

"It's yours," he said and gave the iPad a push in my direction. "You might want to take notes. I never see you taking notes."

"I never think to take notes," I admitted. "I don't know how to use one of these things. I wrote down names yesterday, but should I have been taking notes too?"

"Probably," he said with another amused smile. "I've made up an interview schedule and if you pull it up, you'll find names, addresses and times. Feel free to make changes to it as you see fit as long as you manage to see everyone on the list. I don't mean to cramp your style, but I like to go over the case at night before bed and additional written information from you and Colin would be welcome."

"Did Murphy make you notes?"

"At times, yes. He sent me reports while you were on your road trip and spoke to me on the phone."

"But we weren't working on the road trip." After Murphy's near-fatal overdose in Houston, we'd gone on a month-and-a-half road trip from Texas to Massachusetts. We'd hardly known each other at the start of it, but had been fast friends and bond mates by the time we'd driven into the small driveway of my Boston condo the day before New Year's Eve. I'd known Murphy had talked to Jason, but sent him written reports?

"Up until he quit, he'd send me a weekly report of his activities. Of course, he left quite a bit out during his time in Dublin before I sent you there. It was what he didn't say that roused my curiosity, frankly."

"I never send you reports. Should I start sending you reports?" Was this in the Advisor's manual that I'd never gotten? Had Jason laid out expectations I'd missed somewhere? I felt like an idiot.

"You've kept me apprised of your situation the past three months," he said and took a sip of coffee.

"Because you call me. I never call you unless I'm in huge trouble, like the other day." I moved the iPad closer and eyed it suspiciously. What if I broke the damn thing? I could barely remember to bring my cell phone with me. How the hell would I think to lug this stupid thing with me everywhere I went? I'd need a bigger purse for damn sure.

"I've waited for you to call me, but since you never do, I call you." Jason didn't seem particularly perturbed, but his words still stung like a criticism.

"I guess you never had to tell Murphy to call or send reports, did you? He just sort of knew. Sorry." My cheeks were on fire and I wished I was back on the porch in the cold air again.

"You don't need to be afraid to call me, Stanzie. Even just to talk if you'd like. Or Lauren, for that matter."

I bit my lip.

"Paul didn't like me to call," I whispered. Something clogged my throat.

"Paul can't hurt you anymore. Not in any way. Please call your mother. Don't ask me how she's doing. She has a phone. The number's in another file on the iPad. So is her email address. Calling or writing either of us just because is okay."

I thought of the monthly phone calls I'd made to Lauren and Paul during my two-year self-imposed exile. How after the first two, they'd stopped picking up. I remembered hiding my phone at night after Murphy left me so I wouldn't break down and call him in case he rejected me.

Had I been avoiding Lauren because I was scared she wouldn't answer? Jason too? Did I really think I wasn't important enough to talk to? I guess maybe I did. Deep down inside somewhere.

I snatched up the iPad and keys and bolted to my feet. If I didn't get the hell away from this man, I'd burst into tears. Hell no to that.

"I'll give you a report tonight when I get back." I darted out the door.

* * * *

Colin wasn't on the porch anymore. Neither, thankfully, was Mary. Her cigarette butt floated in the dregs of his coffee, and I grimaced. IPad. How the hell did it work? Maybe Colin was waiting by the car. He might know. I rushed down the steps to the flagstone walkway and followed it to the car park. No Colin by the car.

Stairs leading to the sunken garden beckoned me. I'd seen the garden from my bedroom window, but I'd never had the time to see it up close. Maybe I could take five minutes and wander through the autumn shrubs and flowers before I hunted down Colin. The first interview wasn't until ten and it was only quarter after eight.

Watery sunlight filtered through the dark cloud cover. Maybe it wouldn't rain today. That would be fine with me. I didn't relish driving on wet roads in the pouring rain.

I counted the steps to the sunken garden. Seven, eight, nine, and my boots sank into the soft muddy gravel. The pungent scent of sodden chrysanthemums stung my nostrils. The wind rattled leaves on a twisted oak tree, and drawn by the sound, I turned in that direction.

Colin had Mary pressed against the rough bark of the tree, his fingers tight on her shoulders as he fucked her. Her fingers were buried in his blond curls, legs wrapped around his waist as he thrust into her, his jeans pooled around his ankles. The raw need of their passion nearly flattened me.

I lingered for one shocked moment, then turned and fled back to the car park. Way to stay unbiased, Colin. Perfect start to his Advisor career, the stupid sonofabitch.

I made sure to deactivate the Vauxhall's alarm so it beeped and slammed the door loudly when I climbed into the passenger seat, heart pounding like a drum trapped in my chest.

So they had history. He'd left her and she had a new life now. So did he. If he still loved her, why the hell had he bonded with Devon? Did *she* know how the bastard felt about his ex-bond mate? Did she care? What if Richard wandered into the garden? They couldn't even screw in his room? They had to do it out in the open?

"This is so stupid," I said and beat the dashboard with my fist.

* * * *

I'd worked my way through the iPad's basic functions through a process of trial, error and swearing, when the driver's side door opened and a gust of cold air blew in along with Colin Hunter.

With a nonchalant smile, he reached for the keys dangling from the ignition.

"You might want to comb your hair." I didn't look up from the iPad's screen. He peered into the rearview mirror and frantically brushed at his hair with his fingers. "A cold plunge into the lake wouldn't hurt either," I added.

He froze. "Something the matter, Stanzie?"

"Besides the fact you reek of sex and Mary's perfume and we're supposed to interview members of Mac Tire who will be bound to recognize her scent?" I looked up from the iPad to glare at him.

"I thought I might run into Richard on the stairs or something or I would have showered. Is it that bad?" He had the grace to look ashamed but it was too little, too late.

"What is it with you and Alpha females? You like fucking and fucking over the Alphas in a pack? Does it give you a sense of power maybe?"

His eyes narrowed. "What about those personal boundaries you set the other day? Do they only go one way?"

"Now you're going to hide behind boundaries? After everything you told me last night? You fucked her in the middle of the garden in broad daylight, you jerk. It's like you want to get caught, so don't give me any of that personal boundaries shit." I grabbed the door handle and gave it a vicious pull. "Forget this. I can't work like this. You interview the Mac Tire members and I'll concentrate on Stony Fell. I don't want anything to do with you."

"Why are you so mad?" he asked as I was halfway out the door. "What is it to you who I shag? It's none of your business. We're Pack and we can screw who we want. Richard may not like it much, but we're not breaking any Pack laws and you know it."

"You broke your bond with her. You walked away and now you can't keep your dick in your pants when you're alone with her for five minutes? Why'd you break the bond if you love her so much still?" I shouted.

"I told you why." His jaw was clenched so tightly I could almost hear his teeth grind together. "She's better off without me. She's Alpha now. Everything I couldn't give her, she's got. So fuck you and your holier-than-thou attitude. Have you never been in love? Haven't you wanted the best for someone even if you couldn't be the one to give it to them?"

"I love Murphy the way you say you love Mary. I'd never leave him. Ever. I'm worth something, Colin. Aren't you? I don't understand this self-sacrificing bullshit. All it is, is low self esteem."

"You know nothing about this pack and the hierarchies and the cliques and how your future here is determined almost from the moment you're born. I never had a shot at being Alpha here. I never should have bonded with Mary. She had a chance at it. Her family's old and popular. She was slumming with me and it pleased her for a while, but I never should have bonded with her. I never had a chance at keeping her. You don't understand."

I understood more than he knew. Riverglow hadn't wanted me to be Alpha female because of my wolf, but I never even dreamed of leaving Grey so he could become Alpha without me. Not for a second.

"In the bigger packs, there are betas. People who just don't have what it takes to be Alpha. I'm a beta, Stanzie." Colin stared straight ahead through the windshield.

"Not true. You're Alpha of Riverglow."

He snorted. "Anybody can be Alpha of Riverglow. All it takes to be Alpha of Riverglow is membership. Sooner or later it will roll down to you."

He turned and reached out for my bond pendant. He touched the Celtic knot that hung beside my peridot and pearl pendant.

"You'll be the next Alpha female of Mac Tire and you know it. How could you miss being bonded to Liam Perfect Murphy? It's the same for Mary. Bonded with Richard, she was a sure thing. His family is the closest thing to gods this pack has."

"Everyone has a shot at Alpha. Everyone in a pack is from Alpha stock. Their parents were Alphas, their grandparents were Alphas, and it goes back until the start. So how can you say you're not good enough?" I argued.

"That's not how it works in a big pack. There's a lot of turnover, people moving from pack to pack, there are cliques and alliances formed so certain families keep a monopoly on Alpha. So, yes, my parents were obviously once Alphas, but not of Mac Tire. I'm from a smaller pack called Nightgate. Mac Tire took us over when I was fifteen. Too old to get in with the popular kids and too young to make a name for myself with the older crowd. The only attention I ever attracted was negative. Before I bonded with Mary no less than four duos tried to talk me out of it, the women telling me I was condemning her to a childless existence, the men telling me I would never keep her because they and all their friends would do their best to take her from me. I laughed in their faces because I was in love and I knew she loved me, but fast forward five years and all bets were off because Mary's twin sister was named Alpha and got pregnant during the hunt where we took the pack bond and suddenly Mary realized she was nearly thirty and a full pack member only she wouldn't ever get to have a baby or be Alpha.

"She said it didn't matter, but I knew it did. And nine months later when her nephews were born, the way she held them in her arms and looked at them. It broke my heart. I tried to get into the running for the next Alpha slot, but they laughed at me.

"That's why I wanted to be Alpha of Mac Tire in Ireland so damn badly. A huge sod you to everyone here. It was a sure thing and I couldn't even pull it off." He bowed his head and fell silent. I closed the car door and shut out the restless wind.

I wanted to hug the bastard almost as much as I wanted to knock his teeth down his throat. "The Alphas will all be in the lounge now with

Jason and Murphy. Go shower. We're going to be late, I'll call ahead and reschedule for half an hour later than we said."

Colin thrust open the car door and walked toward the safe house. Just as he reached the steps, fat raindrops spattered against the windshield and turned it into a watery smear.

* * * *

By our fourth interview, Colin and I had the questioning down pat. He let me take the lead, but was there to interject if need be. He knew everyone we interviewed as former pack members.

He grew increasingly moody between interviews and, when I prodded him for the reason, he snarled out that so far everyone on the list the Mac Tire Alphas had given us as might-be candidates for setting the trap had been former Nightgate members.

"That prick, Richard," he muttered as he pushed the Vauxhall into what I considered unsafe speeds since the steady downpour had not let up all afternoon and the roads were slick. "You see how we're second class citizens in our own pack, Stanzie? I can't believe the Irish branch is any less snobby, so I'm assuming you haven't figured out the score yet because of Paddy's death."

"Shut up about Paddy's death and pay attention to the frigging road." I dug my fingers into the upholstery of the seat as I braced myself for the crash I was sure would come.

He shot me a look, but slowed down. My racing heartbeat calmed a bit, but I heaved a relieved sigh when we pulled into the drive of the last interviewees of the day.

Alison James and Garrett Long were in their forties but, as all Pack aged slowly, appeared to be in their mid-twenties. I could only tell their age by their scents and the way they carried themselves. Subtle cues I'd learned to read over the years. Photos of each other decorated the wall above the desk in the front room. A series of shots of them in rock climbing gear on various peaks around Great Britain. No pictures of children. I assumed they'd never been Alpha. I'd met childless women in their forties before, but I'd never assumed they hadn't been Alphas, just unable to bear. My experience as a Pack member in America was vastly different than the UK and Alison brought it home to me in a visceral way I hadn't confronted before.

She was a petite brunette with dark, heavily lashed eyes and he was ruggedly handsome in a windswept way. They looked as if they spent most of their free time out of doors. Looking around their cramped little house, I could understand why. It wasn't so much a home as a place to sleep. Dingy and rather hopeless. Would a child have made a difference? I didn't know.

Neither of them seemed happy to be interviewed by Advisors to the Councils, although they both embraced Colin, and Alison chided him for staying a stranger and not keeping in touch.

"You've really made something of yourself, Colin." Garrett settled us on the sofa beneath the bay window. The rain battered at the glass in hammering gusts blown by the wind, making me shiver. "Alpha of your pack and now an Advisor to a Great Councilor." His expression was hard to read. Was it truly admiration or was there maybe some jealousy as well? "Your parents must be proud. Have you seen them yet?"

"I had dinner with them my first night in town," Colin said, but his tone didn't encourage more questions. Garrett gave him a thoughtful look and fell silent.

Alison brought in a tea tray and set it on the coffee table so she could pour us all fragrant cups of what smelled like Earl Grey tea. Store-bought cookies were scattered across a plate and, for a moment I missed Kathy Manning like hell. She never served store-bought anything. Once a month she sent me a tin of baked goods from Rhode Island. This month it had been snicker doodles, Murphy's favorite, and he'd eaten most of them.

I accepted the brown earthenware mug from Alison's outstretched hand and settled back against the sofa so I could inhale the scent of bergamot and citrus.

Colin hadn't even smiled in acknowledgment of Garrett's praise. Was he embarrassed? Afraid to tell him Riverglow was pitifully tiny with a terrible reputation? Irritation stung me and I struggled to keep from saying something about Riverglow myself. Some of the best memories of my life had happened within that pack and I refused to see why it mattered if the rest of the New England packs looked down their prissy noses at them. Colin was Alpha and he ought to be proud, not mortified every time someone brought up the fact he led the pack.

I focused on the task at hand. For twenty minutes we talked about Stony Fell and Mac Tire as well as the territory dispute. From the very beginning it was clear Garrett and Alison resented Stony Fell's temerity—their word for it. I would have thought they might have been sympathetic, as some of the other former Nightgate members had been when questioned.

Yet when I tried to gauge their feelings about Mac Tire, they were very noncommittal and had nothing overtly positive to say, especially about their Alphas. I got the distinct impression Alison deeply disliked Mary, but it was because of her expressions when talking about her, not her words.

Something nagged at me. They said all the right things in all the right places, but they were anxious for us to leave. Every few moments, Garrett would glance out the window at our car in the drive as if he wanted to usher us out the front door and out of their hair. Alison didn't brew another pot of tea, nor did she set out more cookies even when the last one was consumed.

"Well, I guess we'd better get going," said Colin at last, rising to his feet.

Relief spread across Alison and Garrett's faces.

I put my empty tea mug down on the tray, but didn't get up. "There's something you're not telling us." I kept my voice low, but when I met Alison's gaze, she flinched. Garrett's face blanked, yet I thought he might be debating whether to speak.

Colin froze in the act of standing then slowly sank down on the sofa. He looked at me for direction.

"I don't know what you mean," Alison protested, but her tone rang false. Her cheeks flushed and her hand shook as she reached out for the cookie plate, realized it was empty, and let her hand fall helplessly to her lap. Garrett swallowed hard as if something blocked his throat. He looked at her and she flinched again.

Had they set the trap? My stomach clenched and a wave of sickness swept over me as I remembered Ben's wolf and his agony. The stench of his fear and blood stung my nostrils as if I were still in that forest. Beside me, Colin didn't look much happier. He paled and took a deep breath.

"They were on our land." Alison's voice shook with venomous wrath. "If they want to pretend they have territory and use the land Evie stole from us, then they can hike in through the National Forest side. Let them take four hours to get there. Then maybe they'll understand how ridiculous they're being. Don't they dare use Mac Tire land as a bloody shortcut."

Colin opened his mouth to speak, but fell silent when I put a hand on his arm. His muscles were stiff with shock and at my touch, he leaned so our shoulders brushed. His nearness was comforting as I braced to hear Alison's confession. Did she have any idea what she and Garrett had done to Ben?

"I suppose they whined to their fake Alphas and in turn they complained to Mary and Richard, is that what happened?" Alison demanded, her eyes hot with malice.

"Whined?" Ben hadn't complained to anybody. Were we talking about the same event? "What happened? Tell me."

"Why? They obviously spilled their pathetic, cowardly guts. They didn't even know how to fight properly. So we took them by surprise, they still didn't manage to land even one good punch, did they, Garrett?" Alison turned to her bond mate for confirmation and he jerked his head in agreement. He looked reluctant to speak.

"Fight?" Colin struggled to process, and I wanted to elbow him not to give anything away with his confusion. They didn't know about the trap or they hadn't gotten to that part of the story yet, but I was beginning to doubt they knew.

Alison shoved a lock of dark brown hair behind one ear. "Fine. Pretend you don't know. You've changed, Colin, haven't you? No loyalty to your friends, I see. Being an Advisor's gone to your head obviously."

A muscle in Colin's cheek twitched and I tightened my fingers on his arm so he wouldn't say anything, but I knew her words hurt him.

Alison gave us a disgusted look. "Garrett and I were about to shift three days ago, and along came two bloody twits from Stony Fell, hand in hand, without a care in the world as if they had a right to trespass on our land, on their way to shift themselves. I won't apologize for this. It was egregious cheek. Garrett and I couldn't swallow the insult, so we fought them. I took the woman, he took the man and we had them down and screaming for mercy within three minutes. If that." She flexed her fingers, balled them into fists and looked every inch a predator. I hadn't realized how toned and muscled she was until just now. All that rock climbing kept her in top shape, it seemed.

"What were their names?" I asked.

She blinked at me. "Don't you bloody know? Frazier and Elspeth I think. That's what they called each other anyway. I've seen them at Regionals before, although we haven't ever actually met. What does it matter? They were from Stony Fell and they were trespassing. You've been angling for a confession and now you've got one. So what's our punishment? I can't believe the frigging Great Council is going to go after a duo who were only defending their territory. We didn't hurt them that badly. Scratches and bruises. So there was some blood, but so what? They were on our land, Advisor. We have our rights."

For the first time, I wondered if they wore long-sleeved turtleneck sweaters and jeans to hide bruises, but their knuckles didn't seem abraded, nor were either of them sporting black eyes. Perhaps they were telling the unvarnished truth—the other duo hadn't fought back.

"You just attacked, I guess. You couldn't talk about things?" I asked.

Alison's eyes widened. "What's to talk about? They're wrong. They can't even be graceful about the issue. Do you think Nightgate wanted to be assimilated by Mac Tire? We knew once we attracted their attention it was a lost cause. There weren't enough of us to fight it and there's even less members in Stony Fell. That bitch, Evie, stole that land. She ought to know better. Her, Mac Tire born and everything. Mac Tire owns England and that's all there is to it."

"Alison." Garrett put a hand on her shoulder, but she shrugged it off. Her brown eyes were wild with fury.

"We were Alphas of Nightgate. Did you know that?" She rose to her feet in agitation, her face twisted. "I didn't know I was pregnant until after we'd merged our packs. I did the right thing. I had an abortion. But that fucking bitch, Evie, how can she not know what she's doing is wrong? She'd never make Alpha of this pack and she damn well knew it, but instead of accepting her fate gracefully, she has to go and bond with that bloody Scotch bastard and this is what happens? People like Garrett and me, the ones who know our places and bow down to our fates, have to run across these bastards in our woods when all we want to do is shift.

"Can you understand what an insult that is? Do you have any breadth of understanding or compassion, Advisor? I see that Celtic knot next to your bond pendant. You'll be an Alpha soon. Of bloody Irish Mac Tire. The creme de la creme. You've been handed everything all your life, haven't you? So you don't have the slightest conception of how I feel and what I've been through.

"Get out of my house. Get out. Go tell your bloody Councilor everything I've said and I'll take my punishment the same way I took my abortion. With grace and dignity. You bloody cow, you disgust me. You as well, Colin. You bastard. You sold out. You never were worth shit in the first place."

Alison leaped to her feet and pointed to the door, her face transfigured with rage.

I backed away, unwilling to turn my back to her because I was positive if I did, she'd attack me. Colin kept her in sight as well, his cheeks stained with humiliation and a horrible sort of pity.

The last thing I saw before Garrett closed the door, were Alison's twisted features and the tears spilling down her cheeks.

Colin and I ran through the cold, slashing rain to the sanctuary of the car.

He buckled his seat belt, pulling so hard on it I feared it would snap. I put my hands to my face and bent over, trying to breathe.

"Oh, that sucked," I whispered, rocking back and forth. "That sucked so bad."

He took me in his arms and we held each other for a long time. I burst into tears and he shuddered as he buried his face in my hair.

"I never knew she was pregnant," he kept saying as if he had that would have changed something. He'd been fifteen at the time. It wouldn't have changed shit.

Chapter 9

I consulted my iPad while Colin navigated through the relentless rain. The windshield wipers made a steady *thwack thwack* as they wiped the glass clear. Colin's fingers were white against the steering wheel and his heartbeat thudded so loudly I could hear it without trying.

"Frazier Campbell and Elspeth MacKenzie." I found their names on the schedule. "Shit. Angus's twin sister. Doesn't this just figure."

I'd hoped I would be wrong, but the last name MacKenzie on the iPad's screen burned my eyes like a terrible omen. No wonder Angus had been so reticent to give up the names of his pack. Not that he'd much choice. He'd ended up putting everyone in Stony Fell on the list, except of course, himself, Evie and Ben. Which left it exactly four names long.

Colin sighed. "Jesus, this gets thicker and thicker, doesn't it?"

"Welcome to the wonderful world of being an Advisor." I stared down at the names on the screen as if I could change them with the power of my mind. Fat chance. "After them, we interview Bonnie Patterson and Keith Hastings."

Colin looked away from the road so he could meet my gaze.

"Ben's parents. And they don't know about Ben because Allerton told the Alphas to keep it quiet." Colin tapped his fingers against the steering wheel for a moment as he thought. I only hoped he was paying as much attention to the road as he was to his internal ruminations. "How are we going to play this, Stanzie?"

A small smile curved my lips. "Why do I get to decide strategy?"

"You're the senior Advisor," he said with an engaging grin. For a moment we were on the same wavelength.

"Colin," I said, and our smiles faded. "Shouldn't the bigger pack let the Alphas of the smaller pack they absorb be the next Alphas? Isn't that how it's done? That's what Richard and Mary are offering Evie and Angus. At least the chance at it."

"Alison and Garrett did run for Alpha in the election after Nightgate joined Mac Tire. They were defeated by a landslide. The only ones who voted for them were former Nightgate members. I'd just turned twenty then. My first chance to vote as a contributing pack member. I was so disillusioned." Colin threw me a bitter look. "Nightgate members were second class citizens once the packs merged. I told you that before. When are you going to start listening to me?"

"So why would they even do it Why would they voluntarily become second class citizens?"

"There are perks. Money enough. Food enough. Territory to shift without getting the shit kicked out of you. The Councils always rule in the bigger pack's favor, Stanzie."

"So why are we even bothering? I mean, why'd we come in the first place? Before that damned trap was sprung? Was it just a formality?"

"That's been my assumption all along." Colin took a deep breath and slowed for a red light. "Where are we going? Back to the safe house or to see Frazier and Elspeth? Where are they on the schedule?"

"Tomorrow morning." I consulted the list. "What do you think? What time is it?"

"Almost five. We're due for dinner in Allerton's suite at six. I don't think we have time." Colin drummed his fingers on the steering wheel impatiently as he waited for the light to change.

"I want to talk to Jason anyway. This is bullshit if we came here as a formality. I protest being used like that. If we were." I tried not to lose my temper and leaned back against the seat as the light changed and the car zoomed forward. Colin drove like a speed demon and that was another thing that bothered me. Instead of screaming at him, I stayed silent as he merged onto the highway and flicked the wipers to their fastest speed. They still struggled to keep up. I bit my tongue and tried to relax, but it was impossible.

"My driving makes you nervous, huh?"

"What gave me away? My accelerated heart rate or shallow breathing?"

"Neither. It's that martyred expression on your face," Colin answered. The speedometer needle dropped back five miles an hour or was it kilometers? Whatever it was, it was still too damn fast for the weather.

"You nailed them back there. I was ready to leave. Maybe I don't have what it takes to be an Advisor. I'm already on thin ice with Allerton, thanks to my drinking yesterday. I would have walked away today and been none the wiser. You gonna tell him that?" Colin kept his gaze fixed to the road thankfully, but I had a feeling more of his attention was on me than the road, which made me want to scream.

"You'll catch on. This is your third day on the job." I said. "Plus they were your friends. I understand that."

"That shouldn't mean shit. I should not let friendship influence me. Ben deserves the best I can give him and that was not my best."

"Who are you arguing with? Yourself? Because I think you're being too hard. This is a royal mess we've got here and you were thrown straight into the deep end. This was your pack once upon a time. I have some distance you don't, so just relax, okay?"

He shot me an incredulous look. "You're joking? Relax? I can't even sleep at night, Stanzie. Last night I managed to get drunk enough to pass out, but I wouldn't call it a restful night. And I'm not willing to suffer another hangover tomorrow to black out in a drunken stupor tonight." He switched lanes so he could pass a slower, more responsible driver. One actually taking the rotten weather into consideration.

"You gonna tell Allerton about me and Mary?"

I unclenched my fingers from the edge of the seat, one by reluctant one.

"What the hell, Colin. You must think I'm some sort of spy. Believe it or not, but I wasn't called in on this investigation to judge everything you do and take notes so I can spill my guts to Jason. Screw you."

"I'm hardly distinguishing myself. Don't you think he'd want to know his Advisor nailed one of the Alphas under investigation against a tree in the safe house garden?" Colin asked.

"You think he needs to know so badly, here's a wild thought—why don't you take some self-accountability and tell him yourself?" I suggested.

He gave a bark of reluctant laughter. "Damn. You're hard core. Self-accountability? Men like me are rarely troubled by such things as that. We'd need a conscience to be self-accountable and we tend to travel light. Honor and ethics are rather weighty and among the first things to go."

"Bullshit." I gave him a dark look. "You'd like everyone to think you're a cold, unfeeling bastard, but you've given yourself away too many times to make me believe you're anything but a basically nice guy with a huge inferiority complex. Stop talking shit and start concentrating on your driving. I would like to get back to the safe house in one piece, thank you very much."

"Jesus, you really know how to hurt a man, you know that, Stanzie? Ow. A basically nice guy. The horror." He tried to make it a big joke, but when he slowed the car down and suddenly became a decent driver, I knew I'd touched him.

Maybe we'd be friends yet. Wasn't that a crazy thought?

Chapter 10

Jason had the best room in the safe house. A suite, with a sitting room complete with a marble mantel and working fireplace, and a bedroom and bathroom beyond.

Murphy was already in the suite, drinking brandy by the fireside, when Colin and I walked in. We'd met on the stairs after a hasty retreat to our separate rooms to freshen up. Colin had changed his shirt and I'd traded my jeans and Timberlands for a long, suede skirt and a pair of knee-high leather boots.

On the ground floor, the Alphas dined together at a table for four, and I doubted conversation was flowing as freely as the wine. Their faces had been politely distant as Colin and I walked through the dining room when we'd first gotten back.

They knew better to ask if we'd heard anything interesting on our interviews, but I scanned their faces anyway, on the off chance I might find some trepidation or guilt. No such luck, though, and I'd hurried up the stairs to my room so I wouldn't be late for Jason's dinner.

Colin's gaze had rested just a shade too long on Mary, but Richard hadn't reacted at all. Somehow she'd managed to keep the tryst a secret, apparently, or he really didn't care.

Jason stood by the window in the sitting room, gazing out at the falling rain. His silk shirt was unbuttoned at the collar and tie set aside somewhere, but his trousers had no creases and he looked freshly shaved and handsome. Did he miss Wren? Were thoughts of her even on his radar at times like this? Over time, I'd developed the impression Jason Allerton was a very compartmentalized man and kept different aspects of his life neatly boxed up when he wasn't directly using them. In a way, that was good. It meant when he was with my mother, he was hers entirely without outside distraction. That was more than many women got from their men.

Murphy smiled at me and got up from his armchair before crossing the room to embrace me. For a moment I froze. I wasn't used to him giving me spontaneous gestures of affection, especially in front of other people. Ever since we'd confessed our love for each other, he'd become more receptive to touching. I had high hopes that one day we'd walk down the streets of Dublin hand in hand like actual lovers.

His familiar, beloved scent intoxicated my senses and I buried my face in his neck for a moment before we drew apart.

"Bad day?" He searched my face, his eyes worried yet sympathetic.

"You could say that."

Jason came to attention and turned away from the window.

"Every name on Mac Tire's list was a former member of Nightgate. Colin's birth pack. It was taken over by Mac Tire when he was fifteen," I said. Colin hesitated a moment at the drinks cart where he was pouring himself a soda. No alcohol, I noted with an inward smile.

"Yeah, but their instincts were on the money, weren't they?" Colin asked me. He pointed at the bottles on the cart. "Drink?"

"Brandy." The rainy autumn cold had settled in my bones. Maybe brandy would warm me. Colin obligingly filled the bottom of a balloon glass with Courvoisier and brought it to me.

I cradled the glass between my palms and carried it to the arm chair across from Murphy's. He followed me and resumed his former seat. Colin took his soda to the sofa against the wall which separated the sitting room from the bedroom. Jason remained standing by the window, but his attention was on me. He patiently waited for me to go on with my story, and I knew I had only a finite amount of time before he prompted me.

"Do you think it was good thing for everyone that the former Alpha female of Nightgate had to have an abortion when she joined Mac Tire, Jason?" The bitter accusation jumped off my tongue and Jason's flinch was nearly imperceptible, but I saw it.

"Is that what happened?" he asked. At my nod, his expression became grim. "Sometimes unfortunate things happen, Constance."

"Oh, yes. Unfortunate is the exact word I'm sure Alison James uses when she thinks of that moment."

"Did she set that trap?" Jason apparently decided to ignore my sarcasm and went straight to the point.

"I don't think so," I said, and both his and Murphy's brows knitted in confusion. "They could have but I'm not sure. She and her bond mate kicked the shit out of a Stony Fell duo they found using Mac Tire land as a short cut. Maybe that duo set the trap, but we didn't have time to interview them today. Besides, I wanted to talk to you about it first."

Jason waited for me to go on.

I took a sip of brandy. When I swallowed, the alcohol burned down my throat straight to my stomach. "The duo's names are Frazier Campbell and Elspeth MacKenzie."

Jason didn't look shocked. He never did. "Angus's twin sister and her bond mate. So it could have been Angus then too. I understand your dilemma now."

"I made her cry, Jason." I stared into my brandy glass as if it offered an escape route or maybe a way to erase my guilt. "Alison was holding back telling us about fighting with the Stony Fell duo and I forced her hand and that whole fucking abortion story spilled out of her like rotting garbage. It's not fair that smaller packs can't coexist with larger ones. Mac Tire is a bully of a pack and I'm beginning to be ashamed to belong to it."

"That's a pity, Stanzie, considering you're very likely next in line to become Alpha. If you feel that strongly, maybe you ought to step aside." I'd made Jason angry. I could tell by the clipped tone and his glacial expression.

"I'll tell you one damn thing. If I am the next Alpha, I'm sure as hell not going to crush packs smaller than we are and take away an Alpha's chance to have a baby. That's nonnegotiable."

"There are benefits to bigger packs. You remember how you struggled in Riverglow to make ends meet. Do you do that in Mac Tire?"

"I never went to bed hungry when I belonged to Riverglow. So maybe I wore last year's fashions three years in a row and I never visited Europe, but I didn't suffer. And, by the way, I finally figured out how Riverglow managed to afford to come to the Great Gathering last year. You paid for them, didn't you? Beneficial Councilor Allerton. You wanted to plant a spy in their midst to ferret out Callie and you needed them there so you could introduce one. But I bet Colin was your fall back. Murphy and I were supposed to join Riverglow, weren't we? That's why you told Paddy not to take us back into Mac Tire right away. How close am I?"

"Right on every count," Jason said without hesitation. "Another thing you'll resent me for, I imagine."

"Oh, I don't resent you for the things you hide from me. Not anymore. I got tired of walking around pissed off at you all the time. Now I expect it. Take your best shot, Jason. I don't fall down that easily."

"Which is why you'll make an excellent Alpha for Mac Tire if you don't allow your offended sensibilities to get in the way," Jason told me.

I laughed and drank more of my brandy.

"How does Pack First feel about only Alphas having children?" I asked when my glass was empty.

Murphy winced, but didn't say anything. Colin looked shell shocked. He clutched his soda without drinking it, his gaze moving back and forth between me and Jason as if he couldn't believe I was talking to a Councilor with such brutal familiarity. Or that Jason would talk to me as he would an equal. Colin had no idea how hard-won that familiarity was and what I'd gone through to earn it.

"What do you think?" Jason stared me down until I looked away. But it was a long stare.

"I think they'd damn well better encourage as many new Pack babies as possible if we want to hold our own against the Others," I said.

"If I could change one thing about current Pack culture, every woman being allowed to have a child would be top of the list, Stanzie," Jason said.

"I believe you," I said charitably.

"Thank you," he said drily. "Alphas ought to concentrate on leading their packs, not getting pregnant. If anything, Alphas ought to be the ones discouraged from breeding while they serve. But changing culture that spans centuries cannot be done overnight."

"Are you saying you're campaigning for this change?" I asked.

"No. My energies are focused upon crushing Pack First and their agenda. Then, and only then, will I turn my attention to procreation. My vision is long range and perhaps you find this frustrating, but I hope by the time you're on the Council, Pack First will be a distant memory and you can be on the vanguard of changing the pack structure." Jason smiled at me.

"He thinks I'm going to be on the Great Council someday, Colin." I shook my head. "Isn't that funny?"

"Not hardly," Colin answered. "I rather fancy he's onto something."

* * * *

Jason sent word to the Stony Fell Alphas that he wanted to speak with them. After our dinner of roast pork and potatoes had been cleared away from the table set up in the center of the sitting room, coffee and dessert were laid out.

The cups and saucers were decorated with sprays of periwinkle blue hyacinths, as were the matching dessert plates. Jason handed me a huge helping of trifle and just as I lifted my fork to dig in, a discreet knock sounded on the door.

At a nod from Jason, Colin slipped from his chair and answered it. Angus and Evelyn entered. He looked dour and argumentative; she had her habitually nervous rabbit expression.

"Please sit down and have coffee and dessert," Jason invited.

We'd pulled up two extra chairs, but it was a round table and the sixth chair had to be awkwardly placed at an angle straddling a table leg next to Murphy. Evelyn crept toward that seat and I stifled an urge to snap at her. Why did she always have to be so self-effacing and timid?

"We had it downstairs." Angus had a belligerent glint to his eye, but he did stalk to the chair between Jason and me and sat.

"Evelyn? Coffee?" I saw her eye the silver coffee pot wistfully, but at my words she jerked guiltily in her seat and shook her head. I almost poured her a cup anyway, but somehow forbore.

"Just come out with it. Which one of my people set the trap?" Angus was clearly uninterested in preserving the formalities. "You wouldn't have had us up here if you didn't have something bad to tell us."

The freckles across Evelyn's face stood out in pale relief against the bridge of her nose and cheeks. She clutched at the edge of the table with one hand as if to keep herself from fainting out of her chair.

"Frazier Campbell and Elspeth MacKenzie," said Jason smoothly then even Angus's cheeks went white.

"My sister? Are you saying my sister and her bond mate set that trap?" He tried to sound gruff, but only succeeded in appearing bewildered and a bit heartbroken.

Evie gave a strangled gasp and I looked at her thoughtfully. She flinched when she met my gaze and squirmed a little in her chair. Tell-tale signs she knew something. Would she speak up? I doubted it, but maybe she'd surprise me.

"It appears two members of Mac Tire discovered your sister and her bond mate on Mac Tire land, using it as a shortcut to the disputed territory. There was a fight and Stony Fell came off the worse for it." Jason's cool blue gaze never wavered from Angus's face. "Are you saying you didn't know about this, Mr. Finch?"

"Aye, I am saying that." Angus pounded a fist on the table and the cups and spoons rattled in their saucers. "How can you think I'd hold my tongue about something like that?"

"It seems puzzling," Jason agreed.

"They didn't tell me." Angus's tone was flat and disillusioned. "I can't understand it, Councilor."

"But they told you, didn't they, Evie?" I asked. If I waited for her speak up first, we'd never leave this table.

Dead silence around the table.

Evie quailed under the undivided attention of the entire table. Beads of sweat popped out on her forehead.

"Evie," said Angus.

"I told them not to say anything to anybody," Evie whispered piteously. She plucked at the collar of her blouse. More goddamn ruffles. "I didn't want to cause a scene, Angus. The Council was being called in to settle the dispute and I thought the fewer waves we made, the better our case would look."

"Goddamn it, woman. You sat there all day yesterday when Councilor Allerton was asking us if we had clue who might have a grudge big enough to set that trap and you didn't say anything. Why?" Angus stared at her as if he didn't recognize her.

"Elspeth is your sister. I didn't want to get her in trouble." Tears stood out in Evie's brown eyes and trembled on the edges of her pale lashes.

"You had to know the Mac Tire duo would say something." Angus kept his voice low. He looked like a beaten man who had taken a sucker punch to the gut.

"No, I didn't. I thought there was a chance they'd keep silent. It didn't make them look good, you know. Elspeth and Frazier didn't fight back because of what you told them."

"What I told them?" Angus's expression turned incredulous and slightly scared. "What the hell did I tell them?"

"Not to rock the boat," Evie reminded him.

He groaned. "That doesn't mean not to defend yourself if you're attacked. What a goddamn clusterfuck." He shoved back his chair, but must have realized Jason was watching him and didn't get up. "Councilor, I don't know what to say. If I'd had any idea this had happened, I'd have told you."

He appeared genuine enough. I couldn't smell a lie, but I thought he might be hiding something just the same. Elspeth was his sister. I imagined what Murphy might have felt if someone had kicked the shit out of Fiona in a situation like this. He wouldn't have let it slide. Why had Angus looked scared when Evie reminded him he'd told his pack not to rock the boat with people in Mac Tire?

"Were they badly hurt? I haven't seen Elspeth or Frazier this week. They've been hiding from me, haven't they?" Anger began to simmer in his eyes.

"The Mac Tire duo says it wasn't a long fight," I said. "Just to prove a point. Bruises only. No broken bones."

"Which Mac Tire duo was it?" Angus balled his fists. I'd been careful not to mention names and I sure as hell wasn't going to start now.

"That's immaterial to this discussion," said Jason, and Angus gave him a sour look. Evie knew, that is, if Frazier and Elspeth had names to put to Alison and Garrett's faces from proximity at Regionals, but the thought obviously hadn't occurred to Angus yet.

"That duo was just as likely to have set that trap as my sister and Frazier. Are you gonna grill Mary and Richard the way you just grilled us or is mighty Mac Tire going to be allowed a dispensation because the fight happened on their land? This whole fucking thing has been rigged from the very beginning and I don't even know why I ever agreed to it. Everyone knows when the Councils get involved, small packs' rights dissolve like shit in the rain." Angus rose to his feet and Murphy and Colin tensed, ready to spring into action if Angus was foolish enough to attack.

Jason didn't appear to consider Angus a threat. He kept his seat and glanced at his plate of trifle for a moment before he looked up.

The tension diffused in that space of time. Jason knew exactly how to play the situation. He'd probably had plenty of experience in his service as a Great Councilor. No doubt he was used to handling furious Alphas confronted with crimes against or by their packs.

"As I said yesterday, we are concentrating on discovering the perpetrator or perpetrators of the crime of setting that trap. The territory dispute has been tabled for the time being. It distresses me to think you believe your case is futile, Angus. If you really thought that, why didn't you just agree to merge with Mac Tire? It would have saved us all some time. Perhaps Ben would still have his leg if you hadn't been so stubborn."

I sucked in my breath at that accusation and Angus did too.

"That's low, Councilor," he said.

"I think I have a point." Jason seemed unperturbed. "If this was such a lost cause, why put everyone through it? If you have that little faith in the Councils, why involve them?"

"I'm not the one who called you," Angus snarled.

"Why bother to even present your case? You weren't under any obligation to do so." Jason reached for his coffee cup and lifted it to his mouth so he could take a sip. His calm demeanor was so maddening I wanted to scream and I wasn't on the hot seat like Angus.

"If I hadn't, I would have forfeited Stony Fell's rights. Even a tiny scrap of a chance is better than nothing," Angus answered.

Jason allowed himself a small smile. "Then you do agree the outcome was not rigged after all, don't you? If you had even the slightest hope of a decision in your favor. Right?"

Angus gritted his teeth. "You're the Councilor. I'm a new Alpha of a small pack. It's child's play to twist my words and make me look like a fool, isn't it? Well, you do that, Councilor Allerton. Have your fun at my expense. But it's people like me who depend on the Councils if only to have a place to go so we don't have to crawl to domineering packs like Mac Tire. Evie, let's go, we're through here."

Evie bolted to her feet and when they left, Angus didn't slam the door, but he might as well have.

"Colin, please have the Mac Tire Alphas come up here for a moment, will you?" Jason turned his attention to his trifle and seemed quite intent on savoring every mouthful.

Colin got to his feet, looking a little like a martyred prisoner on his way to the gallows, and left the room.

"Good work, Stanzie," Jason told me after he set his fork down on his very empty plate. "Your instincts are spot on as usual."

"I think you suspected Evie was hiding something too," I said, eying my trifle. How the hell could Jason have demolished his dessert like that? My stomach was in horrible knots. "She acted even more nervous and guilty than she normally does."

Jason gave me an affectionate smile. "Don't underestimate yourself, my dear."

* * * *

Mary and Richard's uneasy demeanor was apparent the moment they crossed the threshold. Colin shut the door behind them and waited for them to seat themselves before he took the last chair. Even though his coffee and dessert plate clearly marked his spot, Mary eschewed the chair that straddled the table leg and took Colin's without compunction. Spoiled bitch.

"Evie bolted out the front door like a spooked horse." Mary accepted the cup of coffee Jason offered her. "What's happened now?"

Richard opened his mouth, probably to tell her to shut the hell up, but obviously thought better of it and closed it again. He declined coffee, but took a piece of trifle, which he left sitting before him, uneaten.

Jason didn't answer until he'd poured himself a fresh cup of coffee.

"It seems one of your duos had an altercation recently with a Stony Fell duo they found walking across your land."

Richard's mouth tightened. "Altercation?"

"Which duo?" Mary demanded.

Colin looked very much like he wanted to say something. By the stormy look in his eyes, whatever he had in mind was no doubt sarcastic, but he kept quiet.

"Alison James and Garrett Long." Jason took a sip of coffee and studied their reactions over the rim of his cup.

"Goddamn them." Mary gritted her teeth. "They knew better. They certainly knew they ought to have come to us after the fact and at least alerted us they've behaved like damn fools."

"I can't think why they didn't. I'm sure you're the most approachable Alpha Mac Tire's had in years," Colin said, and the glittering rage that swept across Mary's face and oozed from her pores smelled like melted plastic. I wanted to sneeze, but held my breath instead.

"Whether I'm approachable or not by your standards doesn't concern me," she said.

"Has it occurred to you that what Garrett and Alison think should?" Colin asked with a maddening little smile.

I expected steam to rise from the top of Mary's skull.

"What are you trying to say? Why don't you just say what you mean instead of leaping around the truth like an irritating River dancer? I'm a cold, unfeeling witch. You've already told me that and I believe I told you exactly what I thought of your opinion." Mary shoved back her chair and jumped to her feet.

She slammed the door so loudly behind her, the reverberations in my skull made me deaf for a few seconds.

Richard rose to his feet and glared at Colin before he turned to Jason "While admittedly I haven't had a lot of experience with Advisors, I'm quite sure Hunter's behavior is not typical. I can at least devoutly hope. I had no knowledge of what James and Long did and I assure you I will deal with it. If there's nothing more you require, I would rather like to leave."

"Is there any particular reason you placed only names of former Nightgate members on the interview list?" Jason's bland smile sent a chill down my spine.

Richard paled.

"Because I'm beginning to wonder if it was for the specific purpose of needling my Advisor, who also, by strange coincidence, happens to be a former Nightgate member." Jason took another sip of his coffee and set his cup down carefully in the saucer.

Richard said nothing.

"Thank you for your time." At Jason's words, Richard wheeled for the door.

He didn't dare slam the door as his bond mate had done, but he was rather forceful.

Jason pushed back his jacket cuff to glance at his watch and I knew it was a subtle signal the night was over. I was on my feet half a second behind Murphy. Colin followed us to the door, but hesitated on the threshold.

"Sir, if I might have a word," he said, turning back.

"Of course," said Jason as if he'd expected it. No doubt he had. Colin gave me an anguished, nervous smile and shut the door in my face before I could go in and offer him back-up support.

Murphy missed nothing that had passed between us.

"What's that all about?" he asked as we mounted the narrow staircase to go up one floor to our room.

"Please don't ask me," I begged. I didn't feel right discussing Colin behind his back. Especially with Murphy. He froze for a moment, fingers tightening around the glossy railing, and then surged forward, shoulders stiff. My heart sank.

"Murphy," I said when we were in our room.

"I'm going to take a quick shower. Don't wait up, honey, okay?" He didn't even look at me when he said it. He just kept walking for the bathroom door.

I'd written maybe six sentences of the damn report I'd promised Jason before the first tears smacked onto the iPad's screen. I rubbed them away with the edge of the sheet and set the iPad aside so I could punch my pillow and pretend I was trying to make it more comfortable to sit against.

Murphy's side of the bed was accusingly empty and the steady gush of water from the showerhead competed with the rain outside the window.

I was staring in a blurred haze at the sheets clenched in my fists, when Murphy's weight sank the mattress down a few inches.

"I guess there's going to have to be some walls between us. You're Jason's Advisor and I'm a Regional Councilor. Obviously there will be things you'll want to keep private. I do understand, Stanzie," Murphy said softly. "It's just when you throw Colin Hunter into the mix, I get a little fucked up."

"I don't want there to be walls or secrets between us." I clutched at the sheets as if I were drowning.

"I shouldn't have asked you that question," Murphy told me. "And your very understandable reluctance threw me for a moment. I'm sorry, honey. Please don't cry."

"I'm not crying." I swiped at my leaking eyes with the sleeve of my nightshirt.

"Then what's this wet stuff on your cheeks?" Murphy teased, leaning close so he could rest his forehead against the side of my face.

"I wish we could go on our road trip." I took a deep, hitching breath and was grateful for his proximity.

"We will," he promised. "As soon as this is over, we'll stop long enough at the apartment to pack eighteen pairs of shoes in two suitcases for you and we'll be off."

I laughed a little. "I might want to bring at least one change of clothes. Maybe my toothbrush."

"Whatever you like." He laughed too. "What's this?" He picked up my iPad and regarded it with an amused smile.

"That thing is not coming with us. It's Jason's latest attempt to get me to make actual reports." I plucked it from his fingers and set it on the nightstand. "But screw him, I don't want to write a report tonight. I want to do something else."

Murphy's lips quirked. "Anything I could assist you with maybe?"

"Definitely." I switched off the lights just before I shrugged out of my nightshirt. So much for my resolve to lay off sex for a bit. My wolf would just have to bite me.

Chapter 11

I was informed at breakfast the next morning I would interview the Stony Fell members on my own as Jason had decided to send Colin off on other errands—ones I suspected had nothing to do with our current case. At least if Colin's downcast expression at the breakfast table was anything to go by.

Jason read the local paper rather than converse with us. Colin bolted his food and when Jason silently placed his car keys on the table without looking up from the editorial page, Colin snatched them and fled.

Murphy looked intrigued and quite inappropriately cheerful as he poured himself more coffee. I crunched through several slices of crisp bacon and gave Murphy my eggs. Without ketchup, eggs tasted like crap.

"You'll use the library for your interviews, Stanzie." Jason flipped from the editorial section to the comics. I knew this because I was shamelessly reading over his shoulder. "I've had Colin call ahead so everyone knows to come here."

He generously handed me the sections he'd already perused. I guessed that meant he didn't want me reading along with him, which was a shame because all I really wanted to read was the comics.

"Any specific questions I should ask Frazier and Elspeth?" I asked.

"I trust your judgment," he said, supremely unconcerned.

"And you know I'm interviewing Ben's parents after that. What should I—"

"Stanzie," interrupted Jason. "I trust you to take the right direction in this."

Great. A test. He was testing me.

Across the table Murphy gave me the thumbs up, and I stuck out my tongue.

Jason rattled the paper as if in annoyance, but he couldn't fool me, I could see his smile.

* * * *

The library was half the size of the lounge, but it had a merry blaze in the fireplace and the salmon pink chintz curtains and sofa cover lent the room a comforting glow. One whole wall was nothing but bookcases crammed with paperback novels. While I waited for Frazier and Elspeth to arrive, I idly examined the titles. Mysteries mostly. Lake District guidebooks as well.

I took one that didn't appear quite as tattered and ancient as the others to the arm chair by the window which overlooked the porch and the front garden. Neither looked particularly appealing. The rain had stopped, but the sky was a sullen, bruised gray that promised more and the shrubs and flowers in the garden had been beaten down into sodden clumps that made me cold to look at them.

With typical British disregard for the weather, the window was open two inches at the bottom and cold air sent a chill down my spine. I set the book on a small mahogany side table and twisted in the chair so I could close the window. I pushed to no avail. The goddamn thing was stuck open and probably had been for decades.

Before I could retrieve my book and find a warmer spot to read, I heard a woman call Mary's name. I recognized the voice but couldn't place it until Mary answered. She must have been sitting in one of the chairs just outside the library window because I could hear her clearly, almost as if she were in the room with me.

"Tracy, I'm over here having a cigarette. Come sit with me. Are you crying? Is everything all right with Ben?" Mary's voice turned sharp with worry.

"No, everything's not all right with Ben, and you damn well know it." Tracy's voice was shrill and Mary made a shushing noise. I sat very still in the arm chair. I knew I ought to move out of earshot, but what was I supposed to do? I had Pack enhanced hearing. With the damn window open, I'd be able to hear them anywhere in the small room. I couldn't leave because Frazier and Elspeth might arrive at any moment. Or so I told myself. Really, I wanted desperately to hear the conversation, but had to rationalize why before I gave myself permission.

"What do you mean?" Mary pitched her voice low, but it carried clearly. So did Tracy's. She'd turned it down a notch or two, volume-wise, but was obviously not much concerned with being overheard.

"Stony Fell can't afford to support him. They can't pay for physical therapy or the prosthetic leg or to assist him if he can't find work now that he won't be able to do construction anymore. So he's agreed to join Mac Tire."

"That's a good thing. We can afford to look after him. Why does this upset you?" Mary tried to sound like she had no clue, but her tone lacked conviction.

"He won't bond with me. We were going to bond. Whatever the hell happened between our packs, we didn't care one way or the other, we were going to bond. But now he won't. Do you know why?" Tracy's fury made her voice sharp as glass.

"Tell me." Mary sounded bitter, as if she'd bitten into a lemon when she'd expected candy.

"He'll never be Alpha of Mac Tire so he won't bond with me. Says I can do better. I don't want to do better. I don't care if I'm ever Alpha. He won't listen to me, turns his face to the wall and shuts me out. Mary, help me. Tell him he can be Alpha someday. Give us a chance. Just because he's missing a leg doesn't mean he can't be bloody Alpha." Tracy sounded muffled. She'd either buried her face in her hands or Mary's lap.

"I can't make that decision, Tracy." Mary's voice was so miserable a lump rose in my throat.

"Can't you? You're Alpha."

"For five years. I don't actually make pack policy. It's already been set and it's definitive. Disabled people can't be Alpha. Not of Mac Tire."

"He can't stay in Stony Fell because they can't afford him. Mary, can't Mac Tire give Stony Fell the money? The trap was on our land. It happened on our territory. Don't we have an obligation to look after him?" Tracy asked.

"Yes, which is why we've offered him a place in Mac Tire. Tracy, love, there will be other men in your life. You're twenty. So young."

"I don't want any other men. I want Ben," Tracy said fiercely.

"You say that now, but wait until you're thirty and bonded to somebody who can never be Alpha. All your peers will begin to have children and you never will."

"I don't care," Tracy cried. "I don't!"

"You will," Mary said gently. "Ben's doing you a favor."

"I hate you. I don't even know why I came to you. You don't care. You don't give a shit about me or Ben. You got rid of Colin quick enough when you turned thirty and realized you'd never be Alpha bonded to him, didn't you?" Tracy's voice was thick with derision and tears. "You put it about that he dumped you, but it was you who hounded him into breaking the bond on his birthday wasn't it? So you could have Richard after he ditched Joanne. You two bloody selfish wankers deserve each other, you know that? So be Alpha and have your precious baby. I'd rather have love. And people like you can't prevent me, no matter what you think. I swear I won't let you. Sod you!"

Thump of running feet on the floorboards, and Tracy was gone. Silence for a moment until Mary began to cry. Hopelessly, desolately.

I sat frozen for a moment before I jumped to my feet and ran out the door, down the hall and through the dining room to the porch.

Mary slumped in one of the slatted wooden chairs just to the left of what I recognized as the library window. I knelt by her and put a hand on her shoulder. She jerked in surprise and let her hands drop away from her face. Her eyes streamed tears, her cheeks were flushed and wet. I dug in my pocket for a tissue.

She snatched it from my fingers and wiped her runny nose.

"How much did you hear?" Mary tried to sound frosty, but only managed weak dismay.

"All of it," I said, and she sighed.

"Just leave me alone. Please. I don't need your sympathy and if you go round spreading this story, I'll bloody well kill you."

"You don't have to worry," I said. "Who would I tell?"

"Just everybody. Him." She nearly strangled on the last word. "What's he told you? That I hounded him into breaking our bond, just like Tracy said? Bloody bastard. I never. I was just like Tracy once, you know? I didn't care if I was Alpha or I had a baby. I just wanted him. I begged him not to leave me, but he'll never tell you that, will he?"

My throat tightened and it was all I could not to burst into angry tears on her behalf. She was a real witch, but it still wasn't fair, what had happened to her.

"I'm damn well going to have that baby. Colin thinks that's what I wanted more than him, so I'll damn well have one." Her face crumpled. "But the real irony of it is, I don't…I don't really want one." She collapsed into my arms and buried her hot face in my neck, shaking with sobs.

I took her into the library with me, sat her by the window so the cold air would cool her heated cheeks and poured her a glass of water. She gulped at it gratefully and hunched in the chair like a frightened bird.

"Please don't tell him I fell apart. I want him to think I'm stronger than this." She set the glass aside and blew her nose. She looked so lost, I wanted to break something. Preferably Colin's stupid head.

"I'm not telling him a thing," I said.

"Sisters?" she asked with a small smile.

"In this, you bet." I knew what it was like to want to appear strong so people didn't think I was weak and needed protection.

"I'm not completely miserable, you know," she said. "Richard and I are comfortable together. Fond of each other. I actually prefer it. It's a much calmer existence than the tempestuous one I led with Colin. Always arguing, always shouting, never seeing eye to eye on anything except sex." Her mouth curved in a reminiscent smile and I grinned too. "We used to argue expressly so we'd have a reason for make-up sex," she confided, and I laughed.

She sat taller in the chair and some of the color came back to her face.

"Elspeth and Frazier will be here soon. I'm supposed to interview them here, but if you need more time, I can have coffee with them in the dining room," I told her.

"No." She rose to her feet and brushed back the hair stuck to her face. "I've got to go repair my makeup. I must look dreadful." Pausing as she passed me on her way to the door, she said, "I'm damn serious about killing you if you breathe a word."

"Alpha, I pledge my discretion," I answered her with one of the Pack's traditional sayings and that made her snort.

"I'm not your Alpha," she said, but sounded pleased, nonetheless.

* * * *

Elspeth MacKenzie had gorgeous red hair and deep green eyes. Shorter still than her twin brother, she barely topped five feet.. She wore her red hair long, pulled over her face as much as possible to hide her black eye and bruised cheek. Dressed in tight jeans and a long gray sweater, she didn't hesitate a second before stepping across the library threshold. I glanced curiously at her feet to see what type of shoes she wore. Sensible flat-heeled black ankle boots jazzed up with a buckled trim. I liked them. I had several pairs in the same basic style but thankfully I'd left them at home. I never liked wearing the same shoes as another woman.

"Advisor Newcastle," she said, reaching out to shake my hand in a no-nonsense fashion. "I'm Elspeth MacKenzie."

On the fast track for the next Alpha female of Stony Fell too, I decided.

Her bond mate, Frazier Campbell, also had red hair, but darker than hers, a rich auburn I envied. I'd always secretly wanted to be a redhead and now I never could even experiment thanks to Sorcha, the redheaded witch. I'm sure me being a redhead would go over like a ton of bricks with Murphy.

Frazier, like Angus, was just about my height, and thin. His handshake was firm and forceful. I sensed coiled muscles beneath his brown sweater.

His eyes were dark blue and the skin around them crinkled when he smiled.

No black eye for him, but he walked stiffly as he made for the closest chair, and I suspected a broken rib or two. That meant Garrett had kicked him, probably when he was down, which was a shitty thing to have done.

I pushed up the sleeves of my sweater when I sat and stared for a second at my right wrist. Three days ago Ben's wolf had bitten me, but this morning I could barely make out the teeth marks. What the hell?

Pack bond. My mind supplied the answer and I sucked in my breath sharply. I'd forgotten about that. God, the day I'd taken it seemed like another lifetime ago, but it had been less than a week.

I thought about Fiona and wondered how she was getting along without Murphy. I supposed he'd called her, but I hadn't been in the room when he had.

Frazier and Elspeth were staring at me expectantly, and I abruptly realized I was daydreaming.

"So tell me what happened in the woods with the Mac Tire duo," I said.

Elspeth took a deep breath while Frazier's eyes went ominously dark. They didn't even pretend to be surprised I knew what had happened. Had Angus talked to them between last night and now? It was a possibility.

"We were walking to our land and we came up to this duo." Espeth's voice was matter of fact without anger or apology. "They were older than us and they'd just about finished stripping down so they could shift. I think that pissed them off too. The fact we saw them practically naked. They started screaming at us that we were on their land and to get the bloody hell off it. Frazier tried to settle them down, we would have turned back even though we were closer to our land than the car park at this point, but they weren't listening. Next thing I knew, I had a fist in my eye and I was flat on my back. It was all I could do to protect my head from being bashed in after that." She flashed me a rueful smile. "We never even got their names."

I didn't enlighten her. "How did that make you feel? Being beaten? Did you fight back?"

Frazier's frown became an outright scowl, but Elspeth continued to smile serenely. Prickles of suspicion wormed down my spine. Surely she ought to be even a tiny bit pissed.

"Angus and Evie want us to keep a low profile until the dust settles on this territory dispute," she said. "Besides, I went down on the first punch. It was a matter of self defense only after that. Frazier, why didn't you fight back?" She turned to her bond mate, who looked ready to hit something.

"I didn't think it would help," was his answer. "I was trying to get to you. That bloody woman was crazy." He switched his gaze to me. "She's the one who caved my rib in. I've been pissing blood for three days as well. Being beaten with a tree branch isn't a hell of a lot of fun, I can tell you that."

"You need to get to a doctor," I told him.

He glared at me. "Stony Fell doesn't have a doctor."

"Mac Tire does."

"So what part of keeping a low profile didn't you understand? Is it our accent maybe?" A belligerent smile curled his lips.

"I understand you perfectly." I made sure not to break eye contact. "Stay here, please. I'll be right back." I rose to my feet and only moved again when he looked away, a tic jumping in his cheek muscle.

Jason was in the lounge across the hall with Murphy. They were deep in discussion in the arm chairs before the fire, but fell silent when I walked in.

"Jason, can you please check out Frazier Campbell? He's got at least one broken rib and something screwed up with his kidneys. He's pissing blood."

Murphy winced and Jason rose immediately to his feet.

"Send him to my room," he said and was gone.

"Asshole won't go to see Mac Tire's doctor and Stony Fell doesn't have one. A fucking Other doctor would have worked just as well," I raged at Murphy, who stared at me.

"Scottish people are proud as hell," he said carefully.

I stamped my foot. "I don't give a shit about that. He's hurt and his fucking Alpha told him to keep a low profile and this whole situation blows, Murphy!"

"No argument there. But Angus didn't know about this. I can't believe he would have told the man not to seek out medical help."

"Angus didn't tell us everything last night," I said, my voice tight with conviction.

Murphy didn't know what to say to that, so I went back to the library.

"For Christ's sake," swore Frazier when I told him Jason was waiting for him in the upstairs suite. "What the hell have you done? Did I ask for your help, Advisor?"

"No, you didn't, you stubborn ass idiot," I snarled at him and his eyes widened. For a moment he looked like a sailboat with half the wind knocked out of its sail.

"Did you just call me a stubborn ass?"

"And don't forget idiot," I said. He bit his lip, but couldn't repress his smile.

"Councilor Allerton is a doctor. I'm not that big of a jerk," I said.

His smile turned into a laugh. "Women. I guess it doesn't matter if you're bonded to them or not, they still want to mother you." He got slowly to his feet and limped for the door.

Elspeth watched him, eyes narrowed.

"I suppose you think we're cowards as well as idiots." She turned to face me.

"Tea?" I gestured to the silver urn on the table by the door and she shook her head impatiently. "Well, I want some." I went to the table and filled a mug with tea almost dark enough to pass for coffee. I doctored it liberally with milk and sugar before I returned to my chair.

"Evie didn't tell Angus what happened," I said.

Her face tightened. "I figured as much." There was a wealth of bitterness in her voice that spoke volumes. "Useless bitch," she added and I was silent.

Elspeth glared at me. Her eyes were really beautifully green. Lovelier than Alannah Doyle's, I decided, somewhat spitefully. "Well, she is. Useless. She's not even pretty so I have no idea what the hell my brother sees in her. Yes, I suppose I do. She has that land. I never should have believed for a moment we had a shot at keeping it. We left the Scottish Mac Tire pack for this. Our mother told us we were fools to leave, but Angus knew damn well neither of us would ever make Alpha." At my frown, she said, "Our father's British," as if that explained everything. Which it probably did, knowing how twisted the politics were in Mac Tire.

"I'll tell you one thing, Advisor, I didn't leave the Scottish branch just to join the British one. I'll be a loner before I ever call Mac Tire my pack again."

"My name is Stanzie," I told her. "If the fact your father's British means you can't be Alpha, how the hell were you ever born?"

Elspeth grinned at me. "Stanzie, that's an easy one. We weren't Mac Tire when we were born, were we?"

* * * *

"Another small pack taken over by Mac Tire." I stabbed my fork into a slice of chicken and Murphy put his hand on my arm.

"Honey, that bird is already dead. Have a care."

I realized I'd splattered gravy all over the tablecloth and put my fork down. Who could eat, anyway?

"What does Mac Tire do? Go out like Napoleon's army and conquer everything in its path? I find it hard to believe that every little pack taken over by Mac Tire had it coming because they trespassed. If I were a little pack in the UK, I'd make damn sure to stay the fuck away from any Mac Tire land. I wouldn't even come to Regionals in case I attracted attention." I grabbed for the wine bottle in the middle of the table, but Murphy got it first and, giving me a look, poured a small amount into my glass. Was he afraid I was going to throw it in his face?

"The fact of the matter is, Mac Tire believe they do own all the land in the UK."

"But they don't," I cried.

"Often they find a way around that."

"Yeah, by taking over the pack who does own the land." I slugged down the wine and banged my glass on the table. Murphy winced. Jason, who had been calmly eating his lunch, moved his plate a prudent few inches away from my side of the table.

"That's just the way it is," said Murphy.

"What? You actually believe that, don't you? You sit there like a smug bastard believing that just because you're mighty Mac Tire, you have some divine right to all the land in Ireland." I glared at him. Who the hell was this man I was bonded with?

"Not all the land, just land wolves can run on," he said and I glared at him.

"You're making fun of me now."

"I am not." He stifled a sigh of impatience. "I don't understand why you're mad at me. I haven't personally taken over anybody's pack and I have no plans to start. Look, I swear if we're the next Alphas of Mac Tire, we will not take over any other pack."

"Well, that's fine for the five years we're in charge, but what about after that?" I demanded.

Murphy looked at Jason for help, but Jason didn't stop shoveling food into his mouth.

"What do you want me to do, Stanzie?" Murphy asked.

"Grow some balls, for one thing," I said.

Jason choked. "Excuse me," he said in a strangled voice.

"Drink some water." I pushed his glass toward him. He picked it up and took a hasty swallow.

Murphy's grin had a dangerous edge to it. "Okay, you won't like what I'm about to say but I'm going to say it anyway."

"Maybe I'd better…" Jason began, but fell silent when Murphy and I both glared at him.

"Go ahead, spit it out." I turned my attention back to Murphy, who still had that same dark smile.

"I think small packs ought not to be allowed," he said and I thought about hauling off and hitting him, I really did. "There are advantages to large packs that far outweigh whatever ridiculous notions of independence small pack members seem to think are so important."

"Getting the chance to be Alpha and have a baby is ridiculous?" My voice spiraled into the upper ranges of sound and both Murphy and Jason winced. Good, I hoped their eardrums burst.

"You know yourself how much better off you are in Mac Tire than you were in Riverglow or your birth pack, for that matter. And it isn't just financial security. It's a community, Stanzie. With doctors and midwives and grandmothers and grandfathers with all their wisdom. It's tradition and security and a pack bond that helps healing, prevents illness and ties people together."

"If people feel so tied together they choke, it's hardly an advantage," I said.

Murphy threw his napkin on the table and shoved back his chair. "I refuse to argue about this with you. Your mind's made up. So is mine. That means it's pointless to discuss this. Thank you for ruining my lunch. And my fucking day." He stalked out of the dining room and out the front door.

"Where do you stand on this issue?" I glared at Jason, who had given up all pretext of enjoying his meal.

"I don't think you'd like my answer, so I'm going to go have coffee in the lounge. By myself, if you please." He left the table and I sat there, fuming, for a long time.

* * * *

Keith Hastings was very handsome with thick black hair and a cleft in his chin that made him look like Sean Connery, only darker. Bonnie Patterson was a redhead with the same pale lashes and freckles that plagued Evie, only she made them look fresh and youthful. Pretty, but not flashy, she smiled as she introduced herself.

I warmed to her immediately, which made me feel guilty for having to ask intrusive questions. However, that was my job as an Advisor. I wasn't there to make friends, was I?

They both made themselves cups of tea from the urn on the table by the door, and balancing cups and saucers, took seats on the sofa. I sat on an armchair across from them.

"Tell me about yourselves. About Stony Fell and why you joined it. What were you hoping to find in a small pack?"

"A chance for my son to become Alpha someday," answered Keith without hesitation. "Have you interviewed the lad yet? Ben?"

I hoped like hell my friendly smile stayed pasted in place. He didn't know about his son's injury. Jason had told the Alphas to keep it a secret, even from Ben's parents.

"I've met him, yes," I said and both Keith's and Bonnie's faces lit with pride.

"Naturally, Elspeth and Frazier will follow after Angus and Evie, but Ben's young yet. Just twenty. He was initiated just before we left Mac Tire to form Stony Fell. He'll need a bond mate, of course, but he met several fine young lasses at the Regional," Keith said.

Did they know about Tracy?

"Anyone in particular?" I asked.

Keith and Bonnie exchanged a private look—one that spoke of the depth of their connection. They didn't need words to communicate. Would Murphy and I be like that someday?

"Advisor, surely he told you about his girl in Mac Tire?" Keith went on the offensive and I liked him for it. These were straightforward people. If they'd set the trap, they would be sly, wouldn't they? Oh, the irony if they had.

"Tracy, yes," I said. "I wondered if you knew and how you felt about that, considering what's happening between the packs right now."

"It could be a bridge, couldn't it?" Bonnie said. "It's been done before, hasn't it? Two packs join and the Alpha duo is made up of one person from each pack. That way everyone gets something."

"Mary and Richard have almost five years left as Alphas of Mac Tire," I pointed out.

Bonnie shrugged. "Ben's only twenty. A few years' wait would be good for him. Tracy as well. She's the same age."

"In a pack as large as Mac Tire?" I wondered dubiously, and some of the optimistic light faded from Bonnie's blue eyes.

"It's been done before, Advisor." Stubborn insistence made her expression hard, but she softened it with a smile.

"That would put a cramp in Elspeth and Frazier's plans, I suspect," I said.

Her smile faded. "We all don't get what we want, do we? Her brother is an Alpha and he can be the father of the family's next generation. And who's to say they wouldn't be Alpha after Ben and Tracy?"

"Or maybe Tracy could join Stony Fell and be Alpha after Elspeth and Frazier," I said.

Keith snorted. "Advisor, please. You know as well as we do Stony Fell will be taken over by Mac Tire. It's the way things go. And Evie's interpretation of ownership of that land is creative at best. We hold land in trust for our packs and when she was given that land, she was Mac Tire."

"So you joined Stony Fell for the express purpose of being taken over by Mac Tire?" I asked.

He stared at me without a smile. "Exactly. My son had little to no chance at Alpha of Mac Tire in Scotland. But at least now he has a shot. Angus and Evie can warble on about co-existing peacefully right next door to Mac Tire, but that is and always was, a pipe dream."

Would they have set a trap? I didn't want to think they would, but there was one sure way to find out if they had. Jason told me he trusted my judgment. My gut was telling me something I thought I ought to listen to.

"There's really no easy way to say this, so please, keep calm. Someone set a trap very near the border of Mac Tire and Stony Fell territory. I'm sorry to have to tell you this, but Ben's wolf was caught in it. His leg had to be amputated, but he'll be all right and the Councils will make sure he's taken care of."

I watched their faces. If they'd set the trap, the guilt would consume them. I did not want to see guilt even though it would be the end of the investigation if I did.

"*Ben!*" Bonnie's cry was one of pure mother's anguish. Grief twisted her features, not guilt.

Keith's face lost all color, even his lips whitened. No guilt at all.

Bonnie began to scream then.

* * * *

"Jesus, Stanzie, what the hell were you thinking?" Rage twisted Murphy's handsome face. Jason had taken charge of Bonnie and Keith and he'd managed to stop Bonnie's wild keening by promising to bring her to her son at the private clinic.

He hadn't said anything to me at all, nor had he looked in my direction. I had the sinking suspicion I'd fucked everything up, and Murphy's reaction underscored it.

"For one thing, they deserved to know. It's their son lying in a hospital bed and it would be nice if he had his parents' support. For another, it was the best way I could think of to see if they were guilty of setting the trap. They couldn't hide that when I told them about Ben, could they?"

Murphy stared at me. "The best way? You were actually cold-blooded enough to watch their reactions for guilt? Who the hell *are* you? This is how you ask questions during an interview? Or maybe you were thinking this was an interrogation. Who's your role model now? Celine Ducharme?"

All the breath left my body. His words were like a punch in the throat.

Celine Ducharme was a manipulative, relentless bitch. I'd been on the hot seat during one of her interrogation sessions and still had the nightmares about it. Calling her my role model was the same as him spitting in my face.

I turned away from him and stumbled blindly for a chair. My legs didn't seem likely to hold me up much longer. I wanted to curl into a fetal ball and cry, but I was damned if I'd let him see me in tears.

"I shouldn't have said that." Murphy was already contrite, but maybe he had a point.

"Why not? She told me basically the same thing herself. Said my interrogation methods were almost as good as hers." My voice broke on the last word and I damned myself.

"What?" Murphy was incredulous and not a little angry. At her, not me. "When did she say this?"

"After what happened with your father," I said and his expression shut down all emotion, leaving him a statue. We'd never talked much about his father's attempt to murder me or the fact he'd been responsible for ordering Sorcha's and Paddy's deaths.

"What did you do? Pissed him off, didn't you?" Murphy's tone was gentle. He sat beside me on the sofa, close enough our knees brushed.

I nodded because I couldn't speak.

"Just went up to him and accused him, huh?" Murphy marveled. "Of course you did. He didn't bother to deny it because you had him cornered and so he tried to kill you to shut you up. Damn him." Murphy gave the coffee table in front of the sofa a vicious kick and sent it careening sideways. I jerked in shock.

"You're not like Celine Ducharme," he said.

I bowed my head.

"She likes to make people squirm and suffer because it makes her feel powerful. You don't like that at all. You just want the truth. That's the difference. Don't listen to me, Stanzie, you do what you need to do. You heard Allerton this morning at breakfast. He trusted your judgment. I ought to do the same damn thing."

"I value your opinion, Murphy." I had to do something with my hands to keep them busy, so I pulled down my sweater sleeve and rolled it up again.

"Well, my opinion is that you shouldn't listen to fuckers like me who don't know what the hell they're talking about." He took both my hands within his.

"I'm sorry about your father." The words burned and choked me, but I got them out.

"Me too," he said. "I wish I knew why the fuck he did the things he did."

I knew. Glenn Murphy told me. He'd done everything for his son. Liam. But I would never, ever, ever tell Murphy that and break his heart even more.

* * * *

I soon discovered after ten minutes of real effort to write a report, the iPad's wireless keyboard and I just didn't bond for extended bouts of typing. I cast it aside on the bed and my glance happened on the desk and Murphy's laptop.

He'd told me nothing on there was secret. He'd even given me his password.

I slid off the bed and approached the desk warily. I'd already fucked up so much today, was this one more thing? What if he'd just said it because he never really expected me to ever touch his laptop?

But I just couldn't sit around doing nothing or I'd go crazy imagining what was happening at the clinic. Angus and Evie had gone with Jason to support Bonnie and Keith. Evie was probably worthless at it. I'm sure Angus was cursing my name right about this second. Maybe they all were.

"Balls," I muttered and pulled out the desk chair.

The desktop icons on Murphy's laptop were neatly arranged across wallpaper of a photo of Mac Tire's castle. Every day he worked, Murphy had to look at a digital representation of the path where Paddy had been stabbed. I swallowed an obstruction in my throat. Was Murphy punishing himself? The spot where he'd stabbed Grandfather Mick to death with the same knife Paddy had been stabbed with was visible as well.

Amy Lee Burgess

He'd quit being an Advisor because he hadn't even hesitated to kill. He thought he didn't have the impartiality and control an Advisor should have had in that situation. I think the fact Allerton had backed him up bothered him as well. Even though I had the feeling vigilantism was frowned upon in Advisors and Councilors, Murphy had never even come close to being questioned by the Councils. Everyone took Jason's word that Murphy had been defending himself and the rest of us who were gathered around Paddy's body in horror. Grandfather Mick had posed no real threat. He'd dropped the knife after stabbing Paddy and Murphy had picked it up and deliberately plunged it into Grandfather Mick's heart. The cold bloodedness of this act had appalled Murphy, but Jason had taken it in stride. Poor Murphy was so confused, and I couldn't blame him.

A folder on the desktop was labeled "Thoughts." I wanted to peek inside, but steeled myself against it. He did keep a journal. Of course he did. Was it filled with self-loathing? Or maybe hope for the future? Fears?

I didn't know and wasn't going to find out. Not today.

I called up Word and began what I suspected was a rambling, incoherent mishmash of words colored more by feelings than logic. Jason would probably wade through this in disbelief tonight and maybe he'd never ask me for another report. That would be a win for me.

Three quarters of the way through my so-called report, Murphy came into the room, tossed his cell phone on the nightstand and said with such loathing I had to stifle a laugh, "Regional Council conference calls. What was I thinking?"

He threw himself on the bed and groaned. If he'd noticed me typing away—and how could he not?—he didn't seem inclined to mention it.

"My iPad sucks for typing reports. I hope you don't mind I'm using your laptop." If he wouldn't mention it, I would.

"How's report writing going?" He must be determined not to say anything about it being his laptop. Maybe he was afraid he would scare me away. I had to admit, I was about three seconds away from powering it down. Guilt scratched at me because I hadn't asked first. I should have asked.

"I'm not a report writer." I grimaced at the hopeless muddle of words on the page and sighed. "I never saw you taking notes." I twisted in my chair to scowl at him. He was propped against the headboard, shoes kicked off so I could see his socks. They had an interesting black waffle weave with the slightest hint of gold.

"Don't need to take notes. It's all in my head." He gave me an outrageous grin and tapped his temple.

I stuck my tongue out at him and turned back to my frigging report. "That's what I told Jason too but somehow it didn't fly."

Behind me, Murphy snorted laughter.

"Fuck this," I said ten minutes later. I closed the document and mailed it to myself and to Jason. I'd named a folder "Stanzie's Horrible Reports" and stuck the damn document in there. I carefully powered the laptop down, sad again when I thought of Murphy torturing himself with the desktop wallpaper of the castle.

When I crawled onto the bed, he opened his arms for me, and after I'd settled against his chest, combed his fingers through my hair.

We stayed that way for a while until he said, "I love your hair. Like muted sunshine."

I shook my head and his chest rumbled with laughter.

"You never will take a compliment from me, will you?" he asked.

I thought of Sorcha's hair—the wild, autumn flame of it. Compared to that, my blond hair was nothing special. A hundred women had the same shade. Muted sunshine. There had been nothing subdued about Sorcha's hair. Or anything about her, from what I'd gathered. Subtle as a hurricane and twice as mercurial. Of course, when it came to being understated, I was hardly a champion.

Why the hell was I thinking of Sorcha? Because of Colin's proximity? Maybe. Probably.

"Why do you have that picture for wallpaper on your laptop?" I blurted. Yeah, the art of subtlety was truly beyond me.

"The castle?" His tone was carefully curious, as if he had no earthly idea what I might be getting at.

"You might as well make two Xs on the damn thing. One for where Paddy went down, the other for Grandfather Mick."

"You think I'm torturing myself with it?" Now he sounded incredulous.

"Maybe," I said, but doubt stabbed at me. What else could it be?

"It's a reminder, Stanzie. Of who I don't want to be and of who I am. It's hard to explain. Mostly, though, it's just a picture. I happen to think the castle is beautiful and there's a lot of Mac Tire history there. Some of my ancestors were born there. And died."

Like his father, for one.

"I don't want to hate the place. It's where we go to shift. Now that I'm a Councilor, I'll be there half the frigging time. There's not room in our apartment for an office for me. I'll need one." He sounded glum.

Amy Lee Burgess

I traced the knitted pattern in his sweater. One of Maureen's creations. Did wearing it make him feel closer to Paddy? Half the reason I wore mine most of the time was because they did do that somehow. I conjured up a memory of Paddy—striding into the conference room in the safe house in Connecticut when I'd been before the tribunal for Nate's death. He'd worn one of Maureen's hand-knitted sweaters and his damn curly hair had been all over the place but he'd still managed to pull off the tired, sexy look. Damn him.

He'd left such a huge hole in my life. The one he'd left in Murphy's had to be enormous. Maybe one that would never fill back in and always remain empty.

"I'm thinking of getting a tattoo," I told him.

"Oh, yeah? Of what?" He sounded very interested. "And where?"

"Ankle," I said. "Very small tattoo of the Mayflower."

"You see," he said approvingly. "You do understand. Family, Stanzie. Pack loyalty."

"Mayflower's not my pack," I reminded him.

"It will always be yours in some ways," he said. I kissed him for that and he whispered my name against my lips, sending a thrill down my spine.

I slid my hands beneath his sweater and he helped me take it off. I tossed it onto the hardwood floor and trailed butterfly kisses down his chest until I got to the barrier of his belt buckle. He undid it himself, but I unbuttoned his fly and we both slid the jeans over his lean hips and down his legs. I stripped off his socks while I was at it, and he grinned at me.

"I only want to feel skin," I told him, and he eyed me up and down.

"Well, then I guess you're a hell of a long way behind me in the stripping department." He had a point. He was now nude and I still had on all my clothes.

"My wolf is going to kill me if I keep doing this and never let her out." I knelt on the bed and slowly pulled off my sweater. Thankfully, I'd worn one of my nicer bras. Lacy and hot pink. Murphy reached out to slide one strap off my shoulder and I threw my sweater in his face.

He knocked it away with a laugh, but settled back against the headboard, arms behind his head so he could watch me strip.

I had to get off the bed so I could take off my jeans with any amount of grace. Murphy's eyes gleamed as I undid the button then very slowly slid the zipper down. I never bothered to match my underwear, but the neon green hip huggers contrasted nicely with the hot pink bra and made my legs look like they went on forever. I'd kicked off my boots earlier, and my ankle socks were boring white, but Murphy wasn't looking anywhere near my feet at this point.

I pretended I was going to take off my panties next, and rolled them down two slow inches, but then switched to my bra, sliding the other strap down my shoulder. The bra fastened in the front and I played with the slide hook as if I couldn't decide whether to take it off.

When I did, Murphy made a sexy growling sound and I turned my back to him and bent over as I slid my panties off.

I never made it to the bed. He had me on my hands and knees in three seconds and was inside me in five. Stripping had turned me on, so I was more than ready for him and he slid in with such slick ease we both gasped.

He nipped my shoulder and I arched against him so nothing separated us and we were skin to skin as I'd wanted.

Concentrated lust made it impossible to speak for several, exquisite moments, but when Murphy whispered, "Bed," in my ear, I was more than willing.

Entwined, we somehow made it to the mattress and I collapsed onto it, him on top of me, and wrapped my legs around his waist.

"I guess this means you're not mad at me anymore." He kissed me hard. I struggled to remember we'd actually been fighting. Oh yeah. Big packs versus little ones. Jesus, that had been an eternity ago.

"Mary says make-up sex is the best. I think she has a point," I said between rough kisses that sent sparks of desire crackling through my veins.

"When the hell have you been talking about sex with Mary?" Murphy paused at a very crucial moment for me and I groaned in dismay. What a fucking big mouth I was.

"Here and there." I tightened my legs around him, but he refused to resume moving.

"You are incredible. You know that?" He rolled his eyes and kissed me again. We forgot about talking for a while.

"Make-up sex between her and Richard? Did you and I come up?" Murphy seemed unable to let it go. I was on top at this point, but he held me still with his hands at my hips and I looked up at the ceiling as if it could help me out. Blank, white and somewhat cracked with age, it seemed to leer at me and if a ceiling could have said, "Big mouth," that one would have.

"It was a personal conversation, Murphy," I said primly. "I'd be breaking the girlfriend code if I gave you any more information than I already have."

"Girlfriend? Since when have you been friends with that bitch?" Murphy gaped at me.

"You don't have to be friends to keep to the girlfriend code," I told him. "You know damn well you have a man code and you stick to it even if you hate the other guy's guts."

"That's different," he said, and I made a sound of exasperation.

"Shut up and fuck me," I said and he grinned. God, he was gorgeous when he smiled. The planes and angles of his face were endlessly fascinating to me.

"You're the one on top," he reminded me and slid his hands to cup my breasts.

* * * *

Dinner was held in the main dining room on the ground floor. Jason was there as well as both sets of Alphas. Jason had a wine glass in hand, half-full. Murphy and I drifted hand in hand down the staircase, and when Jason saw us, he reached for the wine bottle and filled our glasses. Conspicuous in his absence was Colin. He must be in deep shit with Jason to be banished from the dinner table. Was he eating a solitary meal in his room or still running errands?

"Congratulations on scaring the piss out of Bonnie and Keith." Angus was in a surly mood, as I'd suspected he might be. "Don't you think it might have been a nice touch to have their Alphas in the room when you puked out the news about Ben, Advisor?"

"Can I have a glass of wine before I'm ripped to shreds?" Jesus, I hadn't even taken a seat yet.

"I hope you bloody well choke on it," said Angus. Evie flushed and sloshed wine over the rim of her glass when she tried to drink some.

"Watch it," suggested Mary, who sat beside her. How that had transpired, I didn't know. Evie certainly wouldn't have voluntarily sat beside Mary. Perhaps Mary had chosen her seat on purpose so she could needle Evie? I wouldn't put it past her.

Murphy sat between me and Angus to separate us. His gaze traveled between Mary and Richard speculatively, and I kicked his ankle beneath the table. He kicked me back and didn't stop staring.

"What the hell are you looking at, Councilor?" Mary snapped, and Richard winced.

"You're looking lovely tonight, Mary," Murphy said with a grin.

Her irritation morphed into preening pleasure. She did look good. Her teal blue silk blouse was unbuttoned to show a tantalizing glimpse of cleavage. She had her hair twisted up to showcase gold hoop earrings. Effortless and elegant. So not like me. I'd thrown on a long sweater and leggings with my knee-high black boots. To me, it was dressy, but Mary's blouse was raw silk and while I couldn't see if she wore pants or a skirt, I was sure whatever she wore was expensively stylish.

"Have a nice afternoon, Stanzie?" she asked with such archness I had a horrible moment where I was sure my eyes glowed silver blue. My wolf's eyes peeking out because I'd just had some intensely great sex. I'd showered and put on powder and perfume so I knew she couldn't smell it. At least I didn't think she could.

Murphy turned to me with one his sexy grins and I picked up my wine glass.

"It was okay," I said and Murphy kicked me under the table again. "I wrote a report."

"Did you put down in it what a horse's ass you made of yourself during your so-called interview of my people?" Angus wanted to know.

"I must have forgotten. I was too busy writing about how I was definitely satisfied that Keith and Bonnie didn't set that trap." I tasted the wine. Merlot. Fruity. The second sip was just as pleasant as the first.

"Yeah, well, you have a hell of a heavy hand, Advisor," muttered Angus, eyes dark. "And I still think you ought to have had Alphas in the room."

"And I think I heard you the first time you said that," I said cheerfully. "What shall I do, Angus? Roll back time and do it over?"

"Acknowledge the fact you fucked up." He scowled at me and I knew by the set of his jaw, Murphy was having a really hard time hanging onto his temper. Jason drank his wine and said nothing.

I pretended to debate for a moment. "Well, that would be hard for me, you see, because I don't think I did. And I'm not going to say it just because you think I ought to. Can you pass the olive tray? I'm starved."

With a glower worthy of a pirate, Angus shoved the tray in my direction. I plucked two black olives and an almond-stuffed green one from the tray then nibbled on one of the black ones.

Dinner was not the most enjoyable experience. Evie didn't say one word the entire hour and a half. Angus barked out one- and two-word responses to Richard's strained attempts at conversation. Murphy didn't bother to talk to Angus. He was still seething probably.

Jason, as usual, made everything bearable with his social skills. He possessed the ability to make even the worst of enemies relax enough to eat three courses and a pudding, although even he couldn't prod Angus into real speech.

The moment Evie spooned up the last of her sticky toffee pudding, she was out of her chair, murmuring vaguely about a headache and stumbling awkwardly for the stairs. Tonight she wore a truly hideous long patchwork skirt. The garish purple and orange patterns hurt my eyes. The skirt was paired with the inevitable ruffled white peasant blouse, making her a walking fashion disaster.

Mary turned up her elegant nose as she watched Evie's floundering progress and poured herself more coffee.

Angus simply scowled at us all and stomped off behind his bond mate without bothering to say goodnight.

"They are the worst Alphas I've ever met." Mary didn't bother to keep her voice low. I'm almost positive Angus and Evie weren't far enough up the damn stairs to escape hearing and, by Richard's pained wince, he wasn't convinced either. "Is it really too much to expect decent conversation and the barest comprehension of how to dress to impress? That skirt looked like something out of a rag bag."

"Well, when you don't have much money," I began, but Mary held up an elegant, long-fingered hand and gave me a prissy smile.

"Spare me. Second hand shops can be marvelous sources of cast-down designer. There's no reason to dress like an adolescent gypsy. She's nearly forty. And Angus and those damn kilts."

"I had no idea fashion played such a huge role in being a good Alpha," I murmured.

Mary swept a scathing look over my sweater.

"Of course you didn't," she said. I had left myself wide open for that one.

I said, "I just hope the next time you've got a crisis on your hands and someone in your pack needs your support, you're wearing designer. It'll be so comforting for the person in distress to know you care enough to wear the very best. Hopefully they won't be so gauche as to smear snot and tears all over you. That would be a catastrophe. Imagine the dry cleaning bill."

Murphy snorted into his cup and I'm surprised he didn't get coffee up his nose. Jason steepled his fingers in front of his face in his classic pose to conceal his expression.

"You've always got a comeback, haven't you?" Mary fished in her purse and came up with a packet of Players and a lighter. "It must be so amusing to be bonded to her, Liam."

"I've never been happier in my life, actually. Thanks for asking." Murphy lifted his wine glass. "Cheers." He drained the contents and set it down.

"Want some fresh air?" Mary rose to her feet. Belatedly, I realized she was talking to me.

"Sure, why not." I pushed back my chair.

* * * *

Huddled into my jacket, I stood as far back from the chill wind as possible while Mary struggled to light her cigarette. The rain had stopped, but dampness coated every surface—from the wooden beams and floor of the porch to the cushions on the chairs. The windows were smeared with a vaporous, dirty fog that obscured the lights from the rooms within.

"Weather like this makes it difficult to remain a smoker." Mary successfully lit her cigarette and took a long drag. "But not impossible."

I waited her out. She wanted something from me and I was damn sure it wasn't my friendly company.

"Alison and Garrett. Do you think they could have set the trap?" She didn't bother to prevaricate, which I appreciated.

"Of course. Practically anybody in Mac Tire could have set it."

"Jesus, you're deviously literal, aren't you?" Another puff of the cigarette. The end glowed orange in the darkness. "Do you think they actually did?"

"I don't know," I answered. That was the truth.

I couldn't see her eye-roll in the dark, but didn't have to.

"Stanzie, for Christ's sake, Allerton's tying our hands here and I'm tired of being cooped up in this damned safe house. I want this over with and settled. It was a simple bloody territory dispute which everyone knew we'd win and now it's become this tangled, filthy mess and it needs to be cleared up."

"It will be when we get a confession."

"Did you even ask them if they set the trap?" Mary's voice was sharp. "Because I don't believe for a minute you did or they would have come to screaming to me and Richard."

"So sure of that? Don't you agree with Angus that I'm heavy handed and antagonistic in my interview style?" I wondered.

"Angus is a fool," Mary said. "Jason Allerton would not have you for his Advisor if you were an ineffective screw-up. No matter what the rest

Amy Lee Burgess

of us think. There's got to be more to you than the surface. It's clear Allerton has faith you're very good at what you do. I just wish you were a bit more forthcoming."

"I tell him everything." I tried not to let her dismissive remarks about me sting, but goddamn. *No matter what the rest of us think?* Screw you, Mary Lancaster. "I don't work for you, Mary. But I'd tell you if I knew for sure it was Garrett and Alison. I don't. They're strong contenders, but then the only ones I've crossed off my list are Keith and Bonnie, so that doesn't mean shit really at this point."

"Jesus." Mary stubbed out her cigarette in a glass ashtray on a side table. It hissed against the damp condensation. "We're going to be stuck here for ages, aren't we?" She stalked inside without a backward look.

Car tires crunched over the gravel in the car park and the sweep of headlights momentarily blinded me. Then, the *thunk* of an expensive car door slamming and scrunching of gravel beneath booted feet.

Colin Hunter took the porch stairs two at a time and came to an abrupt standstill when he saw me huddled in the corner.

"God, it must be unbearable inside if you're out here in this weather." His breath puffed out in frosty clouds and he stuffed his hands in his jacket pockets.

"Mary wants me to pin the crime on Alison and Garrett," I said. The obscured light from the windows on either side of the front door shed just enough light that I could see his sour expression.

"I'll bet she does. Is there anything left to eat? I'm starved."

"We just finished, but I'm sure Grandmother Nan has something set aside for you."

"Great." Colin took a step for the door then hesitated. "Coming in?"

At my nod, he opened the door and held it for me.

Jason was still at the dinner table lingering over a glass of brandy. Murphy was there as well, but Mary and Richard were gone.

Colin met Jason's gaze across the room and Jason gestured for him to approach the table.

"I guess I'm not exiled to my room with bread and water," he murmured into my ear, one hand on my back. Murphy's eyes narrowed at the familiarity and Colin stepped away from me with an amused smile.

A snifter of brandy waited for me at my place and I took a sip after I settled in my chair.

Colin took Evie's former place, which had been cleared away since my sojourn on the porch.

Grandmother Nan bustled in with a full plate and a cloth napkin wrapped around silverware. Her pink wrinkled cheeks and snow-white hair couldn't disguise her innate prettiness. I'd bet she'd been sweetly stunning as a young woman.

Colin was one of her favorites. She beamed at him as she set a plate of beef wellington and green beans in front of him.

"You look cold and tired, lad." She pinched his cheek.

Beside me, Murphy grimaced into his brandy. He was used to being the favorite with the women. I'm sure the fact Grandmother Nan preferred Colin galled him to no end.

"I am that, Grandmother," Colin agreed, pulled her down and planted a kiss on her soft cheek. For the first time I saw the resemblance between them. I was almost positive she was his blood great-grandmother. No wonder she doted on him. "But this will warm me up nicely. Thank you."

"We're proud of you, Col," she said. "I know you went through some rough patches, but you've landed on your feet. That's a Hunter for you. Just like your great-grandfather you are. Spitting image too."

"So you've always said." Colin's smile faded. Did he not like being told someone was proud of him? "Be a love and bring me some wine?"

"Of course." Grandmother Nan gave him one last affectionate look and hurried back to the kitchen.

I wondered what had happened to Colin's great-grandfather. The grandfather of the triad who operated the safe house was named Neville Jarvis, not Hunter. Nan must be the spare to the pair in their triad. Probably she'd bonded with him and Grandmother Cora after Colin's great-grandfather's death.

I reached for Murphy's hand beneath the table. Please don't let that be my fate. Spare to someone's pair in my old age because Murphy died way before me. I wanted to grow old with him. Please let that be in our future. He gave my fingers a reassuring squeeze as if he knew what I was thinking. Maybe he did.

Colin gave the table a thin, somewhat defensive smile and unspooled his cutlery from the cloth napkin. "Sorry about that," he said.

"What for? She loves you," I said before Murphy could say anything snide. Jason swirled the brandy in his glass until the sides were coated with an amber smear, then took a sip.

Colin fished car keys from his pocket and pushed them across the table to Jason.

"Keep them," Jason advised. Colin grimaced and repocketed them. "Tomorrow's agenda for you is the same as today's."

"What about me?" I asked. Better sooner than later to discover if I was on Jason's shit list too.

Jason gave me an amused look. He knew precisely what I was up to.

"I suggest you wander about and have impromptu conversations with the Alphas."

"That ought to be fun since most of them aren't speaking to me at the moment." I grinned.

"You'll manage." He seemed convinced and, after swallowing the last of his brandy, excused himself from the table and went upstairs

"Bitch." Colin's smile was good-humored as he forked beef wellington into his mouth.

"Shut up. At least you get out of here. I have to make nice with the Alphas."

"But not as nice as me. Friendly warning," he said, and I couldn't help but laugh.

Murphy, left out of the joke, gave us both a thoughtful look.

"I told Ben's parents about what happened to him," I said and Colin barely paused to swallow.

"Good for you." Grandmother Nan returned to the table with a glass and half a bottle of Merlot. She filled his glass, gave him another fond smile and disappeared back to the kitchen. "I didn't agree with the idea to keep it from them. So what did they do when they found out?"

"Fell apart." I sighed. Colin set his fork aside.

"Guiltily apart or parental?"

"The latter."

"Don't worry, Stanzie. Somebody had to do it and Allerton left it to you. You know it was his plan all along." Colin couldn't reach out to touch me, but his smile was warm.

"Damn the man, yes," I agreed.

"Reckon you're happy to be a Councilor and get to the pull the strings rather than dance like somebody else's puppet." Colin regarded Murphy over the rim of his glass before he took a sip.

"If you think I'm not dancing, you're delusional," Murphy said. "You can dance and play the puppeteer at the same time, you know."

"Good luck with that. Cheers." Colin drained his glass and refilled it with the last of the bottle. He switched his dark blue gaze to me. "What about Elspeth and Frazier? You like them for setting the trap?"

I grimaced. "I don't know. They were hurt worse than Alison said. She went after Frazier with a tree branch."

"Jesus." Colin gulped at his wine. "This situation with Stony Fell must be dredging up all sorts of bad memories from when Nightgate joined Mac Tire. I'd hate for it to be her, you know."

"Yeah, well, who would you like it to be? Someone you don't know? Get used to having your heart ripped out and stomped upon in this job," Murphy suggested.

"Look, I got the techno all night extended version of this same song from Stanzie. I understand what I got myself into. When Allerton brought me here of all bloody places, I knew I wasn't in for the pleasure tour." Colin returned to what was left of his meal.

Murphy's grin was sardonic. He so wasn't buying what Colin was selling. I decided to break things up before they got ugly. Murphy followed me up the stairs, as I knew he would.

"Insufferable bastard." Colin got the last word, even if it was muttered beneath his breath.

Chapter 12

Mary had the same yearning look on her face as I suspected I did. We sat on the porch in cold, moist chairs, disdaining the warmth of the safe house so we could get some fresh air.

"I am so sick and tired of sitting around here on my ass," I muttered.

Mary stubbed out her third cigarette in a row and reached for the pack of Players on the table between us. "I'm chain smoking, I'm so bored," she said as she lit up.

The bells above the front door jangled and Evie stepped out onto the porch. Her short hair hung lankly in her eyes, but she made no attempt to brush it aside. My eyes itched just looking at her and I swiped my hair behind my ears as if that would help.

Today she wore a battered sweater the color of weak tea. Though unraveling at the hem, with sleeves bagging at the elbows, at least it didn't have ruffles. When she saw Mary, she paled.

"Sorry, didn't mean to interrupt." She all but bashed her face against the door as she clumsily swung about to duck back inside.

"Sit down," Mary said irritably. "Don't scuttle off like that. You're not a cockroach, for Christ's sake." She looked at me. "It's like we haven't spent every waking moment together for four bloody days now. She acts like I'm her wicked stepmother about to send her off to scrub the floors." She patted the chair beside her. "Cinderella, have a seat."

Evie edged for the chair. I wanted to get up and strangle her. I really had to calm down. Being cooped up in the same place for two days straight was no reason to become homicidal. I wished it was a meal time. At least I would have something to occupy my hands, but we'd just finished lunch and dinner was hours away.

"In any event, it's not raining," Evie said brightly after five minutes of silence punctuated only by my sighs and Mary's smoke-filled exhalations.

"Piss off, Mary Poppins." Mary stubbed out her fourth cigarette, contemplated the pack of Players and hissed something foul beneath her breath. "Look, do either of you want to come for a ride? Arrangements have been made for someone to feed our dogs, but I want to see how far the stream's risen behind the house. We may have to bring them to Roger and Daniela if it's too high. Last time it went over the banks, the back garden was nothing but muck for a week and I don't want the dogs in that filth."

"You have dogs," I said wistfully. Mary turned a genuine smile in my direction.

"Two. Irish setters. Daisy's due to have puppies soon. Another reason to check on her. Come on." She got to her feet and dusted off the back of her jeans, grimacing when she encountered the dampness. "Bloody bollocky rain."

"Do you think we should? Councilor Allerton asked us to stay here at the safe house," Evie, the killjoy, reminded us.

"We've got his Advisor along. She'll watch over us and make sure we don't make a break for it." Mary grinned and Evie's brows drew together in a frown.

"We're not criminals. I just think he wants us to stay here with him."

"Oh for fuck's sake," Mary muttered. "Stay here then. I'm off. Stanzie?"

I knew I ought to stay, but Jesus, I was bored. Hadn't Jason said I was supposed to encourage impromptu discussions with the Alphas? Well, here was a golden opportunity. The fact I was bored enough to consider driving with Mary was another reason I wanted to go. Every step I took toward not being scared of cars was a good one. Wasn't it?

"Hang on one second, Mary." I pushed past Evie as I went into the safe house. Grandmother Nan was sweeping the floor and smiled at me.

"Grandmother, Mary and I are going for a drive to check on her dogs. Will you make sure to let the Councilors know?" I'd learned my lesson the hard way about not telling someone where I was going when on assignment. The last time I'd rushed off without telling anyone where I was going, I'd ended up in a root cellar chained to an autopsy table. That was never going to happen to me again.

"Of course, love," Grandmother Nan promised and I ducked out the door.

Mary hadn't waited for me, she was halfway down the gravel path to the car park but I caught up with her easily.

"Wait for me." Evie boldly hurried after us.

Although I was bored enough to risk getting into a car with a driver who wasn't Murphy, I let Evie take the death seat in the front and buckled myself into one of the back seats. No sense in being completely reckless. Mary looked at me in the rearview mirror after she switched on the Land Rover's ignition and I braced myself for one of her snide comments.

Instead she very carefully backed up the vehicle and pulled forward at a sedate speed my Grandmother Carolyn would have chafed at.

Evie sat huddled in the front bucket seat the entire drive and didn't make a peep. I looked out the window at the tossing waves on the lake and the skeletal branches of the trees. Sometime in the past four days, what was left of the autumn foliage had faded and fallen to the ground. Now everything looked drab and haunted.

The gray clouds overhead gathered in tight groups as if they were conspirators plotting treason. No doubt they would unleash rain upon us. I really hoped we were back at the safe house before then.

Mary and Richard's house was a fifteen-minute drive away. Nestled in the center of a small, wooded lot, the stone house looked snug and inviting. Rock gardens and bordered flowerbeds decorated the front yard. Mary pulled the Land Rover up close to the porch steps and hopped to the gravel drive gracefully. Dogs barked enthusiastically from inside the house. Although there were only two of them, they managed to raise enough of a ruckus that I would have believed there were a dozen.

Mary's face lit up affectionately.

"I'll stay here." Evie clutched at the dashboard. "I'm rather afraid of dogs."

"Bloody hell." Mary stared at her. "You're Pack. You shift into a wolf. How can you be afraid of…never mind." She looked at me in incredulity and I stifled a laugh. Evie's fear was completely absurd, but so was her wardrobe. That's just the way she was.

Mary bounded up the steps and unlocked the front door. Blurs of copper burst onto the porch and much yelping and panting ensued.

One of the dogs noticed me after a few moments and leaped down the stairs. Plumed tail waving furiously, he reared up and braced his paws on my shoulders as he tried to energetically wash my face with his pink tongue.

"Aren't you a beauty." I buried my fingers in his silky fur. "What's your name?"

"Gatsby," Mary called to me as she wrestled with the female dog, Daisy. "Richard's rather an F. Scott Fitzgerald fan."

I laughed. Daisy woofed at me, but didn't leave Mary's side.

"You've got a devoted friend," I said and Mary's smile transformed her into radiant beauty. I wondered if this was the woman Colin Hunter had fallen in love with. I hoped so.

Twenty minutes later the dogs had been fed, watered and had run amok in the fenced back garden until they'd tired themselves out. Mary locked them in the house and I followed her to the front where the Land Rover was parked. With supreme condescension, she marched up to the passenger window and gave it a hard rap with her knuckles. Inside the vehicle, Evie gave a jerk of shock and searched on the door panel— seemingly endlessly—for the window button. When she finally managed to lower it, she peered out at Mary, blinking nervously.

"This is the part where we walk down to the stream. I'm not bringing the dogs, so you might want to stretch your legs and come along. If you're not scared of trees. There will be loads of them. Bring the keys." She'd left them in the ignition so Evie could run the heater if she was cold. Flushing as if she'd been stung by a wasp, Evie snatched the keys from the ignition. "I'll come," she said and thrust open the door straight into Mary, who staggered back and rubbed at her elbow, which had been clipped by the side mirror.

"Watch it, damn it," Mary yelped. Evie bit her lip.

"Sorry." She slid out of the Land Rover and held out the keys. Mary snatched them. Evie flinched when their fingers brushed as if she expected Mary to hit her. Mary probably wanted to, after being smacked with the damn door.

"God, that smarts," Mary complained as she stalked for the gate leading to the back garden. After it squeaked open and we all went through, she latched it and resumed rubbing her elbow. "Right on my funny bone. Brilliant job as usual, Evelyn. Accidents are always happening to and around you, you bloody menace."

"I said I was sorry." Evie kept her head down as she shuffled through the fallen leaves.

"Pick up your goddamned feet. Why are you shuffling like an old woman?" Mary flung a black look over her shoulder at Evie, who flinched. I began to wish I'd stayed in the damn car. If this was how Evie had been treated as a Mac Tire member, no wonder she'd left.

We left the back garden by another gate and followed Mary down a well-worn path that led into the forest. Evie let me go ahead of her, but she still scuffed through the leaves as if her feet were too damn heavy to pick up off the ground.

We heard the savage rush of water before we saw it. The stream was about ten feet wide and I estimated nearly five feet deep when it wasn't swollen with rainwater. At the moment it was a good six feet deep and frothed and bubbled angrily as it roared past us where we stood on the bank. Another four inches and it would spill over the top.

"This is close enough to flood your back garden?" It seemed an awfully long way from here to the stone house, but when I looked over my shoulder I could see still the house.

"It was two years ago. Admittedly, it was a flash flood after two weeks of steady rain, but I get nervous." Mary frowned down at the swirling water. Bits of leaves and twigs whisked past, some sucked beneath the surface where the water frothed white.

Right on cue, a raindrop spattered on my head. First one, then another, and five seconds later, a deluge.

"Shit," Mary swore above the roar of the water. "Come on." She turned and dashed down the path. She had to dodge around Evie, who stood there in the pouring rain like a drowned rat, face lifted to the sky as if in disbelief.

As I pulled up the hood of my rain jacket, Mary screamed. She crashed to the ground and leaves whipped into the air as she twisted her body into amazing contortions. She shrieked again and I stood there, struck dumb. My brain could not process the data. Why was she on the ground? What made her scream like that?

Evie put her hands to her ears and burst into scared tears. The rain beat down in angry, silver needles that pricked my skin, and my paralysis broke.

I threw myself down beside Mary and that's when I saw the bear trap and her foot mangled within it.

"Oh my God," I whispered as Mary continued to scream, the noise drilling into my ears until I wanted to claw them off my skull.

"Stanzie," Mary shrieked. "Get it off. Get it off me! It *hurts*!"

Blood spattered everywhere. The leaves were smeared with it and every time Mary moved, more of it gushed over the teeth of the trap, her booted foot and the leaves beneath them.

"Mary, hold still." I grabbed the trap with both hands. How the *fuck* did it work? I wasn't strong enough, I couldn't shift it and Mary's screams made me believe everything I did hurt. Bad. How the hell had Colin pried apart the jaws of one of these things?

"Mary, I need to go for help. Are your keys in your pocket? I'm going to call for help."

Goddamn me for not bringing my cell phone. Again. Did I never, ever learn? I'd told someone where I was going, but forgotten my fucking phone. Brilliant.

"Don't leave me," Mary begged. Her lips were blue with shock and I watched her struggle against losing consciousness.

"Evie will stay with you." I frantically dug in her pocket for the keys.

"No. You." Agony twisted her face out of recognition. She clutched at me, her fingers digging into my shoulders with uncanny strength. "Don't. Leave. Me."

Shit. Do something. Now.

"Evie, take these keys and go in the house. Call for help. Call Angus and have him bring Jason here." I tossed her the keys, but she stood there with her hands to her ears, her face pale and tear streaked. The keys bounced once on the ground and came to rest in a muddy clump of leaves.

"I'm afraid of the dogs," Evie whispered and I thought about it for one second before I launched myself at her and brought her down, screaming in surprise, to the ground.

"Don't you dare fucking tell me you're scared of the fucking dogs!" I shrieked in her face. I straddled her body and shook her by the shoulders. She bawled in terror like a calf. "Get your ass to that house and call for help."

"I can't think with you on top of me," she wailed. "You're scaring me. You need to calm down. I didn't do anything wrong."

Maybe if I strangled her, she would shut the fuck up.

Mary was dreadfully quiet and I crawled off Evie and thrashed through the leaves to get to her. She was still, her head fallen to a strange angle and for one terrible moment I thought she'd died, but I saw the rise and fall of her chest and heard the thud of her heart although mine was pounding so damn loudly it was a wonder I heard anything else.

"Mary," I whispered. The roar of the stream drowned my voice. I wanted to bring her around, but maybe it was better she was passed out. She couldn't feel anything unconscious, could she? One of her ankle bones protruded a good three inches from her skin and my gorge rose just looking at it. That and the stink of blood and terror made me want to puke, but I was damned if I would.

Evie was snuffling and sobbing into the leaves, rolled over onto her stomach, curled into a fetal ball. I got to my feet and had to really work hard not to kick her.

I spared Mary one last look to make sure she was still out, snatched up the keys then ran like hell for the house. Rain lashed at me and I couldn't see two feet ahead, but I didn't stop or slow down.

I didn't know which key went to the back door, but I did know which one went to the front, so I skidded to a stop at the gate to the front garden, fumbled with it, swearing, until it unlatched.

The rain turned the world surreal and icy cold. I almost didn't see the second car in the driveway, but I heard the door slam shut and then Colin's voice, raised in alarm.

"Stanzie? What's wrong? Are you hurt? You've got blood on you."

"Not mine." My teeth chattered together. "Why are you here?"

"To feed the dogs. Allerton's orders. Stanzie. Focus. What's the matter?"

"Mary." I struggled for breath and Colin's expression altered from scared confusion to outright terror. He shook me until my head spun.

"What about Mary? Is this her blood? Stanzie, goddamn you, answer me."

"She's by the stream. Colin, another trap." I clutched at him, shivering. I was so cold and seemed to be floating somewhere outside my own body. If I let go of him, would I float up into the rainy sky and disappear?

"No!" He let go of me so abruptly, I fell to the gravel drive as he sprinted off, shouting her name.

I struggled to my feet and staggered up the stairs. Please let there be a land line.

There was. My fingers were frozen. I could barely make them work. I blanked on Jason's number, so I called Murphy. He answered on the third ring, his tone politely curious until he recognized my voice.

"Liam, Mary's caught in another trap. You've got to bring Jason and help. It's really fucking bad and I can't breathe." My legs went out from under me and I collapsed into the chair by the phone. The dogs crowded against my legs, whining uneasily. I reached out to one of them and caressed the silky red fur. God, if I could only breathe.

"Take a deep breath, honey," Murphy said, and bless him, his voice was steady, although I could sense the shock beneath it. "We're on our way. Jason's here with me and he heard you. He's on his phone now getting help. Where are you?"

"Mary and Richard's house. We went to the stream to see how close it was to flooding the banks. I didn't see the fucking thing. She just stepped in it, and oh my God, the blood. I can't deal with this."

"Yes, you can. Jason wants to know if you can get the trap off her foot."

"I couldn't, but I think maybe Colin might. He's with her and so is Evie."

"Where are you?"

"In the house. I had to run for help. I couldn't get the trap open. I'm sorry. I'm so sorry."

"It's okay. It's fine. Colin will take care of it. Jason wants you to stay by the phone. He's sending an ambulance and we're coming too. We're in the car right now."

"You don't have a car," I said stupidly.

"We're borrowing Angus's." In the background, an engine fired up. I was eerily reminded of Nate Carver's root cellar. Murphy had driven to my rescue that night too.

Would Mary die the same as Bethany? Why hadn't I seen the trap? Smelled it? Something? Heaving sobs swept over me and Murphy said, "Honey, don't. We'll be there soon. It'll be all right."

Would it be? I looked down and saw I was covered with blood. I scrubbed at the stains on my jeans with frantic fingers, but they wouldn't come out.

"Talk to me," Murphy ordered when too much silence had passed between us.

I took a deep breath. "I'm all right."

Using the arm of the chair for support, I pushed myself to my feet and went to the back window so I could look out. Through the sheets of rain, faintly in the distance, I could see Evelyn standing in the path. Colin and Mary were hidden by a screen of trees. I winced when I heard a scream. Mary was awake again.

"I think Colin's got the trap sprung. I hear Mary screaming." The dogs stood on either side of me, furry guardians. The female, Daisy, was shaking. She heard the screams too, obviously.

"We're coming as fast as we can. The ambulance will be there soon as well."

"Where's Richard?" I asked.

"He's in the back seat with Jason. Angus is driving," Murphy told me.

I wiped my nose on my sleeve. Gross, but I had to do something.

Mary's shrieks reached a chilling crescendo then cut off. A moment later, Colin staggered into view with her in his arms.

"Colin's got her. He's bringing her to the house." In the background I heard Jason say, "Tell her to get some blankets. She'll be in shock and she needs to be kept warm."

A brown and cream afghan was draped across the back of the couch. I snatched it up and another, this one yellow and white, from an armchair.

"Come on, dogs." I led them through the kitchen to one of the bedrooms. I shut them in and they immediately protested with canine yips and barks.

"Do I hear dogs?" Murphy asked.

"Gatsby and Daisy. Irish setters," I whispered. "Daisy is going to have puppies soon. I wish we had a dog, Liam."

"If you want one, we'll get one," he promised me.

The phone was cordless and I carried it with me to the back door, opened it and stood just outside so Colin would see me and bring Mary in. He was halfway down the path, Evie trailing behind him like Banquo's ghost, wringing her hands and stumbling.

Once inside, Colin gently deposited Mary on the couch, making sure to prop her head with one of the throw pillows. He was drenched and dripped rainwater on the carpet.

Mary's teeth chattered and she shook with cold and shock.

"I've got to help Colin with Mary," I whispered into the phone.

"It's all right, honey. We'll be there soon. I'll talk to you then," Murphy said. The phone dropped from my fingers, bounced twice and came to rest under the rocking chair in the corner of the room.

Between the two of us, Colin and I managed to strip off Mary's wet jacket. Beneath it, her sweater was dry. Her jeans were soaked, but there was no way we could get them off her because of her ankle. They'd need to be cut off. We wrapped her in one of the afghans and put the other on top of her, leaving her uncovered below the knee. Each time I saw the white bone sticking straight up like a judgmental finger, I shuddered.

Colin kept up a steady stream of encouraging conversation and, while Mary's responses grew more and more sluggish, she tried to focus on him.

As I went into the kitchen to put on the tea kettle in the probably vain hope Mary might drink something warm, I noticed Evie standing just outside the back door under a small awning that sheltered her from the direct downpour. The wind made sure to gust the occasional spatter into her face anyway.

"The dogs are in one of the bedrooms," I said through the screen door.

"I can smell them." Her lips trembled with the cold.

"Make yourself useful and go stand on the front porch if you can't bring yourself to come in among the dog smell. You can direct people in here. Do something instead of just stand there," I suggested.

She swallowed hard. "Why are you being so mean to me?" Her eyes filled with tears of self-pity.

My conscience nagged me. I *was* being a bitch. How a person reacted in a crisis was a pretty good indicator of their basic personality and my guess was, I wasn't coming off very favorably under stress at all today.

"I'm sorry. Please go stand at the front door. I swear the dogs are locked away and they won't hurt you. I'm making some tea. You want some?"

"Please." She stood there and made no move to come in until I opened the door for her.

An electric kettle perched on the counter by the sink. I filled it, plugged it in and flipped the switch. After I found mugs in the cupboard by the refrigerator, I put them out on the counter and put tea bags in each one from a canister near the stove. I tried not to let my hands shake, but they were not very cooperative.

Fifteen minutes had passed, surely. Where the hell were Jason and Murphy? The torrential rain probably slowed them down. I caught back a terrified cry when the idea of an accident smashed through my mind. No. Fate could not be so cruel. I was just nervous as hell because of Mary and the trap.

"Mary, can you drink any of this?" I knelt on the carpet beside her with a mug of hot tea. I'd put in plenty of milk to cool it down to a drinkable heat and lots of sugar as well. I'd read somewhere sugar was good for people in shock. At least I thought I had.

Colin crouched beside me, unwilling to move very far away. The skin was pulled tight across the bridge of his nose and around his mouth and he was trying very hard to keep a lid on his panic and temper. He shuddered as he leaned against me, seemingly as desperate for touch as I was.

"Stanzie?" Mary turned her head on the pillow and her brown eyes were fever bright. Pain turned them nearly black. She clutched at me, her long fingernails digging into my arm. I tried not to wince or spill the tea.

"I'm here, Mary," I said in as soothing a tone as I could muster. With my free hand, I smoothed some wet hair from her face. She was so cold.

"I want...I'm sorry for calling you a small town, tiny pack nobody." Tears dribbled from the corner of her eyes that weren't entirely due to pain, I suspected. The smell of her remorse lent credence to her words.

"Mary." It was so hard not to cry. The words burned in my throat. How could she be thinking of something she'd said to me two days ago?

Sure, it had been a spiteful, horrible thing to say, but why would she even remember that in the face of so much agony? "I'm sorry for calling you a big city, large pack bitch."

She made a noise that was almost laughter and Colin buried his face in my shoulder for a moment.

"I'm going to die, aren't I?" Her nails dug deeper, but I refused to pull away.

"No. You broke your ankle, sweetie. But they'll fix it. You're not going to die."

"I didn't just break my ankle," she argued. "I can see it as well as you can. Tell me that's…that's just a broken ankle? You're more delirious than me, if you believe that. I don't want to die."

"You're not going to die," Colin said fiercely. "You hear me, damn you?"

"I can't be Alpha like this. You did it all for…nothing, Col. Isn't that funny?"

"They will fix you." Colin's throat worked convulsively until he managed to swallow whatever obstruction had been there.

"I'll be crippled. Maybe I should join your pack. Be a…small town, tiny pack nobody. Like Stanzie. Only for real."

"You won't have to leave Mac Tire, but you will always have a place in my pack," Colin told her. "This is a dumb conversation, Lancaster. You're not dying and you're still Alpha."

"Poor Richard," said Mary.

"They're here," Evie called from the front door. She swung it open and the four men rushed in. Jason and Richard reached the couch first. Jason knelt by Mary's mangled ankle, while Richard thrust me aside none too gently.

Tea sloshed over my arm and dribbled onto the carpet. I stared down at the stain like an idiot until Murphy wrapped an arm around my shoulders and carefully nudged me toward the kitchen, which was separated from the great room by a half wall with an oak railing along the top.

"Sorry it took so long. A tree went down and we had to shift it."

For the first time I realized he was sopping wet, his hair plastered to his skull. Mud and wet tree bark clung to his jeans and jacket.

"Drink this." I thrust what was left of the hot tea into his hands and he took a grateful sip, grimacing at the sweetness. "Too much sugar, I know," I said and bit my lip. Why the fuck was I rambling about inconsequential things like sugar? I was such an idiot.

"Drink some yourself." Murphy handed the mug back and I obediently lifted it to my mouth. The tea tasted spicy, maybe chai, and I couldn't help but sigh when the welcome warmth slid down my throat. I was freezing cold and wet, although nowhere near as drenched as Murphy.

I squeezed my eyes shut when Mary wailed from the couch. Jason's soothing apology shortly followed, but whatever he'd done, I'm sure it had been necessary. Only, what could he do with a bone sticking straight up like that?

Evie had wrapped herself around Angus like a barnacle the second he'd cleared the front door and I watched him trying to ease out of her grip, but having very little success. He was as soaked as Murphy and had a brown leaf stuck to his beard. He must have stood at the top of the tree when they'd moved it.

Brilliant deduction, Sherlock.

Colin lurched into the kitchen. He'd knelt for so long, maybe his legs had fallen asleep. Or it was the shock. Murphy caught him before he fell, saving him from striking his head a nasty blow against the edge of the cabinets.

"You all right, mate?" He brought Colin to a corner between the sink and the refrigerator and Colin leaned into the counter. He appeared dazed and he blinked, clearly having trouble focusing.

I brought him a mug of tea with milk and lots of sugar. I helped him hold it as he lifted it to his mouth. Murphy hovered on his other side, his expression grim.

"I'm getting to be an expert at opening traps." Colin's smile was more of a grimace, and it scared me. "I reckon one more and I'll have it down pat. Either one of you volunteering for the starring role?"

"Colin." When I said his name, his mouth trembled and he set the tea aside on the counter so he could cover his eyes with the palms of his hands. He pressed hard.

"She thinks she'll be a cripple and they won't want her for Alpha." His whole body shuddered.

"That's pack law," said Evie as she and Angus, wound together like two giant squids, arms and legs for tentacles, shambled into the kitchen. "Poor Mary." She burst into tears again and buried her face in Angus's shirt front.

"Fuck your bloody pack law." Colin's voice was savage and when he lowered his hands, his eyes blazed.

Angus took one look at his expression and tightened his grip on Evie. He and Murphy exchanged one of those glances between two men that meant they had each other's backs in the event of violence.

"We aren't going to talk about this right now," I said. "For one, it's sheer speculation and for another, Mary is twenty feet away and this conversation is not going to happen. Now who wants tea?"

"I'd throw up if I drank anything," Evie whined.

"Right, no tea for Evie. The rest of you?" I pinned each of the men with my best don't-give-me-any-shit glare.

I needed to do something productive with my hands so I didn't slap Evie silly.

My temper strained on its leash and I was ashamed of myself. Some people could really get under the skin without even trying. Evie was one of those doomed people, never meaning to be in the way or annoying, but always managing one or the other and frequently both. I shouldn't let her timidity get to me.

I made a lot of tea.

* * * *

Colin stared out at the darkness from the window seat in the library at the safe house. He'd ignored the brandy I'd poured for him and hadn't spoken since he'd refused to go to the clinic to wait for news of Mary's surgery.

Murphy and I brought him back to the safe house, but I hadn't let him go to his room to brood alone and had herded him into the library.

Angus and Evie had returned with us, but had gone directly to their room.

Grandmother Nan brought us homemade oatmeal cookies and coffee, but Colin refused to touch any of it.

I couldn't resist the cookies and in the three hours we'd waited, I'd managed to polish off four of them and two mugs of coffee.

At six, Grandmother Nan brought in a tray of ham-and-cheese sandwiches on thick, homemade bread and a bowl of fresh fruit. Tea instead of coffee.

Murphy ate two of the sandwiches. When I brought one to Colin, he once again ignored me and continued to stare out at the rainy darkness.

I set the sandwich beside his untouched brandy and sat beside him. He had a smear of Mary's blood across one cheek. I got up, went to the table of food, opened a bottle of water and poured some onto a cloth napkin.

Colin flinched when I wiped the blood off his cheek, but didn't push me away. More blood had dried on his pants and sweater. I had quite a bit on me too. Murphy's hair was in desperate need of combing and his clothes were likely still damp. We all looked a mess.

I didn't know how much, if anything, Grandmother Nan knew, but she'd just smiled and given us food. After years of experience running a safe house, she'd probably learned to expect anything and ask no questions.

"I wish you'd eat something." Colin stared out the window and didn't acknowledge me. "Why wouldn't you go to the clinic?"

A shudder ran through him.

"Piss off," he said.

Murphy paused mid-bite of his second sandwich and glanced in our direction.

"She'll be all right, Colin," I said.

"Stanzie, you have no fucking right to say that. You *don't* know that." Colin glared at me and Murphy put down his sandwich and listened.

"You got her out of the trap. You heard Jason say the reason Ben lost his leg is because he'd been in the trap too long. You got her out within the first five minutes."

"Bloody luck," he said.

"Her good fortune. I couldn't get her out."

"You called for help." He shut his eyes for a moment and looked exhausted. When he opened them he said, "Mary kept asking for you when she came back to consciousness. I thought you two despised each other, but you did your best for her when she needed you. Evie stood there sniveling and sobbing, but you got down on the ground with Mary, didn't you? You're covered with her blood the same as I am.

"This is not the bloody conspiracy. This is two stubborn packs going too far across the line." Colin drew his lips back in a snarl, but then the animation left his face and he turned toward the window again. "This was personal against the Mac Tire Alphas. A trap in their bloody back garden, for Christ's sake."

"The trouble is, we've got to figure out who set it." Murphy's tone was grim. "So far you haven't had any luck tracing the traps through antiques dealers or online vendors, have you?

"No." Colin gritted his teeth. In addition to having him feed Mary's dogs, Jason had apparently assigned Colin some research tasks.

We were silent for a moment, the heavy weight of the situation crushing our spirits.

"At least we know it was Stony Fell." Colin's eyes were feral bright.

"Do we?" Murphy picked up his sandwich and took another bite.

"Of course we bloody do," snapped Colin. "Who the fuck in Mac Tire would set a trap in their own Alphas' back garden?"

"I can think of three right off the bat," I said and Colin scowled at me. "Alison and Garrett?" I prompted him. His face lost all color.

"Come off it, Stanzie. They've been Mac Tire for years now."

"Colin, you were there in their house. Did they seem like a happy couple to you? All that talk about accepting their fate gracefully? Did you really buy it? If they had been okay with the past, why did they kick the shit out of Frazier and Elspeth?"

Colin winced, but then said, "There's a duo who has a hell of a lot more incentive to lash out at Mac Tire than Alison and Garrett. Anyway, you said three people in Mac Tire. Who's the third?"

"Tracy," I answered. Colin's face screwed up in confusion, so I told him about the conversation I'd overheard between her and Mary yesterday. I left out a lot of what Mary had said, but I knew Colin read between the lines.

He and Murphy listened intently.

"Just spite? She'd do something like this for spite?" Colin probably didn't want to be convinced, but I saw the dawning horror in his face.

"You heard both Evie and Mary say it today. If Mary's crippled, she can't be Alpha. If Richard had walked into the trap and been disabled, it'd be the same thing. Mary would have to step aside as Alpha. Conceivably, she could break her bond with him and find someone who had a shot at Alpha, but I don't think the pack would look too kindly on her for that, would they? Her chances at regaining Alpha status would be pretty slim," I said.

"That motive works just as well for Stony Fell," Colin said. "With Mary and Richard out as Alphas, there would be a great opportunity for Angus and Evie to step in as the new Alphas if the packs merged. It would solve everything, wouldn't it?"

"Yes." From Murphy's expression, it was obvious he'd been thinking about that very scenario. I hadn't considered that. Would Mac Tire hand over the reins to the Stony Fell Alphas? To keep the peace? Even if a Stony Fell member were responsible for setting the traps in the first place? God, pack politics were diabolical.

"Angus and Evie could have set that trap." Colin took one of my hands between both of his and squeezed hard for emphasis.

"When?" I asked. Jason made sure to have both Alpha duos in the safe house under observation since we'd found Ben's wolf in the trap.

"Jesus, I don't know." Colin sighed.

"Richard told us in the car today that they bring the dogs for walks on that path every day. They'd done it last just before they met you and Stanzie here for the tour in the woods where you found Ben. It doesn't seem likely there was a trap there at that point. If one of them hadn't stepped in it, for sure one of the dogs would have," Murphy said.

"So it's down to Garrett and Alison, Elspeth and Frazier or Tracy." Colin struggled to keep control. He snatched the brandy snifter from the side table and gulped down half of it.

"They seem indicated. Stanzie, who do you think is most likely?" Murphy sat forward in his chair and fixed me with his penetrating dark gaze.

I slowly shook my head. I had no fucking clue. "It seems so cold. Tracy ran out of here pissed off as hell. If she set it, she did it in a white hot rage, but I really can't believe she set the first trap. That means we'd have two potential culprits.

"If Garrett and Alison did it, they could have set both. Alison, especially, has a ruthless streak and Garrett probably follows her lead. If they set the first trap after they had the fight with Elspeth and Frazier, they could have also set the second one.

"And I suppose Elspeth and Frazier might have set the first one as well as the second. But you're forgetting about Bonnie and Keith. They've got the motive for setting this second trap and the opportunity. Nobody's been watching them. But I swear they didn't set the first trap. Both traps looked the same so what are the chances of two different people using the same type of trap? Especially if Colin hasn't found a local store that sells them. But if they did set this trap, we've not solved who set the first one." I buried my face in my hands. What a tangled, fucked up mess.

"And there might be somebody we don't even know about. It's not like we interviewed everyone in Mac Tire," I added.

"Whoever it was, I'm going to kill them," Colin said.

"You don't want to go down that road. *V* for vigilante. It's a one-way street, Colin." Murphy's eyes were dark. Was he reliving the moment he'd plunged the knife into Grandfather Mick's heart?

"Someone is going to pay for what they did to Mary," Colin vowed, and when I looked at him, tears stood out in his eyes, glittering prisms he smashed to bits when he rubbed at his eyes.

I put my arms around him and he buried his face in my neck. I rocked him slowly as he struggled against exhausted, hopeless tears. Murphy stared at the floor.

Colin pushed away from me when he had himself under control. He looked straight at Murphy. "I love Mary the same way you loved Sorcha. Obsessive. Nothing else matters. Do anything for her love."

I really tried not to let his words prick my heart, but they did. I could still hear Murphy shouting at me never to compare myself to Sorcha. Colin didn't include me and how much Murphy loved me because he could obviously tell for himself Murphy's feelings for me weren't nearly the same thing.

"A martyr for love?" Murphy's tone was savage and Colin jerked his head in agreement. "Well, good luck with that, mate. Hope you fare better than I did with it."

"It's the kind of love that never has a happy ending. I know that," said Colin.

"I wonder if you fucking do." Murphy went across the hall to the lounge and returned with bottle of Jameson's and three shot glasses.

Colin took a glass, but I refused the one Murphy tried to hand to me. I turned and looked out the window instead. The wind lashed the rain against the windows and it was impossible to see much, but I made out the smear of headlights. Jason was back.

Colin saw the lights too and went rigid beside me, clutching his whiskey between both hands, face white.

A few moments later, Jason walked into the lounge. His hair needed combing and his shirt was bloodstained and creased. He looked beyond tired as he took the chair by the fireside and reached his hands out to it. How many rooms just like this had he spent his life? His duties most likely rarely allowed him the luxury of being home. What did Jason's home even look like? Had he let Wren redecorate or was she stranded in a sea of things that represented his past?

I gave him my untouched shot of whiskey and when he took it from me, the brush of his fingers against my wrist was deliberate, his smile both grateful and affectionate.

"Thank you." His blue eyes were bloodshot. When he spoke, it was to the whole room, but he kept his gaze on me. "Mary won't lose her foot."

Relief made muscles I hadn't known were tense relax all over my body.

"But will she be crippled?" Colin demanded.

"We think between physical therapy and the pack bond, no, she won't."

Colin slumped against the window. Exhausted, he squeezed his eyes shut, but he still had energy enough to smile.

"Pack bond." I rubbed my wrist where Ben's wolf had bitten it. Mac Tire, both the Irish and English branch, were over a hundred members strong. The more people the bond included, the greater the healing power.

"One of the many advantages of larger packs." Jason reached out for my arm and pushed back the sleeve of my sweater. The skin of my wrist was blameless.

Now was not the time to argue that potentially crippling injuries were rare—maybe infrequent enough to make it worth taking the risk to form smaller packs so women who belonged could have a chance at having a baby, but I still thought it.

"Could Colin and I be the ones to spread the news?" I took the chair across from Jason's, keenly aware of Murphy's gaze upon the back of my head.

Colin opened his eyes, weary relief banished by sharp interest.

Jason downed the whiskey in the shot glass in one practiced swallow and looked at me.

We exchanged a frank and completely unspoken moment of perfect accord. I was no mind reader, but I knew damn well what he was thinking. Depending on the spin Colin and I put on the story, we could be in a very good position to observe reactions from the various suspects.

"I was rather hoping you would. I've got other Council business to attend to tomorrow and you can report back to me at dinner tomorrow evening. Shall we say around six in my suite?" Jason set the shot glass aside and rose to his feet. "Good night. It's been a very long day. May I suggest we all get as much rest as we can tonight? Tomorrow will be equally as long, I suspect."

* * * *

Upstairs, I took a long, hot shower and washed the blood off my face and out of my hair. I threw on a pair of sweats and a t-shirt and combed my wet hair before I went into the bedroom. I hoped I'd find Murphy asleep, but he was at his laptop, the glow illuminating his tired face.

I crawled beneath the covers and shut my eyes. The shower hissed into life again.

When Murphy, smelling of soap and water, came to bed, he curled himself against my back the way he always did. I pretended I was asleep, but I wasn't. I'd been miserably recounting Colin's conversation with Murphy about love. I'd tortured myself with everything I knew about Murphy's relationship with Sorcha. According to him, Sorcha had never slept in the same bed with him, preferring her own. She only spent time in his bed when they'd had sex. He'd never spent the night curled against her back, safe and warm, yet he'd loved her with an obsessive love that couldn't touch the way he felt about me. She'd never loved him and told him so, but he'd never stopped loving her.

I supported him and loved him back and he knew it. I spent every night in bed with him, wrapped my whole world around him, and couldn't even compare myself to her or he'd blow up at me.

"Why are you so tense?" His voice in the dark was soft and concerned. He rubbed my back with the heel of his hand, but I squirmed away.

"I'm not tense, I'm tired. Good night, Liam."

"You're mad at me," he said as if it was a huge surprise.

"I'm not mad." Lie, but I so didn't want to get into it. Besides, I couldn't. I wasn't allowed to compare myself to the exalted Sorcha and therefore my hands were tied.

"Huh. You only call me Liam when you're mad, scared shitless, or feeling especially close to me. I don't think you're scared and I'm sure as hell not feeling the love right now, so that only leaves one option, doesn't it?"

"You know, whatever. I just want to sleep, okay?"

"No, it's not okay. I want to know why you're mad. Do you think I'm going to compare you to Celine Ducharme again because of this scheme you and Jason have to flush out who set those traps?"

He was honestly that clueless. Unbelievable.

"Why are you even here? I know they called in the Regional Council, but what exactly have you contributed so far to this whole thing?" I wondered.

He drew back from me and even though I couldn't see his face, I knew he was staring at me. I could feel it.

"Not a hell of a lot, true." He sounded hurt. "This is Allerton's show and everyone knows it. I'm here to watch, basically."

"Well, good job. Pat yourself on the back for that. Can I please go to sleep?"

"I want to come with you tomorrow when you question everyone. You're putting yourself on the line again and Jason's letting you."

"Colin will be with me. I won't be alone."

Murphy's tone was sharp with aggravation. "I told you I would be there for you and I will be. Let me come tomorrow. Isn't that what you want?"

"No, it is not what I want. You're not an Advisor anymore. The work in the trenches is my job. You're supposed to, I don't know, do whatever the hell a Councilor does. Sit around watching, apparently."

"You don't want me to come?" The scent of his frustration stung my nostrils.

"No, I don't," I answered truthfully.

"Is there something you *think* I should be doing instead because if so, can you please enlighten me?"

"No, watching is good." I inched toward the edge of the mattress.

He inhaled, and a moment later exhaled heavily. "Will you please talk to me and tell me what the hell is wrong? How can I fix it if you won't tell me what I did?"

"You can't fix everything. There isn't a fix for what's wrong and who says I care anyway." With a muttered oath, I threw my pillow on the floor. I didn't need the pillow and I didn't need Liam Murphy.

"Honey, what did I do?" All his frustration melted into genuine dismay. "I'm sorry whatever it is. I didn't mean it."

"Of course you didn't. Just go to sleep, Liam. It's not important."

"I'll go to sleep when you call me Murphy."

"I'm the only one who ever does. Ever notice that? Everybody stares at me when I do. I'm going to call you Liam from now on. That's your name, isn't it?"

"I like it when you call me Murphy." Now he sounded sad and I steeled my stupid heart against him. He'd never love me like he loved her and it didn't matter. Time to stop being jealous over something I could never change.

"Do you want me to go home? Is that it? Stanzie, I can't. I may only be watching events transpire, but I'm representing the Regional Council."

"You don't have to explain it to me. I know why you're here. Please, can I just sleep?"

"Sure, fine." He rolled to his back and fell silent. I smelled his confusion and hurt anger, but blocked it out. Tomorrow I wouldn't be angry, I would be resigned. And cheerful as hell. But I would not call him Murphy.

Chapter 13

Murphy was deep into whatever he was doing on his laptop the next morning when I woke. I listened to him type for a few moments before I stretched beneath the covers and sat up, rubbing my eyes.

"Hey," he said when I blinked away crusty sleep and could focus. He'd turned away from the laptop with a wistful smile.

"Hey." I smiled back at him. He got up and came to sit beside me on the bed so he could pull me into his arms. I went willingly enough, but a part of me felt so much like crying I had to shut my eyes.

"I love you." His arms were so tight I could barely breathe.

"Love you too," I said because I did.

"Then we're all right?" he whispered.

"Yeah." My stomach gurgled and he laughed. He kissed my hair before he reluctantly let me go.

"I smell bacon. Hurry up and get dressed. I'll let you have half of mine if you give me a kiss and call me Murphy."

"Bribing me with food. That's bad," I teased. I kissed him, but didn't call him Murphy. His face fell, but he didn't push it.

I threw on a pair of jeans and the dark plum sweater Maureen had knitted for me. After I pulled my hair back into a pony tail, I traced eyeliner and eye shadow around my eyes. Screw lipstick. Which shoes to wear gave me a few moments' pause, but I went with the black knee-high boots. I cursed the fact I'd brought only six pairs of shoes with me. Two were evening wear which left me only four pairs to wear by day and I'd already worn the boots before. Twice. I needed to go shopping. Or go home.

Halfway out the door, Murphy pulled me back and pressed me against the wall so he could melt against me, his mouth against mine. So possessive, my knees nearly buckled under his sensual assault. I kissed him back, twining my tongue with his.

"I love you," he said again, a hint of desperation in his voice.

"I love you too," I whispered against his lips. "Now are we going to breakfast or back to bed?" My stomach growled again and he laughed.

"I guess that's the answer." He stepped back, but didn't release me. His eyes were dark with passion and the barest hint of baffled hope.

His cheek was smooth beneath my fingertips, betraying the fact he must have shaved before I woke. How long how he had been up?

"Didn't you sleep well?" I asked.

"No. I didn't. I was worried. About us." He turned his face so he could kiss my palm.

"Don't be," I told him. "I'm sorry I was such a bitch."

"Are you ever going to tell me what I did wrong?"

I shook my head. "Forget it. Really, it's not important. Certainly nothing that should have ruined your rest. Sorry for that too. Come on, I want that bacon."

Murphy followed me down the narrow staircase to the ground floor. Angus and Evie ate breakfast at the table beneath the window where I'd sat with Colin the first day. Both looked morose.

Richard sat with Colin and Jason at the table in front of the fireplace. His handsome face was drawn with exhaustion and worry. A plate of untouched food rested in front of him, eggs cold and congealed.

I slid into the chair beside him and gave him an impulsive hug. He relaxed against me immediately, seemingly grateful for the touch.

"Thank you for being there for Mary yesterday." When he straightened, he reached out a shaky hand for his tea cup.

Across the room, the sound of Angus's and Evie's chairs scraping the floor as they stood up was almost as loud as the crackle of the fire in the grate behind Jason. The bells above the front door jangled, and I turned to the window to watch Evie and Angus walk down the stairs toward the car park.

"They're going to the clinic to visit with Mary and, I presume, Ben," Richard said when he noticed my attention had wandered.

"They were very relieved to hear about Mary," said Colin from around a mouthful of rye toast. His gaze met mine and I knew he'd tell me more when we were alone.

Lying awake half the night being jealous of a dead woman had caused me to oversleep, it seemed, but thankfully Colin had taken the lead this morning.

Grandmother Nan hurried to the table bearing a tray of two full English breakfasts and a pot of coffee. She'd soon learned my preference for that caffeinated elixir in the morning. In addition to the bacon, spicy links of sausage steamed on the plates next to mounds of creamy yellow scrambled eggs. Baked beans as well. I'd never get used to beans at breakfast, but Murphy piled his on top of a buttered piece of toast and bit into it hungrily.

He picked up both slices of his bacon and put them on my plate. I gave him my eggs and beans. Colin watched the exchange with a bemused expression while Jason immersed himself in the paper as usual. Richard stared into space. His skin was gray with exhaustion and fine lines radiated from the edges of his lips.

"You really don't look well." I put a hand on his arm to get his attention. "Did you sleep at all last night, Richard?"

He came back to himself with a start and sloshed tea onto the tablecloth. He grimaced. "No."

"You should go back to bed," I suggested and Jason observed us both over the top of his paper. Murphy busied himself with his toast and beans and Colin helped himself to coffee after draining the tea in his cup.

"There's so much to do. I have to get back to Mary." Richard's voice was gravely with weariness.

"You just told me Angus and Evie went to visit her. Colin and I are going too. Aren't we, Col?"

Colin nodded as though he'd known that had been plan all along although I'd just that minute decided our course of action.

"She doesn't like to be alone. I spent the night sitting up with her, but this morning she made me come back here to rest. Only, it feels callous to sleep when my bond mate is lying in a hospital bed in great pain."

"She's not in much pain, Richard. She's sedated to take the edge off," Jason told him. "You're about to fall out of your chair. Go upstairs. Liam and I will be here all day and if you're needed, we'll let you know."

Richard didn't argue. He used the table for support as he stood then stumbled toward the stairs. I watched him intently, ready to spring after him if he tripped. I doubted he'd even bother to take off his clothes before falling into bed once in his room.

"About me staying here all day," said Murphy once Richard was out of earshot and before Jason could return to his paper. "I thought maybe I'd go with Stanzie and Colin instead."

He kept his gaze fixed on Jason, not me, but I knew damn well he was vitally aware of my reaction to his words. Was he expecting me to argue as I had last night?

"For what purpose?" Jason's tone was politely curious. He no longer had jurisdiction over Murphy and couldn't precisely boss him around, but he was a Great Councilor to Murphy's Regional. A request from Jason was as good as a command and by Murphy's determined expression, he was well aware of that.

"He thinks I'm going to put myself in danger," I said before Murphy could answer.

Murphy glanced in my direction then back to Jason. "Yeah, that."

Colin snorted into his coffee.

"I was under the impression Colin would be with her." Jason rustled the paper as he turned a page, but I was pretty sure he wasn't reading.

"Me too." Colin gave Murphy a challenging grin which made Murphy grit his teeth.

"I just thought maybe I'd tag along."

"I'd prefer you to stay here. There's a Council conference call at ten and I suspect the Regional Councilors who plan to be on it will be expecting you to be there as well."

"Goddamn it," Murphy muttered, trapped. He turned his smoldering attention to Colin who wore a *bring it on* grin that only made Murphy angrier.

"You." Murphy pointed a finger at Colin menacingly. "You don't leave her side for one minute today. You hear me?"

"What if she needs to go to the bathroom?" Colin asked, straight-faced, and I thought Murphy would launch himself over the table top. Jason's blue eyes twinkled, but he managed not to laugh.

"You stand outside the goddamn door until she comes back out," snarled Murphy.

"Is this per order of the Regional Council or overprotective bond mate?" Colin wondered.

"Neverfuckingmind by whose order, you just do it. Got me?"

"Sure." Colin gave him a mock salute with two fingers to his forehead.

Murphy's laugh sent a chill down my spine. "Go ahead, fuck with me. You're not always going to be sitting at a breakfast table with a Great Councilor to hide behind, you bastard."

"Liam. I will not leave her side." Colin became deadly serious in an instant. "I promise."

"Yeah, your fucking promises mean a lot to me." Murphy glared at him. "If something happens to her, I'm gunning for you, Hunter. You understand?"

"Perfectly." Colin glanced at my plate, saw it was empty, and shoved back his chair. "Stanzie, let's go."

"'Bye, Liam." I turned to Murphy and brushed a kiss across his smooth cheek. A little qualm of conscience struck me because I didn't call him Murphy, but I squashed it.

"Stanzie." Murphy took my face between his hands. "I'm serious. Be careful. Please?" His voice was gruff with worry and I kissed him again, this time on the lips.

"Tonight at dinner, you watch, I'll have this thing solved. I want to go on that road trip and I'm getting tired of waiting."

He grinned at me, but worry still shadowed his eyes.

"Just come back in one piece, will you? If there's anything risky to be done, you let Hunter stand in the line of fire. He's expendable. You're not."

"Oi," said Colin.

"I'll be careful," I promised.

Murphy did not look convinced. I had to pull his hands away from my face, and even then, he twined his fingers with mine and squeezed as if he couldn't bear to let me go.

"I'll be careful." I pried my fingers from his. He let me do it, but the worry and fear in his eyes was a silent reproach as I hurried out into the cold autumn morning, Colin hard on my heels.

* * * *

Ben and Mary had rooms in a small private care facility where the Mac Tire pack doctor and both nurses worked. Another Mac Tire member worked as a physical therapist. Pack from all over the UK were transferred to this facility if their injuries were severe enough. I was more than a little impressed one pack would boast not only a doctor but nurses and a physical therapist as well. Another positive for larger packs?

The door to the private, four-room wing where Ben and Mary convalesced was locked, but the visitor passes Colin and I were issued at the reception desk opened it via a small badge reader.

Inside, the corridor smelled of disinfectant and tears.

We found Tracy huddled in a small waiting room furnished with six chairs, a round coffee table and a repurposed desk which held urns of coffee and tea, a tower of paper cups and a tin of cookies. Biscuits. This was the UK.

The sight of her strawberry blond hair sent a chill down my spine. Callie's hair had been almost the same shade. Dressed in jeans and a wrinkled blouse, she looked as if she'd grabbed the clothes from a hamper waiting to be washed. She needed a shower. A mound of used tissues littered the carpet around her booted feet and an empty box rested on the chair beside her.

"Maybe he'll see you, but he won't let me in the room anymore." Tracy spoke to her knees, not us. A curtain of lank hair concealed her expression.

"We want to talk to you, actually." I moved the empty tissue box to the coffee table and sat beside her. Colin went to the desk and fixed us coffee. For a moment the only sound in the room was the squeak of the desk drawers as Colin opened them to retrieve, sugar, creamer and stirrers.

I tucked a strand of Tracy's hair behind one of her ears and she looked at me. Her blue eyes, red-rimmed and swollen, made mine ache in sympathy. God, she was young. I had to remind myself she was twenty because stripped of makeup and full of despair, she appeared to be in her teens. Surely this girl had not cold-bloodedly set a trap for her Alpha?

"Did you know Mary was here too?" I asked her.

Her mouth got small and sullen. "That bitch. I hate her. I suppose she's come to work out the details for Ben to join Mac Tire. I would have thought Richard would do that. Mary's purely ornamental and twice as useless." She shot a vindictive look at Colin, who calmly continued to stir sugar and creamer into one of the coffees.

It had been nearly five years since he'd been bonded with Mary in this pack, but Tracy would remember, even if she had been an adolescent at the time.

"Someone set another trap, Tracy," I said. She went very still, as if straining to hear something no one else could. "On the Mac Tire Alphas' property. Mary was caught in it yesterday."

Shock made her gasp. Dark gladness glowed across her face, but tears of grief also stood out in her eyes. I could smell her sorrow, she couldn't fake that, but was it for her Alpha in general, or Mary in particular? For herself, for what she'd been pushed into doing?

There was no question she was glad, on some level, to hear the news and that made my heart squeeze into a painful ball.

"Did you set it?" Colin thrust a cup of coffee at her and she took it automatically. Her lips parted, but no sound emerged.

"Did you?" Colin's expression was terrifying. Tracy put the coffee down and shrank against her chair. The thud of her heart was clearly audible.

"Why…why would you think I did something like that?" Tracy licked her dry lips and scooted toward me as much as she could so our arms brushed. Did she think I'd protect her?

"You just said you hated Mary." Colin stepped closer so he towered over us, his blue eyes stormy with menace. He set the other two cups next to Tracy's. Fingers curled into fists, he made even me nervous.

Tracy's mouth tightened and the defiant look she gave Colin tempted fate. "I hate her because she won't help me with Ben. She says a cripple can't be Alpha. Well, then, she can't either anymore, can she? Serves her bloody well right."

The heat of Colin's fury was blistering.

If he went for her, I'd have to get in the middle. Murphy would kill me if I came back to the safe house bruised and bloodied, but what else was I supposed to do?

"For your information, you pathetic little cow, Mary's not going to be crippled," Colin said. "She has the pack bond to fall back on, remember? Which your boyfriend would have had if he hadn't left his birth pack."

"You're one to talk, Colin Hunter. You left your birth pack and now you're Alpha of another one and an Advisor to a Great Councilor. If you're trying to say Ben was an idiot for wanting some of things you've managed to get for yourself, you're a bloody hypocrite, aren't you?" Tracy had no room to stand, but her fear had been replaced by burning rage. If she leaped at Colin, I would also be forced to throw myself between her and Colin or there'd be a bloodbath. Murphy was really going to be pissed off, I just knew it.

"Did you set that trap, Tracy?" Colin loomed over us.

"Go fuck yourself." Tracy wasn't backing down.

Good thing we were in a private health care facility because it seemed likely one or more of us would end up requiring medical help.

Incredibly, Colin threw back his head and laughed. "A simple no would have worked just as well. More polite too. Remember, I am an Advisor and older than you. Not that it counts for much, but I'm Alpha of my pack too. A little respect, Tracy."

"I will give you respect when you give me the same in return. Advisor doesn't translate into bully, does it?" Tracy clutched the arms of her chair so tightly her fingers looked cramped. I winced and flexed mine.

"I had to be sure, love." Colin sat beside her, apparently ready for a long chat. My heart still raced sickeningly and I wished I could change emotional gears so damn quickly. How the hell did he do that?

"I didn't set a trap. After what happened to Ben and seeing firsthand what one can do, I would never." Tracy's lips trembled and she hid her face in her hands.

Colin made a soothing sound and put his arm around her. She crawled over the arm of the chair into his lap and sobbed into his shoulder while he murmured comforting words and patted her back.

I snatched one of the coffees off the table and gulped at it. Maybe they had prior history together I didn't know about.

The anger in the room dissipated and Tracy's choking sobs gradually tapered off, but Colin made no move to shift her from his lap.

By this time, I'd gone through all three cups of coffee and my bladder was screaming.

"Colin, I'm running to the rest room. Meet you in the hall?"

He acknowledged me with a nod. He knew as well as I did we had more people to interrogate. He might be convinced Tracy didn't set the trap for Mary, but I wasn't sure I was. Men could be so blindsided by women's tears. Especially the tears of pretty women who crawled into their laps.

* * * *

"I don't think she did it," Colin told me when I emerged from the restroom.

"So all a girl has to do is crawl on your lap and sob and you'll take her off the suspects list?" I asked. "That's rather unfair to the men. Unless you'd like them to cry on your lap too?"

"Piss off." Colin rolled his eyes. "You jealous?" The thought seemed to scare him. Probably he was thinking of Murphy.

"Colin." I took a step closer to him. He backed away uneasily. "Get real. I'm just pointing out that women can be devious."

"Tracy didn't do it." Colin's expression turned stubborn.

Whatever. We didn't have the time to argue this.

"Are you going to pull the he-man-rip-you-from-limb-to-limb-if-you-don't- answer-my-question routine on everyone we see today?" I asked. "Do you think you might be able to be a bit less aggressive and a little more objective?"

"What?" He stared at me. "Are you insane? We're talking about Mary here. Someone hurt Mary. No, I'm not able to be objective about that and the day I can be is the day I really do become a monster."

A twinge of pain vibrated through my skull and I rubbed my forehead. Great, a headache. Just what I needed.

"Let me do the talking from now on. You stand there and glower, okay?"

"Sure. Good cop, bad cop. I can do that," he agreed.

"This isn't a cop show."

Colin became serious in an instant. "I know. But I respect your experience. I'll follow your lead from now on, I promise."

"You're just as much Jason's Advisor as I am. And you're an Alpha." I was aware that stomping on people's egos rarely went well.

"Please." Colin flashed me an attractive grin. "Every card in your hand trumps the ones I hold. You're right, I should be objective. But I can't be. I'm telling you so you'll know. Mac Tire was my pack once. I watched Tracy grow up. We used to catch fireflies together by the lakeshore. I taught her how to whistle." His smile turned wistful, and my heart clutched.

I put a hand on his arm. "You're doing fine, Colin."

"Bollocks," he said with a snort. "Not according to Allerton, I'm not. He reamed me out badly after I confessed to shagging Mary against that tree. After I researched where a demented psycho might purchase an antique bear trap, which was an exercise in complete futility, I spent most of the rest of yesterday dealing with Allerton's dry cleaning and ringing his bond mate to make sure she was having fun in London. The most engaging thing I did yesterday was give her a few tips on places to visit and where to eat."

My expression must have changed because he dropped the rueful woe-is-me act and frowned.

"Wren's in London?" The idea fascinated me. Hurt a little too. So close, yet I wouldn't see her. Once this case was settled, Murphy and I would go back to Dublin.

"She *is* your mother, isn't she?" Colin asked. I nodded. "She's very shy. I spent forty minutes on the phone with her and I swore I was talking to myself except sometimes I could her breathing."

"She's all alone? Isn't there anyone from Mac Tire who could show her around? Or another pack in England? There's a Councilor who lives in London, isn't there? Couldn't his bond mate give her a tour of the city?"

"She wasn't available and Lauren was spending the day alone."

"What? To prove she could do it? Is this one of Jason's schemes to improve her?" I bit my lip and cursed my stupid tendency to speak before I thought.

Colin's eyes widened, but he didn't say anything.

"Wren was rather sheltered for many years with my father," I said. "She does need to come out of her shell, but alone in a big, foreign city? That seems extreme."

"On her own yesterday," Colin said. "*Yesterday*, love. She's with the Councilor's bond mate, but there was a conference or something she had to attend yesterday. Some charity she's involved in."

"Charity? Some Other charity?" I shook my head, unable to comprehend.

"If we ever do come out to them, wouldn't it be nice if we could prove we're philanthropic and we don't discriminate?"

"But we do," I argued. "We're Pack and we stick together and no Other could ever come between Pack members."

"Don't be too sure of that one," Colin suggested. "There are many people who have turned their backs on the Great Pack so they could live with their Other lovers."

"That's stupid, Colin. We don't age like them. They could keep it up for maybe twenty years. Then their lovers would suspect something."

"Not if they already knew," Colin said, as if that weren't such extreme heresy that I was halfway surprised the lights didn't blow out and lightning strike him down in front of me. He frowned at me. "Are you telling me you've never heard of anyone doing this?"

I shook my head.

"You spent two years alone, didn't you? Did you never take an Other lover?" He seemed incredulous.

"No," I said. He didn't believe me because I'm sure he smelled my guilt. I had slept with an Other once, but not during my self-imposed exile. I'd had a one-night stand the evening I'd quit as Jason's Advisor after he'd announced he was bonding with Wren. Jason had let me go without a fight. I'd gone crazy, gotten drunk at a beach bar. I woke up in bed with an Other I'd sworn the night before had been a dead ringer for Murphy but in the harsh light of day had not even come close.

"It's nothing to be ashamed of," he said.

"Can we please get on with what we're supposed to be doing?" I snarled.

He took a step back and nodded. Great. Now he thought I was a secretive, lying freak. Just the rapport we needed to be partners.

Something he'd said earlier struck me. I blurted, "Are you Pack First, Colin?"

He laughed. "I'm Jason Allerton's Advisor. Would I be if I were Pack First?"

"He might want to try to change your mind," I said. How the hell did he know so much about Jason's position as the leader of the Guardians? Had Jason told him? He'd never told *me*, I'd had to find out from somebody else months after I'd begun working for him. Why did that man never tell me anything? Anger spurted through my veins.

"Keep your friends close, your enemies closer?" Colin laughed. "With Riverglow's history, do you really think Jason would have put a Pack First sympathizer there?"

"Yes, I do," I said. "You were put there to draw out connections Riverglow had with the corrupt sect of the Guardians. How better than to be Pack First? Make yourself a target."

"Diabolical. Your brain works the same way his does. So what if I am Pack First? Would that change anything between us?" Colin asked.

"What do we have between us? We barely know each other." Would it matter to me? Would it affect how I saw him? Interacted with him?

He laughed again, but this time I saw hurt in his eyes. "I've grown rather fond of you, Stanzie. I'd hate for something else to come between us. We've already got Liam making things difficult, it not impossible, for us."

"I can handle Liam," I said.

"But can you handle Pack First sympathies?"

I looked at him. "I don't know."

"Fair answer." He ruffled my hair. "Fine. I do believe Pack First are right. We need to integrate with Others and stop living in the shadows. Allerton and I have had some spirited conversations around this topic and he has some good points, I'll give him that, but so do I."

"We're not going to talk about this. You and me," I decided. "I'm confused enough as it is."

"Hiding your head in the sand doesn't do shit except leave your backside exposed," Colin said. "But right now I guess we should concentrate on the task at hand, no?"

I looked at him and for a moment didn't trust him at all. Pack First. He was in league with people like Celine Ducharme. My conscience pricked me. So was Kathy Manning and I trusted her, didn't I? But we had history. She'd protected and stood by me. Colin Hunter had screwed Murphy over badly. He was an opportunist and had self-esteem issues. That did not seem like a healthy mix to me, especially when combined with the Pack First agenda.

What the hell was Jason thinking?

* * * *

"Hello, Ben." Colin cruised confidently into Ben's small room as if he'd been there before. Perhaps he had. Another of Allerton's errands?

Ben had curly reddish hair and a face more pretty than handsome. I hadn't seen him in human form before today and his male model appearance threw me for a moment. He looked so damn fragile in the hospital bed. The stump of his amputated leg was bandaged and had various tubes sticking out of it for reasons I didn't really understand or want to know. I tried to keep my gaze on his face, not his leg but it wasn't easy.

Bonnie and Keith had pulled up uncomfortable-looking plastic chairs to the bedside and, by their expressions, hadn't been having much luck engaging their son in conversation.

Colin ignored the lack of greeting from Ben and his parents and pushed the remaining chair in the room to the other side of the bed. He gestured for me to sit and I did, but I wasn't quite sure what I would say.

"Still trying to force feed you apple sauce, I see." Colin gestured at the uneaten breakfast tray and rolled his eyes. "At least it's not Jell-O."

"That's for lunch," said Ben, and Bonnie's eyes widened at the sound of her son's voice. "Disgusting crap. Can you get me out of here, Colin?"

"I'm working on it," Colin said cheerfully. "You've got to heal a bit more, is what they keep telling me. You should take the Mac Tire pack bond. That ought to speed things up."

"Sod the pack bond. And Mac Tire." Ben flashed me a sullen look, as if just realizing I was there. "Who the hell are you?"

"Stanzie Newcastle," I said. His nostrils flared as he took in my scent. Recognition flooded his face.

"You held my wolf down," he accused. I flushed. "He bit you. Can I see the wound?"

I pushed back the sleeve of my sweater so he could inspect my unblemished wrist.

"Pack bond?" he guessed as he scowled at me. "What pack are you from?"

"The Irish branch of Mac Tire," I said and felt dirty somehow.

"Bloody hell." Ben's frown intensified. "So if I'd still belonged to the Scottish branch, I'd have my leg, wouldn't I?"

His parents winced, and tears glazed Bonnie's eyes. Keith put a hand on her shoulder, but she seemed barely aware of it. Their guilt must be intense.

"I don't know," I answered, because I didn't.

"Well, I do. I would. My parents convinced me to join Stony Fell so I could be an Alpha someday and now look at me. Prime Alpha material, huh?" Rage coated Ben's voice and twisted his features.

"I'm sorry, Ben," I whispered.

He sighed in disgust. "I don't give a shit what you are. I wish you'd leave."

I pushed back the chair so I could get to my feet. I couldn't think of anything else to say, so I left.

Outside in the hall, I leaned against the wall and struggled against tears. So not good.

Bonnie and Keith appeared at Ben's door.

"Thought we'd get a coffee," Keith said. "Would you join us, Advisor?"

I shrugged and followed them to the small lounge. Tracy was gone. Had Colin convinced her to go home? Maybe she was in the restroom. What did it matter where she was?

Bonnie slumped into a chair, head down, while Keith went to the desk to pour coffee.

"I know you helped our son." He stirred sugar into one of the cups. "We'd like to thank you even if he won't."

"It's okay," I said. "I understand his bitterness."

"It's all our fault," whispered Bonnie. "We only wanted the best for him."

"We could not have anticipated something like this," Keith told her. "Stop blaming yourself, Bonnie."

"I'll blame myself as long as he does." Bonnie clenched her hands into impotent fists.

"Thank you for coming to visit him." Keith handed me a cup of coffee. My bladder twisted in horror, but I took a sip so he wouldn't feel bad.

"Another trap was set," I said. What the hell. How could I tiptoe around this? Colin was just down the hall. If Bonnie and Keith turned violent, one scream would bring him running. I hoped.

"Was someone else hurt?" Keith's fingers tightened around the cups in his hands and one of them crumpled. With an oath, he dropped it, splashing coffee across the cuffs of his pants and the carpet at his feet.

"Mary," I told him, and he turned so pale I feared he would faint.

"Oh my God." Bonnie put a hand to her heart. "Is she all right?"

"A badly broken ankle, but she'll recover." Colin walked into the room and took in the scene without blinking. The pulse beat visibly in his throat, the only sign of his coiled anger. "You two happen to know anything about it?"

So much for me doing all the talking.

"What the hell kind of question is that to ask us?" The fury in Keith's voice was razor sharp. He set the cups on the coffee table and took a step toward Colin, who stood his ground. "You've seen my son in that hospital bed. What kind of a bastard would ask us a question like that?"

"Me," answered Colin. "Someone set that trap. Someone angry that their son would never be an Alpha, perhaps?"

"Why would we go after Mary? The only thing that would make us go after her would be the knowledge she set the trap that hurt Ben. And if she'd done it, I wouldn't be so bloody cowardly as to set a trap for her. I'd confront her face to face and kill her with my bare hands." Keith took another step toward Colin and I got scared. He meant business and I wasn't sure I could do a damn thing to help Colin if there was a brawl.

"Did Mary set the trap?" Bonnie's eyes glowed with rage that matched her bond mate's. I very slowly got to my feet so I could be in a position to at least run for help from the pack doctor if I couldn't physically do anything.

"That's not the question, is it?" Colin spared her one brief, amused glance as Keith took another menacing step.

"We've answered your question, now you answer ours," Bonnie demanded.

"I haven't the slightest fucking idea who set the first trap," Colin confessed. "Are we going to fight, Keith? If we are, let's bring it outside."

"You are not going to fight. We are all going to sit down and shut up for a moment until we get ourselves straight," I said.

Colin obediently took a seat even though it exposed him. Keith growled beneath his breath, but he, too, sat. Bonnie had never gotten to her feet, but some of the wrath died from her eyes.

We sat in a strained silence until Keith said, "You're the only one Ben's currently talking to. Did you know that?"

"I figured," Colin answered. "I sat with him for several hours yesterday morning."

"You were at his side when we got here," Bonnie said. "I apologize, Advisor. I'm ashamed of myself. I swear to you I didn't set any trap."

"Nor did I." Keith's voice was gruff. "How did you get him to talk to you?"

"Just lucky," said Colin.

"You got him out of the trap," I said. "His wolf must remember that."

Colin shrugged, making light of his actions.

"Another reason we owe you." Keith cleared his throat and got to his feet. He walked to Colin and extended his hand. Colin shook it without hesitation. "We're not ourselves, Advisor, as you can well imagine."

"I understand," Colin said. "I'm going to find out who set those bloody traps. I won't rest until I do. Stanzie and I take our jobs very seriously. She downplays her role in Ben's rescue, but you ought to know she held his wolf down, even after he bit her, so I could get the trap off and then she shifted and ran for help. For a while there, she was the only person around who had any sort of idea what to do. She kept calm and got us all through it. I played a very small role. She's the one whose hand you ought to be shaking."

"Advisor Newcastle." Keith held out his hand and I grasped it. He pulled me to my feet and enveloped me in a hug I think he needed so much, he was willing to force me into contact regardless of my feelings. I didn't mind though. I needed a damn hug too.

* * * *

After we'd declined an early lunch with Keith and Bonnie at the pub across the road, Colin and I entered Mary's room.

Evie and Angus were sitting bedside with her. Evie, as usual, hunched in her chair as if trying to become smaller. Angus was discussing a recent football match with Mary, who looked dazed and very out of it.

"I don't even know why I'm bothering to talk to her," Angus told us as Colin and I approached the bed. "Should she be on such a high dosage of whatever pain medicine they've given her?"

"Mary?" Colin's voice was sharp with concern and I debated looking for one of the pack nurses.

"Col?" Mary blinked her eyes as she tried to focus.

Colin sat at the edge of the mattress and took one of her hands within both of his, careful of the IV feed.

"Col, don't leave me." Mary struggled to regain more than a soupy consciousness, her eyes darkening. The pungent scent of her fear permeated the room and I held my breath to escape it.

"I'm right here." Colin gave her hand a squeeze.

"Should I get one of the nurses?" I asked.

When Evie's spoke, her voice was tentative, as if she was used to having her opinion squashed. "One came in here a little while ago. Mary didn't want to take her pills, so she gave her a shot. I think that's why she's so out of it. Maybe the shot was stronger than the pills?"

"She did kick up a ruckus about the pills," Angus confirmed. "And she keeps asking not to be left alone." He looked at me as if I might have a clue why, but I didn't. Maybe Mary didn't like the feeling of being sedated. I didn't. I flashed back to the castle after Glenn Murphy had tried to strangle me. Jason kept me pretty drugged up for at least twenty-four hours and I remembered the punch-drunk surreal quality of consciousness. I'd hated it, but there had been nothing I could do to fight against the feeling.

Mary clung to Colin's hands weakly, but he made no move to let go. His unguarded expression was way too revealing, and I caught Angus staring. Evie was oblivious, as usual.

"Colin, we're supposed to feed Mary and Richard's dogs soon, aren't we?"

Colin frowned at me. "They can wait a couple of hours."

I moved to the window and glanced out. Brooding clouds massed together. More damn rain. Would it never end?

When I turned to the bed, Colin was stroking Mary's cheek with the back of his hand. Now even Evie's attention was riveted.

"I think we should go now."

"I don't want to be alone," Mary whispered and Colin glared at me.

"We could stay," Evie offered.

"I want you, Col." Mary turned fretful.

"Do you want a lift to feed the dogs?" Angus gave Colin and Mary a pointed look, then fixed his gaze on me. He looked very anxious to leave. I supposed he had as little desire to watch Colin and Mary bill and coo as I did.

"I'm afraid of dogs," Evie objected.

"You can sit in the goddamn car." Angus moved for the door as if I'd already agreed to let him drive me.

I waited for Colin to remember his promise to Murphy not to leave me alone, but Colin had already returned his attention to Mary and was completely oblivious to mere nuisances like me. Jesus, I wanted to hit him. But I also felt guilty. Mary was in pain and scared, and if she wanted Colin to be with her, who was I to object? She couldn't have Richard because he was sleeping at the safe house and who better to comfort her than the man she really loved?

Why the hell had she let him leave her? I knew she hadn't had a choice. No one in the Pack was ever forced to stay with somebody. That's why we had the option to break our bonds on every birthday. But couldn't she have made him understand how much she wanted him to stay with her?

Yeah, I was a fine one to talk. I'd let Murphy walk out on me six months ago without a murmur of protest and I'd loved him. But I'd gotten him back. Mary had bonded with Richard, and Colin started a new life with Devon.

Anger sloshed in the pit of my stomach. Large packs might have their advantages, but in my heart I suspected I would always champion the smaller ones.

Chapter 14

The autumn air was layered with the scents of wood smoke and cold lake water. Angus unlocked the doors of his station wagon and waited impatiently for Evie to get in the passenger's side. Her expression was a mixture of mutinous and nervous.

"Were you bitten by a dog before or something?" I buckled my seatbelt in the backseat.

"When I was little, the kids in the pack thought it was funny to hold me down so this big dog Richard's parents had could lick me. I didn't like it and they laughed." Evie struggled to fasten her seatbelt and I sighed. I really had to do something about my impatience. As an Advisor, I needed all the serenity I could muster. People would continually challenge and try to thwart me. I intimidated others just by the very fact of my position. What good would I be if I let myself become so easily frustrated by timid people like Evie?

"That was twenty years and more ago," Angus reminded her, as if they'd had this discussion before. He twisted the keys in the ignition and the engine coughed into life. Random raindrops spattered the windshield as the car warmed up, but never developed into a full-fledged shower.

Angus met my gaze in the rearview mirror, and yet again, I received the impression he wanted me to understand something he was not saying. I frowned and gripped the edge of the seat when he abruptly shifted into reverse and zipped out of the parking slot, making my heart leap into my throat.

What the hell had I been thinking, to drive with him?

The sky darkened and whitecaps rose on the lake's surface. We followed the shoreline until Angus made a right-hand turn and left the lake behind. Trees hemmed us in, closing over the road like a canopy. In summer, tree limbs must have formed a leafy arch, but today in the autumn, bare branches scraped against each other, tossed by the fitful wind.

The gravel drive in front of Mary and Richard's house was soft and muddy. I sidestepped a puddle and hurried up the front steps, digging in my purse for the house keys Colin had absently pressed into my hand before I'd left.

Inside, the dogs set up a barking ruckus. Evie stayed locked in the car while Angus lit a cigarette and leaned against the back fender, head tilted so he could look at the tattered gray clouds, harbingers of rain to come.

The moment I opened the door, both dogs rushed out and jumped on me, yelping frantic greetings. Gatsby, the male dog, gave me a canine hug, his front legs wrapped around my hips as he tried to kiss my face with his tongue.

Daisy clearly expected to see Mary and when she didn't, rushed down the steps so she could inspect the car. Evie shrank down in her seat.

"Aren't you a bonnie lass," said Angus as she investigated his boots, tail wagging politely. At the sound of his voice, she pressed her head against his hip and he gave her a pat.

Gatsby left me so he could attend to pressing business with the flower beds and tree trunks in the front garden and I went inside to fill food and water bowls.

The sofa in the great room had splashes of dried blood on the fabric, but someone had removed the afghans we'd used to cover Mary. I gulped and averted my eyes. That nightmarish afternoon was something I wanted to forget, not relive. I made a mental note to talk to Jason about arranging for the sofa to be cleaned and opened cabinet doors until I located the dog food.

The dogs bounded inside when I called them ten minutes later and I locked the door behind me.

"Do you mind if I go check the stream?" Angus was still contemplating the gray sky, but at the sound of my voice, fixed his attention on me. "Mary's nervous it might flood the banks and if it does, I'd like to arrange for the dogs to go stay with one of the Mac Tire duos."

"How about if I walk with you? I could use the exercise." Angus straightened out of his slouch against the back of the car and followed me to the back gate.

When I had my hand on the latch, he said, "Advisor, I'd like to talk to you. I need to tell you something." The guilt in his voice made me stiffen. Was he about to confess to setting the trap? But how could he have? When had he the opportunity? Maybe he'd set the first one, but not the second one? Or maybe he was going to tell me something that didn't have anything to do with traps at all. Leaping to conclusions was a bad habit. Dangerous too.

Before I could respond, the car door slammed and Evie rushed to catch up with us. I tried not to let Angus see me sag in relief. I didn't want to be alone with him. Why the hell had I allowed myself to be separated from Colin? Fear spiked my veins and I fought against it before the scent oozed from my pores and alerted him.

"Where are you going?" Evie didn't exactly demand an answer, but she was obviously not pleased we'd left her behind.

"Just to check the stream." Did I sound nervous?

"Aren't you afraid there might be another trap?" Evie's brown eyes were huge in the paper-white oval of her face.

"The area was checked thoroughly," I said. "There was just the one trap. But we'll stick to the path anyway, how's that?"

"What if it starts to rain?" Evie didn't want to go, that much was clear.

"Then we'll get wet. Why don't you wait in the car?" Angus suggested impatiently.

"No, she can come," I said. Hopefully not too quickly.

Angus blew out an impatient breath. He stared at me as if I'd betrayed him, and I was more than ever resolved not to be alone with him. Something weird was up. I patted my purse where I had my cell phone. I could call Murphy in a pinch if I got really nervous. Not that he could do anything but yell at me for leaving Colin with Mary. By the time he got to me, whatever Angus meant to do to me would be long over.

I gulped. Angus was not going to do anything to me. I was being ridiculous. He was not Nate Carver or Glenn Murphy. My hands shook as I unlatched the gate and I hid them by angling my body so Angus couldn't see. My boots squelched in the muddy grass as I hurried across the back garden and unlatched the gate that opened onto the forest path.

"I really need to talk to you." Angus said, voice pitched low. He matched his pace to mine as we walked down the leafy wet path. The muted roar of the stream grew louder with each step.

"When we get back to the safe house." If he wanted to confess to something, he could damn well do it when I had back up.

"But, damn it…" Angus trailed off hopelessly and stalked ahead of me.

"Careful, Angus, there might be a trap," Evie called. She was several prudent paces behind us, hands stuffed into her jacket pockets. Her red hair needed to be combed and her eyelashes were so pale as to appear nonexistent. God, I wished I could sit her down behind a vanity so I could put some mascara on her. And maybe insert a backbone while I was at it.

Angus, head down, bulled his way along the path as if he had a personal score to settle with it. Stopped short by the bank, he hurled a rock into the depths and the sound of the splash was swallowed by the water's rough roar.

"Okay, I'm not fucking around anymore," he said when Evie and I were within hearing distance. He turned around, his face twisted with a strong emotion that hovered between rage and suspicion. "I want the truth and you'd better tell me because I'm through with all this bloody confusion. I can't sleep at night anymore because my mind keeps going round in trapped circles. Where the hell were you that afternoon? You tell me where the hell you were." He stabbed a finger at me and I gaped at him. What the hell?

Then I realized Evie stood right behind me and maybe he was pointing at her, not me.

I swallowed with difficulty. Fear, huge and slithering, blocked my throat.

Evie stared at me as if she waited for my answer.

"Don't look at her, look at me and answer me. Mary wasn't afraid to be left alone, was she? She was afraid to be left alone with *you*." Angus's breathing was ragged, as if he found it difficult to drag the air deep enough into his lungs.

Tingles of horror pricked up and down my spine.

"You kept trying to send me out of the room. Coffee. A biscuit. The doctor. What were you going to do if I'd gone, Evie? Tell me what you were going to do," Angus demanded.

A strange sound escaped Evie's throat. At first I thought it was a sob of disbelief, but then I saw her sly smile.

"What do you think, Angus? I was going to take a pillow and press it against her face. She was supposed to step down from being Alpha. *We* were supposed to take her place. Don't tell me you didn't know the plan. You never asked me where I was the day before we took the Advisors for that little walk in the woods. You never asked me where I went for two hours when we were supposed to be packing to stay at the safe house. You gave your implicit consent and don't try to weasel out of it. We're both in this together."

"You said you needed something from the store," whispered Angus. "That's what you said."

"And you believed me? Because I don't think you did, not after Mary was trapped. I saw you looking at me when you got here yesterday. Don't think I didn't notice you didn't sleep in the same bed with me last night."

Evie gave a cunning little laugh, and a cold tingle shivered down my spine.

"I didn't want to believe any of this." Angus moaned and pulled at his hair as if he could make everything go away if he hurt himself hard enough.

"Believe it. I did it for *us*. You knew Mac Tire would take us over. I knew it too. The plan was never to have our own pack, but to take over Mac Tire. You *knew* that, Angus."

"I didn't," he cried. "I wanted Stony Fell to succeed. Jesus, Evie, you set those traps. You've *destroyed* Ben's life. Your own pack mate. He looked up to you as Alpha!"

"He wasn't supposed to be where he was. You told everyone to lie low and he didn't. Neither did your sister and Frazier. Always thinking they know better than everybody else. I was glad when they got the shit kicked out of them, you know that? She's never liked me. Women never like me." Evie's voice shook with resentment. She glared at me as if realizing I was there for the first time. "You despise me too, don't you, Advisor?" She made the title sound like a curse. "Admit it. You think I'm a sniveling, weak coward. But I've shown you what I am and what I can do. Do you think a coward could set traps like that? Come up with a plan to take over a pack the way I have?"

"Yes, I do. I think being a coward would be essential to a bullshit plan like that," I said, and Angus winced.

"Shut up," Evie screamed, her face transfigured with rage. "Who asked you?"

"You just did," I pointed out, and Angus drew in his breath with a hiss. I think he was trying to tell me to quit antagonizing her which was probably a very good idea. Unfortunately, I rarely held onto my tongue when I was pissed off. "You're pathetic. They'll exile you for this. I hope you understand that."

"I'm not going to be exiled. I'm going to be Alpha of Mac Tire," said Evie with the complete conviction of the utterly insane.

"In what world? Angus doesn't seem likely to keep silent about this anymore and I sure as hell am not. You've just admitted you set those traps and you can't take it back. Said and witnessed by an Advisor to the Great Council. It's a done deal. You're screwed."

"They picked on me as a child. Bullied me because they thought it was fun to see me cry. I got them back, though. Accidents always happen around me. People get hurt, sometimes me too, but when I do, someone else gets blamed."

In my mind, I saw a wine glass spill. What I'd thought was clumsiness, had been very carefully engineered. And Mary's elbow against the SUV's door. Another staged accident. Hadn't Evie stood in Mary's way in the path, forcing her to go around and, in so doing, Mary stepped into the trap? Jesus. No wonder Mary hadn't wanted Evie around her in the hospital room. Instinctively, she'd known. Maybe she'd always had a bad feeling but hadn't known what to do with it and could never prove anything.

"Everybody thinks I'm such a loser." Evie's eyes glittered with malice. "All the kids in Mac Tire conspired against me all my life so I never had a chance to be anything. Especially Mary, the cunt. I've hated her for years. Years. I've hated Richard too, even Colin, although he was nicer to me than anybody else. I had the biggest crush on him when he first joined the pack. He didn't know I was a loser at first and he was nice." Evie shook her head. "But then he fell for Mary. Every boy in the pack did. It wasn't fair. She's not even that pretty. You're prettier than she is." She pointed an accusing finger at me as if being pretty was a crime. "When you put makeup on me that night and let me borrow your dress, I saw Colin's face and Richard's. They thought I was attractive. For the first time ever." Her smile was demented, and I slowly moved my hand inside my purse for my cell phone.

"I think we need to go now," I said,.

Evie laughed. "You're not going anywhere." In a perfectly normal tone of voice as if she were ordering off a menu at a restaurant, she said, "Angus, kill her. You're stronger than me."

"Evie." Angus said, her name a hopeless plea.

"Nobody knows what I've done but her. If we kill her now, we can make it look like an accident." Evie smiled at her bond mate, who recoiled.

"I'm not killing anyone," Angus said. "It's over, Evie."

"It's not over!" Cords stuck out in her neck and her face turned a mottled red that made her freckles disappear. "Everything I've done, I've done for us. You can't back out on me now. Don't be a bloody coward, Angus. Kill her!"

I closed my fingers around my brush. Fuck. Where the hell was my phone?

"Evie, no," said Angus.

"You're in this as deeply as I am. You covered for me. I'll swear you knew everything. This is the only way." Evie took a step toward him and he backed up. His heels were dangerously close to the edge of the bank. One more step and he'd be over.

"I'll take what's coming to me," Angus declared. "I didn't want to believe what you'd done and I didn't know for sure until now you had, but I suspected, that much is true. I'll take my punishment."

"You bloody idiot," snarled Evie just as I triumphantly gripped my phone.

The full force of Evie slamming me took me completely by surprise. I'd been focused on the phone. I took two stumbling steps backward, then the ground fell from beneath me.

* * * *

Icy cold numbness. Breath shocked from my body. Water closed over my head and darkness claimed me. The roar of the stream was inside me now. I screamed, and frigid water rushed into my mouth and nose before I could clamp my teeth shut. Was I dying? *No*, I didn't want to die.

I struggled to find the surface, but everything was so black and the weight of something big held me down. Fingernails dug like needles beneath my skin. The pain was only thing keeping me conscious.

I thrashed and my foot hit something hard. A rock? The bottom of the stream? I was in the stream. Evie had pushed me in and I was drowning.

Again, I fought to find the surface. If my foot hit the rock on the bottom, the surface was in the other direction. But I couldn't get there because something heavy held me down. The fingernails in my skin. They weren't mine. Evie. She was on top of me, holding me down. Had she meant to come into the water with me?

Her fingernails hurt and I reached out, found her flesh, and pinched hard. I was free and I rocketed up. My head broke the surface of the water. Black tree branches, swirling water, Angus screaming Evie's name, one sucking, painful breath and then hands wrestled me down again. No. No!

I wrapped my arms and legs around her and tried to sink us both. If I drowned, so would she. Panic gave me strength and we zoomed down until my back scraped against the rocky gravel of the stream bed. My sweater rode up and the pebbles abraded my bare skin as the raging current swept us along the bottom.

Evie kicked and clawed at me until I released her and I was blessedly free too. My feet were deadened from the cold and I tried to kick off the bottom so I could shoot to the surface, but I had no sensation in my feet anymore. My lungs burned and I clapped a hand over my nose and mouth before they could turn traitor and try to breathe. My hands were numb. The sucking awful cold took over everything.

"Murphy." My lips moved and maybe I said his name aloud or maybe I didn't. Everything was so mercilessly cold and dark. Maybe if I just gave up, it would all go away.

* * * *

"*Breathe*, damn you." Angus screamed into my clogged ears. "Stanzie, breathe. Breathe!" Air flowed down my throat, but stopped halfway. My lungs were on fire and my stomach was a ball of agony.

I gave a great, whooping cough and cold water burned up my throat and through my nasal passages. I threw it up in a great, wrenching gush that twisted my insides until I wanted to shriek, but couldn't because the water kept coming and coming until all I could bring up was bile.

Angus belted me between the shoulder blades and more water burst out of my mouth and, disgustingly, my nose.

"Get it up, get it all up," he crooned in my ear and when he was certain I had nothing left, rubbed my sore back. My stomach and abdomen muscles cramped and I curled into a sobbing, fetal ball. Every part of me hurt. Agony to breathe, anguish to move. The stench of blood gagged me. Was I bleeding? Cold numb pain cut my muscles like a knife.

Angus was soaked to the skin too. Had he jumped in after me? He must have. I rolled onto my back so I could see his face. His beard dripped water onto my chin and I'd never seen anyone look so scared and bedraggled in my goddamn life. What the hell did I look like?

"Evie? Where is she?" God, I croaked like I had after Glenn tried to strangle me. Panic clawed at me again and I forced myself to lie still. How could I run when I couldn't even feel my fucking feet?

Angus shook his head. More water drops rained down on me.

"Didn't you save her too?"

He stared at me and took a hitching breath. "I could only save one of you. I had to choose." His face twisted and tears poured down his cheeks. "I don't understand how she did those things. Oh, God." He put an arm across his face, both to stem his tears and hide his shame. I tried to speak, but huge shudders quaked down my spine and I couldn't breathe.

Angus swept me up into his strong arms and ran down the path. Once he fell to his knees, crying out when a rock shredded his jeans at the kneecap, but he was up and running again in an instant.

I couldn't stop shaking. Blood squirted into my mouth when my teeth clamped painfully on my tongue, and I squealed.

"Almost there." Angus propped me against the gate as he struggled to unlatch it. Something dug painfully into my side, but the pressure eased when the gate flew open and he ran across the yard to the back door.

"The…keys…in my purse," I managed to say.

"Your bloody purse is halfway to hell by now." Angus set me down on the flagstone terrace and used his elbow to smash the glass in the small window on the back door.

Snarls and growls from inside.

"The dogs," I whispered as Angus reached through the broken window and fumbled open the lock.

He yelled something and, miraculously, the dogs shut the hell up.

"I'm so fucking cold." I couldn't help the tears streaming down my face. I hurt and was freezing and couldn't feel eighty percent of my body, but I could smell my blood.

"It's warm inside." Angus opened the door and the dogs blurred around his legs as they arrowed toward me. Gatsby licked the tears off my cheeks while Daisy whined and tried to crawl into my lap. Maybe they were trying to warm me?

Angus scooped me up in his arms again and I smelled his blood. His arm was bleeding from breaking the window. Shards of glass crunched beneath his boots as he carried me inside and put me down on the sofa.

"Liam," I whispered, and Angus smoothed the wet hair from my cold forehead.

"I'm ringing him, love. It's just…I don't know the number." His breath caught in his throat and for a moment he hovered on the edge of tears, but he recovered.

"I know the number." I recited it between my chattering teeth. The dogs piled onto the sofa and curled up on top of me.

* * * *

I was sitting up with the comforter from Mary and Richard's bed wrapped around me, the dogs on either side, when Murphy and Jason burst through the front door. Marginally warmer thanks to a hot shower Angus and I had taken together—he was as cold as I was—I still couldn't stop shivering.

Murphy gently nudged aside one of the dogs so he could sit beside me. He pressed his forehead against the side of my face and I could tell by the way he breathed, he was trying hard not to cry.

"Aren't you going to yell at me?" I'd wanted him so much, but I'd been equally afraid he'd shout at me when he came because he'd told me to be careful and I hadn't been.

"You? No." His lashes brushed my cheek and he leaned back so he could look at me. "I am going to yell at Hunter though. I'm going to hit him too. Repeatedly."

A small, watery giggle escaped me and I brushed tears from my eyes. Murphy crushed me into a hug that drove all the breath from my body.

"You scared the hell out of me, Stanzie." His voice was a choked sob and he cupped my face with his hands so he could stare in my eyes. "I felt like I was dying all the way here."

"Angus saved me," I said.

Angus huddled in the rocking chair in the corner. He looked small and defenseless in one of Richard's robes and a blanket from the bed. Jason stood beside him, a stricken expression on his face.

"He had to choose between me or Evie and he chose me." That thought still fascinated and festered too. Because of me, Evie was dead. Wasn't she?

"We need to look for her."

"I'm on it," Jason said. "I've got people looking downstream."

"She might still be alive," I said.

"I hope not." Angus stared blankly at the wall. Jason moved toward me and gestured for the dogs to get down. They obeyed instantly even though he didn't say a word. He sat beside me and very carefully drew the comforter away from my shoulder.

"Your back's pretty torn up," he said. "Will you let me put some antiseptic on it?"

"I'm so cold," I told him, and Murphy drew me closer.

"I know." Jason's expression was so kind, I wanted to cry. He looked so gentle and affectionate. And sad.

Before Jason tended to my back, he made us all tea. I sipped mine gratefully, cradling the mug between my palms even though Murphy told me it was too hot to do that. I didn't think so. Maybe my hands were still numb?

When the tea was gone, Jason took my mug to the sink and returned with a small leather case. His doctor's bag, I guessed.

Whatever he put on my back stung. I leaned over my knees, back bared so Jason could see, and gritted my teeth against the pain. Murphy sat beside me and held my hand. I squeezed his fingers instead of screaming and he didn't wince or pull away.

Jason went as quickly as he could, but he didn't miss a single cut. The rocks and gravel on the stream bed had been brutal. When he was finished, he helped me put on one of Mary's soft cotton nightgowns then wrapped the comforter around me again.

"Angus hurt his knee," I said.

Angus sighed from the rocker. "Don't worry about me. I'm fine."

"He's got a black eye too," Murphy said, staring at him critically. I looked and noticed it for the first time.

"Did I hit you?" I must have, with a flailing fist or elbow.

"It's nothing," he said.

"Jason, please check on him," I insisted.

Jason squeezed my shoulder and went to Angus.

"He didn't know anything she did," I said.

Angus groaned. "I had my suspicions, love. Don't cover for me. I told you I'd take what was coming to me and I will. Exile, I know it."

"Bullshit," I argued. "Jason, we are not going to let Angus be exiled. Suspicion is not the same thing as…" I struggled to find the word. Where the fuck was the word? The cold was eating my brain and all the words I knew. For a moment I felt like my wolf when she didn't know the name for something, and I wanted to howl in frustration.

"I can't think straight." Cheated tears clouded my eyes and Murphy hugged me close.

"Stanzie, stop," he whispered, rocking me.

"I'm willing to listen to his story." Jason examined Angus's bloody kneecap. "Yours too, but I want you to rest now, Constance."

When he called me Constance, he meant business. I might not be able to think of the right words, but I was damn sure Angus was not going to be exiled for the things Evie had done.

"Honey, why don't you lie down?" Murphy tried to move so I could, but I clung to him. I didn't want him leaving me. He ended up lying with me beneath the comforter, me on the inside, snuggled into the crook of his arm. I relaxed against him, my head on his chest so I could hear the reassuring beat of his heart. Gatsby curled up on our feet.

I jerked in shock, ripped from near sleep, when the front door slammed open. Colin blew into the room accompanied by wind and rain. He struggled to shut the door behind him and when he turned around, he looked consumed with guilt.

"Jesus, Stanz, are you all right?"

"You'd better fucking stay over there," Murphy snarled at him. "She's fine, no thanks to you. Where the hell were you, Hunter? I ask you to do one fucking thing and you can't do it. Worthless piece of shit."

I hung onto him so he wouldn't get up and start one of his Irish brawls, but he didn't seem in a hurry to leave me.

"Mary was afraid," Colin said. "And too drugged up. I was scared for her."

"You sonofabitch," said Murphy. "I don't want to hear it."

"Too drugged?" Jason turned away from dabbing antiseptic onto Angus's nasty looking knee.

"That damned nurse gave her a shot when she wouldn't take pills." Colin wiped rainwater from his face and grimaced.

Jason didn't look very happy about that.

"She was scared of Evie," Angus muttered. "She didn't want to be left alone with Evie, but she was too out of it to say what she was afraid of, poor thing."

"I didn't want to leave her. I thought Stanzie would be safe with Angus and Evie. They couldn't have set the trap Mary stepped into, they didn't have the opportunity." Colin's tone was weak.

"You are so frigging stupid," Murphy told him. "Even if you did believe that, they could have set the first one, you fecking idiot. Ever think of that?"

"I'm sorry." Colin peeled off his jacket and it dripped all over the floor.

"Apology not accepted. Go fuck yourself." Murphy was tense against me and his heartbeat galloped so hard I'm sure the entire room heard it.

"The next time, Jason, my gut tells me to go with Stanzie, I'm fucking going. And you aren't stopping me." Murphy turned his wrath toward Jason, who bore it without a protest. He neither agreed, nor disagreed and went back to ministering to Angus's injuries.

"Colin, go help look for Evelyn," he said without looking at the man. Colin grimaced. "Where am I supposed to look?"

"Downstream," said Jason shortly. "Start at the end of the path and follow the stream. You'll eventually come across the three people I've got looking already. Janice Montgomery and Frazier and Elspeth."

"Oh, hell, not my sister." Anguish made Angus's voice tight.

Jason's mouth tightened. "I was rather short of options. They were on hand at the safe house waiting to be interviewed." He looked over his shoulder at Colin. "Janice is a nurse. She has medical equipment and she can use it, as you know. Find her and don't come back until you've located Evelyn, one way or the other."

Colin paled at the terseness and hastily thrust his wet jacket on.

"I didn't know it was Evie Mary was afraid of. If I had, I never would have let Stanzie leave with her."

"Now, Colin." Jason's glare was chilling. Colin fled.

"Am I in trouble too? If he's in trouble for letting me leave without him, I ought to be in trouble for leaving in the first place." I struggled to get the words out. Warmth flooded slowly through my body, little electric charges that sent bolts of sleepy pleasure through my system.

"Your loyalty does you credit, Stanzie, but I'm not sure it's well placed in this instance." Jason's smile was affectionate, but anger lurked behind his blue eyes as well.

"I am." My jaw nearly split with the enormity of the yawn that swept over me. "Jason, did you put something in that tea?"

"Go to sleep, Stanzie," was the last thing I heard for a long time.

Chapter 15

Evie's drowned body turned up two miles from where we'd both gone into the stream. Colin found her and Murphy was vindictively pleased about it, from the grim smile that played about his lips when he told me.

Whatever Jason put in my tea knocked me out and by the time I woke again, Angus's fate had been decided.

I didn't fuss about being left out because the Councils decided not to exile him, but Stony Fell had been disbanded.

After much pleading, I persuaded Murphy into the shower. I didn't think he'd slept even an hour of the twenty-four plus I'd spent unconscious and he needed to shave, comb his hair and have a moment to himself without worrying about me.

When I was sure he was engrossed in the rush of hot water, I carefully dressed and crept out of the room. I needed space too. And food. Had I ever been so ravenous in my entire life? I couldn't remember a time.

The mouthwatering scent of sausage and mashed potatoes lured me down the stairs to the dining room, where I found Jason and Colin indulging in huge plates of bangers and mash.

"God, I hope there's enough for me." I nearly tripped over my damn feet in my rush to get to the table.

Both Jason and Colin stood and all but battled each other to get to me first. Colin won only because Jason pulled up short, probably to see what we'd do together.

Colin swept me half off my feet into his arms and buried his face in my hair.

I hugged him back. Somewhere along the line, I'd grown really fond of the bastard. I even think I liked him.

"Come sit down. There's plenty to eat. Do you want some wine?" Colin wouldn't let go of me and all but sat on my lap as he settled me into a chair.

"I don't want anything that will make me sleepy or woozy. Jason, damn you, you put something in my tea."

His blue eyes twinkled. "A little wine won't hurt, Stanzie. It's a rather nice Cab and it's a shame to waste it all on Colin. I can't drink the entire bottle myself."

Colin snorted in my ear and I grinned.

Grandmother Nan swept to the table bearing a tray with a steaming plate for me and an empty wine glass, which Jason promptly filled.

"Are you still an Advisor?" I asked Colin when my hunger had been somewhat appeased by a few huge bites of bangers and mash.

"Barely," he said.

"By the skin of his teeth," Jason added, and his expression was ominous enough that my stomach knotted for a moment.

"I will never disregard a Councilor's direct orders again." Colin held up his hand in a solemn pledge, but Jason didn't look particularly convinced.

"Liam told me Angus wasn't exiled," I said around a mouthful of food. I rinsed it down with some wine and discovered Jason was right—it was good.

"No. As a matter of fact, he's coming back to Connecticut with me to join Riverglow. If Devon's agreeable, we're going to form a triad." Colin spoke nonchalantly, but I could tell my reaction was important to him.

"Colin, that…that's very generous of you." I was impressed. I touched his hand and he smiled at me. He was gorgeous when he grinned like that.

"The rest of Stony Fell are also going to join Riverglow." Colin squeezed my fingers. "Including Ben and Tracy. After Elspeth and Frazier, they're going to be Alphas."

I squealed and leaped out of my chair so I could throw myself at him. He caught me and pulled me onto his lap, laughing in delight.

"You are so fucking awesome, Alpha." I wrapped my arms around his neck and pressed my forehead to his. We stared into each other's eyes happily until Colin abruptly went rigid against me and his smile died.

I wriggled around in his lap until I could see what he was looking at. Murphy. Standing a few feet away. He carefully walked around us and took the chair opposite mine. His smile was strained.

"What are we celebrating?" he asked.

"Colin is taking everyone from Stony Fell into Riverglow. Including Ben. He and Tracy will be Alphas there one day." I moved Colin's arms away and climbed out of his lap so I could sit in my place again. My dinner was growing cold. Plus, I didn't like the hurt shining in Murphy's dark eyes.

"Great." Murphy helped himself to the wine bottle and an extra glass Grandmother Nan had thoughtfully put on the table when she'd brought mine. "What's that make, Colin? A grand total of six people in your pack now?"

Colin's smile looked more like a grimace. "Eleven, actually."

"Pardon me." Murphy took a gulp of wine, and I doubted he even tasted it. "Riverglow's really coming up in the world. Congratulations." He raised his glass in a mocking toast and took another sip.

Colin's jaw jutted. "Look, I know compared to Mac Tire, it's a load of crap, but it's my load of crap. I'm making the most of what I've got and I'm not doing badly actually, so to hell with you, Liam Murphy." He shoved back his chair and stalked off.

Murphy didn't seem to like my expression. "What?" he demanded. His hair was wet and he still needed to shave. He'd probably panicked when he'd come into the bedroom and hadn't found me there. His clothes were obviously the ones he'd thrown to the floor before getting into the shower. At least he'd paused to dress in his headlong rush to find me.

"It is a big deal, what he's doing." I struggled against a burst of anger. I loved him, but damn it, he could be such a stubborn sonofabitch sometimes. "Ben would have been less than nothing here in Mac Tire. He's giving him a chance to be Alpha."

"Being Alpha is the ultimate of Pack existence, I suppose," Murphy remarked. "I guess things like financial stability and basic support don't matter a damn as long as you get to call yourself Alpha."

"The Councils are going to help with Ben's financial support," I reminded him. I wondered if now was the time to mention the money I'd pledged to give Colin. Probably not if I wanted Colin to keep his head on his shoulders.

"Yes, and don't let that prick convince you that didn't factor into his generous as hell offer to take the boy in." Murphy's disgust was evident in his expression and tone.

"He's in love with Mary. How could you expect him to have left her alone? If I'd pleaded with you to stay with me, would you have left me? Yeah, I forget. *You* would have. You have a history of walking away, don't you?" The food I'd eaten sat like lead in my stomach and I wanted to throw what was left on my plate in his smug face.

The color leached from Murphy's cheeks and left him looking vulnerable and small. Shame licked at me.

"Constance, Liam didn't leave your side for a moment these past twenty-four hours." Jason's tone was softly chiding. Like I needed a lecture from him.

"One time he sticks around. Does that excuse the times he didn't?" I snapped.

Murphy bowed his head so I couldn't see his face anymore.

"You're together today because he didn't abandon you. If you don't recall that scene with Celine Ducharme, I surely do." Jason tossed his napkin on his plate and gave me a reproachful look as he got to his feet. Without bothering to excuse himself, he left the table.

"He shouldn't have said that." Murphy still wouldn't look up. "I know I've let you down more than I've ever been there for you. It's okay, Stanzie. I'm a frigging hypocrite, expecting Colin Hunter to do something I can't even do for you, aren't I?"

"I don't want to fight." Tears burned my eyes. "I know you didn't leave me last night, Liam, not even for a second. And I'm sorry I left the room without telling you. I was so hungry."

"I'm sure you wanted a break from me." He tried to laugh, but it stuck in his throat. "Either I'm not there at all or I'm smothering. There's no in between with me, is there?"

Grandmother Nan approached the table with a plate for Murphy. Her steps were hesitant until I waved her over with a small smile. "Thank you, Grandmother Nan."

"Can I get you some coffee, love? Some chocolate cake perhaps?"

"Just the coffee would be good." I didn't really want coffee, but she looked so eager to help.

"Eat." I looked at Murphy's plate and he picked up his fork but didn't take a bite. "Please, Liam. I'm sorry."

He shook his head, smile bleak, but he did eat after that, although I suspected he forced it down only because I'd asked him.

Later that night, in bed, I turned to him and tried to make everything I'd said up to him with my body, and he participated willingly, but I knew I'd hurt him and maybe some injuries weren't so easily healed.

Chapter 16

Colin stood by the front door of the safe house, his suitcase at his feet. He wore the same tweed jacket he'd worn that first morning at breakfast. It had obviously been dry cleaned because Ben's wolf's bloodstains were gone. Somehow, he was no longer a hostile stranger. He'd become a friend and a partner.

I wanted to hug him goodbye, but Murphy stood beside me, so I didn't. Colin seemed to understand, if his smile was any indication.

"I guess I'll be seeing you again at some point, Stanzie. When Allerton trusts me enough to send me on another case. Take care of yourself." Colin bent to retrieve his suitcase and, when he straightened, he stepped forward to offer Murphy his hand. "You too, Liam."

Murphy shook his hand, but didn't say anything and, with a last smile in my direction, Colin walked out the door. Angus, Elspeth and Frazier waited for him in Angus's station wagon. They were all traveling to Connecticut with him. Ben, Tracy, Bonnie and Keith were going to join them later, when Ben was cleared for long-distance flights. He and Mary had a lot of physical therapy to do. Richard and Mary had offered to put him and Tracy up at their house for the duration, and turn one of the spare bedrooms into a therapy room. Bonnie and Keith had taken an apartment nearby.

Evie had been cremated and her ashes scattered by Angus and Jason earlier that morning. Angus hadn't wanted anyone with him, but somehow Jason had wangled his way along. I was grateful for that. No one should have to scatter their bond mate's ashes alone. Especially under circumstances like these.

Murphy and I had our suitcases in hand too and I knew Murphy wanted to wait for Colin to be gone before we left.

"I smell coffee. You want me to track some down for you?" I touched the back of my hand to Murphy's smooth cheek and he turned his head so he could plant a kiss against my wrist.

"Don't you think we've put that road trip off long enough? You still want to go, don't you?" he asked.

"Are you kidding? It's all I've been dreaming about since I got here."

Behind us, the stairs creaked as someone descended and we turned to watch Jason take the last five steps with easy grace, suitcase in one hand. His moss green suit was flawlessly tailored and his shoes gleamed with fresh polish. Had he made Colin shine his shoes as well as take care of his dry cleaning? The thought made me want to giggle. I must have grinned because Jason's lips twitched into a friendly smile and he set his case down so he could stand beside us.

"Hunter gone?" he asked and Murphy nodded, but remarkably forbore from saying anything snarky. "Have you two got a spare couple of days you could spend in London, by chance?"

Murphy opened his mouth to say no, but I jumped in before he could.

"Is Wren still there?"

Jason nodded.

"I'd like that. Liam, can we?" I turned to Murphy, who looked thoughtful. Of course, he agreed we could.

Chapter 17

Wren's hair was shaped around her face and the ends blunt cut to just above her shoulders. Wispy bangs fluttered across her forehead in the cold breeze. She stood outside a trendy wine bar near St. Paul's Cathedral where we'd arranged to meet.

My father, Paul, had liked her hair long and her dresses girlish and frilly. Today she wore a shark skin gray skirt suit. The blazer was double breasted, the skirt just above the knee. Black tights and charcoal suede ankle boots made her legs seem endless. A black Coach purse and diamond earrings added chic accessories to an already powerful suit. She was every inch a Great Councilor's bond mate, this woman who stared at me, her flawless face smooth with perfectly applied makeup.

Beside her, I felt downright frumpy in jeans and one of Maureen's sweaters. My favorite plum one had not survived the plunge into the bone-chillingly cold stream. This one was red and the pattern reminded me of the one Paddy had worn the first day of my tribunal. My hair desperately needed trimming and blew around my face in the ill-tempered autumn wind. My lips were chapped—another result of the icy plunge I'd taken.

"Wren, where's your coat? It's thirty-five degrees out here." I had on a leather jacket and gloves. She looked cold but elegant in her suit.

"Inside. I've got us a table, but I saw you through the window and I couldn't wait to come out here to meet you." Even her voice was different. Confident. Happy.

The last time I'd seen her she'd been glowing with joy at her bonding ceremony, but this happiness was mellow as if it were an everyday experience, not something fleetingly felt at times of celebration.

Flanked by Murphy and Jason, I felt trapped and uncertain. Wren and I stared at each other, neither one making the first move.

"Let's go inside, shall we?" Jason nudged me with his shoulder, but I hung back, unaccountably shy and more than a little suspicious, so he stepped forward and Lauren kissed him on the mouth. It was not a passionate, cinematic gesture, but the love between them was plain and shining.

My throat ached and I put a hand to it. I clutched at my bond pendant, grateful for Murphy's shoulder against mine. He took my hand and walked with me up the three steps into the wine bar.

I took the seat across from Lauren on the inside by the window and Jason went to the bar to order us wine and food. He might have asked me what I wanted, but I was too dazed to know for sure. Who was this woman across from me? Where had my mother gone? Everything about her screamed red flag alert to me. Was this Wren or was this Lauren Newcastle, Councilor Jason Allerton's bond mate? I couldn't quite believe Jason had been the one to initiate the wardrobe and hairstyle changes, but I suspected Lauren may have done everything to please him, not herself. The more things change, the more things stay the same.

"I'm Liam Murphy, Lauren. It's good to meet you." Belatedly, I realized I hadn't introduced them. Murphy grinned across the wooden table at Wren and she smiled back, but the frost was unmistakable and Murphy's smile faltered.

"I'm angry at you," Wren told him. "You broke my daughter's heart. I wanted to help her pick up the pieces, but she wouldn't let me in. She never does. But I saw her suffer and it was all your fault."

"Wren." I gasped in dismay. This was a hell of a first impression.

Instead of backing down with flustered apologies, Wren stood her ground. "He did hurt you, Stanzie. And there's still some of that same sadness in your eyes right now. If he doesn't make you happy, why are you with him?"

"He does make me happy." I'd sounded defensive, and the last of Murphy's smile died.

"I know what I did was unforgiveable," he said. "I had my reasons, but they were more justifications than anything else. Insecurity. I didn't know she loved me. My Alpha was in trouble and I didn't want Stanzie to get hurt. I didn't think it was her battle."

Wren considered his words, but her cold demeanor didn't thaw.

"I heard about Paddy. I'm sorry," she said. "He was your best friend too, wasn't he?"

"Best I ever had next to your girl here." Murphy's voice was rough with emotion. I found his hand with mine beneath the table.

"I don't know from a first-hand perspective, of course, but from what I understand her first bond mates made Stanzie very happy. I want you to make her at least as happy as she was with them. Can you do that, Liam?" Wren asked.

"I'll spend my life trying," he said, and I sucked in my breath so I wouldn't make a spectacle of myself and burst into tears.

"Will you two stop talking about me as if I wasn't sitting here too?"

Wren's smile was astoundingly beautiful. Every man in the wine bar stared at her, but she was oblivious. No, not oblivious. Unaffected. None of them mattered to her. But when Jason came to the table with a bottle of wine, four glasses and a stand-up flag marked with the number six, she glowed.

"I've just given Liam a piece of my mind," she told him as he set the flag at the edge of the table so the wait staff could find us with our food. "I'm not sure I like him yet."

"Me either," Jason said, eyes twinkling.

* * * *

Wren smelled like Guerlain's La Petite Robe Noire. It was a very Jason Allerton scent, much different than the girlish scents she'd worn for my father. She held me close for a moment while Jason waited by the taxi outside our hotel. She and Jason were taking the Council's private jet back to Montana, while Murphy and I were taking a later commercial flight back to Dublin. He and I had the afternoon left to wander London's streets. I had yet to buy a pair of shoes and aimed to remedy that as quickly as possible.

The four of us had spent a hectic two days sight-seeing and dining in impossibly upscale restaurants. The night before we'd seen a play in the West End—a comedy—and I could still hear the novelty of Wren's loud, unrestrained laughter ringing in my ears. I'd never heard her laugh like that in my entire life.

I still wasn't sure who she was, and while I hadn't rejected her friendly overtures, there was a strangeness between us that never existed before and neither of us seemed sure how to handle it.

I didn't want to let her go into the taxi with Jason and out of my life again. What if we lost touch again? When would we see each other next? How would I satisfy myself she was changing for herself and not Jason if I didn't spend more time with her?

"Stanzie, please tell me you'll call me sometimes. I feel like I'm going to get into this taxi and never speak to you again until Jason can maneuver us together somehow." Wren spoke my fears aloud and when I heard them, they seemed so damned stupid.

"The phone works both ways," I reminded her and she patted my cheek. I wanted to melt under her maternal touch, but something held me back.

"You're right," she agreed. "But somehow I get nervous and tongue tied and I think you don't want to hear from me." This sophisticated woman in her tailored pantsuit and designer pumps didn't seem as though she was ever unsure of herself. The admission spooked me, rather than reassured me.

"Why would you think that? I always want to hear from you." My tone was brusque.

She frowned. "Then why don't you call?"

"Because you might not answer," I said. "There were so many times you didn't, I'm afraid to call now." I bit my lip. I'd said it.

"I'm not that person anymore." Wren's answer was too quick, too pat and I knew she must be reciting something somebody else had told her. Someone like Jason. "I'm different now."

"Nobody can change completely," I said. "You put on a good front, Wren, but you're still the same frightened woman deep down."

"The things that frightened me are gone now," she insisted. But she wouldn't say his name. If Paul was gone and she wasn't afraid of him anymore, why wouldn't she say his damned name?

"Bullshit," I argued. "In the dead of night, you still wake up screaming. You're lying if you tell me you don't."

Her face went pale beneath the mask of expensive makeup.

"Why do you always have to ruin everything with your questions and your accusations? I'm still not good enough for you, am I? I'll never be a good enough mother. You'll never forgive me for not being there when you were a teenager and things were hard for you." Her hyacinth blue eyes glittered with self-pitying tears. Here she was. Here was the Lauren I knew had to still exist.

"Say his name, Mother." I clenched my hands into fists so I wouldn't scratch her. Anger swept through me. Jason Allerton could not remake my mother into somebody completely different and totally confident. Not in two months, he couldn't. It was a sham. She was a shell just trying to please him and if he couldn't see that, I could and damn him for it. Her too. She ought to have taken her opportunity for self-reflection and run with it, not thrown it away to become just another man's image of the perfect bond mate.

"No." Her expression turned mulish. "You selfish, small person. You want everyone to be as miserable as you are, don't you? Well, I'm not miserable anymore. I'm happy. Jason is the best thing that ever happened to me and if you can't be happy for me, shame on you. You're making Liam suffer too. You'll never forgive him for not being there either, I suppose. Everyone around you is supposed is drop everything and rush to your side whenever you snap your fingers. You're more like your father than you'll ever admit, you know that?"

The sound of my palm striking Lauren's faultless cheek was as loud as cannon fire. How dare she compare me to that man? I'd gotten free of him and made something of my life and she'd stayed with him and been submissive until I'd rescued her. She'd still be under his fucking thumb if I hadn't freed her and her whole goddamn pack as well.

Just because she was now the bond mate of one of the most influential men on the Great Council, it did not give her the right to stomp all over me and tell me I was like Paul Benedict. I was me, Stanzie Newcastle. I wasn't some fucking sham of a half person like she was. I didn't define myself by who I was bonded to. That was her neat little trick. Bitch. How dare she? If I ever had a daughter, I would *never* forget she existed the way this woman forgot me whenever I got too inconvenient.

"I do everything for everybody and I get nothing in return," I shouted. The hand I'd slapped her with burned and I wiped it against my jeans, but couldn't erase the prickly sensation. "I constantly think of everyone before myself and all I get is shoved aside when somebody more important comes along. I wait and I wait and I'm tired of being grateful for the crumbs. I want the whole fucking cake. I want it all, not just little bits and pieces. You want to swoop in and bring me to plays and out to dinner every six months, go ahead, but don't expect me to throw myself at your feet in gratitude. You want to hear from me, *you* pick up the fucking phone and make your scared little fingers push the buttons. You don't let your bond mate figure out a way to get you in the same goddamn city as me. I'm not calling you. I did call you. Over and over and over again and you let the phone ring. You stood there and let it ring. So screw you, Lauren, and your perverted power plays. Just because Paul's not here anymore to boss you around, don't you dare start giving me orders. You hear me?"

The imprint of my hand stood out red against her white cheek. She stared at me for a moment, but didn't say anything.

Very deliberately, she turned her back on me and got into the taxi. Jason followed her. He stared at me through the window, but didn't roll it down or say anything to me. Of course he'd choose her over me. I was always everyone's afterthought. Screw him too. He should have known better than to bring me to see his little Lauren puppet. I wanted a mother, not another man's toy. A moment later the taxi pulled away from the curb and disappeared into the London traffic.

I whirled around to confront Murphy, who stood staring me as if he didn't even know who the hell I was. "And that goes double for you," I shouted and ran. I had no idea where the fuck I was going, all I knew was that I wasn't going to stop until my legs gave out.

The city turned into a kaleidoscopic blur around me. Cold air burned my lungs and made my eyes water, but I didn't slow. Others dodged out of my way with stifled oaths and I knocked one woman down, her packages scattering everywhere. I was vaguely conscious of Murphy behind me, stopping to help her, and my fury doubled. Even helping some goddamn Other woman in the frigging street was more important than pursuing me. He'd never catch me now, he'd given me too much of a head start.

He did catch me, though. Halfway through some damn park, my legs rebelled and went out from beneath me and I went ass over teakettle into the dry autumn grass. I dragged myself onto a bench and sat hunched over my knees, gulping back tears and gasping for air. His shadow cut across the weak autumn sunshine and he sat beside me. His breathing was almost as ragged as mine, but his jeans weren't grass stained and ripped like mine. He wasn't crying either, damn him.

"You think if you keep bludgeoning us with the same damn accusations over and over again that it's somehow going to change history?" he asked when he'd gotten his breath back. He unbuttoned his jacket. Sweat gleamed on his face. "You keep giving it your best shot, but it still doesn't change anything. Except every time you do it, the wall between us gets bigger and darker. Maybe you want that. Do you?"

"Shut up." I wiped my runny nose on my sleeve and ignored the tissue he tried to hand me.

"I love you, Stanzie, but it's getting harder and harder to figure out what the hell you want, and it scares me."

"I told you what I want. I want to come first and I never will with you. So why shouldn't I build a fucking wall? It's my protection. It's for me."

"You do come first," he said.

"Liar." I wiped my nose again and wished I was dead. Why hadn't I drowned in that goddamn stream?

"I know you understood why I spent so much time with Fee," he told me. "You think I didn't know you were there, but I always knew. You took care of us. You made sure we ate, had clean clothes, went to bed at semi reasonable hours. You cared for Will like he was your own son. You think I didn't see that?"

"Children are always taken care of in packs," I argued.

"You love that little boy and you know it."

"I promised Paddy." I stole a look at Murphy and, just as I'd suspected, his face was shuttered against all emotion.

"You see? I can't talk about him. I can't talk about your father or anything that happened. You listen to Fee, you listen to her, let her talk, but not me. Why not me? Because I didn't know him as long? Because he wasn't my best friend or my bond mate? I try to understand, but I don't. I just don't."

"You got to be with him." Murphy stared at the empty bench across from us, not me. "You were the last person he talked to. I'm jealous and I'm guilty and I squandered my last chance to be with him so I could stab that bastard old man to death. And I can never get that chance back. Paddy wanted to come with us to the frigging airport to pick up Allerton and I wouldn't let him. If I'd let him come, Stanzie, he'd be alive right now. Don't you get it? It's not because I don't want to talk about him with you. It's because I don't want to talk about him at all. You were there in the room when he begged to come with us. Fee wasn't. She has no idea how much I contributed to his death. I can't look you in the eye because you *know*."

"It wasn't your fault." His guilt caged him, made him a prisoner and I'd been too damned selfish to see it until just now. "Remember how he asked me to stay with him at An Puca? If I had, he might be alive. So I'm just as much to blame if you are, if that's how you think."

"No," he denied. "You wanted to stay with him but you came with me because you knew I wanted you with me. You not staying with him is my fault too."

"You didn't kill him."

"*I fucking did*," he shouted at me. "I did! He wanted to tell Allerton. Way back at Bethany's funeral he wanted to tell and I talked him out of it because I thought I knew best. I didn't know shit, Stanzie, and I got him killed."

"You didn't." I tried to put an arm around him, but he shrugged me away. I moved to the edge of the bench, as far away from him as I could get. He didn't want me. He never wanted me when he hurt inside.

I waited, but he didn't say anything or move closer to me, so I got up and walked away. I had no idea where I was going, but that seemed par for the course in London. God, if I ever got out of this goddamned city, I would never set foot in it again if I could help it.

The wind sent leaves rattling down the path ahead of me. They swirled in a brown blur and I kicked them out of my way, crunching them beneath my boots.

Murphy matched his stride to mine. One moment he hadn't been there, the next he was.

"I wasn't even talking about Fee, you know." I concentrated on stomping as many damn leaves as I could reach before they blew out of my path. "I admit I felt invisible sometimes, but I always understood how you needed to be there for her just as much as she needed you. You two are twins and Paddy was always there, your whole lives. Of course you'd turn to each other when he wasn't anymore."

"Then who?" Murphy deliberately brushed his shoulder against mine. Other people held hands as they strolled through this damn park, but not us. I was supposed to be grateful for a shoulder brush. Fucking hell.

"You'll get mad," I predicted.

"So let me get mad."

"I'm tired of being yelled at."

"I'm not particularly a big fan either," he said.

"I can't talk about this because you've made it plain I'm not supposed to compare myself to her. I don't know how I'm supposed to tell you how I feel if I can't." Crunch. Two leaves at once. Double points.

"Are we talking about Sorcha?" He stopped dead in his tracks, but hurried after me when I continued without him. He grabbed me by the shoulders and forced me to stand still, facing him. "Stanzie, talk to me."

I shrugged out of his grasp, but didn't turn away.

"Of course we're talking about Sorcha. She's the frigging invisible elephant in the room everywhere I go with you. You heard Colin that night. How he loves Mary the same way you loved her. I was standing right there and if you think that didn't hurt, fuck you. You didn't say a word about me. It was like I didn't even exist. I know damn well I'm only the best you can do since she's dead and you can't have her. I tell myself how unfair I am to want you to love me the way you loved her. I don't have the right to dictate your feelings to you, but I do have the right to my own feelings. And I'm tired of not measuring up, no matter what I do. I thought loving you would be enough. Being loved back. Most days it is, but lately all I feel when I look at you is sick to my stomach because I can't be like her."

"I was obsessed with Sorcha." Murphy's expression was bewildered and tears gleamed in his eyes. "You want me to be obsessed with you?"

"A-do-anything-for-her love," I quoted Colin. "If Sorcha had been facing a tribunal, you'd have been there. You would never have left her alone after Bethany's funeral and everything that happened. You see how fucked up I sound? I *know* it's irrational, Liam. If you just let me work this out on my own, I'll be fine."

"So you can decide how I feel about you without my input? How I felt about her? So you can make yourself sick with uncertainty? Paint yourself into a corner and never let anybody help you out? Why? Why do you have to do this on your own? Could the truth of my feelings for Sorcha be any less devastating than what you've imagined?" Murphy tried to touch me again, but I danced out of reach.

"All right, tell me. Just tell me. Say it and get it out there and then I can deal with it. Maybe you're right, maybe I need to hear you say it once and for all and kill the last bit of stupid hope I still have. Look me in the face and tell me you loved her more." I clenched my fists tightly and braced myself.

Why had I opened this can of worms? What on earth was I thinking? If I heard him say it, wouldn't it change everything? I wouldn't be able to stay with him. I'd have to leave. I'd lose everything again because I couldn't keep my goddamned mouth shut.

"I let you go because that's how *much* I loved you. No, I wouldn't have walked away from Sorcha, you're right. Because I was damned if I would give up my ideal of who she was and who I wanted her to be. Who I wanted to be to her." Murphy's eyes were so dark and determined. I couldn't look away, although I wanted to.

"Stanzie, when she died I realized how selfish I'd been for ten years. Holding her back from going after someone she could love. In all those years we were together, the happiest I ever saw her were the last four months when Hunter was around. And I couldn't even let her have him the way she wanted. I had to be in the mix somewhere there too.

"It hurt so much to give you up, but I didn't want to ever do to you what I did to her. You know why?"

"Because you don't love me as much as you loved her. Why don't you just say it?" I demanded.

"Because it's not true. I don't love you anywhere near the same way I loved her. Jesus, sometimes I don't think I loved her at all. I loved being in love. She was the placeholder. It's more complicated than that. I can't explain it very well. All I know is that you taught me what love really was. And it's not clinging selfishly to somebody and making it all about myself, but making it about you. What you want. What you need."

"You think I wanted you to leave? That I needed you to leave?" I gaped at him in shock. "You are *always* deciding what I need. Why don't you try letting *me* decide for a change?"

"I will if you ever frigging tell me what the hell you want instead of figuring I ought to know somehow," he said.

"What part of 'stay with me, don't go search the Archives' didn't you understand? I know I said it, I didn't just *think* it at you," I shouted.

"What part of I'm not going to lose you no matter what I have to do didn't *you* understand?" he shouted back.

"Wait?" I mentally replayed our conversation. "What do you mean, you sometimes think you didn't love Sorcha at all? What the hell does that mean?"

"What the hell does it sound like, woman? I'm telling you I *really* love you and if that's not good enough, then you need to walk away. Turn around and walk, and this time I won't come after you. You decide where we go from here. You want the power, take it."

"I only want to walk away if you don't love me as much as you loved Sorcha. But you won't answer that. You give me this crazy bullshit about not loving her at all and expect me to swallow it? Jesus, Murphy, what are you doing?"

He grinned at me and I stared. Was this a time for grins?

"This is funny now?" I asked.

"You called me Murphy," he said. What a lunatic.

"I call you Murphy all the time."

"No. Not since that night you got mad at me. Now I know it was because of what that bastard fuck said about Sorcha, and as a side comment, I am sick of him coming between me and women. He never wanted Sorcha and he doesn't want you either."

"Of course he doesn't want me. He's in love with Mary. He's always been in love with Mary."

"I don't give a fuck about him, Stanzie. I don't want to talk about him."

"You brought him up."

"And I'm telling you to drop him. Call me Murphy again. I want to hear it."

"I won't." I glared at him. He grinned at me again, the sonofabitch.

"Come on. Say it. Murphy. Two syllables, it's not that hard."

"Asshole is also two syllables and it fits better," I said and he burst into laughter.

"You're a lunatic," I told him. He took a step closer to me. I moved backward.

"Call me Murphy."

"It just slipped out. I don't want to call you that anymore. It's a dumb nickname."

"How can someone's real name be a nickname?" he asked.

"Your real name is Liam."

"Liam *Murphy*," he stressed. "Come on, Stanzie, either you call me Murphy or I will call you Constance all the damn time. Every chance I get."

"I hate that name," I snarled.

"I know." He grinned. "So, last chance, Constance. Call me Murphy."

"Are we going on that road trip or not? I hate London and I want to leave," I said.

"You gonna call me Murphy?" he asked.

"I'm sorry I'm jealous of Sorcha. I'm an idiot. I know." My throat ached unbearably. I wished I'd taken that tissue when he'd offered it. "You shouldn't have to explain anything. You shouldn't have to talk about her."

"Why?" he asked, totally serious now. "You never talk about Grey and Elena either. You told me how they died, but you've never told me any stories about them when they were alive."

I bit my lip. "Why would I?"

"Because you loved them. Because they were a huge part of your life? Because I love you and I want to hear the about them? Like Lauren said, they made you happy. You shouldn't have to keep them locked away inside yourself all the time. Maybe you'd like to talk about them sometimes."

"I don't want you to think you don't make me happy," I whispered. "Because you do. When I'm not being a complete imbecile and shoving you away, that is."

He stepped closer and this time I went into his arms instead of backing away.

"I don't want there to be walls between us, Stanzie. I don't want you to keep things from me about your past. I don't want you to go around being jealous of Sorcha. I'll tell you anything you want to know about her. Maybe if you knew how it was with her, you'd *see* how much I love you. You'd understand.

"I've waited and waited for you to talk about things with me. Not just Grey and Elena, but what happened in that root cellar with Nate Carver. About Callie shooting herself in front of you. Remember the day we took the pack bond? You as much as told me you wanted to talk to me, but you've kept silent. You lock so much inside and you don't have to."

"Because I'm afraid. Because people go away. There wasn't anyone to talk to for so long, I don't know how to do it anymore and I guess I expect you to know how I'm feeling even if I don't say." I buried my face in his shoulder and he stroked my hair. "Murphy, I don't want to fight anymore. I want to go on that damn road trip and see parts of Ireland I haven't seen. Our first road trip was so much fun. I want to have fun with you. I don't want to worry about anything or anyone."

"Then, let's get back to the hotel and get our things. The sooner we leave, the sooner we can start on all our fun." He pressed a kiss to the side of my face and wrapped his arm around my waist so we could walk close together.

"Do you think it might be fun to stop at a shoe store on our way to the hotel?" I asked. "Because I kinda do."

"I love you so much, but I am going to have to buy a separate apartment just for your goddamn shoes, I swear." Murphy kissed my temple again.

"Maybe we should get a house. I really only need a walk in closet for my shoes, not a whole entire apartment," I mused.

"I'll get you anything you want," he promised.

I leaned into Murphy as we walked.

"You going to call your mother?" he asked as we left the park and headed down a crowded urban street. Cars whizzed past us, and to my eyes, they were all on the wrong side of the road. I would never get used to living outside America.

"No, she's going to call me," I declared.

Murphy shook his head. "You're so goddamn stubborn, Stanzie."

"You don't think she's just being what she thinks Jason wants her to be?" My voice wobbled and Murphy pressed his forehead to the side of my face for a moment as we continued to walk.

"I don't know her well at all. I can't judge," he said.

"I just want her to be herself. Why can't she be who she really is and not what other people want her to be?"

"I think she's scared maybe," he said. "She's trying, honey. The way she looks at you when you don't know she's watching you. It breaks my heart. Love and guilt and fear all wrapped up in a sick little ball. And you treating her like you're not sure who she is."

"I'm *not* sure who she is," I cried. "And Jason is no help, throwing us together and then standing back and watching. Did you see the way he looked at me when the taxi pulled away from the curb? Like I was a stranger or something. He didn't even say goodbye." A tear trickled down my cheek and then another and another.

Murphy groaned and stopped walking so he could hug me. I buried my face in his shoulder and inhaled the sweet, safe scent that was uniquely his.

"You two need to work this one out on your own. Jason's a Councilor. He knows how to sit back and let two people work out their differences without his interference."

"Oh, hell, Murphy, he's the one calling the shots in their relationship. Do you think she dresses that way because she likes the look? It's pure powerhouse Councilor's bond mate attire. And that hair." I shuddered and his arms tightened around me.

"You think I'm calling the shots in our relationship? Ever notice how much red you've got in your wardrobe these days? Because I told you I liked you in red. And you were talking about cutting your hair until I mentioned how much I loved it long and the next thing you know, you'd canceled your hair appointment," Murphy remarked. "And me wearing crew neck sweaters every chance I get because you once told me how sexy you think they are. Remember my goatee? I worked hard on that damn beard and you told me it made me look like a stranger to you and I shaved it off. Months of hard work gone in fifteen minutes.

"People like to dress to please their bond mates. It's not a crime. I think it's kind of nice, myself."

I groaned when I realized my nose was buried in one of his crew neck sweaters. The green one I particularly adored. Damn him.

"Paul always made her wear frilly dresses and keep her hair long and loose. If she bought clothes he didn't like, he made her bring them back to the store," I said.

"Do you honestly think Jason would make her do shit like that?" Murphy asked.

"No, but I do think she'd watch to see what styles he admired and take all his compliments to heart and then arrange her whole wardrobe around him, regardless of whether she liked any of it or not." I said. "I love my red dresses and sweaters. I know you like me in red, but I like the clothes I buy."

"Have you ever asked Lauren what styles she liked?" he asked.

"We never talked about clothes and hair and stuff like that unless it was because of Paul. When I was fifteen, I wanted a pair of Doc Marten boots so badly I could taste it. I saved all my babysitting money and bought a pair at the mall when Lauren took me shopping. She told me not to do it, but when her back was turned I ran back to the shoe store and bought them. I tried to hide them from Paul because I knew he'd hate them, but he found them. I think she told him. She must have. He made me bring them back and I had to buy some little girl shoes I hated instead." God, Murphy must have thought I was a baby hanging onto to old grievances from when I was fifteen, but it still hurt.

"Every time I buy a pair of boots that aren't soft and feminine, I always think of him. I always think 'Screw you, Paul' and I wear the hell out of them," I muttered.

Murphy laughed in my ear, but it was a sympathetic laugh.

"Give her time, honey," he said. "Maybe it pleases her to dress as Jason likes. It's all she knows how to do right now, but maybe if you just give her time to figure herself out, she'll surprise you."

"That's what I wanted for her. Time. On her own. Not bonded to Jason," I whispered. "She'll never find herself because she'll be too busy being what she thinks he wants her to be."

"You don't know that. I can't imagine Jason will let her do that. For all his faults, Stanzie, he loves her. That much is plain every time he looks at her. You believe that, don't you?" Murphy asked.

I shrugged. I didn't want to admit it, but I had to. He was right. Jason loved my mother and she loved him back.

"I guess I ought to stick to trying to work out my own relationship issues instead of trying to fix hers," I said.

"We've got so many, have we?" Murphy sounded mournful and I gave his chin a remorseful kiss.

"It's all on me, Murphy. Not you."

"Someday you'll let yourself rely on me. I swear, I'll drop dead of the shock too," he said with a disgruntled sigh.

"Then I hope it never happens. I don't want you to drop dead." I gave his chin another kiss and he grinned.

"You're not alone," he told me, serious again. "I love you, Stanzie. I'm here for you. You don't have to do everything on your own. That's all I'm saying."

"I love you too, Murphy. So much."

He pulled me against him and we began walking again. We were so close we almost tripped each other.

One year ago I'd been lost and lonely. Today, thanks to Murphy, I was surrounded by people who loved me, none more than the man by my side.

What a difference three hundred sixty-five days could make.

I had no idea what the future held. I hoped in time I could work things out with Wren and with Jason too. One thing I did know was that Murphy would be with me wherever I went, whatever I did. And that's all I really needed.

Meet the Author

Amy Lee Burgess lives in Houston, Texas with two spoiled dachshunds. She adores paranormal creatures and scary things that go bump in the night. Wolves and Celtic mythology are her current passions. Her writing has led to her many fascinating destinations including Paris, Edinburgh and a small town in Colorado where she met real, live wolves in a sanctuary. She's always up for a conversation about Stanzie and Murphy, Ireland or the Walking Dead, so please drop her a line at amyleeburgess99@gmail.com

Turn the page for a special excerpt of Amy Lee Burgess's

Beneath the Skin

If you could shift into a wolf, what would you discover about yourself?

Two years after the deaths of her bond mates, Constance Newcastle is ready to start over. The problem? The rest of the Great Pack, gathered in Paris to shift into wolves together, is not so sure she deserves the chance. Although the Great Council ruled the car crash an accident, even Constance blames herself. She was driving, after all.

Treated like a pariah by those she longs to rejoin, Constance reunites with an old lover. Everything looks promising until he mysteriously dies. Accused of his murder and desperate to clear her name, Constance joins forces with handsome, confident Liam Murphy, a former Alpha pack leader with a past as tragic and troubled as her own. Guided by the mysterious Councilor Jason Allerton, Constance and Liam discover they are not alone-- throughout the Great Pack, people are dying. Can all the deaths be accidents, or is something more sinister going on?

On sale now!

Chapter 1

Run. Run, run, run. Scared. Littles hide, no scrape legs, no make noise. Wind no push things. Fur stick up. Me scared. Me follow scent. Her. Me love Her. See big hard thing. Pushed in. Black water drip, drip, drip. Blood. Smell blood. Drip, drip, drip. Scared. See Her. See Her in big hard thing. Her two legs now. Her eyes no see Me. Look up to Big Shiny and little shinies. No see. Smell blood. Smell Her. No hear beat thing. No hear blood move under skin. Her no move no more. Her gone. Me look up see Big Shiny. Me cry loud.

* * * *

When I jerked awake, a smothered scream on my lips, the digital clock on the nightstand read five thirty-two in the morning. I rolled over and reached out instinctively for the reassuring warmth of Grey's body, but of course he wasn't there. He never would be there again.

Two years, I told myself as I threw back the covers of the single bed in a small, unfamiliar Paris hotel room and staggered for the bathroom to splash cold water on my face. The dregs of the dream slipped away under my fingertips as I massaged my cheeks and forehead, blond hair spilling over my shoulders into the wet stream of the water.

My hair was getting long. *Two years*, I told myself again, bitterness twisting my face.

I scowled into the mirror and saw my own reflection—as familiar to me as anything in the world. I thought of the wind, the trees at night, the scent of the pine needles embedded in the soft earth of the forest.

Everything conspired to create a wall between me and the rest of the world. I hadn't connected with anything or anyone for so long I barely remembered what it felt like not to be alone.

My thirty-second birthday had come and gone three months earlier. Once upon a time there would have been a celebration. Grey and Elena would have been there with me. Presents. Cake.

Instead I'd sat in a dark theater and watched a horror movie while secretly envying all the couples who sat around me.

When I saw people in love, a strange, isolating ache gripped my whole body.

Two years, I told my reflection in the mirror.

Grey used to tell me I was beautiful. He loved to trace the contours of my face with his fingers—my high cheekbones, my full mouth, my eyelids and forehead. Even my nose, which I thought was too big but he pronounced elegant. Ha.

He was the elegant one with his sensitive mouth and long, thin fingers. A poet's face. Hollow cheeks, dreamy eyes.

Elena had been the beauty in my opinion. Blond, like me, only hers was so fair it was nearly white. The milky translucence of her skin made me think of women in castles in the medieval days, women who stayed behind the castle walls and never saw the sun because of the feuds and fights their men waged for them.

Grey and Elena—my bond mates, my lovers, my friends.

There had also been Jonathan, Nora, Callie, Vaughn and Peter. Grandfather Tobias. My pack.

Two years ago, that is.

When everything stopped.

* * * *

I spent the day shopping. I ended up at Au Printemps on the boulevard Haussman where I sorted through a bewildering array of bright, modern dresses and used my limited French with the saleswoman who tried to steer me away from black toward something brighter.

"*Tout le monde préfère des robes noires, mais, pour vous, madame, je pense rouge! Voila!*" She produced a shimmering red gown with a plunging sequined neckline and a nearly indecent slit up the right thigh.

I had thought something a little plainer. Something that would allow me to blend into the background, because I wasn't sure I wanted attention.

Two years, I heard my own accusing voice say in my head then, abruptly, I agreed to try on the dress. If I didn't like it, I would stick with the original plan.

Ten seconds after staring at my reflection in the three-way mirror in the dressing room, I abandoned my idea of blending into the background. I looked gorgeous. Gorgeous, hell. I hadn't even felt pretty in so long. The crimson color made my blond hair glow and darkened my eyes to navy. I looked regal and self-assured. It was a dress that would force people to take me seriously. For two years I'd felt invisible. In this red dress that would be impossible.

Of course it wasn't cheap and I winced at the hit on my bank balance as I paid. Back in my little hotel room I had a new pair of fantastic cherry red stiletto pumps that would be the perfect accompaniment. Paris was proving to be an expensive adventure.

As I left, the saleswoman wished me a good afternoon, and that she hoped I would enjoy myself at the party tonight.

Party. I nearly snorted aloud at the idea. It was a not a party. No one there would dream to call it something as frivolous as that, even if there would be canapés and cocktails, three or four different types of music, candles and designer clothes. People there would laugh and flirt, dance and drink, but it was not a party.

It was a gathering. The Great Gathering.

So many of the Great Pack would be there from all over the world, maybe including people I hadn't seen in five years, since before Grey and Elena had died.

There I would be in a bold, sexy red dress without them, and everyone would see me. My stomach lurched. What was I thinking?

I turned around on the sidewalk so I could return the dress. I should be in mourning still. I should wear black. What kind of a message would I send with a red dress? Could I afford that message? After all, everyone thought—my own former pack even—it was my fault they were dead— Elena and Grey. Of course I thought so too.

After all, I had driven the car that night.

My pack's eyes had been so cold when they'd severed ties with me. Jonathan's, especially. He was Alpha, the leader, but Grey had been a favorite in the pack, even if he hadn't been Alpha. He could have been, but he didn't want to. He said no when Vaughn asked. Everyone had been a little shocked he'd turned it down. After all, everyone wanted to be Alpha at some point in their lives. But then he explained it to me. Some people needed to lead more than others, and that popularity didn't prove the best indicator of need. Jonathan needed to lead. If he'd been under another male, he would have chafed at it, and the bonds between us all would have suffered. Besides, Alphas rotated. We'd get our chance. Let Jonathan go first. Grey had been so wise. So good. He would have made a much better Alpha than Jonathan, and now he would never have the chance.

It was November in Paris and cold even with the wintry sunlight filtering down through the clouds. A gust of wind rattled the plastic bag in my hand and blew the skirt of a tall woman who walked in front of me. She squealed a little, and held it down while her companion laughed indulgently beside her and said something in rapid-fire French.

The sun struck her hair and lit it up into a white-gold halo around her head and, for a moment, I thought of Elena. The sun used to turn her hair into a white-gold halo too sometimes.

My heart hurt so badly inside my chest I couldn't breathe, and I stopped dead on the sidewalk and squeezed my eyes shut against the sudden blinding burn of tears.

Two years. When would it ever stop? When could I walk down the street and see the sun hit some woman's hair and not be overcome with grief? When could I wake from a nightmare and stop reaching out for somebody who wasn't there?

When would I run through the forest on all fours, fur whipping back against the wind, knowing I was with my bond mates, safe and secure, and above all, loved?

Even though my hotel was only a few streets away, I didn't feel like walking. Yet I wanted to escape the Paris afternoon where everyone was happy and be alone with my thoughts of dead connections.

Instead I found a sidewalk café and ordered hot chocolate. I sat on the cold wrought-iron chair in the Paris sunshine and shivered a little in my navy blue pea coat as I people-watched until my drink arrived.

It was sweet and warm, and I tried to convince myself I deserved to live again and to be happy. Over the past two years, I'd paid my dues to the Great Pack, to everyone, and tonight was my chance to start over again. I was not the same as I once was, but I could start over again. The invitation to the Great Gathering proved it, even though it was my right to attend, because the two years had been up three months ago, on my birthday.

The clock always reset on birthdays. It was a day to examine yourself and your ties and bonds, to renew them if you wanted or dissolve them, if you could. At least start the process if it wasn't a mutual agreement.

My pack had severed our ties on Jonathan's birthday. It was the first pack birthday after the accident and they only waited that long because they had to. The accident had occurred on the night of my birthday, and by the time they all knew about it and the circumstances surrounding it, it was already past midnight and the chance to dissolve then had passed.

They'd formally severed ties on Jonathan's birthday, because that was how our laws worked. They'd blamed me for the accident, and instead of offering me comfort, they'd condemned me.

I hadn't protested back then. I was too shocked—too shattered by the knowledge Grey and Elena were gone. I had felt guilty because I had been driving and it had been my idea to go to the club that night. Why shouldn't we have gone out? It was my birthday. I was young and happy and I loved to dance. So why shouldn't I have wanted to go to a dance club?

I saw their hostile faces as I had been interrogated by the Councils at my tribunal, after they'd had time to think about it and talk about it among themselves without me. I smelled them too and I knew. They smelled of the same despair and grief I gave off. But they also smelled of anger—against me.

One thing about being Pack, we could smell emotions. We could try to mask our feelings from each other, but our scents usually gave us away.

Others, people who weren't Pack, couldn't do this. It was one of the things, besides shape-shifting, that made us different.

All my life it had been drilled into me that the Others would not understand our kind. We would be persecuted and bullied, isolated and studied. Perhaps even exterminated. I was kept away, home schooled when I was little. The only people I knew until I was eight or nine years old were the members of my birth pack.

One day my mother brought me to a grocery store. All the Others scared me, I remember that. A world that had consisted of twenty-four people who were Pack had suddenly changed and twisted. My insular little existence had been shattered, and the idea of the Others scared me. They outnumbered us. They always had, they always would. Somehow we had to coexist. We could know about them, but they could never know about us.

My father made me watch werewolf movies so I would understand that I needed to keep silent about what I really was. I didn't like the way those movies made me feel. Hunted, persecuted. I wasn't a bit like any of the monsters in any of the movies or books, but he told me the Others would not see the difference.

We had no special protection in wolf form. We didn't bite people, or change them into wolves like us. We didn't even call it *werewolf*. We called it being Pack. You had to be born Pack, or you would never be Pack.

The legends of being bitten by a werewolf then turning into one were just that—legends. The grandmothers and grandfathers said the legends protected us. Spread false information about something real and you could hide behind the legends. Twist it just enough so no one would believe you, even if you told them the truth. Not that we would. Who would believe, and what profit would come of it if they did?

Some of the Pack, especially the older ones, thought my generation was soft and the ones after us only getting softer. We were losing touch with our beast natures and becoming weak. We used our ability to shape shift as if it were a hobby, as if we were in a secret club. Our nature no longer defined us and gave us strength and purpose of will. Or so the grandfathers and grandmothers said.

I supposed modern life had made things easier. I'm not sure about softer. In the modern world it was harder to disguise the fact we aged much slower than Others. We lived in isolated areas. Switched jobs often, changed social security numbers and passports. Of course most of the grandfathers and grandmothers disdained such things. They usually lived under the radar. They preferred not to have *Other* identities. They might live in cities but they didn't vote or own businesses. They did nothing but exist on the fringe. If they traveled, they paid cash and used transportation that didn't require ID. Or, if they still were up for it, they traveled in shifted form.

They had jobs, but menial labor, under the table. Or they stole, begged or borrowed.

Most Pack members were particularly adept at pick-pocketing and sleight of hand. Lots of the grandfathers and grandmothers gambled for a living. They ran shell games or dice or any game of chance.

The younger generation liked material comforts. We didn't want to live in squalor, or squat illegally on somebody else's property, or rely on someone "legit" in our pack to provide us with housing. Lots of the old grandfathers and grandmothers lived in homes owned by their children and grandchildren.

Since we weren't the Alpha couple in our pack, Grey and I hadn't been allowed to have children. In the old days, if you got pregnant and you weren't Alpha that meant going to an old grandmother for a potion to miscarry. Nowadays we had modern birth control, thankfully. Not that the old grandmothers endorsed such things. They had herbal concoctions but their efficacy was not as reliable as the Pill.

The old ways were good enough for us, they lectured. They should be good enough for you. But why not use something better if it was available?

That's how I thought anyway.